DR. YURIY SHCHERBAK

Realm of Darkness

A novel

Translated by

Stephen Komarnyckyj

KLP
Kalyna Language Press Limited

First published in the UK in 2016 by Kalyna Language Press Limited

This paperback edition published in 2016

Originally Published in Ukraine in 2011 as Chas Smertokhrystiv: Mirazhi 2077 roku by Yaroslaviv Val

Acknowledgements:

Cover Design by Yaroslaviv Val

About the Author

Yuriy Shcherbak is the author of more than 20 novels, numerous short stories and screenplays. A writer, a soviet dissident, who was persecuted for his political views, a medical doctor and a former ambassador to Canada, Israel and the USA. He is the head of the Shevchenko Award Committee and was awarded the Order of Freedom in 2016.

About the Translator

Stephen Komarnyckyj is a poet and translator who was born in Yorkshire, England and maintains strong links with Ukraine, where his family live.

For there shall arise false Christs, and false prophets, and shall shew great signs and wonders; insomuch that, if it was possible, they shall deceive the very elect....
Wherefore if they shall say unto you, Behold, he is in the desert; - go not forth: behold, he is in the secret chambers; believe it not. For as the lightning cometh out of the east, and shineth even unto the west; so shall also the coming of the Son of Man be. For wheresoever the carcase is, there will the eagles be gathered together.

The Gospel According to Matthew
Bible, King James Version

A mirage is an illusion, a phenomenon caused by the anomalous refraction of light when a person sees, in addition to objects as they are really are, an unreal and distorted image, wherein real objects may be rotated, increased or diminished.

Ukrainian Soviet Encyclopaedia 1982, Volume 7 Page 29

Russia ... that realm of darkness which oppresses Ukraine.

Ivan Franko

CONTENT

Part 1

THE RETURN

1

20 April 2077
Encrypted Telegram 63-80/CSNA
From: The Embassy of Ukraine
To: The Confederation of States of North America, Washington
Top Secret
Destroy after Reading
For the attention of the Chief of the Scientific and Technological
Bureau of Ukrainian Military Intelligence (UMI) - I. P. Haiduk

Dear Ihor Petrovych
I am writing to inform you of your promotion to the rank of
major general and to offer our congratulations. In connection
with the emergency situation, I order you to return to Kyiv
promptly to receive your new commission. The period allowed
for the fulfilment of this order is between one and three days.

Signed: His Excellency, Hetman of Ukraine, General Kuzma-
Danylo Makhun

2

Haiduk awoke at dawn when the spring sky above Washington
had begun to fill with a muted and, at first, barely noticeable
lustre. The screen of his alarm clock presented a figure that was
new and unsettling to him, 04:00, and he came to with a start;
anxious and unable to comprehend where or who he was and
what was happening around him. He only rarely fell into a black
hole of oblivion as a result of exhaustion or physical trauma

after the effects of crossing through several time-zones when he travelled from Washington to Tokyo and then to Canberra.

It seemed to Haiduk that there was someone else in the room apart from himself and Linda. He had temporarily forgotten yesterday's encrypted telegram and the simultaneously startled and frightened gaze of Belkin, the cryptographer. The coded telegram was shocking to Haiduk because it drew a line under the carefree life he had enjoyed until now.

He felt as if someone were watching him attentively from the shadow of the bedroom and saw a drone half a metre from the bed. It was the size of a tennis ball, but not springy or downy, instead it was metallic and its lens glittered evilly. Haiduk froze and waited for the shot with a resigned fatality. In February he had sent the Centre a description of this new killer-drone, code-named 'Sparrow', which was capable of destroying the leaders of terrorist organisations, high-ranking officers in enemy armies, and other foes of the Confederation.

His Puerto Rican lover, Linda Kenworthy, slept peacefully by his side; her belly was barely covered by a white sheet. She was on her back, breathing quietly and happily, in the deep sleep that comes after a night of making love, and her breath sounded like a breeze wafting gently through a child's harmonica. Her body was black in the dusky room. Her heavy legs were only slightly bent at the knee, and below the grey strip of the sheet were her naked torso and full breasts. She was resting her head on her left arm and there was an air of utter tranquillity and defencelessness about her.

The drone continued to hover motionlessly before Haiduk, like a globule of dark energy. He knew that the centre of its metallic sphere was seething with electrical life. The unseen operator from the Central Security Service was sitting not far from Annapolis, yawning in front of the monitor and swallowing cold coffee as he studied the nocturnal life of Haiduk and Linda, with all its trivial and shameless details, and deciding whether to reduce them to ash or grant them a little more life.

Haiduk's paralysis fell from him and he made a barely perceptible movement with his left hand towards the pillow, under which was an old, but reliable, storm pistol loaded with self-targeting bullets. It was a type favoured by marines, the Beretta M9A11. The drone reacted immediately, darted to the ceiling and blinded him with a flash, which filled the room with an agonising, mercurial light and transfixed the newly promoted major general. When an all pervasive and oppressive darkness came in place of that light, without any intimation of dawn, Haiduk realised the drone was no longer in the room.

He recollected that he had been invited to the White House today and realised there was a direct connection between that invitation, the encrypted telegram and the drone raid. Subsequently, he thought about how, in Kyiv, he would have to order major general's uniforms in camouflage, staff, and parade ground formats. The idea disgusted him. He had forgotten when he had last been forced to wear a uniform; perhaps it was during his service with the Spetsnaz unit of military intelligence at the end of the Romanian-Ukrainian war. Then there was Boston.

Linda moved and quickly opened her eyes, as if to question what was happening. He gently kissed her eyelids, her nose and her lips.

'Go back to sleep. Everything's fine.'

What would become of her when she was again just a cashier in the Continental Bank on M Street? He had grown accustomed to the passive and reticent Linda Kenworthy. Perhaps he loved her. Suddenly, feeling disgusted with this spring morning when Japanese cherry trees bloomed on the banks of the Potomac, he swore under his breath, 'Fuck it!'

3

Haiduk's service automobile remained parked on Dupont Circle. He had run out of fuel vouchers and so had to hail a taxi on Canal Road, near to the smallish, two-storey building he rented, which was not far from Georgetown University and was secreted among the green recesses that meandered down to an expanse of water. The taxi driver, a Pakistani man in a light green *kufi*, who had the appearance of a typical officer of the Islamic Information Service seen everywhere in Washington, at first refused to travel as far as the 'Sleeping Pterodactyl' at 1600 Pennsylvania Avenue. This was the name given to the gigantic, deformed, concrete structure with its chimerical sharp angles, which hid the White House, the D. Eisenhower Executive Office, where the War Ministry used to be located, the Blair House Government Residence, and the Ministry of Finances. Government functionaries insisted that the 'Pterodactyl' would withstand a strike from a ballistic missile with a nuclear warhead, though no one believed this.

The taxi driver haggled over the fare for a long time, like a stall-holder on a bazaar, until Haiduk offered to pay in globos rather than ameros or yuan. When they had travelled along F Street as far as 18th Street, the taxi driver saw some black police terrapins, which threw a protective circle around the 'Pterodactyl', and refused to go any nearer.

'The cursed police,' he said, and explained that when they saw his *kufi* they would arrest him and confiscate his licence. The driver grabbed the twenty globos note, adorned with the image of Bill Gates, from Haiduk and left swiftly without handing over any change.

Haiduk had to walk two blocks before he drew near to the security checkpoint. It was 14:00 and the police officers were becoming fatigued with the temperature and were enfeebled by post-lunch drowsiness. The spring heat was exacerbated by their bullet-proof helmets, armoured waistcoats, knee pads, the long electric prods, the chains, and the powerful, short-barrelled, NK MP 5/11 automatic weapons. They looked menacing if you were unaware that China had refused to supply the Confederation with armour-penetrating bullets. The electrically charged prods and rounds were useless against bullet-proof plastic.

The police spent a long time inspecting Haiduk's passport. They checked the biometric information it provided on the computer and peered into his pupils. All this just to hand him into the charge of a fat police officer who swayed flabbily as she walked towards the central control admissions point, which could only be accessed by a long, concrete labyrinth concealed in the recesses of the 'Pterodactyl'. Haiduk emerged into the open again and finally saw the White House beneath its huge, domed-concrete pavilion. The pallid, ornate building seemed to Haiduk like a decorative trinket immersed in the perpetual polar night. It was lit by projectors, like a corrective facility in North Canada.

The third security check would take place in the midst of the White House itself. Haiduk was provided with a set of sterile clothing, blue trousers and a top with the letter V on the left breast pocket. Bitchy Washington journalists wrote that visiting dictators were provided with a bright red uniform, Islamic autocrats with a green outfit, European democrats with pale blue, and Russian oligarchs with a striped outfit. Only the Chinese were not compelled to strip and redress. The uniform was introduced after the previous President of the Confederation of States of North America had been contaminated with Josser Disease, which had been virus borne into the building by an Emir from one of the Arab Emirates on his luxurious gold-green robe. The White House had to be closed for three months for disinfection and an inoculation programme.

Haiduk dressed in the tight-fitting clothing, which made him resemble a patient at the Bethesda clinic. He smiled to himself as he thought about how he really needed to be dressed in a flowery smock which fastened at the back and made it possible to see his bare backside. He passed into the neighbouring room, which had an old-fashioned melange of oak panelling and heavy furniture. A rosy-cheeked giant was sitting in front of the monitor. He was dressed in a white, peaked military cap and a blue greatcoat, with red cuffs and gold buttons, white trousers and well-polished black shoes. As far as Haiduk could see, this titan was not carrying any weapons. A skinny grey-haired woman with comically childish plaits and vivacious black eyes appeared in the doorway and gave Haiduk a welcoming smile before she pronounced ceremoniously, 'Mr Haiduk, the first lady, Senator Van Lee, is waiting for you.'

This was Martha Jefferson, the chief aide to the wife of the President of the Confederation, Shirley MacDowell, as was, now Senator Shirley Van Lee.

Haiduk stepped towards the door, almost catching himself against the oak stool on which the rosy-cheeked giant was sitting without making the slightest movement or taking his eyes from the monitor.

4

15 April 2077
Top Secret (One Copy)
For the personal attention of His Excellency, the Hetman of Ukraine, General Kuzma-Danylo Makhun
A report with exceptional importance for the state

I inform you that the Overseas Intelligence Service of the State Guard of Ukraine (OISSGU), with the permission of the GPU from 2075, has undertaken an operation to monitor the chief of the second (scientific-technological) bureau of the military intelligence section of the AFU, Lieutenant I. P. Haiduk.

Haiduk was born in Kyiv on 12 February 2027 and attended a specialised computer school before studying at the Kyiv Polytechnic University in the Faculty of Missile Control Systems. He revealed himself to be a gifted engineer and has two inventions to his credit. During the period of Romanian aggression against Ukraine (2048-2052), he served in military intelligence and became a staff officer of the Ukrainian military intelligence service. In 2055 he completed his studies at the General Ye Marchenko Intelligence Services Academy, thereby acquiring the rank of captain. In 2057, in the framework of a programme of student exchange, and under a resolution of the leadership of the Ministry of Defence, K. D. Makhun, and the State Guard, Yu. Merezhko, he was dispatched to the Confederation of States of North America to study at the Massachusetts Institute of Technology, in the faculty of Space Technology, Control and Communication, where he emerged as one of their ten best students. He is a Doctor of Philosophy and a Doctor of Engineering Sciences. After completing his studies at MIT, and while still on Confederation territory, he engaged in intelligence work under the cover of his post as the Executive Director of the Ukrainian-American Bureau for Scientific and Technological Exchange.

In 2058, while he was a student at MIT, he entered into an intimate relationship with an American citizen, who was also a student at the institute, Shirley MacDowell. Three years later she became the wife of the future President of the CSNA, Andrew Van Lee, and is currently one of the most influential Confederation senators.

The Overseas Intelligence Services has information which demonstrates that Shirley MacDowell, during her years as a student, became an agent of the Central Security Service of the Confederation. She operated under the pseudonym 'Baby' and, during the course of their intimate contact, recruited I. P. Haiduk, who was given the pseudonym 'Icarus'.

I. P. Haiduk created the impression that he was successfully acquiring information useful to the Ukrainian State regarding the newest scientific and technical products in the sphere of information communication and new kinds of weaponry, such as the Fountain, Terrapin, Coyote, Swallow and other projects. However, he was really working for the Confederation and did a huge amount of harm to the defence preparedness and the science and technology of the Ukrainian State. It has been proved that I. P. Haiduk engaged in providing the Americans with information on such promising projects in the sphere of Ukraine's defence-industrial complex, as a new kind of fuel for solid fuel missiles located in space and at sea; these being the SS-32 and SS-52, and anti-corrosion for ocean based platforms of strategic importance, super-sensitive radar installations of the Mantle type, and new principles for the manufacture of gas turbines and plasma engines, and others. A list of the criminal and treasonous activity of I. P. Haiduk is included separately.

While handing over these and other technologies and products to his American masters, I. P. Haiduk embarked on a path of personal enrichment, accumulating, in fake accounts in Panama, significant sums of money totalling approximately sixty-million globos. Haiduk leads an amoral life, being engaged in an extra-marital relationship with a cashier at the Continental Bank, Linda Kenworthy, who is an agent of Brazilian intelligence and is used for illegal monetary operations.

The facts in the possession of the State Guard are sufficient to reveal the treacherous anti-state activity of I. P. Haiduk.

In connection with the situation outlined above I propose the following:

. To immediately recall I. P. Haiduk from the Confederation using a persuasive pretext - a promotion.

. To arrest him immediately on his return to Kyiv and create a special military tribunal for the trial of I. P. Haiduk.

. As an exceptional punishment, to sentence I. P. Haiduk to death by the Argentinian execution method of throwing him from a plane at a height of five thousand metres over the Ukrainian soil.

. To honour the agents of the Overseas Intelligence Service (Pseudonyms 'Imperator', 'Axe', and 'Chess Player'), whose work led to the exposure of I. P. Haiduk.

The Director of the State Guard of Ukraine, Yulii Merezhko
Determination on the basis of the document to V. Ya Klynkevych

I. P. Haiduk to be promoted to the rank of major general and recalled to Kyiv
Hetman K. D. Makhun
16 April 2077

5

Haiduk entered a large, mirrored hall. It was illuminated by the light from three chandeliers, which highlighted numerous porcelain Chinese vases on the tables and piano. All were filled with a pleasing mixture of pink and white gladioli. They're fake, he thought, because not one of the strangely tenacious petals had wilted. The flowers were uniformly magnificent and perfect.

The First Lady of the Confederation of States of North America, which consisted of the former USA, Canada and Mexico, Senator Shirley Van Lee, was waiting with a welcoming smile. She proffered her hand. She was almost unchanged from those long-ago times, only her beautiful face, the face of the queen of those student balls, had lost its aquarelle freshness and the imprecise half-tones of youth; these had been etched with the sharp pencil of time and cosmetic operations. However, none of that detracted from her looks; she remained the most beautiful senator in the history of America.

'I am delighted to see you Mr Haiduk,' she said, smiling enchantingly, though her gaze seemed perturbed to him. Her dark chestnut hair, once so gorgeous and untamed, had turned fair and was carefully groomed and plaited into a tight bun, ballerina fashion, behind her head.

He thought of Lara.

'Senator Van Lee this is a great honour for me, both your invitation and this meeting.' In his agitation Haiduk floundered, then managed an utterly sincere compliment, 'You seem much younger than …'

'Than when?' the First Lady of the Confederation flashed him a relaxed smile.

'Than when we wiped the nose of George Eastman.'

'I'm afraid his nose disappeared long ago,' said Shirley, beckoning Haiduk to sit on a special, two-seater bench, upholstered in dark red and blue striped fabric of the type so beloved in official Washington, where buildings were decorated in the style of the eighteenth century.

Shirley was sitting in an armchair to the left of him. Martha Jefferson was sitting on a stool behind her, with a notebook in her hand, and added, 'They have recently welded a new nose for Eastman, made out of some hard alloy.'

'I heard you were leaving Washington,' Shirley continued. Haiduk saw her touch her left elbow with the palm of her right hand, which he knew was a sign of anxiety. 'In the name of the President and Senate of the Confederation, I wish to thank you for your contribution to the development of Ukrainian-American relations. The president places a high value on your strenuous efforts in this regard and sends you his best wishes. The experience of the last few years illuminates just how fruitful our cooperation in the sphere of science and technology has been. You will leave a big gap in Washington.'

Haiduk remembered the time of their crazy, besotted love; when they lived in neighbouring rooms in a complex at Southgate, on the banks of the Charles River, with a view of Old Boston town gracing their windows. Shirley, a captivating, dark-haired American from New England, had made a deep impression on young Haiduk's heart, so much so that he forgot his oath to the Spetsnaz and the Ukrainian Intelligence Service, and indeed his own goal of simply studying missile guidance systems in the best university in the world. He had forgotten all the injunctions of Counter-Intelligence Captain, Yulii Yulianovych Merezhko, to the effect that his first visitor, his first student friend, the first girl in his bed, the first acquaintance in a student bar, would be an agent of the intelligence service of the Confederation and, as a matter of course, he would have his own personal 'curator'. All these forewarnings and injunctions flew out of his head when Shirley MacDowell knocked on his door and asked him to help sort out her computer.

She was a second year student on course 21F in foreign language and literature. The course focused predominantly on Spanish, but she was also interested in Russian, Polish and Ukrainian. She had even tried to say something in a bizarre mixture of Slavic languages until he started to laugh and interrupted the flow of her words with an embrace and kiss. He was envious of her precise English, the language of white, New England aristocrats, the last legacy of the linguistic architecture of Shakespearean times, which was being eroded by the wave of Indian, Chinese and Mexican accents, and the barbarous computer slang that rolled across the American continent. Later, Shirley admitted she was aroused by his strange accent, which seemed like an echo of the far Eurasian Steppes. At that time she could not have imagined where Ukraine really was, and he could not have imagined what she would become.

'Do you know where in Kyiv you will be working?' she asked.

'Not yet; I'll rest at first and maybe go fishing in the Dnipro.' He had once told her that he hated fishing. She had not forgotten and shot him a sharp glance, and her right hand touched her left elbow once more.

'I have the great honour to present you with a parchment that commemorates and acknowledges the service you have given to both our countries,' Shirley said, rising from her seat.

Haiduk rose from his seat, realising this was the last time he would see her. She gave him a soft leather folder with the parchment enclosed. 'I also request that you present this gift to the wife of your president, your military leader,' she said with the customary captivating smile.

'The hetman,' whispered Haiduk.

'The wife of the hetman, Lady Natalia, I remember her hospitality in Kyiv.'

Haiduk took a heavy package wrapped in paper from her hands, it was adorned with the image of the White House and tied with a bow of pink ribbon. He felt something hard through the paper, perhaps a small wooden box. Haiduk stood to attention, like a proper general, and even clicked his heels.

'I wish you every success,' said Shirley, squeezing his hand tightly, as if she did not wish to let him go. It seemed to Haiduk that tears glittered in her eyes.

'I'll show you the way out,' said Martha Jefferson.

The rosy-cheeked giant stood to attention and immediately saluted when they came out of the first lady's chamber. Why was he so quick off the mark, wondered Haiduk, was it because he saw this award from the Confederation President in my hands or do they have a protocol about greeting guests like that when they are leaving the White House for the last time?

'You may remain in those clothes,' said Martha, gripping his elbow with her strangely dry hand. 'Keep them as a souvenir. Your clothes are in the car.'

Haiduk wanted to say that there was no car waiting for him, but Martha, gripping his elbow tightly, led him to the parking area under the 'Pterodactyl's' protective shield and said quietly, but firmly, 'They want to kill you. You have to flee. Don't ask any questions. The car will take you to Canada where there is a plane waiting. Open the package there. My one request - no I don't request this, actually, I am begging you - my niece, Bozhena, is travelling with you and will also be flying to Kyiv. Look after her, I will always be grateful if you can do that. She ...' Martha nodded towards the White House, 'loves you. Enough, I will say goodbye now. Don't forget to open the packet.'

Martha Jefferson nudged him towards a black, armoured limousine, which had a White House number plate. Instead of a roof-box, the limousine was topped with a machine-gun turret in which a gunner sat. It was reminiscent of an old bomber aircraft he remembered from the computer games of his childhood. Nothing was visible through the darkened windows of the limousine; no police terrapins nor taxi cabs, nor the bums on the lawns in Lafayette Park. The killer drone, which was controlled by the White House guards, glittered in the sun and docked by the traffic light. It looked like an ordinary camera used by the police to monitor traffic, but it was also invisible from the car.

Haiduk settled into the seat of the limousine which was immersed in darkness. Suddenly, he saw the barely noticeable lights of the armrests, the crystalline glasses of the mini-bar and the coloured glowing buttons of a remote control. There was a person silhouetted on the seat before him, with their face turned towards Haiduk.

'Are you Bozhena?' he asked.

She nodded. The limousine jolted sharply as their brief attempt at conversation ended.

6

The indicator lights of the remote control glittered to Haiduk's left. He felt for the barely illuminated GPS button and looked at the screen while trying to work out their escape route. Instead of travelling to Baltimore and exiting on Highway 95, which led to New York, the limousine was battling along the beltway and towards roads crammed with smelly, old Chinese bangers, which used a mixture of oil and alcohol as fuel and were spluttering along at thirty kilometres an hour, north-west towards Pittsburgh.

Haiduk's first thought was that they were heading across Cleveland towards Detroit, which had been destroyed by war and repeated insurrections. They would take the tunnel under the River Detroit to travel to Windsor, a Canadian town of other worldly tranquility. He was convinced the tunnel had not suffered as a result of the war because the bridge over the river had been destroyed three years ago and had not yet been restored. The information about the condition of the tunnel was subsequently classified.

However, the on-screen chart of their hypothetical route showed that after two hours of slow progress towards the north-west, they had turned sharply right towards the south-east. It was possible they could travel to Huntington, take the 81st to Syracuse, and then make it to Canada.

They travelled along pot-holed, rural roads, on which even their super-modern limousine, with its water and hydrogen-powered engine, jerked and swung on its suspension. The darkened windows did not permit him to even imagine the world that surrounded them outside. Through the armoured glass, the emerald spring fields of Pennsylvania, the red farm buildings, the granaries, which resembled missile defence batteries, and the white protestant churches, groomed for Easter a few days ago on April 11, were denuded of colour; the shadowy forms left by a solar eclipse.

Bozhena had not uttered a word since the beginning of their journey and was now lying on the seat before him with her back towards Haiduk as she slept. He could not see her face, but he noted she had wrapped her head in a scarf, like some Muslim women do. A journey to Kyiv with this sombre entity, silent and unfriendly, was, to Haiduk, yet one more sign, not the most terrifying but certainly not too pleasant, of the catastrophes that engulfed him. A feeling of foreboding had pursued him recently, something had broken in the debugging mechanism of the Bureau and UMI.

He extracted a crystal carafe from the mini-bar, poured some dark liquid into a glass and tasted it. It was bourbon. He was unable to find any ice and so he gulped it down.

A quiet voice resonated from somewhere above him, 'Sir, if you want ice please open the fridge below the mini-bar. There's soda and sandwiches with ham and cheese in there.'

'That's all great,' replied Haiduk cheerfully, although he was in despair. Don't give in to panic, Haiduk ordered himself. The drone could have reduced you to ashes, but you are alive. What happened? Why? Who is your enemy? There are many enemies, but who is the main one? Who is my mortal enemy?

***

Haiduk's bureau was an entirely legal and respectable body, established in one of Washington's most respectable districts, where Connecticut and Massachusetts avenues merged into a single, sharp pencil point and pierced Dupont Circle. Building number 1369 was painted a brilliant yellow and as a result had come to be known as 'The Chicken'. Its architectural style, which incorporated ceramic decorations, was reminiscent of a Kyiv merchant's house. It was a very convenient building and had a large underground garage for Haiduk's clients. Despite its prestige, Dupont Circle was one of the most infuriating areas for Washington's motorists; a blood clot in the heart of the capital.

Haiduk loved the place because however hot it was he could feel a coolness wafting from the fountain, built in honour of Admiral Du Pont, freshening the air, and the trees created a quiet and tranquil shade. The fountain was borne aloft by naked boys and girls, representing the sea, the stars and the wind. The water, generously cascading over the yellowed statuary, served to symbolise America's naval prowess. It was here, on the bench by the fountain, that Haiduk had made the acquaintance of Linda Kenworthy.

Haiduk diverted his thoughts from their lyrical vector into a more serious direction. There were five people working at the Bureau, including Haiduk, his chief deputy and old friend, Viktor Bezpalii, and UMI Lieutenant Colonel Kostiantyn Slisarenko, a doctor in physics, mathematics and technology. Slisarenko clearly did not belong to any of Ukraine's intelligence agencies because he was an exceptionally disorganised and forgetful person who displayed signs of genius. He lived from binge to binge. There were two Americans working at the Bureau: Carl Thomson, a technical expert, phlegmatic and steeped in knowledge about the latest Confederation weapons systems, and attractive, plump Nicole Cohen. She was their translator and secretary, who organised rumbustious barbecues that were always a good place to hear interesting gossip and strike mutually profitable deals. Haiduk assumed that all the men in his office had slept with Nicole.

The operations of Haiduk's company were conducted in accord with part three of the Confederation Law regarding national security, which covered 'the protection of sensitive and dual-use technologies'. He divided the possible reasons for his now undoubtable calamity into several categories. Economic - Perhaps some company had lost profits and markets previously secured for them by Haiduk's partners in Japan, Singapore or

Africa. Perhaps it was personal - Someone had not received the promised funds in their offshore account. Or perhaps they had been paid in full and greed had taken over. Who? Political - Perhaps Haiduk and his office had begun to hamper someone in the political game of chance when the map of the world was being re-drawn and the fourth world war was slowly gathering momentum. Who? The stakes for the life and death of states had never been as high.

The last possibility - Some entity at a high level had decided to slit his throat. Which - political, military or intelligence? For what? To take his place? It was not a particularly prestigious position in the state hierarchy, in fact quite the contrary; it demanded specialised knowledge, quick wittedness and abstinence from many of the allurements of a normal life; and was regarded in intelligence circles as one of the more dangerous postings. Any unwary step might prove fatal.

Haiduk began to analyse possible variations of the subsequent development of events. The message regarding his promotion to major general, which in other circumstances would have gratified his vanity, did nothing to improve his mood; on the contrary, the promise of his new assignment only strengthened a depression against which mouthfuls of bourbon proved powerless.

The sound of gunfire, which suddenly rang out from the turret on the back of the limousine, dispelled his dark thoughts. It told Haiduk this was the latest anti-aircraft weapon, which could fire a wave of small homing mines that could destroy any airborne weapon within a ten mile radius.

Bozhena jolted with fear and, without saying a word, reflexively covered her head with her hands; the naive gesture of a defenceless child.

'Sir, Ma'am,' a voice rang out from above, 'don't worry. It appears that someone is attacking us, but everything is okay.'

'It's me they are hunting,' Bozhena muttered, barely

audibly, as she crossed herself, Haiduk noted, from right to left. He offered no comment on her words, knowing who was really the main target.

They halted half an hour after the shooting.

'We are stopping here for twenty minutes. There is a toilet at the end of the hangar and coffee on the table by the wall. We are on the Mansfield Military Airbase and are well protected. Nothing threatens us here. Please get out of the car.'

Someone opened the heavy, armoured doors and Haiduk exited the limousine, followed by Bozhena. He stretched his legs. The lights were shining fully in the hangar and darkness was already falling outside. There were two burly men in black, special-forces clothing, smiling welcomingly at the refugees; an African-American, with black gloves, probably the driver, and a white man; this was their guard.

There were no aircraft in the hangar, only the intelligence terrapins, which were shaped like flying saucers, near which bustled a team servicing them. The gunner sat on the roof of the limousine, dangling his legs in the opening in the turret. A mechanic in a grey jump-suit, adorned with the emblem of the National Guard of New York State, assisted with replenishing the ammunition of the anti-aircraft weapon.

There was a wide table against the wall of the hangar, which was heaped with tools for repair, dirty technical instruction manuals with drawings and diagrams, filthy rags and spare electronics boxes for the terrapins. Someone had also covered part of it with paper serviettes and placed a large jug filled with coffee, some milk, cans of China-Cola and hideous American cookies sprinkled with chunks of chocolate, like the speckles of fat in cheap, deli sausage.

Haiduk swallowed the coffee, which did not seem too bad, and approached an electronic notebook that was working on automatic. He tapped the keys and checked out the world news. It was all mundane and wearisomely familiar:

The Union of States of the Horde (USH) has announced its intention to hold a representative international conference in Batii-Hrad in December, at which a number of historic peace initiatives will be announced.

Columbia has left the military alliance of South America in protest against the hostile policies of Venezuela, and intends to join the Commonwealth of the Celestial Empire.

And now the news from Washington:

President Andrew Van Lee has flown to the West Coast this morning in connection with the increasingly tense international situation and is now in the vicinity of Santa Barbara, at the Vandenberg Space Station. He is there to examine the battle readiness of the missile protection system …

Now the crime reports …

Haiduk's gaze was riveted to a report from the police in Washington's Colombia District:

Today, at 13:00, the body of well-known businessman, Viktor Bezpalii, was found in an apartment in Springfield …

As if in some horrible dream, he automatically clicked the button for the TV images. He saw how they wheeled the gurney, bearing a corpse in a black plastic body-bag, from the familiar passage way. He saw the mask of fear on the faces of Bezpalii's wife, Nina, and their terrified children, Mariana and George. This image passed in a moment and a doll-like reporter, with the blank eyes of a fish, appeared on the screen reading, so obviously, from an auto cue:

'The murdered Bez... Bez... paLII,' she uttered with the accent on the last syllable, barely defeating the unfamiliar surname, 'may be connected to the arms trade. The police suspect I. P. Haiduk, the director of a Ukrainian-American company, of the murder.' His photo-portrait, taken from the company website, hung statically on the screen; black hair, with the first signs of grey on the temples, cut short, dark, deep-set eyes, and a boxer's flattened nose, lips tightly closed, and a heavy, suspicious glance. A typical Italian Mafiosi, thought Haiduk, or an ancient Roman Centurion.

'Haiduk,' continued the all-knowing reporter, 'fled from his Canal Road residence today. His neighbours saw him depart in a taxi belonging to a Pakistani company suspected of being connected with the Muslim extremist movement Al-Karim ...'

So that's where they're placing me, thought Haiduk. Maybe I should really go to Islamabad.

The reporter sprayed words rapidly without a pause:

'It has become known to the police that there was a long-standing conflict between Haiduk and the murdered man. The company was ruled by an atmosphere of enmity and mutual accusations ...'

One of their guards delicately touched his shoulder. 'We need to go now, don't pay any attention to that, we are protecting you. This business stems from Fiery Sara and her people.'

Haiduk slowly walked in the direction of the limousine, as if recovering from a heavy blow, feeling tediously weak. If only he could suppress the urge to vomit. He knew that if he did not defeat this overwhelming terror he would perish. He looked at Bozhena and saw that neither the big, dark glasses nor the black headscarf, which had covered most of her face, could conceal the sad fact that Martha Jefferson's niece had been savagely beaten. There was white tape with plastic rollers on her swollen nose for stabilising her nasal bones. Bruises seeped beyond the periphery of her dark glasses, and there was a split, smeared with grease, in her lower lip. Blue stripes, indicating strangulation, wreathed her neck. Bozhena was dressed in a long frock of dark denim, which bore a strong resemblance to a convict's attire, and hid all the particulars of her figure and movements. But it was not hard to observe that the girl could barely move as she slowly sat in the limousine. Haiduk suggested she could sit on the back seat, but she refused.

The car headed towards the Canadian border, which they had to cross in the Ogdensburg district, somewhere between Kingston and Ottawa.

7

In the darkness of the car, for night now ruled outside, it was easier to concentrate and understand the situation. Of course Haiduk knew how dangerous Fiery Sara was. The vice-president of the Confederation, Sara Lou Lane, who they called 'Fiery', not only for the bright red colour of her hair but also for her explosive temperament and her inflammatory, aggressive speeches against the Jewish, Chinese, Russian, Mexican, Indian, Brazilian, and whatever Mafia ran Washington. Fiery Sara had done more than just concentrate in her hands, well, more accurately in the hands of her husband, the trade in all the narcotics substitutes manufactured by the pharmaceutical corporation NOP; from 'no pain', but also associated with NOPAL, named after the Mexican cactus from which they manufactured the most powerful narcotic.

She was preparing to monopolise the development and production of new arms systems and it was here that her path had cut across the interests of Haiduk's bureau.

As early as the second day after her election to vice-president she had begun a campaign against the Chinese mafia, which was evaluated by observers as the beginning of an open campaign against the president. Haiduk knew how ferociously she hated the first lady. She had extracted, from the historical chronicles, some fragments about the white colonisers, Shirley's ancestors, who had mercilessly destroyed the Native-American population during the deportation to Oklahoma. Sara began a loud campaign for the admission of guilt by the White American establishment, emphasising the necessity of material compensation for a crime committed in the seventeenth and eighteenth centuries. The contemporary heirs of those accused of the genocide of Native Americans would have needed to pay as well, of course, and only a Supreme Court verdict halted Fiery Sara's deranged onslaught.

However, Haiduk did not quite believe in his white guard's statements. Such soldiers, without a game plan confirmed by someone, or an order from their leaders, did not have the right to cast such information towards those they were protecting. There was another principle driving the events that had come to pass.

Suddenly, Bozhena's quiet voice rang in the darkness. She spoke, not the diaspora Halychinian-Polish-Ukrainian but the language of the central Dnipro regions. 'I've been there before, in Mansfield, stuck in a military prison. They tortured me there. Three days ago Auntie Martha took me from there to Washington.'

Startled, he replied to her in English because he had almost forgotten Ukrainian. Everyone in the embassy spoke Russian and at gatherings of the CUC (The Congress of Ukrainians of the Confederation) American-English predominated. However, Haiduk only rarely attended gatherings of the CUC because he had no desire to draw the unnecessary attention of the Military

Intelligence Services of the Confederation of States of North America. There were more than a few Ukrainians among his agents, who for ideological considerations provided him with necessary information. 'Don't say anything,' he said in a tone of command. 'They are listening to us.'

'I am afraid of no one,' the girl continued stubbornly. 'This Cadillac took me to Washington, the same people guarded me then. They know everything.'

'Why are you going to Ukraine?' he asked, while still thinking about Fiery Sara.

'Because I cannot live in this cursed country. It is ruled by oppression and lawlessness. I hate America. There is no worse country in the world. They kill innocent people here.'

They kill innocent people here, Haiduk repeated in his thoughts, but where don't they kill them? 'Have you visited Ukraine before?' he asked her.

'Never, but my brother, Askold, lives there. He says there is no better country in the world.'

'And what does he do there?'

'He fought against the Muscovites. Now he's a potter. He moulds pots and whistles from clay. He got married and is happy.'

Both of them fell silent and did not speak as they reached the Canadian border, which they crossed at 04:00. A whole day had passed since the drone had hung in the air above Haiduk and Linda. Bozhena again settled herself to sleep on her seat and Haiduk dreamed until he fell into a profound sleep.

8

21 April 2077
09:07
Secret
For the President of the Confederation of States of North America: Andrew Van Lee

Sir

I consider it my duty to inform you of the events connected to the American-Ukrainian Bureau of Technical Exchange, which has always been at the forefront of our intelligence forces' attention. The directorate of strategic operations at the Central Security Services monitors both the character of the contacts made and the specific details of the activity undertaken by the bureau, headed by I. P. Haiduk. According to our information, Haiduk is a colonel in Ukraine Military Intelligence (known as UMI) and the manager of one of its directorates. A message from the president (hetman) of Ukraine, decrypted by the National Centre for Processing Information, which reached the Ukrainian Embassy yesterday, 20 April, indicates that Haiduk has been promoted to the rank of major general and simultaneously recalled to Ukraine.

According to sources among agents controlled by the Central Security Service of the Confederation, in the special section under the president (hetman) of Ukraine, the situation in Kyiv has become extremely tense. This is as a result of the growing opposition between the Union of States of the Horde, who have gathered around the leader of the Movement for Four Freedoms, and Ukrainian Aeropagus member, M. Basmanov, supported by the State Guard of Ukraine, and the group orientated towards the Greek-Polish-Lithuanian-Scandinavian Union, headed by the speaker of the Upper Chamber of the Sejm (parliament) of Ukraine, Indira Holembiyevska. She is supported by Ukrainian Military Intelligence and the Ministry of Defence of Ukraine.

The president (hetman) of Ukraine, K. D. Makhun, occupies a cautious position, striving to prevent either group from gaining an advantage and seizing power in the country. According to our agents, I. P. Haiduk is a highly qualified technocrat who does not participate in political conflict and is uninterested in internal Ukrainian affairs. The bureau headed by him works for the benefit of the strategic partnership between the Confederation and Ukraine, realising an array of mutually advantageous scientific and technical projects in the defence sphere. However, I. P. Haiduk's future role in Kyiv is unclear.

Admiral Stanley Fisher, Director of the CSS

Cryptogram from aboard AF No. 1
21 April 2077
10:00
To: Admiral S. Fisher

What do you know regarding the intention of the Union of States of the Horde to conduct a summit of the states of the USH in Kyiv (Batii-Hrad)? What decisions will be approved there? I require you to strengthen your surveillance of the president (hetman) of Ukraine. What role will Haiduk play? Inform me immediately.

President Van Lee

21 April 2077
15:00
Secret
To: President of the Confederation of States of North America,
Andrew Van Lee

Sir

I am writing to inform you that at approximately 11:30
V. Bezpalii, I. P. Haiduk's deputy, was murdered in his
apartment in Washington. The nature of the murder is being
analysed by experts at the central laboratory of our research
department. Haiduk, who is continuously under surveillance
by the responsible services of the CSS Research Bureau of
the Confederation, has a cast-iron alibi. We are working on a
number of versions of the murder, which include the possible
cooperation of people known to you.

Haiduk had a meeting at the White House with the
first lady from 14:00 to 14:30; visual and audio recordings
were made of the conversation. He left the White House at
14:45 in the first lady's limousine, and under the protection
of her personal bodyguard. In accord with national security
directive No. 1278-X/68, a force-field was activated around the
limousine of the first lady, which rendered it neither possible to
bug the conversation nor effectively target the limousine with
drones.

The limousine took the following route: The Mansfield
Military Airbase, the Canadian border, the General U. Clark
Secret Confederation Airbase.

I will inform you of the subsequent course of events.

Admiral Stanley Fisher

21 April 2077
16:30 local time.
Top Secret (One Copy)
To: His Excellency the Hetman of Ukraine, General Kuzma-Danylo Makhun

The Embassy of Ukraine in the Confederation of States of North America respectfully informs you of the emergency events that have occurred today:

1. The Deputy Director of the Ukrainian-American Bureau for Scientific and Technological Exchange, Colonel Bezpalii, Viktor Ivanovych, born in 2042, was murdered in his apartment in Washington while engaged in a radio communication with Kyiv. He was on the balcony of a twelve-storey residential complex. The Criminal News TV Channel (WCN) announced this in broadcasts at 15:00 and 16:00, reporting that I. P. Haiduk was allegedly implicated in the murder. The embassy reacted immediately, directing the consul to contact the police and establish the details of the murder, while undertaking all the necessary formalities.
2. We have lost contact with Haiduk and his present location is unknown. I have personally instructed the embassy staff, security officers of the OIS SGU, and the UMI military mission in the Confederation to use all means to establish the location of I. P. Haiduk and his possible involvement in the murder of V. Bezpalii.

Although the bureau represents the interests of Ukraine it is not a sub-division of the embassy. Ukraine will not suffer any damage to its reputation as a result of the scandal. I will inform you regarding the further course of events and am awaiting for your directives.

With Respect, the Ambassador of Ukraine, Ruslan Foshchenko

22 April 2077
02:00
Encrypted Telegram 63-84/CSNA
For the Ambassador of Ukraine in the Confederation of States of North America, R. V. Foshchenko

You will pay with your own skin for what has happened. Who killed Bezpalii? Where is Haiduk? I'll show you the 'spotless reputation of the embassy'. You're off to Sierra Leone, faggot face.

Hetman of Ukraine

9

They did not notice when they crossed the American-Canadian border; in reality there was no boundary between the countries. Passing over an old bridge, which linked the banks of the Saint Lawrence River, they halted at the edge of the forest, where there was an old, timber hunting lodge occupied by sleeping Canadian militiamen. They consisted of students armed with ancient M-24 rifles. The serving adult personnel of Canada's regular military forces were participating with American and Mexican troops in three global operations: the Southern, Operation Cockatoo, which saw battles occur mainly in Brazilian jungles; the Eastern, Operation Silk Road, where mobile Confederation forces operated in Szechuan and Tibet, and undertook incursions into the sphere of the Horde-Turkestan and the Caucasian-Caliphate; and the Middle East, Operation Grail, where the Confederation's elite military seized bridgeheads in Beirut, Damascus and the Negev Desert, along with the high ground around Jerusalem, in an attempt to save the remnants of the Israeli State from being overwhelmed. The Pentagon and the Organisation for Global Security, having taken account of the geo-political situation, were working on the plan for Operation Stalingrad, which would see a new theatre of military operations in Europe.

On hearing the limousine's horn, a sleepy young man in grey-green military underclothes emerged from the booth and raised the bar, which was weighted with the wheel of a jeep that had been blown apart by a nearby mine. The limousine moved slowly through the epizootic barrier, which consisted of a fetid quagmire poured into a tailor-made concrete trough, and entered Canadian territory. Haiduk was awakened by the horn and remembered the diplomatic passport he was entitled to, in accord with the agreement on Ukrainian-American cooperation in the sphere of science and high-technology. The document was stashed in the outer pocket of his new blue jacket. However, the guards did not check his passport. Haiduk subsequently recollected the package given to him by Shirley, and Martha Jefferson's words. He picked it up, untied the ribbon and tore open the gift wrapping paper around the parcel. He wondered if it might contain a porcelain Chinese vase or an Inuit stone idol. He switched on the reading light in the roof of the limousine. Bozhena slept with her back turned to him.

A ray of light picked out the cherry-coloured leather box engraved with the emblem of the president of the Confederation, which was essentially identical to the one known since the period of the USA; an American eagle with an olive branch in its right talon, a clutch of arrows in its left, and a white tail, and the inscription, E Pluribus Unum. Over its head were arrayed the white American star, the red star of Canada and the green star of Mexico. He opened the box to reveal a finely crafted, gold butterfly adorned with emeralds, destined for the proud bosom of Natalia Havrilivna Makhun, the first lady of Ukraine. Then he saw his old familiar Beretta M9A11 with three reserve magazines and an envelope containing his cash and bank documents. He wondered when they had managed to acquire these riches from the building on Canal Road? Below them, in the depths of the box, he saw an unfamiliar device akin to a wristwatch with a huge dial. He raised it to his eyes and the watch suddenly glowed with the blue transparency of a screen on which various symbols emerged, including a drop of water. Haiduk realised that in his hands he held the most recently produced gadget for secure global communication. Any signal produced by this device: telephone, television, computer or satellite, could not be detected, thereby preventing it from being targeted and destroyed by a volley of self-navigating missiles. He could only dream of a better gift. Haiduk's agents had informed him of this new toy, manufactured by Four Apples, which the Americans were issuing in limited numbers for the use of the Confederation's civilian and military functionaries. A deranged thought flickered through his head, he could ring Fiery Sara right now and ask if her people had murdered Viktor Bezpalii.

As he thought about Viktor, he could not believe he was no longer among the ranks of the living. As recently as yesterday, or the day before yesterday, after the receipt of the encrypted telegram from the hetman, he had a good chat with Viktor as they drank to Haiduk's promotion. They were in the O'Connor, an Irish pub in Springfield, drinking Bily Orel Polish vodka and good, black *Guinness*. They had agreed that Viktor would take on all Haiduk's responsibilities and his contacts with the network of agents. Haiduk had promised to return from Kyiv soon, to hand over his affairs to Bezpalii and organise everything necessary for his departure. They had said goodbye … and neither doubted that after Haiduk's exit Bezpalii would become the director of the bureau. He imagined Viktor, with a gunshot wound to his head and a yellow tag tied to the big toe of his right foot, in the morgue of the central laboratory of the Bureau of Investigation at Quantico, where the FBI Academy had once been based; he was certain they would have taken Bezpalii's body there. He thought about Nina, helpless and paralysed with grief, her face swollen with tears; George, curly haired and petrified, and tearful Mariana.

Haiduk, for the first time in the last deranged twenty-four hours, felt acutely what it was to lose someone close to him. For him, both as a soldier and a scientist, the conception of 'my team', 'my people', 'the people you can trust' was sacred. Neither the family nor any party nor political movement, a rabble of treacherous bigmouths, united, or more accurately, disunited by a lust for power, had any value for Haiduk. He never had any sentimentality towards relatives such as cousins or uncles, who had often manifested enmity towards him, taking Haiduk for a vain, power-loving savage and self-absorbed egotist. He disregarded all parties and had no belief in any of their leaders. His intelligence work and the opportunity to become familiar with the most secret files gathered by the main directory of military intelligence and the special division under the hetman had denuded Haiduk of any illusions concerning Ukraine's past and present political leaders. He believed only in his friends and fellow agents on whose help he could rely in any fatal situation and with whom he had passed more than one ordeal. He knew those tried and tested colleagues, who belonged to 'his team', he was proud of them and helped them whenever he could. Viktor Bezpalii had been one of Haiduk's most faithful companions.

Day was already breaking when the limousine transporting the fugitives reached Smith Falls, where the secret General U. Clark Airbase was located. A report on this base, prepared by the Ukrainian Military Intelligence resident in Canada, had passed through Haiduk's bureau in 2075. It was a pretty superficial document; the activities of the resident agent in Canada, in general, summoned up many questions for Haiduk. However, now, as he dug in his memory, he recollected that, according to the report, the base was allocated for secret operations in the Arctic, Siberia, Pakistan, China, India and Afghanistan.

The routes taken by strategic bombers and military cargo planes traversed the North Pole and the territory controlled by the Union of States of the Horde. There was no reference to the base in the American or Canadian press, or on the internet.

There was just one occasion when a large Lancaster-37 bomber had crashed not far from Ottawa, in Gatineau, the city's French district, which had ignited a scandal. The French-controlled area of Quebec accused the authorities in Ontario of a deliberate act of sabotage against French interests. The explosion destroyed a scientific research centre for the manufacture of high-tech warheads, situated in the Gatineau foothills. The Parisian press even suggested that the Lancaster may have been carrying nuclear weapons because the explosion was so powerful, but the affair swiftly faded. The Confederation had paid Paris a robust sum in compensation, and provided the French with armed assistance in the conduct of their punitive operation against the self-proclaimed Arab Caliphate in the Yvelines district, thereby saving Versailles from the green banners of Islam. However, the analysts at UMI had been able to draw some conclusions as a result of minor observations regarding the coordinates of the bomber's take off point, its military load and the trajectory of its fall.

Morning broke and the sun emerged from the stone bastions, where the Atlantic Ocean ended, and rose above Newfoundland and Labrador. In the chilly, spring fog, the grey-blue silhouettes of huge aircraft were imprecisely sketched. Haiduk automatically reckoned their number; there were over thirty. In the eastern sector of the airport F-160 vertical take off and landing bombers were kept, which looked like black, flat, featureless platforms and ruled the stratosphere. The air-traffic control tower pierced the fog. The taxi-ways were still marked by blazing, nocturnal-blue lights. Heavy munitions trucks lumbered across the field. The limousine traversed the runway and reached the end of the airfield.

Not far from the powerful radar antenna stood an aircraft, the kind of which Haiduk had only ever seen in pictures. It was a huge, old Lancaster-27; a legendary transport bi-plane with eight engines in two rows of four on each lower wing. The plane was constructed forty years ago when deranged greens had seized the UN and tied up humanity with suicidally low quotas for carbon production and fuel consumption under the pretext of combatting climate change. The dark grey, two-storey fuselage of the plane was painted with a huge red cross on a white background. The flying hospital, which could simultaneously transport up to four hundred wounded, was equipped with two operating theatres and three treatment/dressing rooms.

The limousine drew up under the open belly of the plane, part of which lay on the ground and served as a bridge for loading containers painted in desert camouflage colours. There was the usual bustle that accompanied this kind of scenario. The sergeant supervising the loading of the containers was swearing at the drivers to pressure them not to imbalance the plane's centre of gravity. Two searingly yellow fuel cisterns were suckered by hoses to the left and right wings, along which mechanics ran or worked around the engines. Haiduk observed a special path, fenced off with netting, which ran along the lower wings, and wondered if they might even go out onto the wing during flight.

No one paid any attention to the arrivals, who stood in silence near the limousine. Bozhena kept herself apart and arranged her headscarf in order to avoid revealing her face. Finally, an older man wearing the uniform of an intelligence officer of the Air Force of the Confederation approached Haiduk, saluted and asked to see his passport. He typed something on his laptop and said, 'I recommend you discard your clothing. It contains some homing devices.'

Haiduk silently proffered the officer the packet with

the clothing in which he had travelled to the White House. A decent two hundred globos dark blue suit, a light pink tie and new shoes.

The officer rubbed his palm in his grey beard, 'Please let us hold onto the box during the flight. We will return it to you later.'

Haiduk handed him the box with the pistol, the first lady's gift, and the certificate of the president of the Confederation. He had prudently concealed the cash and communication gadget in his pocket.

'Where are we flying to, Captain?'

'We are flying to Europe, but I don't have the right to say where exactly or, more accurately, I don't know. Everything depends on the situation. You must know there is war in Europe.'

In fact there was war everywhere. A war that no one had officially declared, a creeping, permanent, global war.

The warmth of the sun devoured the fog and the roar of the engines filled the runway as bomber after bomber started up and flew in the direction of Hudson Bay, and from there to the Northern Circle. A feeling of solitude and hopelessness seized Haiduk.

The forest around the base was still circled with a strip of snow, as if it were the Taiga, while on Canal Road in Washington small pink and yellow asters, carefully watered by Linda, bloomed. His life remained there.

The cisterns slowly moved away from the aircraft, leaving a hot trail in the cold territory of the airport. The grey-haired officer raised his palm to the visor of his old aviation cap in salute. 'Please board the aircraft now ladies and gentlemen. I welcome you on board the 'Lame Dragon' on behalf of the 'Flying Tombs' airline. We will be flying for a long time, up to twenty hours. Whether we will reach our destination is unknown. Our route is dangerous, but the crew are reliable, jolly and young, even if all the pilots are older than me.' He winked merrily at the silent Haiduk and Bozhena, 'There's plenty of alcohol and some tasty food. Please Mademoiselle.'

He gallantly allowed Bozhena to board first. Haiduk waved farewell to the gunman, who was on the roof of the limousine, and headed for the ladder into the uninviting belly of the 'Lame Dragon'. The huge hatch immediately began to close and darkness gripped the interior of the aircraft. Just a second before the door closed, a small drone flew into the aircraft and hid in the operating theatre on an unshaded surgical lamp. The plane moved slowly along the taxi-way to take its place in the departure queue with the bombers, which one after another roared into the cold Canadian sky.

10

22 April 2077
Operational Order No. 1377/2554 OT
Secret
To: All border facilities, points and posts at the transit areas of the state border, and all intelligence sub-units of the border service
To: All area and district offices of the State Guard of Ukraine. All agents of the SGU, police officers and serving employees of the military police

The executive director of the Ukrainian-American Bureau for Scientific and Technological Exchange, Major General Ihor Petrovych Haiduk, also of the main directory of military intelligence, fled from the capital of the Confederation of States of North America, Washington, on 21 April for an unknown destination. He is accused of involvement in the murder of the bureau's deputy director, V. Bezpalii, and other serious crimes against the state. He will attempt to enter Ukrainian territory.

In the event of an attempt by I. P. Haiduk to cross the state border of Ukraine, or his appearance on Ukrainian territory, I direct that he is apprehended and transported to the headquarters of the SGU, Kyiv, Volodymyrska Street 33/37.

Haiduk is armed and extremely dangerous, and has military experience as an officer of the intelligence Spetsnaz. You must inform me personally of any suspicious movements or attempts to cross the state border.

The Director of the State Guard of Ukraine - Yulii Merezhko

22 April 2077
10:00
To: President of the Confederation of States of North America, Andrew Van Lee
Secret: Of the highest significance for the state

Sir
We have just obtained information from reliable sources that Sara Lou Lane is preparing an exceptionally dangerous provocation, capable of destabilising the foundations of the Confederation's state system and significantly weakening our international position, not to mention the catastrophic consequences for you personally.

Yesterday evening (21 April 2077, at 22:00) in the headquarters of the United Forces Submarine Navy of the Confederation, a recording was made of a television, radio and press interview with the vice-president. The recording will be distributed to leading media outlets, including *The Washington Post*, *The New York Times*, *Globe* and *Mail*, *Mexico News*, *The Guardian*, *Der Spiegel* and *Kyiv-Star*. Her interview contains serious accusations directed at the first lady, Senator Shirley Van Lee, in connection with her relationship with the resident agent of the Union of States of the Horde (USH), Major General Haiduk, who allegedly obtained the most sensitive, secret information connected to the national security of the Confederation via her. The interview contains falsified information regarding numerous meetings between Haiduk and the first lady, of a blatantly sexual character, in safe houses. The interview has the addition of, unfortunately, genuine video recordings of an intimate nature from twenty years ago, when Shirley MacDowell and Haiduk were students at MIT.

During the interview, Sara Lou Lane demands that this scandalous affair be passed to the special prosecutor of the Confederation, Steven Goldman. She also demands the immediate arrest of Haiduk and the first lady. The main aim of the interview is to achieve the impeachment of the president of the Confederation; the first phase of which must be the immediate removal of your authority and the transfer of all your powers to the vice-president until the details of the case are clarified. You will be presented with an ultimatum to this effect today. In the event of your refusal to act in compliance with the demands presented to you, the interview will be made public tomorrow, or at the latest the day after tomorrow.

Admiral Stanley Fisher

P.S. Haiduk, whom I mention above, reached the Clark AF Base (Canada) today and flew to Europe at 09:30 on a hospital plane, a Lancaster-27 of the Confederation Air Force. The plane will land, depending on the operational situation, at the secret Rostock base in Germany or at the Mazury base in Poland on the 23 April, at approximately 15:00 European time.

Stanley

22 April 2077

12:30

Top Secret

To: Commander in Chief of the Space and Air Defence Forces of the Confederation, Air-Marshal Alex Joseph

It has become known that an exceptionally dangerous criminal, the resident agent of the Union of States of the Horde, Major General Haiduk, flew to Europe today on board a Lancaster-27, while in possession of the strategic plans for Operation Silk Road. If these plans fall into the hands of the enemy they will deliver a huge blow to the national security interests of the Confederation, as a result of which tens of thousands of our military personnel will perish and the losses will amount to billions of ameros.

I therefore order you to locate and destroy the Lancaster-27 hospital plane above the Atlantic Ocean. The collateral damage from the loss of the plane and its civilian team does not bear comparison to the strategic catastrophe that is threatened by the hand-over of these documents to the enemy. The aircraft must be destroyed outside the territorial waters of the Confederation and its economic zone. You must inform me immediately of the fulfilment of this order.

President Andrew Van Lee

CNN TV Channel Report

22 April 2077 (11:00 Washington time)

President Andrew Van Lee, for reasons unknown, has suddenly departed the Vandenberg base and flown to Washington. Neither the president nor his entourage have commented on this situation. It is the opinion of various experts that the departure of the president is connected to a sharp deterioration of the situation in the Middle East. It has become known, from unofficial sources, that a military contingent of the Confederation in Beirut has sustained heavy losses.

11

They were quartered on the second storey of the aircraft, in an empty ward for wounded Confederation officers. It was an ascetic, grey environment, scented with iodine and disinfectant, and had four beds. Two portholes revealed a view of the right wings of the airplane. The little table, like the beds, was welded fast to the deck, while four metal chairs were held in place by electro magnets. There was a wall cabinet with crockery and medication packages, and a drawer with old books and magazines.

The jolly, grey-haired officer entered the room and introduced himself as Senior Steward Blanchard before setting the table. He presented them with a standard array of food in plastic containers; salads, ham, cheese, tuna, shrimp, cold buns, milk and strawberries. Not bad at all, thought Haiduk, recollecting the miserly food rations that Linda had brought back to the Canal Road flat on Fridays when she returned from the bank.

Bozhena immediately headed for the shower next to the ward, and Captain Blanchard explained the specific details of their flight to Haiduk. The 'Lame Dragon' had a relatively low speed of three hundred and twenty to four hundred kilometres an hour and a low-flight ceiling of up to three kilometres, though sometimes the plane flew at an extremely low altitude of one hundred and fifty to three hundred metres. This gave them a significant advantage insofar as the stratospheric interceptors of the Horde, with their cosmic rapidity, were designed for battle at high altitudes and were often useless against the slow, almost unarmed Lancaster-27s. In addition, Blanchard imparted the secret that the 'Lame Dragon' usually flew in a stealth regime, becoming invisible not only to high altitude interceptors but also land and sea based anti-aircraft rockets with which terrorist formations were armed en-masse. The crew maintained radio silence, which helped overcome the danger of travelling long distances over the ocean. 'And yet,' Blanchard said, as he shook his head morosely, 'every journey undertaken by the flying hospital carries a substantial risk.'

Bozhena returned and politely declined breakfast. She only drank some milk before lying on the upper bunk.

How am I going to get this tormented being to Kyiv? Haiduk wondered. He understood, though not to its full extent, that he had jumped into a pretty horrible mess, and began to draft some alternative plans for safely reaching Ukraine with Bozhena after they had landed in Europe.

Haiduk refused alcohol, although Blanchard tried to persuade him. The cold food, denuded of any flavour, did not summon up any appetite in him. There was no hot coffee, which he would have liked, because the system for heating the water tanks for beverages was not working.

'That outfit is too tight for you,' Blanchard cautioned him. 'Where did you get it?'

'They gave it to me at the White House.'

'Oh, it's an exhibit. And what does the letter V mean? Victory?'

'Visitor.'

'Do you want to swap? I'll take your costume, it will suit me, and I will give you an officer's camouflage uniform in exchange. I think the size will be okay.'

'Okay,' agreed Haiduk, who was irritated by the 'pyjamas' from the White House.

Blanchard left the room and returned swiftly with the camouflage fatigues. 'Here, try on these.'

It wasn't a bad outfit, jacket, pants and sturdy shoes.

The camouflage colour and pattern changed automatically, depending on the theatre of military operations, from arctic conditions (white tinged with light blue) to desert (yellow with bluish swatches) and autumnal forest (predominantly yellow with hot crimson tones).

'I thank you profoundly,' said Haiduk, lightly casting off the gift from the White House and swiftly redressing. Wearing it had made him feel like a buffoon.

Bozhena slept quietly on the upper bunk, lulled by the humming of the engines and the slight trembling of the fuselage. Haiduk transferred his passport, money and gadget to one of the pockets of his new outfit. The fatigues certainly had sufficient pockets, many of which served no discernible purpose. Blanchard was also satisfied, not every officer of the Confederation could own a cheap but chic suit, with a gold letter V on the left breast pocket, from the White House. It was a good deal for Blanchard because he had obtained the camouflage from the room where they stored the possessions of dead patients. Blanchard, bursting with pride at his new attire, decided to head for the pilots' cabin to swagger in front of them in his new outfit. His pilot friends were confidently steering the aged Lancaster-27 from the coast of Labrador to the coast of Greenland.

The pilots were drinking hot coffee, because they had their own facilities in the cabin, and the fragrance of the espressos summoned an additional wave of enthusiasm in Blanchard. He strutted before them in his new presidential garb, and by way of thanking the pilots, who shared their coffee and warm crisp croissants with him, proposed showing them a new blue movie that would surely stimulate these jaded air force veterans. He extracted a little disc from a pistol holster fastened onto his right-hand side.

The pilots, as always, welcomed Blanchard. They knew this shyster was an unsurpassed master of dirty jokes and a renowned financial intermediary, who could secure the best exchange rate for ameros against globos, yuan or rupees during the brief stops made by the 'Lame Dragon' at Confederation bases around the world. Blanchard's talents were held in high regard, not only by the pilots but among the teams of surgeons and nurses, whose personnel were changed regularly. A sunny day broke, because the murk of Europe was still some distance ahead, and the ocean below the plane was sprinkled with thousands of glittering sequins, which were extinguished momentarily as the shadow of the 'Lame Dragon' skated over the waters.

12

A Lancaster-27 hospital plane, known as the 'One-eyed Dragon', crammed with the wounded from the Beirut operation, was returning to the Confederation along the usual route from the coast of Greenland to Labrador. The plane travelled at the upper level of its flight ceiling, three kilometres above the ocean's surface. The surgeons in the operating theatres worked at full capacity, in spite of the slight turbulence generated by the chill, polar wind surging to meet the plane from the Canadian coast. Groans and imprecations were heard in the hospital rooms where injured men and women were lying with missing limbs, some of whom would die. The nurses did not skimp on the narcotics they administered in order to reduce the suffering of the soldiers. The military chaplain was tired-out with running between hospital departments, absolving sins and administering the last rites to the dying. The bodies were carried to a platform from which they were lowered in plastic body bags into the refrigerated compartment; the realm of the dead.

The captain of the 'One-eyed Dragon' knew that after two hundred and forty kilometres, the route of his plane would cross the route of the 'Lame Dragon' on its way to Europe.

Perhaps, if the weather was right, it would be possible to see its silhouette from above. The 'Lame Dragon' was piloted by his brother. When the 'One-eyed Dragon' reached the intersection point with the route of the 'Lame Dragon', its captain, who had not seen his little brother for a year, broke radio silence and pushed the button on the inter-plane communication device, 'Hello, it's Vancouver One here. Are you receiving me?'

The 'Lame Dragon', Vancouver Two, maintained radio silence, although the signal was quite audible.

'Gerry, it's Sam here. Everything's okay with me, but I'm missing you. I'm having a holiday after this trip and I'll wait for you to return … Love you, bro.' The connection ended.

Gerry was silent because his captain waved his fist threateningly. The 'Lame Dragon's' commander did not approve of disobeying orders.

The captain of the 'One-eyed Dragon' was still smiling blissfully, imagining his brother's delight, when a terrible crack ran along the fuselage, as if a tin opener blade were tearing open a can of sprats. The debris from the wings, the hot engines, medical equipment, corpses in black bags, and the bodies of the wounded all dropped into the ocean, along with surgeons in green caps, masks and scrubs, nurses in yellow overalls, and pilots in blue uniforms. All fanned across the sky until they hit the 'concrete' ocean surface like bugs on a windscreen.

The 'Lame Dragon', which had not revealed its position over the Atlantic, had managed to fly some sixteen kilometres from the area where the debris of the flying hospital fell and was unaware of the other plane's fate. An atmosphere of gentle euphoria reigned in the cabin where the silence was broken by the passionate cries of the protagonists in the porn movie they were watching.

'I always take a break with him in Victoria,' the junior pilot said dreamily. 'After I return I'll take my vacation immediately. He promised to wait for me.'

The captain and Blanchard did not react because they were concentrating on the screen where the film approached its crescendo. Blanchard was seized with sweet, sexual dreams and remembered that nursing sister Monica Harodi was flying on this shift to Europe. Her fantasies surpassed the primitive situations depicted in the film. He needed to track her down.

The pilot of the F-160 fighter bomber was Confederation Air Force Major Dick Strindberg. He was the best fighter pilot of the Confederation. Having dropped the three rockets, he rose to twenty-seven kilometres and the plane, black and as flat as a folded flick-knife, hovered triumphantly over a planet covered with the dark waters of the ocean and the stark, smooth silhouette of Greenland. Dick Strindberg selected the code for the secret communication channel with Air-Marshall Alex Joseph and gave a brief report, 'Sir, the task has been executed.'

In reply he heard the high-pitched, almost boyish, voice of Air-Marshall Joseph, 'Congratulations Major, nice job.'

The F-160 headed back to the General U. Clark Confederation Airbase.

13

Haiduk rummaged in the drawer where a stack of publications was kept. There were well-read erotic magazines, Chinese military publications, European, mainly French and German, economic reviews, and reports issued by the Global Security Organisation. Finally, he extracted a copy of the Russian journal, *Nabat*, and began to read an article by an archpriest called Father Borisogleb Chikirisov.

THE NEWPEOPLE AS A SIGN OF OUR TIME

Humanity is living through one of the most crucial periods in its history. A time of which the significance can only be compared to the revolution of that time when the axis of history turned in the VIII-IV centuries BC and led to the creation of the world's religions and the philosophical foundations of humanity's awareness. The stars drew nearer to the earth and God appeared in heaven. The deity illuminated not only the sky but also pierced the souls of people. They became aware of the conception of good and evil and trembled with the bloody weight of sins, which they had committed in the past, for the first time. The apex of that revolution and its ultimate culmination, which marks the beginning of the modern era, became the birth, missionary activity and martyr's death of the Jewish dissident, Jesus Christ. The fundamental terrestrial teaching on which the Christian church was built became faith in the divine origin and resurrection of Christ and His ascent into the Kingdom of God and His long-awaited second coming, the return to our brutal world where He will judge the living and the dead and grant each reward or punishment, according to their thoughts and deeds. This doctrine seemed immovable for centuries.

The belief in Christ's resurrection and, as a consequence, their own immortality, warmed the souls of the faithful and became a source of inspiration for artists. However, it should be recognised that the events of the XX and especially the XXI centuries led to a crisis in Judeo-Christianity. They almost destroyed, over most geographic territories, the teachings of the Christian church regarding the immortalities of the spirit and the resurrection. The Judeo-Christian edifice tottered under the blows of the monstrous, mass killings of innocent people, unthinkable by the standards of that earlier revolutionary time, during the course of world wars. These resulted from the atrocities of totalitarian regimes, genocides, and the consequences of massive transportation and industrial catastrophes. All these brought billions of deaths in their wake.

The second brutal blow to classical Judeo-Christianity, if we may call it that, was delivered by the combined forces of aggressively liberal Judaism and secularism, in other words, militant, market-

orientated, hedonistic atheism. The Christian church was driven to the periphery of society's spiritual life as a result. If, as Oswald Spengler affirmed, Christianity died in Europe, this is not our concern. Instead, we have the agony of the remnants of Judeo-Christianity on the battlefield, in military and paramilitary structures, concentration camps, entertainment centres, the throes of sexual ecstasy, in the drugged haze of brothels, in the gangs of a youth culture committed to violence, in the comfortable surroundings of shopping centres, and videos brimming with illusions.

And so, just when it seemed that humanity was mired in the darkness of spiritual chaos and a new barbarism, blessed tidings came from Kyiv, the capital of Russian Orthodoxy, the cradle of a true Russian faith. We mean the globally significant discovery of arch-monk Father Kalerii, or to give him his worldly name Sygismund Sansyzbayev, in one of the remote caves in Kyiv's Pechersk-Lavra monastery. He is the greatest authority in the sphere of Christian history and archeology. While undertaking research there with a team of the warriors of light, the holy fathers and guardians of the faith, Father Kalerii found the actual remains of Jesus Christ.

Haiduk put the journal to one side and looked askance at his surroundings. Was all this a dream? This stark room for wounded officers on board the Lancaster-27, the view from the porthole, with the bi-plane wings shearing through small clouds as the plane shuddered; the monotonous soothing hum of the engines. Did he, Ihor Haiduk, exist now in the real world or was this just some turbulent vision? He flexed the fingers of his left hand, as if feeling and seeing them for the first time, and touched his unshaven cheek. So he did not feel utterly insane he compelled himself to think about the simplest things, such as the sterile packet of shaving paraphernalia that had been prepared for him and placed on the shelf in the narrow toilet-shower area next to their room. Bozhena, who was lying on the

54

upper bunk, did not make the slightest sound. What was it with her? Was she gulping tranquillisers, because she slept all the time? He remembered Linda, her soft, sleepy, nasal breathing and snoring, and her white, toothy smile, her … he signed and finally returned to reality where he was impelled to read more of the newspaper's verbiage.

Father Kalerii produced irrefutable, verified scientific evidence that Christ was a normal man and perished on the cross. He did not rise from the dead - that is the chief discovery of the great Russian monk/researcher. The comparison of various texts from the lists of apocryphal gospels and, in particular, the gospel of Jacob the grave-digger provide clear evidence that the body of the deceased Nazarene was stolen from the tomb at Golgotha on the second day after his death.

The members of his sect bribed the guards and temporarily buried him on the Eastern slope of the Temple Mount, not far from the Golden Gate. At the beginning of 70 AD, which was approximately 37 years after the death of Christ, his body, now mummified, was smuggled out through the ring of Roman soldiery, which besieged the city and was preparing for the destruction of Jerusalem, and transported to the then little-known city of Byzantium. At that time a secret sect of Deathchristians was already at work. These contrasted with other Christians, let us call them Risenchristians, because they believed in the death of Christ the man and the impossibility of his resurrection. Only a small number of families of Deathchristians would preserve the terrifying secret and the location of Christ's burial for generations. No one has ever preserved so vast a secret as they.

According to sources, which have been discovered in the chronicles of the time, the real reason for the crusade into the Roman State in 1204 was the desire to besiege and capture Byzantium, which at that time had become a powerful walled-city, and a powerful imperial capital, Constantinople. The crusade was intended to seize and destroy the remains of Christ. Thus, they hoped to preserve the myth of the man-god and his resurrection, which then utterly dominated the mentality of Europe's inhabitants. A special order of fanatics was created from among these Christian warriors and particularly the Norman soldiers, which today we would refer to as special forces, the order of Christseekers.

The Deathchristians were aware of the potentially fatal danger hanging over the secret of the New Truth. They kept faith with their oaths and in turn transferred the remains of Christ on an Imperial warship across the Black Sea and docked at Crimea. They guarded the body and kept it safe in mountain caves for a short time (less than a year). The remains of Christ were then transferred to Kyiv and found their resting place in one of the remote caves in Kyiv's Pechersk-Lavra monastery. The branch from the main cave where Christ's remains were kept was a dead end and usually walled up, particularly during the war years and the occupation of Kyiv. However, from time to time, the members of patriotic Russian families who defended this precious relic (we may now name the family, they are the descendants of Nazar Potapenko, who kept the body of Christ safe and entire until the present day) came to examine the mummified body, which was perfectly preserved, and, if circumstances demanded, change the location of Christ's grave.

'Where am I going back to?' Haiduk sighed as he answered his own question. 'To a crazy country where such rubbish is published.'

Haiduk was a technical and pragmatic individual who was indifferent to religious matters, despite his mother having him christened as a child. He remembered the tranquillity and light of the small, empty Greek-Catholic church by the square in Lviv, and the incense fragrance of the vestments of the young priest who had baptised him. Yet he still found the entirety of Christianity, with its gospels, its confused confessional affairs, conflicts, prayers and rituals, incomprehensible. It was all embodied in his mother, Maria Yuzefivna Haiduk, or Marisia Horol as she had been called prior to her marriage.

She was born on the Polish-German border, between Catholic and Protestant cultures, and had married Petro Haiduk, an aviation engineer from the Antonov company. She had, over time, absorbed more and more of the Greek-Catholic outlook, however, it was not her affiliation with any denominations but her gentle kindness and patience that made her a genuine Christian. She was able to forgive the sins and weaknesses of both those close to her and total strangers. She patiently endured the angry outbursts of her husband, the indifferent, and often irritating, nature of her children, Ihor and Katerina, the obnoxiousness of her daughter-in-law and the chilliness of her son-in-law. She endured the privations connected with the quasi-military existence of an Antonov company family. Maria Yuzefivna had managed all this by praying every day. Easter, which she referred to by its Polish name of Wielkanoc, was the most sacred event for her. She believed absolutely in the resurrection of the Son of Christ. She usually celebrated this festival twice, according to both the Catholic and Orthodox calendars. Although the children ironically asked, 'So when did Christ actually rise?'

Maria Yuzefivna said, her face gleaming, that the date did not matter, the main thing was that he rose from the dead.

So now Haiduk, in whom a feeling of tenderness towards his mother, whom he had not seen for several years, was awakening, along with a feeling of guilt that tormented his soul, was compelled to read more of this contemptible rubbish.

The identity of the body of Christ, which is preserved in Kyiv, has been fully established by scientific research, including a DNA comparison of Christ's blood from the Turin shroud with the DNA of the remains of the corpse, and during the course of other recent scientific research. The discovery by the arch-monk, Father

Kalerii, shocked the religious world. It raised anew the issue of what Christianity is today and what it might become tomorrow in a society with an increasing population of Newpeople.

Father Kalerii's discovery leads us to the point where the teachings of the Deathchristians emerge from the deep underground of religion and cease residing within a small group of conspirators. The newly emerged doctrine initially captivated the intellects of the ministers at Kyiv's Pechersk-Lavra monastery. It is continuously developing and is augmented with new postulates. The teachings of the Deathchristians have spread triumphantly beyond the walls of the Lavra monastery. They have seized, with the swiftness of a Steppe fire, such established Russian monasteries as Chernihiv, Makhnograd, Dnipropetrovsk, Khorkovsk, Ternovenetsk, Lemberg, Minsk and, even further afield, Suzdal, Vladimir, Novgorod, Ryazan and Arkhangelsk.

The situation itself, the factual proof of Christ's death as an ordinary person, compels a complete rethink of the original project.

The establishment of the indisputable fact of Christ's physical death has led to the emergence of a new evolutionary era; a new paradigm in the development of humanity. Father Kalerii's discovery has evoked a new split in humanity and one that is no longer between races, ethnic and national groups, religions or political parties. Humanity is now divided between Newpeople and Oldpeople in a manner that fully accords with the split between Deathchristians and Risenchristians. It would, finally, be wrong to assume that Newpeople appeared only in the second half of the XXI century. No, the origins of Newpeople are lost in the mists of time. Ultimately, the first Newman known to us was Pontius Pilate, who did not believe in the essence of Christ. He was not convinced by the spectacle involving the disappearance of Christ's body, supposedly as a result of his resurrection. Pontius Pilate provided the world with an example of genuine spiritual freedom because he made a responsible decision and did not yield to the pressure brought to bear on him.

On every historical occasion, when huge personalities such as Ivan the Terrible, Peter the Great, Napoleon, Hitler, Stalin, Mao Tse Tung and Kara-Khan have appeared, they did not fit into the Judeo-Christian context. These people created a new conception of the world, terrifying their friends and enemies with freedom and fearlessness in their actions. We may say with certainty that these individuals were Newpeople.

A vast, and as yet not fully comprehended, process has commenced. We refer to the reproduction of Newpeople who do not fit into the framework of fallacious Judeo-Christian doctrines. In other words, the Deathchristians' movement and its new canons are surprisingly fitted to the beliefs and spiritual needs of Newpeople, as if these developments were made for each other. We see before our faces the chaos and utter confusion of humanity, which it would seem present insurmountable contradictions and uncertainty. It resonates menacingly with the challenges of the new revolutionary time, a period of fundamental changes, where old beliefs perish and new truths are born. The boundaries of this new time, ruthlessly bisect continents and billion-strong masses of humanity. They shear through families, permanently destroying family ties and presenting every individual with a stringent examination of their own powers - Do they meet the criteria of Newpeople or do they belong to the world of the past, ordained to certain death?

The teachings of the Deathchristians are clearly very new and the psycho-sociological characteristics of Newpeople are insufficiently studied. However, Father Kalerii has attempted to define some special features shared by the new generation of this revolutionary epoch which is being born before our very eyes. It is not about the individual essentially or about the various qualities of individual people but about the mass process capturing millions of our citizens, the process of conquering new spiritual terrain. The core of these special features is as follows:

1. The death of Jesus Christ. God has departed into his hinterland of energy, Jesus is dead and man is now free. Free for the first time in two and a half thousand years.

2. The individual has the right to a free existence. However, they may only realise this inalienable right through the path of struggle, including self-defence and attack, conflict and violence. The core of the Newpeople's faith is that violence is limited by nothing and no one. It stands in opposition to the unnatural moral prohibitions of Judeo-Christianity, which have shown their unsuitability for the new world.

3. The new humans themselves create their moral norm, which is more in accord with their interests. This human is free to speak and act as dictated by the necessities of their struggle and survival. The concept of 'untruth' is deleted from the Newpeople's dictionary, as archaic, devoid of content, and is replaced by the more scientifically precise term 'information'. If you wish to vanquish your enemy, to destroy him, you have the right to utilise any lies, half-truths, denunciations, slander and defamation because the goal of the Newpeople is victory and victory alone. The value of triumphant information is determined, not by its truthfulness but by the force with which it is proclaimed by the energy of its conviction, the power of the information stream in the battle between Deathchristians and Risenchristians.

4. Life without God is the unusual and wonderful state enjoyed by Newpeople. It frees them from the degrading conditions of that existence, life with God, where in the name of the mythical, heavenly kingdom they would have to eke out some servile existence beseeching alms of the 'Son of God' with no guarantee that His mercy will be allotted to them. No one and nothing, no Judeo-Christian religious, moral, tribal, national or other taboos obstruct the great path taken by the Newpeople as they head for the future.

These are the main implications of the discovery of Father Kalerii, although at present it is clearly difficult to evaluate the full depth of the consequences and changes that will be produced by the revelation

60

of this humble monk. Only one thing is clear - today the Russian city of Kyiv is already the capital of the world, the capital of the Deathchristians of all the planet, the capital of the Newpeople. It remains only for the whole world to decide the fate of the Nazarene Christ's body. In our opinion, it would be fitting for the corpse to be entombed in a grand mausoleum in the grounds of the Pechersk-Lavra monastery on the hills above the Dnipro with the inscription 'From now on everyone is free. Christ has died.'

Arch-Monk Borisogleb Chikirisov

'Fucking priest,' Haiduk muttered irritably, casting the journal back into the drawer.

As the plane imperceptibly immersed itself deeper into the night, anxiety gripped him again. The slow flight of the aged contraption over the ocean engendered a feeling of hopelessness and solitude. The silence was broken abruptly by frantic knocking at the door of their ward and a scream from outside, 'Help … there … there …'

Bozhena darted from her bed onto the floor. Haiduk was startled because her movement displayed none of the previous lethargy nor any confusion, but automatic, trained reflexes. It took him by surprise and he wondered where she had learned to react like that.

The fragile doors shook with the racket, and the screams from the corridor became louder. Haiduk opened the door and a naked woman, covered in blood, stood before him. She sobbed, moaned and pointed her finger into the bowels of the aircraft, 'There … there …'

14

Maurice Blanchard, a captain in the intelligence services of the CAF, was seized with sweet expectations as he embarked on the search for nursing sister Monica Harodi. He peered into the 'mess', a room on the first floor, where the hospital personnel rested when they were off duty. Surgeons and nurses were already mingling around a table laden with food and drink to suit all tastes. People talked over each other, shouted jollities and roared with laughter. All to defeat the lurking anxiety. They squeezed up close to each other and some put their arms around the shoulders of their friends. On seeing Blanchard in his wondrous attire they waved and invited him to join them, but he evaluated the situation with a wary eye and, not seeing Monica, closed the door. He plunged further into the dark belly of the Lancaster-27, opening the doors of the offices and dressing wards on his route. But he did not find Mademoiselle Harodi.

Although not in the first flower of youth, Monica had never been married because her unstable, itinerant profession, her lust and her desire to be with as many men as possible mitigated against betrothal. She enjoyed pilots and surgeons, dark-skinned soldiers with minor wounds, teenage volunteers, old generals and captured soldiers, who were often transported in the prison room onboard the 'Lame Dragon', ... mechanics on military bases, addicted soldiers undergoing rehabilitation, French Gendarmes, Neapolitan refuse collectors … and none of this would help her in the tedious stability of married life.

Blanchard found Monica in a darkened, empty operating theatre, which was lit by only one small, illuminated panel. She was changing her clothes and this process aroused Blanchard still more. The dimly lit features of her plump body summoned longing in him. He seized her large breasts from behind and whispered, 'It's me.' She silently finished undressing, switched on the surgical lamp and pushed Blanchard onto the operating table. She lay him on his back and sat gently on top, so she did not suffocate the skinny intelligence officer, and felt something hot well up inside her, making her yearn to scream.

'Quietly,' said Blanchard as Monica continued to moan softly, already remote from all mundane concerns.

His eyes were wide open. He was staring at her massive legs, feeling her breasts and thinking that she was not heavy at all. He tried to recollect if he had closed the doors. At the moment Monica began her orgasm, he also moaned with pleasure and as he did so he noticed the cold eye of the drone directly above him. It hovered alongside the surgical lamp, studying the blue presidential jacket, which, in his haste, Blanchard had not removed.

What? What does it want? Where does it come from? Blanchard managed to think before feeling the laser turn the tissues in his neck to ash. A fountain of blood spattered Monica, who still sighed with ecstasy until she saw she was sitting on a crimson-soaked corpse. Blanchard's bluish lips still moved, as if he wanted to inform her of something very important.

15

Haiduk and Bozhena ran towards where the naked woman pointed as she shivered with fear, and saw the unusually savage crime scene.

Could that naked old girl really have done this? Haiduk wondered, approaching the table and the remains of Blanchard, together with his lowered trousers and blue, White House jacket soaked with blood. There was no sign of the murder weapon. All the surgical instruments were stored in sterile boxes in special military, medically sealed packs. Haiduk observed characteristic traces on the remains of the deceased's neck, as if the head had been severed with a blow torch.

'Laser,' he said, comprehending what had occurred, and he raised his head to study the crime scene. This was the work of a drone. The surgical lamps dazzled him. The ceiling of the operating theatre was swathed in darkness and he noted nothing suspicious.

Meanwhile, terrified surgeons and nurses were scurrying around him. One of the nurses led the unfortunate Monica to a shower cubicle to wash off the blood, administer an injection against shock, and wrap her in a pale blue towel emblazoned with the Confederation Air Force logo. She held Monica tightly, waiting for the injection to take effect and wondering where Mademoiselle Harodi had found the strength to take off the head of this petty loan-shark and womaniser, God rest his soul.

The security officer was summoned to the operating theatre and acted as if he suspected them all of simultaneously committing the crime. He wanted to grab Haiduk, but at that very moment the displays in the aircraft flashed red with the alarm signal and the voice of the 'Lame Dragon's' captain spoke over the loudspeakers, 'Attention crew. Battle alert. Everyone take up your positions. We are in the operational zone of the Karakorum enemy platform. Prepare to fend off an attack.'

Haiduk took advantage of the commotion and ran along the central corridor into the tail of the aircraft from whence the canon fire sounded. A hatch on the left side of the Lancaster, in the part of the fuselage where the red cross was painted, had opened. A terrible racket emerged from the six-barrelled, seventy-five millimetre automatic Howitzer aimed through it by one of the onboard mechanics. He sat on the saddle, which was akin to a motorcycle seat, and swung in unison with the cannon while looking at the computer screen. The cannon fired rounds of incendiary ammunition whose burning trails flew downwards toward the ocean surface.

Haiduk positioned himself parallel with, but behind, the mechanic so he did not hamper him, and tried to observe the alternations of darkness and the flare of ammunition. At first he understood nothing and was deafened by gunfire, but, after a moment, he saw an incendiary substance flare in a pillow of fire covering some rectangular surface similar to a runway. Fear gripped him when he saw how low they were flying over the oil-black waves of the ocean on whose peaks, like in distorted mirrors, reflections of fire flared and were extinguished. The glow of battle illuminated their aircraft with a purple radiance.

Haiduk had heard of the Horde's legendary Karakorum platform. It had been created in the pre-war years as a civilian oil rig and oceanological research centre. As they prepared for the war, all the major countries had positioned such platforms on strategic routes in the Atlantic, Pacific and Indian oceans, near the North Pole and the Antarctic. The platforms had a standard pattern of construction. They provided, at twenty metres above the ocean, a concrete take-off and landing strip, radar station, and antennae for controlling military satellites. The lower levels, which were encased in a thick hide of composite concrete, concealed anti-aircraft missiles and fighters, which, in a process similar to that on aircraft carriers, would be raised to the take-off strip by special elevators. Underwater warehouses had been constructed and stocked with ammunition, fuel and food. Special rooms for the personnel of the platform to relax, hospitals and even kindergartens had been created in that quiet, underwater world.

The platforms served as bases for submarines. MOPs, military ocean platforms, whose positioning had been sanctioned by a UN resolution, played a significant role in preserving the balance of power between the forces of the Horde, the Confederation, the Celestial Empire, the Organisation of Global Security, and other unions of states. It was thanks to these entities that almost all trade via ocean freight had been halted and the world was subject to a global blockade.

Having ignited the upper platform of the Karakorum with napalm, the mechanic switched to another kind of ammo, concrete piercing, which was intended to penetrate deeply and ruin the innards of this artificial island. It was unlikely he would succeed in doing the platform a great deal of harm because the hospital plane lacked sufficient firepower.

It was suddenly silent. The battle between the 'Lame Dragon' and the Karakorum had barely lasted a few minutes but it had seemed like an eternity to Haiduk. The island smouldered with fire in the wake of the aircraft. Haiduk clutched a handle by the hatch and stuck his head outside. The air blasted him and he saw underneath, but nearby, the restless intermingling of the waves lit briefly by a signal rocket fired by the platform in the wake of the aircraft. It seemed to him that he smelled the aroma of the ocean and his face was wet. It had begun to rain. The mechanic cast off his helmet and turned a youthful, smiling face towards Haiduk.

'What a thrashing I gave 'em! They weren't expecting that. We agreed with the pilot that we would fly at ninety metres or they would have spotted us; we couldn't fly around them.' The mechanic added, seemingly reading Haiduk's mind, 'Fuel must be conserved. Even more so because there are so many of them here … You can't fly around them all.'

The mechanic left the cannon, which was still hot from being discharged, and carefully pulled the left door closed. The Howitzer was positioned on a special mobile mechanism and was very comfortable to use. Fire could be directed just as easily out of the left or right hatch and, if necessary, its elevator platform could be raised into the lantern in the upper part of the fuselage to direct fire towards airborne targets. Although the Howitzer was old, it was greatly to Haiduk's liking. It would be worth arming our Antonov 250s with those, he thought.

'I'm going to check out the wings and engines for damage,' the mechanic informed him, showing Haiduk the respect due to an unknown, but high-ranking, officer of the Confederation.

16

22 April 2077
20:00 Washington Time
Report of the President of the Confederation of States of North America: Andrew Van Lee

An old image of the White House, depicting it without the concrete shelter popularly known as the 'Pterodactyl', appeared on the screens of the Confederation and fifty other countries. The camera solemnly conducted viewers to the Oval Office where a youngish man with lush, dyed-black hair sat at a modestly sized writing table. His Manchurian eyebrows and narrow eyes, glittering from under weak, barely perceptible spectacles, gave the president an intelligent appearance. Van Lee's face was painted with sorrow, concentration and resolve. His pudgy hands lay motionless on the polished surface of the writing table.

'My Fellow Americans,' the president intoned solemnly. 'I address you as our great country experiences a difficult time and many trials. The headquarters of the Air Force of the Confederation has informed me of an unprecedented and senseless act of barbarism that occurred over the Atlantic Ocean today. Our Lancaster-27 hospital plane, which was returning to the homeland with wounded soldiers onboard, was attacked. These strong, brave men and women had participated in the operation to establish peace and democracy in the Middle East. As a result of the attack …' Van Lee paused at this point, because the auto-cue, from which he did not shift his gaze for a second, displayed the word 'PAUSE', and his face assumed a tragic appearance, 'three hundred and eighty-six people died … the wounded, medical personnel and the crew of the aircraft. This is a huge loss for the armed forces and the people of

North America. I express my deepest sympathy to the families of the victims and declare Friday 23 April a national day of mourning. We are undertaking a thorough investigation of the circumstances surrounding the tragedy. The initial findings show that the hospital plane, which had all the necessary identifying markings on the wings, fuselage and tailplane, as required by the Geneva Convention, was attacked by an unknown military plane with no markings. We have strong evidence this blatant act of international banditry was undertaken by a power hostile to us, which, without declaring war, has set its course on global hegemony. They are conducting an undeclared submarine war against the supply of energy and other natural resources necessary for life on Confederation territory. It is they who mercilessly destroy the Confederation's maritime trading vessels and civilian passenger airliners; it is they who direct fire on our coastal areas, terrorising us with waves of cyber attacks, undermine our military bases and take our citizens hostage. However, their latest crime is also the most heinous; the destruction of a hospital plane. This state of affairs cannot continue. Our patience is not inexhaustible. I have convened a meeting of the High Council for National Security tomorrow, in order to develop adequate counter-measures and punish the aggressor. I have ordered the Armed Forces of the Confederation to adopt the highest state of battle-readiness. This evening, we have also undertaken several rounds of rocket strikes against the enemies' Military Ocean Platforms in the Atlantic and against terrorist bases on territory occupied by them.'

The president's soft palm flapped decisively over the table as if finally swatting the enemy. Swatting the menacing Celestial People's Democratic Empire and the Horde, whose combined forces were waging an undeclared war against the Confederation and striving to sever America from sources of oil and strategic raw materials in Asia and Africa. Everyone listening to the president knew this just as they knew the Celestial People's Democratic Empire was led by someone who looked very similar to Van Lee, as if they were two peas in a pod. The same black dye tinged their hair and brows, and they wore the same intelligentsia-style spectacles on the same immobile face. The enemies of President Van Lee even spread the provocative rumour that the Chief of the Empire was his twin brother.

'And now, My Fellow Americans,' Van Lee continued, 'I want to turn to a no less painful theme. I am talking about a savage act of terrorism inflicted against the family of the vice-president of the Confederation, the highly respected Sara Lou Lane, my good colleague and friend. As we know, the vice-president's husband, their two adult children, daughter-in-law and three grandchildren, aged three, five and eight years, were kidnapped today by a criminal gang, while visiting the Grand Canyon. According to reports from the Confederation's Bureau of Investigation, none of the hostages has sustained any harm, but their psychological state is serious. It is unclear what the kidnappers, who are communicating directly with Sara Lou Lane, want to achieve. She has cancelled the press conference scheduled for today and travelled to Arizona. All necessary force and means available to the Confederation will be deployed against the criminals and their masters. The investigative group will be headed by the General Prosecutor of the Confederation, Enriko Pekenya, who has outlined some versions of these events. The most probable is that this was revenge by the narcotics mafia on the vice-president's husband in connection with his business. We all pray the hostages will be released and that Sara Lou Lane returns to the execution of her duties as vice-president as soon as possible. Goodnight Fellow Citizens and God Bless America.'

The president's image vanished and was replaced by his seal on a dark blue background.

17

Their plane flew over Europe. Below them, in the idyllic, misty-azure depths, the circle of fire tightening around Paris glowed like a branding iron. The military forces of the French-Arab Caliphate were striving to take by siege a city, which, at low altitude, seemed bereft of life, a carefully executed architectural maquette. However, the reality of the image was attested by the ruins of the Champs Elysees, the scorched zone in the central quarters, and the broken spire of the Eiffel Tower, whose remnants swung on a twisted armature. Motionless automobiles were chaotically strewn along and across the streets and squares of the city, which Islamists had renamed Lyutetsiy. Europe already knew about the tragedy of the Lancaster-27 hospital plane and the French bombers they passed waved their wings sympathetically. The pilots and crew of the 'Lame Dragon', sealed off from the outside world, were focused on the problems that had emerged within the aircraft after the skirmish, and the dangers dogging their journey.

Bozhena, sitting by the porthole, gazed in terror at the landscape over which they flew. 'My God,' she murmured. 'I dreamed so much of being in Paris. In the Louvre ... What can we call this place now?' Her hand touched the circular pane of glass.

'It's called a change in the revolutionary epoch of humanity,' Haiduk replied, catching himself thinking that the oppressive text of Arch-Monk Borisogleb Chikirisov dominated his memory.

Although Haiduk had convinced himself of the mendacity of this falsified work, to which no one would pay any heed, he now asked himself which group he belonged to, the Deathchristians or the Newpeople?

A ring-tone sounded and Bozhena pulled up the long sleeve of the right arm of her dress. Haiduk saw the pulsating screen of the communicator gadget, exactly the same as the one he had been presented with at the White House. Bozhena pressed the gadget to her ear, but had to remove the headscarf to hear and in doing so revealed close-cropped, dark auburn hair shaved on the crown like a monk's tonsure.

'Yes, it's me,' Bozhena uttered, quietly listening attentively to the voice from the gadget. 'It's okay, Tyotyu,' she said, using the Ukrainian word for aunt, 'all is under control.'

Was it Martha Jefferson speaking? What had happened? The thought troubled him.

Martha Jefferson's monologue persisted for quite a while as Bozhena listened without interrupting, only saying at the end, 'He's very reliable. Don't worry about me. Bye-bye.'

Bozhena looked silently at Haiduk, as if deciding what to say and what not to say to him. 'Auntie Martha phoned. She said they have issued an official order in Ukraine for you to be found and apprehended. You must decide what to do. Perhaps you will stay in Europe for a while?'

'And you? What have you decided?'

'I may try to reach Ukraine on my own through Poland. Buses travel from Krakow to Lviv.'

Her face, partially covered by the dark glasses, was impenetrable, and Haiduk could not discern the expression in her eyes. He only saw his reflection in her spectacles. A man in a foreign officer's uniform.

'I think,' said Bozhena contemplatively, 'it is better for us to keep together. However, you can decide how it will be.'

'Okay. I'll think about it,' he replied, cursing the lack of backbone shown by his inability to rid himself of this unfortunate girl. Nothing was preventing her from travelling comfortably to Ukraine on her own. No one was hunting for her. He recollected again the death of Bezpalii and the absurd accusations tightening around him, like the circle of fire around Paris. Haiduk understood someone from Ukraine was behind this murder. Someone who wanted to destroy him.

He was unable to develop this line of thought further because the battle-stations signal sounded and the racket of the six-barrelled Howitzer throbbed again from the tail of the fuselage. An unseen force propelled the plane upwards and then, with a rapidity that might arrest the heartbeats of its passengers, cast it downwards. The fuselage crackled but the bursts of anti-aircraft rockets, which broke up against the Lancaster-27's defence field, were not as fearsome as at night over the ocean. On the contrary, they seemed like the merry addition to a spring afternoon; as harmless as streams glittering with sunshine.

The clock showed it was 16:35 Central European Time and the pilots of the 'Lame Dragon' saw the green fields of Poland before them. Their route was between Wrocław and Częstochowa, to the north-east. A cargo wagon on the highway beneath them unfurled its canvas awning, transformed into a mobile anti-aircraft complex, and fired at the hospital plane. The Lancaster-27 entered a deep dive, of a kind not recommended for this type of aircraft, to destroy the truck with its on-board Howitzers. During the manoeuvre the outer engine on the right wing, which had been damaged during the flight over the Atlantic, exploded.

Bozhena and Haiduk were not flung head over heels because they were tied, crisscross fashion, with safety straps pressed against the porthole. They watched fire blossom in place of the engine and black smoke tail upwards, marking out the trajectory of the Lancaster's fall. The other engine on the wing caught fire.

'I'm scared,' Bozhena screamed, clinging with all her strength to Haiduk's hand.

'Hold on there,' he instructed himself rather than her.

'Lower your head to your knees and cover it with your arms.'

She gripped his hand even more tightly. The anti-aircraft complex was transformed again into a mundane canvas awning, covered with a blue canvas and adorned with big yellow letters that spelled 'Friedman'. The wagon merged back into the weaving traffic of the motorway and disappeared under a wide overpass. The burning aircraft pulled out of the dive and now flew to meet a field of fresh winter wheat. The pasture seemed ideally level, but the pilots knew this was not the case. The junior pilot of the Lancaster-27 mentally said farewell to his older brother. He would not be going on holiday to Victoria with him this year. The captain of the 'Lame Dragon' prayed for the forgiveness of his sins of which he had committed sufficient in his wretched life.

The Lancaster-27 fell on its huge belly, which crackled and splintered as it ploughed a deep furrow through the Polish wheat. Black ribbons of fuel smeared the ditch along with sacks torn to shreds, which had contained the corpse of the unfortunate Blanchard and stocks of medicine and laundry. Along with them were strewn the bodies of those on board, and the mutilated parts of the fuselage. The lower wing rose in the air and backwards; the upper wing dragged in the earth until it was torn off. Haiduk and Bozhena were saved because they were on the second storey of the aircraft. The terrible, impact that followed caused both of them to lose consciousness.

As he recovered, Haiduk saw a pillar of sunlight. The fuselage was sheared in half. Bozhena was sitting and did not move in the safety straps.

'Get up quickly,' bellowed Haiduk, as he tried vainly to wake her. Then, cursing, he failed to unbuckle the steel fastening of the strap across her chest. He realised the aircraft would explode and tried despairingly again. Finally, the steel plate came off the strap and he grabbed Bozhena and carried her over his shoulder. She seemed amazingly light and he was able to reach the left-hand part of the aircraft through a rift in the fuselage. The ground was very close. He could see the stalks of young wheat, which reminded him of childhood, and smelled the aroma of ploughed earth. The remains of the aircraft were immersed in the field, like a boat sinking into a green lake. Haiduk leaped cumbersomely onto the ground and ran, hauling Bozhena with him, to the forest behind the area where the plane had crashed.

There, where there were fragments of the Lancaster-27's tail section, he saw the mechanic who had been thrown ten metres to the side, along with the Howitzer. He remained seated on the motorcycle saddle; his head had been thrust into the computer screen, which had taken off half his skull. The helmet was nowhere to be seen and the wind ruffled the fair hair remaining on his scalp.

Breathing heavily, for Bozhena became heavier with every second, Haiduk ran to the ditch at the edge of the field, beyond which the forest began. The force of the blast shook everything nearby, lifting aloft the remains of the plane, the soil and the roots of young, winter wheat. Black smoke obscured half the sky. One of the unobserved, but significant, consequences of the blast was the loss of the drone which had melted in the fire that engulfed the crash site.

'What? Where are we?' Bozhena opened her eyes. Her dark glasses had been lost somewhere and Haiduk was also bereft of his favourite pistol. He didn't even think about the Confederation President's certificate or the first lady's gift.

'We have to get out of here,' he said. 'Are you up to that?'

'I'll try.'

He helped her to her feet.

'Where to?' Bozhena asked.

'South-east,' he said decisively, even though shortly before he had been unable to decide what to do with Bozhena.

They traversed the forest until they saw the motorway. It was absolutely empty and the surface was cracked, as if no one had driven there for a long time. They saw a rusted and peeling motorway sign showing the route for Opole-Sosnowiec and travelled alongside the road in the direction of Sosnowiec, ready to hide at any moment from ... in fact they did not know why they needed to hide.

18

23 April 2077
16:45 European Time
Exceptionally secret
To: Air-Marshal Alex Joseph

The task has been executed. No one remains alive.

Major William Crawford, Commander of the X-139 individual mobile battery of the space and air defence forces of the Confederation in the Central European Sector of the Theatre of War.

24 April 2077, Saturday
08:00
To be delivered personally to His Excellency, Hetman of Ukraine, General Kuzma-Danylo Makhun.

According to absolutely reliable intelligence sources, yesterday, at 16:45, a Lancaster-27 hospital plane crashed in the vicinity of Wrocław. I. P. Haiduk, who stands accused of treason, was on board the aircraft. All the crew and passengers of the aircraft perished, thereby removing the issue of I. P. Haiduk from the agenda. I propose we dispatch our military attaché in Warsaw to the crash site in order to identify Haiduk's body and arrange for his remains to be repatriated and buried with all the honour due to a major general, in the alley of the Heroes of Ukraine.

Director of the State Guard of Ukraine
Yulii Merezhko

Determination on the document: to V. Ya Klynkevych

I agree. Prepare all the necessary funeral arrangements and allocate a special pension for I. P. Haiduk's mother.

Hetman K. D. Makhun, 24 April, 09:00

19

The steam-powered tractor and trailer slowly rumbled along the narrow track which threaded between little mining towns. The driver, an ageing Polish farmer, was returning home after buying fertiliser and weed killer in Legnica. He chatted unhurriedly with Haiduk. Haiduk, thanks to his mother, spoke Polish with a soft, eastern accent that did not evoke any inconvenient questions from the farmer. Haiduk presented himself as Yezhi Sokolsky, an inhabitant of Przemyśl, who was returning from working in Germany. A Ukrainian woman was accompanying him on the road, a distant relative from Halychyna, and they had heard that work was to be found in Ruda Śląska. It was unclear whether the word relative had convinced the farmer they were kin, but he was not unduly interested in the travellers' cover story and anticipated earning at least a few globos from them. The driver cursed everything on the earth; the bosses, the weather, prices, the children who had abandoned the farm and set off for Australia, and the poor quality of the coal he threw into the furnace of his antediluvian steam-powered tractor,

76

which resulted in thick, toxic smoke pouring out of its funnel.

Bozhena sat between the farmer and Haiduk and dozed. She understood nothing in Polish, even more so since the farmer spoke the strong dialect of the area. They agreed he would drive them to Ruda Śląska. In the outskirts lived Haiduk's cousin, Marek, a nephew of his mother, who had lived there before moving to Kyiv. The farmer travelled along the A4 and they reached Ruda Śląska late at night. Haiduk gave the tractor driver ten globos adorned with Adam Smith's image. The driver's delight knew no bounds, but he stared suspiciously at the image of this Adam (it definitely wasn't Mickiewicz). Then he kissed Bozhena's hand and thanked Haiduk. They made their farewells and the farmer embraced Haiduk while breathing a clinging mixture of the aromas of home-brewed vodka, tobacco and China-Cola, which sustained him on the road, onto his face. He poured some more coal into the tractor's furnace and headed to Mysłowice.

Haiduk and Bozhena headed south-east along the badly lit, seemingly dead streets of a strange town. He had turned on the navigation system on his gadget, but they barely managed to find Marek's two-storey house in the outskirts. Luckily, a light was still shining in a window on the first floor. Haiduk knew this home well, having stayed there fifteen years ago with his ex-wife, Lara. He carefully circled the yard around the house to check if there was anywhere an assailant might be hiding. Then he climbed onto a bench and peered into the window of a room where a light was on. This was the kitchen and he saw a large, cast-iron stove and a dining table on which there was a computer monitor. Marek was sitting heavily and looking tired as he stared at the screen; his face seemed illuminated by moonlight.

Haiduk activated a programme on his communication gadget that allowed him to see a real-time thermal image of the building in which only the glowing orange figure of Marek was depicted. And where are his wife and children? Haiduk wondered as he tapped quietly on the window. The lights at the entrance to the house flickered on and Marek appeared at the threshold with a pump-action shotgun.

'Who's there?' he asked in Polish.

'Your cousin, Ihor,' replied Haiduk in the same language.

'Is it really you, Ihor?' Marek sounded delighted. He carefully set down the gun and embraced Haiduk as if he were not at all surprised by the nocturnal visit of a cousin who lived in America and never called to mind his relatives from Ruda Śląska. Marek was not in the least offended by his cousin's neglect; he accepted the world as it was, without any pretensions, demands or expectations.

'No one has come to you to ask after me?' Haiduk enquired.

'No, what has happened? I returned from my travels the day before yesterday and know nothing.'

'Everything's fine.'

Marek explained that his wife, Henya, had gone with the children to stay at her mother's in Gliwice for three days and he was having to work pretty hard. He was a long-distance lorry driver with the German-Polish-Russian-American-Ukrainian firm, Friedman. Their wagons could travel unhindered across the whole of Europe after treaties between the warring parties. They transported grain, foodstuffs, equipment, clothing, weapons and ammunition from the Urals to the Pyrenees. Although the work was dangerous because of bands of pirates, who did not respect any treaties, it did not pay too badly. He could make a living and pay for his twin daughters to study at an accountancy college. Marek showed his guests photos of his wife and his daughters, Maryla and Kasia, on the screen. Then he put a bottle of vodka and a few bottles of Egyptian beer on the living room table before frying some German sausage in a hefty pan.

Haiduk said nothing about the Lancaster to his cousin, but Marek had heard something about a catastrophe that had befallen an unknown plane carrying gold to the Horde. Haiduk said that over the past year he had been working for a German-American electronics firm in Dresden and was travelling to Kyiv, but the bus had been hijacked so they had been forced to hitch. Bozhena, a Ukrainian, migrant worker, was travelling with Haiduk on the same bus, returning to Kyiv to recuperate after an accident at the manufacturers where she worked. They urgently needed to change their clothes, buy documents and ammunition, and, above all, sleep.

Marek conducted Bozhena upstairs to the children's bedroom, then returned to stay downstairs with Haiduk in the living room. He made-up an old leather armchair as a bed for Haiduk and, after clearing the dinner things into the kitchen, lay on the settee. Haiduk had barely put his head on the pillow before he fell into a deep, dreamless oblivion, untroubled by the early morning insomnia that often affected him in Washington. It was a sleep like the sleep of death.

20

His excellency, the Hetman of Ukraine, General Kuzma-Danylo Makhun, measured out the office in the hetman's palace with heavy steps. The building, which resembled a flying saucer, was nestled on a legendary hill above the Dnipro, a few kilometres away from the ancient Trypillian area. Here archeologists had discovered the first settlement of Ukrainians who had migrated from India six thousand years ago. They asserted that the first Ukrainian borshch was cooked here and hence the village was known as Borshchiv, and the hill where it was situated was Borshchykha Hill.

The hetman was a sturdy, masculine figure. His masterfully dyed, dark brown moustache, which formed a horseshoe around his mouth and chin, gave him a resemblance to his glorious hetman predecessors. They stared at Makhun from portraits where dark brown and black tones predominated.

He measured his office once again and was persuaded that the dimensions of the room remained unchanged. It was forty-nine metres long and thirty-five metres wide. On reaching the observation deck, which hung over the precipice below, the hetman pressed his brow against the reinforced panoramic glass, and its pleasant coolness slightly stifled his anger. It was a sunny day of the kind that makes you glad to be alive.

'Fuck,' he said hoarsely. 'I'll have their heads and balls for this.'

The hetman looked at the Dnipro, its expanse was brimming with the waters of spring as it unfurled at the foot of the hill beneath him. The white blossom, which made the trees seem snow covered, awoke troubling, bitter-sweet memories. In the distance, on the opposite, level side of the river, control towers protruded into the air. They were intended to deter anyone from thinking about aiming a portable hand-held, anti-tank rocket at the palace and firing a missile into the heart of the people's leader, the immutable hetman and liberator of Ukraine.

The hetman lumbered heavily, as if weakened after his wrath had flared up, towards the long meeting table where twenty monitors were arrayed. They displayed various secret information or communicated with secret services. He pressed the button of the monitor marked with the acronym UMI, Ukrainian Military Intelligence. A crimson, Cossack cross with two crossed swords appeared on the screen. This image was then replaced by text, the sense of which the hetman tried to comprehend as he read the report for the third time:

25 April 2077
10:30
Top Secret
To: His Excellency, the Hetman of Ukraine, General Kuzma-Danylo Makhun

The thorough searches undertaken to recover I. P. Haiduk's body at the site where the Lancaster-27 hospital plane, which was en-route from the Confederation to Beirut, crashed have not generated any results. The bodies of the aircraft's crew and the hospital staff have been identified. Haiduk is not named among the lists of passengers. The possibility that he is still alive cannot be excluded.

Colonel S. Ignatenko, Ukrainian Military Attaché in the Polish Commonwealth

Fuck, the hetman swore in his thoughts. The State Guard says one thing, those faggots say another. Maybe you could order the tax investigators to get involved and really mess it up? Then he bellowed out loud into the microphone built into his wristwatch, 'Vitold.'

A handsome, young lieutenant general appeared in the doorway. Vitold Klynkevych was the hetman's personal adjutant, his general clerk and the manager of the hetman's bureau. He, like the hetman, was dressed in a *zhupan*, a Cossack mantle. Makhun's *zhupan* was black, whereas his adjutant's was dazzlingly white with gold epaulettes, knots and embroidery on the sleeves. The sunburned face of the lieutenant general, who spent all his spare time fishing on the banks of the Dnipro, was also adorned with a horseshoe moustache, which, unlike the hetman's, was not dyed but left its natural deep black hue.

Vitold bowed his head respectfully. 'I am listening, Father.'

'Find Natalia Havrilivna and bring her here.'

'I'll do it immediately,' Vitold said, bowing his head again. 'And what about the reception? There are plans for ten men to attend.'

'Fuck 'em,' said the hetman, glowering darkly.

'I get it,' said Vitold, swirling away like the wind.

The hetman, with a reluctance due to his loathing of tedious bureaucratic work, approached the writing desk on which lay a bundle of papers bearing the label, 'For the immediate signature of His Excellency'. A bronze bust of Winston Churchill, a gift from the King of England, stood on the desk. The hetman rubbed his knuckles hard against the lofty, brass brow of Churchill, but the bust's expression remained unchangingly ironic and sombre. Makhun signed numerous decrees, directives, honours lists, orders and other material necessary for the existence of the state. He signed them mechanically and without consideration because he was focusing on the incomprehensible events connected to Haiduk, which had thrown all his plans into disarray. Only one document caught the hetman's eye, a proposition from the head military hetman, Otaman Pryadko, and the chief of the State Guard, Merezhko, to appoint the military attaché in Singapore as Haiduk's replacement to head the scientific and technical division of Ukrainian Military Intelligence. The attaché's Chinese wife was the State Guard's resident agent in the Celestial Empire. The hetman crumpled up the request and threw it into the wastepaper basket under his desk, thereby breaking his own rule of shredding documents where necessary. It's too soon for that you sons of bitches, he thought.

The secret door into his office, which bore a massive pendulum clock that chimed gently every half-hour, swung open. Natalia Havrilivna Makhun appeared on the threshold. The hetman's servants referred to her behind her back, with a combination of fear and respect, as Grandma Hetman.

'What's happened? Have you done an "Austria" again?' she asked, understanding that he had summoned her urgently on some serious matter. During a meeting with the Austrian President, Von Zaydenberg, the hetman had stubbornly referred to the country as Australia.

The hetman rose and feigned kissing Natalia Havrilivna on the cheek, though in reality he had forgotten when he had last kissed the wife, whom he loved greatly and feared even more.

'Natalochko, does Haiduk's mother know what has happened to him?'

Natalia Havrilivna shrugged. 'No. I issued an order that nothing should be said to her and all the information is blocked. Your numb-skulls, Pryadko and Merezhko, were ready to arrange a state funeral. We must treat her sympathetically and not rush to deal with this.'

'I think so and it's even more necessary in light of the conflicting information I'm receiving.'

He lit up the screen and showed her the report from Warsaw.

'So you see,' she said delightedly, 'it's too early to bury him.'

It was a closely guarded secret that Natalia Havrilivna was the best friend of Haiduk's mother. They had met in their student years when they had both studied singing under Professor Slonymska. Maria Yuzefivna had a soft, lyrical, soprano voice and Natalia Havrilivna was categorised as a lower, mezzo singer. However, neither had embarked on an artistic career.

Maria Yuzefivna had given birth to two children, who occupied all her time. Natalia Havrilivna had met the gallant tank-commander, Kuzma-Danylo Makhun, and shared with him all the delights of a harsh garrison life. The lack of a home, the chronic lack of money, and the drunkenness of his fellow officers were enough to destroy any marriage, but theirs survived. Natalia began to give solo performances with a guitar in Ukrainian garrisons and became very popular in military circles. She caught the attention of the commander of the airborne troops, who subsequently facilitated Makhun's transfer to Kyiv, where he became a general inspector of tank forces. He was also endowed with a nice apartment on Povitroflotskyi Avenue and the title of general. The two women renewed their friendship following their return to Kyiv.

Natalia Havrilivna loved little Ihor Haiduk like her own son. She did not have her own children and helped the Haiduk family greatly during the years of global depression and war. Although the narcissistic and proud engineer, Petro Haiduk, did not love this overbearing dark-eyed 'Gypsy lass with a moustache' as he called her, Maria Yuzefivna would have given up her soul for this woman. Ihor would certainly not have received such an education in the most expensive Ukrainian and American schools if it were not for her. His studies at MIT had necessitated a resolution from Kuzma-Danylo Makhun, who was at that time a deputy to the minister of defence.

A whole array of political considerations compelled the friends to keep their relationship secret, as Makhun had ordered. They met up, only rarely, in government apartments. Natalia Havrilivna was transported to these assignations under the protection of Georgian cavalry troops who could be trusted with the secrets of the hetman's family. Natalia decided how to deal with her friend now. 'I will speak with Maria and keep her calm. I am afraid your idiots might already have whispered something to her about the accident.'

The hetman agreed. The monitor on his desk, which displayed the information from the State Guard, had not transmitted Operational Order Number 1377/2554 of 22 April 2077, with Yulii Merezhko's signature, requiring the arrest of I. P. Haiduk in the event that he should cross the state border of Ukraine. They had probably decided not to report this measure to the hetman in order to avoid diverting his attention from far weightier affairs of the state.

21

Haiduk and Bozhena spent two days in Ruda Śląska, recovering from their nightmarish journey to Europe. Haiduk considered using the gadget to contact his colleague, the military attaché in Poland, Serhiy Ignatenko, because its location could not be traced by his pursuers, but something held him back. His reluctance to phone the attaché was strengthened by his growing trust in Marek, who had revealed himself to be what the Polish call a *chlopek-roztropek*, a smart, energetic lad.

On the evening of the second day he had brought home two bags with clothes, documents and hair dye; one each for Bozhena and Haiduk. Ihor had decided to be blonde, in line with his false Polish passport in the name of Yezhy Sokolski, and his trucker's license for the Friedman company. Marek had also included a special case containing a short-barrelled NK-MR 5/11 automatic with Chinese bullets carefully packed into three magazines. The case also included Haiduk's favourite storm pistol, a Beretta M9A11, along with ordinary ammunition rather than self-targeting bullets. Marek had also included neuro-paralysing police grenades and two anti-infantry grenades with particularly high-explosive power. Finally, there was a Confederation marine dagger, equipped with a wide razor-sharp blade, and a razor whose handle contained five 'disintegration on impact' bullets.

'Wow,' Haiduk whistled, as he gathered up the weapons, which seemed to be fresh from the warehouse. 'You've given us something here Marek.'

'It's pretty cheap,' Marek said with satisfaction, 'in terms of cost and reliability, unlike the stuff you get from Romanian speculators. They sell you a fake dagger that can't even slice liver sausage, and pistols that overheat and jam after five shots.'

'Have you been a specialist in this area for a while?'

'That's what I was compelled to do. Anything can happen in life.' Marek sighed.

The biggest gift was not weapons, clothes or documents but Marek's report that tomorrow, at dawn, a convoy of Friedman wagons and two buses was heading to Ukraine. The cargo's final destination was Chyngiz-Saray, the capital of the Horde on the Ural River, where the Russian city of Orenburg had once been located. Bozhena listened to this news delightedly. Haiduk had barely recognised her after she had changed out of the dirty dress. He was presented with a girl who was almost taller than him and slim. She was wearing blue jeans and a dark blue soccer jersey emblazoned with the inscription 'Friedman'. Bozhena had put on make-up, insofar as she was able, in a way that masked her bruises, and stripped the plaster from her nose.

She went to prepare her supper and it soon became clear she was a skilful cook. There were tastier things than German sausage to be found in the fridge crammed with products left by Henya. Beefsteaks, pre-prepared potato fries, which just needed dipping in the pan, fresh tomatoes, onions, cucumber and pepper for salad, and chocolate ice-cream in the freezer. Bozhena also found a packet with the enticing inscription 'Ukrainian salo' and immediately longed to carve the pork fat into slender petals like her mother had taught her. However, on seeing another inscription on the package, 'Made in China', she changed her mind. They accompanied their meal with Californian Merlot rather than the pungent vodka or weak alcohol-free beer they had previously drunk with Marek. The taste made Haiduk yearn for that lost American paradise with his tender Linda and her passionate lovemaking. He even ached for his company and Viktor Bezpalii. Everything had been ruined in an instant and forever.

Marek now gave them the best of his gifts. He told

them he had reached an agreement with the owner of one of the firm's garages in Katowice; instead of driving to the Pyrenees he would be part of the Chyngiz-Saray convoy and would drive them to Kyiv.

Haiduk was ashamed that he had not previously recollected his Polish relatives, or indeed his Ukrainian ones, for he regarded such contacts as sloppy sentimentality. His life was guided by the principle of achieving short-term goals that were entirely subject to the strategic importance he attached to them. If he was developing an operation, such as the exchange of technology for the manufacture of water-powered engines for the terrapins, which only a few years ago had been absolutely secret, he would forget about everything else on the earth. At such moments he was oblivious to reports from his home country, what events shook the state, what agitated people, or which of his relatives had married or died. Martha Jefferson, who facilitated his contacts with the first lady, was of more significance in his life than all his relatives, any acquaintances or strangers, and, in particular, distant and incomprehensible, Ukraine.

At the end of the evening Marek ceremoniously presented Haiduk and Bozhena with blue uniform jackets, which bore the inscription 'Friedman' on the back in yellow letters. Bozhena raised her arm as she tried on the jacket and Haiduk saw a tattoo above the elbow. It was of the world with wings and there was a sword and a crimson star above it. This was the emblem of an elite sub-division of the Confederation's space forces, the Mars Legion.

22

26 April 2077
Secret
Member of the Aeropagus of Ukraine, Muscovite Boyar, Prince of Chernihiv, Tsar of Voronezh, Ryazan, Stalingrad, Khan of Ulan Bator and Aral, Chief of the Order of Light, the Sacred Priests and Guardians, His Highness Mintimer Nykonovych Basmanov

Your Highness
I wish to update you in connection with a matter which is of interest to you. I am in contact with Air-Marshall Alex Joseph, who responded very positively when your wishes were conveyed to him. He has informed me that on 23 April 2077 your request was fulfilled. Unfortunately, one of our best agents, 'Imperator', who controlled the situation in the bureau, died on 21 April 2077 of unknown causes.

I request you, Your Highness, to protect me from the brutish onslaughts of the hetman, who has threatened to dismiss me from my post in Washington.

Glory to YeDRON!
The Ambassador of Ukraine in the Confederation of States of North America, Ruslan Zoshchenko

23

Dawn broke above Ruda Śląska with a pure, translucent light. The two-storey, redbrick house with its flat roof, which Marek Horol had built fifteen years ago, seemed new and had a jolly, toy-like aspect. Perfect harmony reigned too in his yard. A small carousel intended for the girls, though they did not ride it anymore, shone with fresh paint and seemed ready to begin swirling at any moment. The blue plastic container used for his coal sparkled and not even a single black chunk had fallen from its maw. An old, wheel-less Mazda, its bodywork perforated with holes, stood at the entrance to the yard without spoiling the overall picture of prosperousness and good housekeeping.

Marek went into the centre of town to pick up his wagon. Haiduk and Bozhena breathed in the sweetness of the chill, spring air as if it were an elixir of life and freedom. Bozhena concealed the shaven tonsure on her head by wearing a blue Friedman cap with a gold letter F. She was again wearing dark glasses, which Marek had purchased at her request.

'What's the haircut about?' Haiduk asked, touching his own head and feeling the harshness of his dyed hair.

'Torture by electrocution,' she replied, reluctantly letting it be understood that she would not continue on this theme. She fell silent for a moment before adding, 'Please excuse me, these are very painful memories, but I want to thank you. You saved my life. I don't know if it was worth it … but all the same, thank you. Yesterday, during the night, I called Auntie Martha and told her about our soft landing and about everything you have done for me. Up until yesterday, I no longer wanted to be alive. But today … a morning like this … I grew up on a farm in Illinois very similar to this one; only the roosters don't sing here.'

As if he had heard, a rooster, perching on the chicken coop at the end of the yard, gave a full-throated greeting to the morning and Bozhena laughed for the first time on their journey.

Marek returned. He was driving a Volvo wagon and they clambered into the cab, which was similar to a steam tractor's. Marek sat at the wheel, with Bozhena alongside him and Haiduk to the right. He stashed his weapons in a secret hiding place below the seat. Marek brazenly held his pump-action shotgun, which the Friedman company allowed him to carry. He crossed himself and they set off.

24

The twenty wagons, with their blue canvas awnings and yellow Friedman logos, and two armoured buses, topped with gun turrets, at the front and rear of the column, were heading for Kraków, Rzeszów, Jaroslaw, Przemyśl, and then the Ukrainian border. After entering Ukraine they would pass through Lviv, to Zhytomyr and then to Kyiv. From Kyiv the convoy would have to go to Kharkiv before traversing the wild steppes to Stalingrad. After the Volga area, their path led to the Urals and Chyngiz-Saray, the capital of the Horde and the final point on their four thousand kilometre journey.

Wagons travelled from all over Poland to Krakow and assembled in a long line on the empty highway before Tarnów. Administrators in blue uniforms linked them with chains so the distance between the vehicles was no more than twenty metres. The column was now transformed into a seamless, steel serpent that could only be split apart with great difficulty. Steering the wagons in these conditions demanded extreme concentration and co-ordination from the drivers.

The crew of the armoured bus leading the convoy used the intercom system to inform the drivers how to guide their vehicles and of the dangers on the road. These cargo columns traversed Eurasia day and night, terrifying drivers who, on hearing the klaxons and seeing blue and red emergency lights, pulled over to the roadside so as not to be crushed under the wheels of this rampant Armada. Individual bands of thieves were reluctant to attack these convoys as a rule, in spite of the potential treasures they offered, although they did not have an agreement with the Friedman empire. Those who did attempt to attack the caravans encountered resistance in the form of volleys of fire from the armoured brigades. People said that the caravans incorporated well-disguised military wagons armed with rockets, but no one knew where they were hidden among the monstrously huge blue and yellow trucks.

Marek Horol, one of the best long-distance lorry drivers in the Friedman column, travelled at number seven in the convoy. The thirteenth place in the wagon-train was occupied by William Crawford, commander of the X-139 individual mobile battery of the space and air defence of the Confederation in the Central European sector of the theatre of war. Marek, who regularly travelled in such convoys, could spend hours telling tales of captivating adventures along these Eurasian routes, but he sat silently, listening to the commands of the convoy co-ordinator through his headphones and watching the rear of wagon number six. Shunting the wagon before you or breaking the chain was regarded as a severe infringement of the company rules and would be punished mercilessly with fines or dismissal.

Marek did not divulge interesting tales about the Friedman company and how they pitilessly exploited their drivers by forcing truckers to drive continuously for twenty hours. The bosses saved money on food by provisioning drivers with preserved horse meat, which was sold to them cheaply by the Horde, and the disgusting China-Cola. He could have told them of how drivers, who made some loose comment about the type of cargo in these wagons traversing war-torn Eurasia to the places of on-going conflicts, disappeared secretly and forever. However, he kept shtum because he knew the cabs of these wagons were bugged, and his cousin and his companion did not need to hear these tales. He had told them all the details of how to act when crossing the border during their last evening in Ruda Śląska.

The average speed of the convoy, only fifty to sixty kilometres per hour, was not as high as Haiduk had imagined, because the highway was packed with steam-powered tractors, horse-drawn wagons, old cars and new armoured vehicles bearing the troops of the Organisation for Global Security to the East. He wondered what was going on. Even though he was aware of the situation from analytical reports and secret documents, what he saw in Europe was deeply disturbing. Although none of the blocks, the Confederation, OGS, Horde, Celestial Empire, or South America had formally declared war, and all maintained diplomatic relations, in reality the past two years had seen the commencement of a fourth-level war. This war was fought by giant competing corporations, liberation movements, individual criminal formations and local irredentists.

Haiduk would never have imagined he would be languishing in a Friedman convoy and have become a small particle of the international power that sowed fear among the governments of states that formally still existed, business competitors and the population of territories it had conquered. This is some ironic jest of fate, Haiduk thought as he was lulled into drowsiness by the monotonous movement of the wagon, the roar of the engine and the skittering of the chain on concrete, which seemingly struck sparks, or perhaps it was the heavy, steel links, polished by the friction, scraping against road surfaces that were glinting in sunlight. He reflected on the most valuable part of his wealth, which guaranteed him simultaneously both death and survival, the 'Haiduk file', collated by him, bureau colleagues and UMI over the past five years. The archive was where he had accumulated compromising material on members of the Ukrainian Aeropagus and other governing structures that represented the interests of big-wigs. The file could also be potentially harmful for multi-nationals who, in pursuit of their profit margins, endangered society. The archive was hidden in a secure location and only Viktor Bezpalii had known of its existence. However, he had not known where it was hidden, even though Haiduk had thought about the destiny of the file more than once. What would be done with it? Would it all just disappear if something happened to him? Who would the file be handed to? When would it be revealed? Haiduk assured himself now was not the time to expose its contents.

Bozhena lay her head on Haiduk's shoulder as she slept. Her blue pilot's cap had slipped and was skew whiff on her head, until he carefully removed it and placed it in the glove compartment. Her hair, as short as brush bristles, tickled his face. Bozhena's shaved tonsure had begun to sprout a covering of auburn down and her bruises were almost fading into the whiteness of her skin. She radiated the fragrance of cosmetics, awakening half-forgotten memories, simultaneously agonising and happy, in Haiduk's soul. Bozhena's arm pressed against his hip and Haiduk remained in an uncomfortable posture so as not to rouse the sleeping girl.

The convoy reached the Ukrainian border during the evening. The blue and yellow inscription on the gate of the 'holding tank' read 'Merry Ukraine Welcomes You!' The tank was a huge, concreted field near Krakovets, where streams of convoys and individual long-haul travellers from both east and west congregated. A specially fenced-off section had been allocated for the Friedman convoy so as not to plague the well-respected company with the pointless bureaucratic procedures of passport control and customs inspection. The area was decorated with huge portraits of the Ukrainian Hetman, General Kuzma-Danylo Makhun, and his renowned slogan of the three Ds - Defence, Discipline and Dynamism. The notices from Ukraine's border service warned foreigners on Ukrainian territory of the necessity to strictly adhere to all its laws, principles and instructions. Another placard informed travellers they were now entering the territory of the Great Slavic Unity and the inspections would therefore be undertaken by joint Russian-Ukrainian-Kazakhstan teams. In order that no one should have any doubt, a few peeling, ancient placards, whose red, blue, azure and yellowy-green hues created a chimerical hybrid of tones, pronounced, 'Our Future - UROD'. The acronym unfortunately read like urod, the Ukrainian word for freak. It was decoded underneath for the benefit of dim-witted foreigners and read in English, 'Ukrainian-Russian United State'.

It was an unusual occurrence, but a customs inspection was held on that day. Three armed individuals in black uniforms, with red epaulettes, cuffs and lightning emblems, approached their vehicle. Haiduk thought they must be EnROS troops. EnROS or *Energia Rossii*, Russian Energy in English, was one of the largest global companies engaged in the extraction, transport and sale of gas, oil and arms. The EnROS troops were holding powerful YiZh 107 automatic rifles fitted with grenade launchers.

The soldiers unceremoniously opened the right and left doors of the cab simultaneously, and aimed their weapons at the occupants. 'Documents,' they barked in Russian.

'Please would you tell me, Sir, where are the Ukrainian State border guards?' Marek asked in Polish with the utmost politeness, as he reluctantly extracted his documents. This was the first time they had ever been inspected on this border. Marek was sure these were self-proclaimed border guards.

The fat skin-headed brigadier in charge snarled at Marek in Russian, 'Shut the fuck up you rancid Polack. Your lazy *Khokhols* have gone to get drunk. Give us the documents.'

A trooper accosted Haiduk through the right-hand side of the cab. 'Are you also a Polack?'

Haiduk stared at the man, who was short and skinny. He looked as if he had a gastric ailment, his face was sweaty with alcohol, and his eyes were red, 'Yes, I am a Pole and work at the Friedman company,' Haiduk replied, calmly handing the red-eyed man his passport in the name of Yezhy Sokolski.

The guard flicked through it, stared long and hard at the photograph, compared it to an image on a small notebook computer attached to his left shoulder strap, then commenced studying Haiduk's visage. Haiduk had shaved carefully so his black stubble would not contrast suspiciously with his fair hair, but nevertheless the guard clearly disliked something about him.

'Where do you live? In Przemyśl?'

'Yes sir.'

'Tell me then, on what street is the mayoral building located?'

'On Wałęsa Square,' Haiduk replied firmly, regretting that he had concealed the weapons in the truck's secret hiding place. He did not know where in Przemyśl that infernal mayoral building was situated.

'He wants a bribe,' said Marek quietly. The brigadier and the other guard had moved on to check other wagons and this '*gnojek*' Haiduk called him inwardly, his mind having switched over to Polish, was still hassling Ihor.

Haiduk extracted ten globos from his pocket and handed them to the guard, adding, 'Please Sir, accept this small present from Przemyśl.'

The gift from Przemyśl was so much to the guard's liking that he decided to put the squeeze on Bozhena.

'Who are you? A Pole? Hand over your documents.'

It would have been dangerous to present Bozhena's American passport to this bandit.

'I'm Ukrainian,' she said, 'returning from Germany and my passport was stolen.'

'Aha, a *Khokhol* lass,' the guard laughed with satisfaction. 'Then you can pay, if you like, in the natural manner.'

Bozhena understood little of this and looked fearfully at the EnROS trooper. Haiduk, with a swiftness that surprised even himself, twisted the strap of the automatic rifle around the trooper's neck and grabbed his prod from its holster, poking the sharp end into his gut. He turned blue and gasped in Haiduk's choke-hold.

'You fucking son of bitch,' Haiduk whispered into the soldier's ear in English, before adding in Russian, 'do you want me to take off your head?'

The soldier shook his head and Haiduk continued in Russian, 'I am a friend of Friedman himself. Do you know who that is?'

The trooper nodded emphatically.

'There are fifty Chechens in the convoy. If I whistle now, they'll cut off your head and the heads of your colleagues. Do you understand? So just fuck off quietly and don't say anything to anyone. I gave you some cash?'

'Yes, yes, thank you.'

'So, get away from here. And forget what I said.' Haiduk released the blue-faced, red-eyed trooper.

The EnROS soldier could barely stand and headed, with an uncertain tread, to the other end of the holding area and the building where the Ukrainian border guards and customs staff had been drinking since lunchtime. The EnROS soldiers and fuel hauliers from the Horde were their drinking companions and had brought various precious gifts for these defenders of the border.

The Horde was an updated version of the Mongolian Golden Horde by whose rules they lived. The Eurasian fuel corporation they had created was known as OrdOil.

The trooper wobbled onwards, glad that he was still among the living and had earned some cash. He knew the locals certainly would not have advised EnROS to tangle with one of Friedman's convoys and now he knew why. There was only one thing he didn't understand, where that cursed Polack had studied Russian?

25

THE HAIDUK FILE
15 October 2075
Absolutely Secret (One Copy)
To the Head of the Scientific-Technical Division of Ukrainian Military Intelligence (UMI): Colonel I. P. Haiduk

Operational character report on Friedman, Rafael, Hariyevych, a citizen of Ukraine, Israel, the Confederation of States of North America, Canada and Switzerland. Member of the Aeropagus highest state-political organ, Ukraine. Member of the World Government, the so-called Locarno Club, in Switzerland, Baron Bukovinskyi, Podilskyi, Gomelskyi, Smolenskyi, Lublinskyi, Count Marburzskyi, Honorary Professor of Harvard and Yale Universities, Honorary Consul of Panama and Columbia in Ukraine, and Head of the Ukrainian Bible Fellowship.

Friedman was born on 9 July 2026 in Chernivtsi, Bukovyna. His father was Harry Friedman, a jazz pianist, and his mother, Esther Nauman, was a librarian at the Ze'ev Jabotinsky Hebrew University. He was distinguished by notable mathematical gifts from childhood onwards and triumphed, on more than one occasion, in global student mathematic olympiads. He graduated from the Cybernetics Faculty of Solomon University in Kyiv when he was eighteen.

When he was twenty he defended his doctoral thesis concerning the problems of magical mathematical cycles of history, which concerned the methodology of associative encoded prediction, and as a result was honoured with an award from the British Royal Society.

Friedman's life was marked by tragedy in 2048. During the Romanian occupation of Chernivtsi, the occupiers and their supporters among the local population organised a Jewish pogrom, in the course of which his parents perished, along with his grandfather, two grandmothers and numerous relatives. R. H. Friedman left Ukraine and spent three years in Israel, where he graduated from a military studies course at the IDF Special Forces School in Netanya. In 2051 he left Israel for the United States, where he worked as a stockbroker on the American-Chinese-Japanese global stock exchange. During the period of transition to a single international currency he acquired a personal fortune of ten billion globos through illegally manipulating currency exchange rates. He was accused of financial speculation that undermined the exchange rate of the yuan. However, the New York Financial Appeal Court acquitted him of the charges in 2054.

In 2055 he reached a truce with the government of the Celestial People's Democratic Empire and was appointed to the post of African Director, responsible for the supply of strategic metals and energy resources to mainland China.

He returned to Kyiv in 2058 and established the Friedman transport company, which was soon transformed into a supra-national corporation, one of the ten wealthiest such entities in the world. The creation of the company was accompanied by large-scale crimes, falsifications, corporate raids and murders. Friedman's actions were particularly savage in Bukovyna, where he seized 80% of the industrial and 95% of the agro-industrial potential of the area and obtained a licence to personally own the population of 736,000. (See the documentation on the crimes of R. H. Friedman in annexes I-IX.) By working with the same methods of bribery, blackmail and terror, R. H. Friedman seized land and industrial and agricultural resources in the Podilia, Gomel and Smolensk regions, Lublin Province and Marburg, Germany. He simultaneously created the Ukrainian-European level political party known as the Freedom Party, which achieved 38.75% in the Ukrainian parliamentary elections of 2060 and 15% in the European parliamentary elections. He is one of the co-authors of the new constitution of Ukraine (2068), according to which the country is a Military Cossack-Feudal State with a strict militarily vertical system of power, within which the supreme body is the Aeropagus, which elects the Hetman of Ukraine. (The word 'Feudal' had been crossed out and 'Federal' written in its place in Haiduk's hand.)

According to UMI and the State Guard's reliable sources, R. H. Friedman was involved in the 2066 murder of the Ukrainian president, Federico Garcia Kostyuk - see annexes X-XIII. In 2070 he became a member of the World Government - the Locarno Club. The personal fortune of R. H. Friedman, according to the International Currency Bank, is in excess of globos 600 bn, or 900% greater than Ukraine's GDP. R. H. Friedman has extracted his base capital from Ukraine and pays taxes of globos 6000 annually as the manager of a low-profit transport agency and head of the Ukrainian Bible society.

Friedman is on his fourth marriage, on this occasion to an Indonesian citizen, and has nine children from his previous marriages.

He appears kind and gentle during social interaction. Although he is a key Ukrainian political figure, R. H. Friedman conducts himself as a non-public person, eschewing discussion and refraining from public statements, interviews and participation in television talk shows. His private life is shrouded in secrecy. Friedman's private residence is situated not far from Kaniv, in the Pekari-Khmilna district, on the right bank of the Dnipro and Sushky on the left bank. The property is comprehensively guarded by the private military formations of R. H. Friedman.

Friedman is vindictive, cruel and capable of any crime. He is an enthusiast both of the ballet and ancient Jewish music, and sponsors the Kyivski Lebedi International Ballet Festival.

Senior Analyst Maximilian-III

26

The caravan halted just over forty kilometres from Kyiv, in the grounds of Kalynivskyi International Market. The market was the largest trade, retail and transport hub in eastern Europe, with the status of a free economic zone. The concreted field at Krakovets seemed small by comparison.

He gave Marek two 'clean' phone numbers belonging to a safe apartment, the existence of which was unknown to his colleagues in the State Guard or UMI. He had bought them with his own funds through intermediaries. This covert refuge was located on the second floor of a multi-apartment block on Protasiv Yar and was distinguished by having two exits. One of these led to the highway linking Heroyiv UPA Street with Pechersk. The second was on the slope of Baikova Hill, which was covered in ancient oak trees and from where it was possible to slip unnoticed onto Nikolaya Amosova Street and the Baikove Cemetery. The apartment was registered in the name of a businessman, Mr Orlenko, who worked in Mexico and paid all the bills regularly. Haiduk had decided to use this property because all the other safe apartments belonging to UMI were kept under close surveillance by the State Guard.

Marek sighed with relief when his replacement driver, who would have to accompany him to Chyngiz-Saray, came to him from vehicle number ten.

The parting with Marek was emotional, Haiduk would never have believed he could be so moved by a farewell. However, he only said, 'Goodbye old mate, kiss the wife and kids for me,' as he patted Marek on the shoulder.

Marek dabbed away a tear with a chubby finger as Haiduk and Bozhena disappeared into the crowd. They headed for the rear of the convoy where old vehicles were being sold in a separate area. Friedman's convoy was being rapidly loaded at that moment. Special trolleys bearing large cardboard boxes with the inscription 'Irpin Fridges' were being wheeled to the wagons. Haiduk recollected that the commercial division of Kyiv's Artemida factory traded under that name. The firm was the main manufacturer of the Khars, the most modern system for missile targeting. Haiduk practically whistled at this revelation, imagining the arrival of the most modern, autonomous guidance system in the capital of the Horde, whose power menaced the whole planet. The Kyiv manufactured guidance system was being pursued by intelligence services across the world and empowered rockets to destroy the most well-protected targets anywhere on earth. The manufacturers of Khars refused to participate in the programme accepted for the arms of the Confederation (VxWorks/HurriKane) and the OGS (ADA-105). They utilised an entirely original principle of control through bio-electronic intelligence.

Haiduk slowed his stride a little as he tried to memorise the inscriptions and codes on the cardboard packaging. They heard American-English near vehicle number thirteen and saw four men and one woman in camouflage fatigues of the same kind Blanchard had given to Haiduk. The group laughed as they watched long, dark green cartons bearing a smallish symbol, a red triangle in a white circle, being ferried to their vehicle. There could be no doubt that these were MXAir-Cleaner 124 surface to air missiles, the product of another Kyiv manufacturer, the Arseniy factory. Bozhena suddenly seized Haiduk's hand and squeezed it painfully.

'Let's get past here faster.'

On the contrary, he wished to look at the boxes on this peaceful international exchange of consumer goods as closely as possible. However, Bozhena dragged him sideways, away from the convoy and towards the flames and pinkly glowing balloons of the Eurodrome. This consisted of an array of pavilions, including some where girls were presented for sale.

Bozhena headed to the sign inscribed 'Auto-Motor Products'. They entered the area displaying old cars, mopeds, bicycles, motorcycles and scooters. Here people wearing greasy jackets, who were as old as all this gear, roamed among the relics.

'Major William Crawford was standing with that group of American military personnel. I spotted him because we served together in the space forces, he's scary; a thug,' Bozhena said.

Haiduk had heard about William Crawford, indeed he occupied a place in the Haiduk file. 'And what is he?' he asked.

'A red-neck pig. He likes groping women and telling dirty jokes.' Her face seemed to have grown older with lines of sorrow etching themselves near her lips.

Haiduk negotiated the purchase of a German motorcycle, a yellowy-grey Zundapp KS, manufactured in 1943, for four hundred ameros. He had decided to save his globos for now. He put Bozhena in the side car and lashed the bags with their stuff to the rear seat. He had packed away the blue Friedman company jacket and dressed in his camouflage jacket, packing its countless pockets with weapons. Bozhena remained in her Friedman attire. The vendor, an old guy with the appearance and aroma of a Washington bum, presented himself as a former polytechnic professor; the words pierced Haiduk's heart as they called to mind his own father. The old man was the owner of the largest collection of antique motorcycles in Ukraine, which he was now selling in order to survive. He poured some stinking, brown liquid into the tank and the motorcycle stuttered into life after several coughs and firing a few blanks.

On leaving Kalynivskyi Market they did not turn right onto the strategic east-west road but headed among the forests and rarely travelled roads that were used by cyclists who wanted to experience nature. They reached an area of huge shopping malls where a ring road, similar to Washington's Beltway, commenced. Haiduk decided not to risk going here because the ancient motorcycle would draw attention. He knew their presence at the market might be remembered because Haiduk had knocked down the price on the rare motorcycle in front of a few onlookers. He and Bozhena might also have caught someone's attention when they bandied around a few English words. He knew also that the parking area at the mall was monitored with numerous surveillance cameras. So, he halted the motorcycle among some damp aspen, inserted a rag from a torn shirt into the opening of the fuel tank and set it on fire. Bozhena and he left swiftly, leaving the museum-worthy Zundapp burning reluctantly.

They agreed that they would each make their way to Kyiv by different routes on buses that rarely went to the malls, where lines of shoppers with heavy bags queued for them. Haiduk slung his pack on his shoulder and said farewell to Bozhena who, in her blue jacket and pilot's cap, resembled an air stewardess martyred by her life of demanding, shrieking passengers. They agreed to telephone each other only in the event of dire necessity and by using their secure communications gadgets. So, he said farewell to this marvellous girl who languidly squeezed his hand and only walked a few steps before suddenly turning and kissing him. They stepped onto the asphalt car park and silently headed for separate places in different bus queues.

Springtime Kyiv met him with shadows and a solid wall of snow that engulfed the city from the east and transformed the high-rises on Borshchahivka into grey apparitions. Haiduk saw the characteristic silhouette of a Mormon church on the right. The huge structure, built according to the canonical style of Mormon churches all over the world, was topped by a tall, sharp spire on which an angel with a trumpet heralded the end of the world. It was weird how, even in the sky dense with falling snow, the angel glimmered like a fire lit in warning. Haiduk believed that the surveillance camera would be unable to pick up the face of the solitary man with a dark green Polish army bag on his shoulder, standing in line for the bus, in the sudden engulfing obscurity of the snow.

When the bus came for Protasiv Yar, through the KGB Victims' Square, people in the line jostled each other as if they were undergoing an evacuation, but they all squeezed into the home-made bus, which was without seats. The owner of the vehicle had fashioned it from an old Chinese ShangTse wagon and thereby tripled its profitability. It cost one globo for a journey and, ironically, it was not possible to pay the fare in yuan.

Well, here comes Kyiv, thought Haiduk sombrely. Hello my native town. How could I not love you … my Kyiv? As the bus lumbered off, a plump woman stood on Haiduk's foot. She apologised immediately and tried to strike up an acquaintance. Fuck you, he thought irritably, without replying.

27

The Ambassador Extraordinaire and Plenipotentiary of Ukraine in the Confederation of States of North America, Ruslan Vitaliyovych Foshchenko, sat portentously in his office on the fifth floor of the embassy on M Street. A huge portrait of the Ukrainian Hetman, Kuzma-Danylo Makhun, hung behind him. The Ukrainian leader was smiling, a rare enough event, and wearing a black *zhupan* with gold epaulettes, embroidered with two crossed maces and a marshall's star. The hetman's PR people had thoroughly worked on the portrait, removing any unnecessary wrinkles and adding a touch of transparency to the cunning, narrow eyes.

The hetman was satisfied with this portrayal, which successfully united the grandeur of the state, the indomitable strength of a military leader, and the kindliness of the nation's

104

father. The portrait, produced by the popular photographer, Colonel Pavlyuk, in the most contemporary, three-dimensional format, was personally approved by the hetman. Copies were distributed to all offices and foreign-based institutions of the UMCFS (the Ukrainian Military Cossack Feudal State) by Ukraine's General Clerk, Vitold Klynkevych. The circular accompanying the portrait stressed the unacceptability of maliciously damaging the image, especially in the lower section, which iterated the fundamental principles of the hetman's work, the 'Three Ds' - Defence, Discipline and Dynamism. The circular clearly had in mind the malicious campaign against the hetman that caricatured the 'Three Ds' as Decapitation, Dumb-assness and Disorder.

On the same wall, but to the left of the portrait, a soundproof blind completely covered the window, which Foshchenko opened from time to time to get some fresh air. He liked to bask in the wonderful view of the 14th Street Bridge over the Potomac River and the glass structures of Virginia on the other side. He particularly loved to observe how, at 10:00, the black terrapins, usually three in number, one of them bearing President Andrew Van Lee, headed from Camp David to the White House.

Ambassador Foshchenko was proud of the photograph, which in truth was not as large as the hetman's portrait, in which the presidential couple, smiling widely, welcomed the Ukrainian diplomat and his wife to the White House. The Ambassadorial couple were wearing identical blue suits of Chinese manufacture, emblazoned with the letter V on the left breast pocket.

Ruslan Foshchenko, by contrast with the hetman, always smiled at official meetings with Confederation big wigs during his journeys across this vast land that stretched from Canada to Mexico, or at private lunches with businessmen and working meetings with Embassy colleagues. While he was still at the Yuri Andropov Intelligence Operatives' College near Moscow, and they were preparing him for the Pakistan residency, Foshchenko practised how to smile so that attractive, boyish, dimples appeared in his rounded cheeks. Functionaries from the Confederation's State Department, for the governance of 'transitional countries', Ukraine, Kazakhstan, Palestine and Colombia had named the ambassador 'Dimple'. He was so accustomed to his own mask that even now, sitting in his empty office, he smiled pointlessly, even as anxiety gripped his heart, because he was well acquainted with the hetman's vicious temper.

Foshchenko was troubled by the history with Haiduk, who was outside of his control because he worked in the Confederation. The ambassador did not really understand what had happened to Haiduk; whether Air-Marshall Alex Joseph's people had eliminated him or whether, as was possible, he had successfully evaded his just punishment. Foshchenko's future depended on Haiduk's fate. He regarded himself as his intellectual and professional superior by several degrees and did not forget the personal humiliation inflicted on him. A satanic pride and disregard for others were firmly ensconced in his soul despite the perpetually smiling exterior.

During a visit to Washington, Hetman Makhun had taken Haiduk to negotiations at the White House, instead of Foshchenko. President Van Lee and the director of the Confederation's Central Security Service, Admiral Stanley Fisher, had participated from the Confederation, while the hetman and Haiduk had spoken for Ukraine. Casting aside his dimpled-cheeked mask, Ruslan Foshchenko had sat morosely in the service room of the White House and waited for the negotiations to end. He had thrown imprecations at Haiduk as soon as he emerged from the Oval Office. 'What are you, some self-proclaimed tinpot emissary?' he had yelled, disregarding the surprised glances of the Americans. 'You know that I ... I am

106

the boss here. Did you read the law about diplomatic service?'

'Ruslan, button it, for fuck's sake, and sit quietly,' the hetman had placidly replied while he walked hurriedly past to a meeting with the vice-president in the neighbouring building.

Haiduk had grabbed Foshchenko by the lapels of his waistcoat, choking the ambassador, and said, 'Listen, Smiley, there are things that can't be made known to you. You're a lackey. And lackeys aren't trusted. Get lost.'

Thrusting Foshchenko aside, he had run after the hetman.

Foshchenko remembered the boxer's look in Haiduk's eyes, that of a fighter placing his next blow. Fear and doubt had settled in his soul for a long time afterwards, even though he was the Ambassador of Ukraine, the intelligence operative of the Horde in Ukraine and the Confederation, and the trusted confidante of Aeropagus members Kreyda and Basmanov. His visceral hatred and envy of Haiduk was due to his rival's success in securing high-level support for the bureau's trade with the Confederation through the purchase and sale of high-tech, primarily military, products. This trade was in fact originally the ambassador's achievement as the head of the mutual trade commission. He simultaneously informed his bosses in the Horde about the new arms systems that were being exchanged by Ukraine and the Confederation. An old treaty regarding the strategic partnership between these states was then in force, although Ukraine had long ceased to be within the Confederation's sphere of interest.

Everything rolled along with a weird inertia, although former geo-political unions and ties collapsed. A new, global conflict approached, an Armageddon wherein Ukraine might be wiped off the face of the earth by a one mega-tonne bomb of the SOD-666 Scythe of Death category with which both the Confederation and Horde had armed themselves in 2075.

Foshchenko pondered geo-politics sombrely as he

decided where to take his children and grandchildren, who were currently in Ukraine. Where was a safe place to be found on this earth? Might it even be Costa-Rica? He smiled at this, checking with his fingertips whether he had summoned up his trademark dimples. A drunken American had once said to him that with dimples like that he might become the hetman. The phrase had lodged itself in Ruslan Foshchenko's memory. He phoned Air-Marshall Alex Joseph's aide to arrange a special meeting between Foshchenko and his boss. At the meeting they would discuss the schedule for the arrival of the Ukrainian Air Force in the Confederation, the events planned for the delegation during their stay and the preparation of a joint communique. He managed to agree the meeting with Joseph's aide, but his mood did not improve.

There was a quiet knocking at the door, although he had instructed that no one be allowed to see him. A face, as white as a washed, peeled and scrubbed potato, peered around the door; it was the embassy's cryptographer. 'Excuse me Your High Excellency.'

'What is it?' barked Foshchenko, wiping the smile from his face.

'There,' Belkin pointed downwards with his index finger, 'is a phone call.'

Foshchenko realised from the movements of Belkin's lips just who was phoning. He leaped from his chair and flew across his spacious oak-lined office to the door, almost concussing Belkin and Sveta, the voluptuous secretary. He ran to the staircase, jumped down several steps at a time and spun around the sharp bends in the stairwell. Belkin trotted after him almost inaudibly. Below, in the antique part of the embassy where Washington had worked in March 1791, in the room where he signed the decree establishing the federal capital, was a half cellar, the so-called 'Stone Hall'. This had once been the room for slaves ferried here on barges that traversed the canal alongside the Potomac. They had now transformed it into a special room for cryptographers and set up a steel compartment there, two metres by three metres, for secret discussions and transatlantic phone calls with Kyiv.

The compartment had the necessary systems for protecting the secrecy of conversations, though the same could not be said about the transfer of the signal between Washington and Kyiv. The signal used a special high-fragmentation voice encoder, which shifted codes every 0.1 second. It had been devised by Ukraine's best mathematicians. However, the fifteen thousand American mathematicians who worked in the National Data Processing Centre near Annapolis had not been sitting on their hands either. With the assistance of the most powerful computer in the world, the ZEUS-MD 17/35, they could easily decode these encrypted reports and conversations. They only did so rarely because Ukraine generated little anxiety in the leadership of the Central Security Service. On this occasion the CSS was interested in the conversation between Kyiv and Washington. Foshchenko grabbed the phone with sweaty fingers and said, 'I'm listening.'

'Is it you Ruslan?' asked the familiar throaty bass of Basmanov.

'Yes, yes, I am working on that issue,' Foshchenko replied.

'Chill. According to Merezhko's information, he's made it to Kyiv.'

'Jesus,' said Foshchenko, with genuine terror.

'Don't be scared. It's our problem now. I discussed you with the hetman. It is time you changed jobs.'

Foshchenko went cold. His worst forebodings were being realised.

'What are you doing there? Have you nodded off?' Basmanov asked agitatedly.

'I'm listening,' the ambassador said quietly and

fatalistically, envisioning presenting his credentials to General Mguanbo in Sierra Leone, who often became besotted with ambassadors of any gender.

'I think it's fitting you have another appointment.'

'But I'm in place here and we are preparing for your visit.' Foshchenko began to push back, 'I have agreed things with Fiery Sara and she will receive you.'

'Oh what an idiot you are,' Basmanov interrupted him angrily. 'She won't receive me, I will receive her, if I want to. I think it is time to appoint you as Minister of Foreign Affairs. I hope this has the hetman's support. Have you understood me?'

'I understand.' Foshchenko came to himself, still unable to believe in the reality of the conversation or Basmanov's proposals. 'Glory to YeDRON,' he said, referring to the Single Russian People's State.

'Get ready for some great work, son of the great YeDRON,' said Basmanov, ending the conversation.

Long signals pulsed along the line from Kyiv to Washington.

When the Ambassador emerged from the compartment the encryptors understood that something bad had happened. He was pale and unsmiling and his eyes had changed colour. One of them had brightened from grey to almost white, while the other had almost turned black. His hands trembled as he wrote up the journal entry for the conversation.

Part 2

INSIDER

28

29 April 2077
Confidential
To: His Excellency, the Hetman of Ukraine, General Kuzma-Danylo Makhun

Report

Father, as you will be aware, January 2078 will see the completion of your term in office as Hetman of Ukraine. There is no doubt regarding your re-election by the Ukrainian Aeropagus for a third, six-year term or the endorsement of their choice by members of all chambers of parliament, the representatives of Ukraine's military administration, and the free electorate of Ukraine. However, in my view, it would be appropriate to begin preparations for this significant political event in order to prevent the destabilisation of Ukraine. This is particularly significant in light of the exceptionally complex geo-political, economic, internal-political and social situation of Ukraine and the rest of the world.

The main issue is that it is unlikely the next elections can be conducted on a sole-candidate basis. According to the intelligence sources of the hetman's division, two other individuals wish to contend for the title of Ukrainian Hetman. These are Aeropagus member and leader of the Movement for Four Freedoms, Mintimer Basmanov, and the speaker of the Sejm, Indira Holembiyevska. Unfortunately, the position of Aeropagus member R. H. Friedman, whose support will be decisive for the outcome of the elections, is unknown.

According to our sources, preparations have already begun in the headquarters of both pretenders, including propaganda plans for the campaign and the preparation of press releases, declarations and manifestoes. It is known that M. Basmanov's main slogan will be 'UROD is our future', referring to the plan for a Ukrainian-Russian United State, and 'We will create UROD and be happy'. I. Holembiyevska will conduct her campaign under the slogan 'Ukraine with a woman's face'.

We cannot exclude the possibility that other pretenders to the hetman's mace might emerge and exploit the difficult political situation. They may utilise populism, demagoguery and criticism to present themselves as candidates for the post of hetman. Taking into account the above, I propose:

1. To immediately begin preparation for a mass-scale information campaign for your re-election. All state, military, Cossack, agricultural and other mass-communication channels will be deployed for this aim. These tools will convey your accomplishments in the name of the Ukrainian people, with particular emphasis on your role in securing victory in the Ukrainian-Romanian war, and the consolidation of the people to preserve the unity of the Ukrainian State during the period when the Muscovite State collapsed. They will also emphasise your reform of the healthcare system and your peaceful independent state policy of joining neither the Organisation for Global Security nor the Union of Horde States.

2. The preparation for a massive, popular information campaign to secure support for you as the irreplaceable, undisputed people's leader for whom there cannot and will not be an alternative.

3. Simultaneously, in order to forestall any hostile accusation from the oppositional groups to the effect that you have infringed the constitution that limits the duration of an individual hetman's rule to a maximum of twelve years (two terms), I propose that you announce the name of your successor. They will become the

hetman of Ukraine in 2084, following the completion of your third term in office. Your young successor will not be chosen, of course, from the opposition. They will be of one mind with you, someone close to you to whom, over the period of the next five years, you could transfer your rich experience as Head of State. You will thus instantaneously defuse any social tension regarding your re-election, along with accusations of infringing the constitution.

4. In tandem with the announcement of your successor, you are obliged, in my view, to organise several changes in the leadership of the state. You must appoint young people loyal to you to key positions, to strengthen the system of governing the country and the people's trust in you. Attached to this report is a list of senior personnel aged 80-90 years whom it would be appropriate to replace with younger, promising individuals no more than 60 years of age.

5. Particular attention should be paid to R. H. Friedman, on whose position, in a large degree, rests the fate of the historic choice of the Ukrainian people and the Ukrainian Military Cossack Feudal State. Only your intellect and your diplomatic talents might secure the support of Friedman and the world government in Locarno for your candidacy in the next elections.

6. In order to strengthen your high standing internationally, I propose that we organise a series of foreign visits to destinations, including Chyngiz-Saray, the capital of the Horde, and to Suzdal, the capital of the Russian-Tsarist State. We would also schedule visits to the Confederation capital, Washington, Beijing, the capital of the Celestial People's Democratic Empire, and Berlin, the capital of the territory now controlled by Fortress Germany. The summit of states of the Horde, which will be held in Kyiv (Batii-Hrad) in December 2077, has acquired particular significance in light of your speech there, which will determine both your fate as the hetman and the geo-political destiny of the union. It is essential to commence preparations for this event

immediately.

Glory to the Hetman!

General Clerk of the UMCFS, Lieutenant General Vitold Klynkevych

29

Haiduk knew that on the Saturday after Easter, which was celebrated by Greek Catholics and Orthodox believers, the *hrobky* or graves ceremony of remembrance would have been held in Baikove Cemetery for all who were buried there. It was the same date as when he had travelled to Ruda Śląska on the steam-powered tractor with Bozhena. Haiduk knew his mother never visited his father's grave on that day. She disliked the huge crowds, the atmosphere of a sunny pagan banquet on graves, the lurid painted shells of the eggs, and the drunken grins of people glad they were still alive. It seemed blasphemous to Maria Yuzefivna, to be drinking *horilka* and gorging on food on the graves of loved ones. The sombre rain-sodden Catholic festival of All Souls, on 1 November, was much more suited to the nature of her grief.

Haiduk remembered that she always went to his father's grave on Friday, every week, every month. She could not conceive of life without this ritual. Therefore, at 14:00 on 30 April, having rested and caught up on his sleep, he slipped unnoticed from his apartment-cum-hiding place on Protasiv Yar. He headed up the hill and crossed the road, where it looped between the institutes of cardio-surgery and bacteriology, and reached the Baikove Cemetery. He walked in the direction of the Polish section where his father rested, but came to an abrupt halt when he saw that a six-lane road ran across the cemetery. On its eastern side there was the ten-storey, pyramid-shaped Baik Entertainment Centre, which glimmered with advertising.

Haiduk trod confusedly in front of the fence that divided the cemetery into the upper and lower parts.

He was barely able to orientate himself and went alongside the road to where there was a small island of the dead, which was overgrown with trees. He saw the sign 'Polish Section', and sighed with relief. Everything was covered with snow, which was exceptionally white and pure where it smothered the graves and the ancient, ruined tombs. He made his way through the virgin whiteness and wondered if his mother might not come here in such weather.

Looking down the hill, he recognised the place where his father's grave was situated. It was mounted with a huge, oak cross entwined with wild vine that resembled wire. He saw no fresh tracks in the snow, not even on the path that passed by his father's grave. With the help of his gadget he checked the possibility of there being surveillance cameras nearby, but detected nothing suspicious. Haiduk approached the old, Polish tomb, which had once belonged to the Izdykovsky family, and stood by the entrance like a guardian angel, so as to remain unseen.

At 15:00 he saw his mother moving slowly along the path. Her hands gripped a small wreathe of green pine branches. No one accompanied her. She came to the tomb, opened the cast-iron gate in the fence and laid the wreath on the snow-capped sepulchre. She extracted a small candle in a glass holder, lit it and placed it on the grave. Crossing herself in the Catholic manner, from right to left, she sank deeply into her thoughts.

'Mum,' said Haiduk in a voice brimming with tenderness for his mother, and guilt. His mother slowly and confusedly turned towards the sound of his voice.

'Mum, it's me, Ihor.'

His mother had aged greatly during the years he had not seen her. She was wearing the long, old, brown overcoat he had bought her from America ten years ago, and her head was swathed in a grey, fluffy headscarf, like a village woman.

'Mum, don't be afraid, it's me.'

His mother slowly sat in the snow, while trying to arrest her descent by latching her hand onto the fence around the tomb. Haiduk ran to her, picked her up and began to dust the snow from her coat.

'Ihor ... son ... you're alive,' she moaned softly.

Haiduk kissed her cheek, which was wet with snow. 'I'm alive. I've come back.'

'They told me you were a criminal. Some young officer came to tell me. Later, they told me you were dead.'

'Are they watching you?'

'They hang around the building but they don't follow me to the cemetery.'

'Contact Natalia Havrilivna in person immediately, do not use the phone. I will tell you everything later. There is no time now. Let her tell the hetman I have returned. If he wants to see me, let him send a signal.'

'How?' asked his mother, unable to believe she was seeing her son alive.

'Ask the hetman to come to the apartment on Sunday at 16:00. He knows where in Lypskiy Lane. I only need a signal. The clock on the National Bank must be five minutes slow between 14:00 and 16:00. Have you understood all this, Mum?'

'Yes'

'Can you remember?'

'The clock must be five minutes slow,' his mother repeated, 'and the apartment on Lypskiy Lane.'

The apartment was a safe-house belonging to the hetman's special division and outside the remit of the State Guard, but under the protection of the hetman's bodyguards.

Haiduk again kissed his mother, who sat on the fence around the tomb as she dabbed away the tears with a handkerchief. 'Leave now, son. I'll stay here a while longer and pray.'

Haiduk returned up the slope, striving to step in his own footsteps, and reached the panoramic view of Kyiv at the summit. He looked at the one hundred-storey skyscrapers in the town's business district, where the Volodymyrskiy market had once seethed with life. They were akin to huge icicles, and from a distance snow-covered Kyiv resembled a Carpathian village. To the left, on Batyieva Hill, a huge yellow structure arose, surmounted by a tower with a dome. It resembled a mosque and was Batii-Hrad, the venue created by the Horde for the summit of their alliance of states the USH.

30

'Your good health,' the hetman greeted him sonorously, in a manner that was a touch theatrical. He smothered Haiduk in embraces at the threshold of the safe-house. Makhun had reached the property through a subterranean passage from Bankova 11, the ancient building where the hetman's special division was based. The apartment, with its secret access, was exceptionally convenient for covert meetings with those individuals whose presence he did not wish to highlight at the presidential palace. There were always journalists at the hetman's official premises, taking it in turns to wait for a sensational story. The apartment was utilised for informal, friendly meals, such as the hetman loved, and for other purposes that were concealed from Natalia Havrilivna.

'I've been waiting for you,' said the hetman, stroking his moustache, which had been dyed and trimmed that very morning. 'And all the time I waited, you didn't come. You are really necessary to me now.'

What a great theatrical talent, Haiduk thought, he would be a great actor. He asked in a restrained fashion, demonstrating his respect and devotion, 'Were you waiting to have me arrested?'

'You are being abrasive.' The hetman laughed, although his eyes flashed in the manner carefully deleted by his PR staff from all his portraits. 'What arrest are you talking about?'

'Well, there are rumours circulating, but I don't believe them.'

'Don't believe it.' Kuzma-Danylo placed his hard, hetmanly hand on Haiduk's shoulder and led him to the dining room where a dining table, set for two, sparkled enticingly with crystal and silver.

Well, this doesn't look like an arrest, thought Haiduk as he sat opposite the hetman. 'Sir Hetman …'

'You don't need to be so official, call me by the name you used to use.'

'Father,' said Haiduk, who was actually touched by this, 'thank you for everything you have done for my mother; both you and Natalia Havrilivna.'

The hetman dismissively waved his hand, 'It was nothing, no more than my duty to her.'

They were served today, not by the taciturn, trained officers of the Marchenko Intelligence Services Academy but by talkative, beautiful Motrya. This snub-nosed favourite of the hetman's wore a white blouse with a plunging neckline, offering a prospect that caught the eye of every heterosexual man she encountered.

'Motrya, pour out our favourite,' the hetman ordered.

She poured a transparent, icy stream of Kozatska Hetmanska *horilka* into the glasses. The bottle was adorned with the image of an unknown hetman, who bore a strong resemblance to K. D. Makhun, but who was wearing a fur hat adorned with feathers, and a fur cape.

'Well, let's drink to our meeting.' The hetman downed his glass in one gulp. Haiduk just drank a little of his. Motrya immediately poured some more *horilka*, serving the hetman then Haiduk. She had previously been an officer of the State Guard until the hetman saw her and ordered a transfer to his special division. While drinking his second glass, the hetman said, 'What arrest were you talking about?'

'The clock on the National Bank wasn't five minutes slow as agreed. It was five minutes fast. I thought …'

'But that's what Natalia told me. Five minutes fast.'

'Mum made a mistake, poor lass,' Haiduk said when he realised. He extracted a little packet wrapped in gift paper. It contained a little box, inside which was a tiny, blue velvet pillow where there rested a gold butterfly adorned with emeralds. He had purchased this replacement for the first lady's present, which had been lost in the crash, at the market in Kalynivskyi. 'This is a gift for Natalia Havrilivna from the first lady of the Confederation.' Haiduk had removed the tag inscribed 'Made in China' when he had prepared the gift at his apartment.

Having drunk three glasses of *horilka*, the hetman asked Motrya to leave them until summoned to return and he produced a packet of papers, 'Read this.' It was Vitold Klynkevych's report.

Having read the material attentively, Haiduk handed back the papers to the hetman. 'I completely agree. Though in truth I am not very well orientated in the internal political situation. However, some intelligent steps are proposed here.'

'Of course,' the hetman agreed ironically, 'particularly regarding the succession. Don't you get that Vitold wants to be my successor?' He looked sternly at Haiduk, who shrugged his shoulders and replied, 'Well, he is entitled to dream.'

'To dream, to dream,' the hetman said, reddening. 'It's too soon for him to think about that, much too soon. Who and what is he? A fetcher and carrier; an errand boy … Motrya, bring the borshch,' bellowed Makhun.

After they had tasted the red borshch and *pampushky*

with garlic, they feasted on lamb chops and *varenyky* with cherries. Haiduk told the hetman about the situation in the Confederation and Fiery Sara's struggle with the legitimate president. The hetman shook his head understandingly and said that the same chaos and struggle for power was everywhere.

They moved to a round table and sat in leather armchairs where they drank coffee and cognac. The hetman foreswore the traditional Cossack pipe and lit a Cuban cigar. Haiduk had obtained pungent Cuban cigars from the Confederation's occupying military group in Cuba and, from time to time, sent them to the hetman. However, Haiduk was still anxious because he did not know what this sly man wanted. Makhun was in love with power and the opera theatre scenery he arranged around himself. Eventually, the hetman looked sharply into Haiduk's face. 'Work is needed now, Ihor. The state is dying. Will you help?'

'I am an officer,' said Haiduk, 'and you are the commander in chief.'

'I appoint you my aide for national security and, simultaneously, the secretary of the national security council. In a month you will be promoted. Oleksa!'

The hetman's younger adjutant, a captain in the Airborne Troops, appeared on the threshold. He was holding a coat hanger from which hung a snow-white dress uniform with gold thread and epaulettes adorned with a little mace, crossed with a horsehair flail, and one star.

The hetman rose heavily and Haiduk stretched and stood. The adjutant gave the hetman a blue folder embellished with a raspberry-red Cossack cross, which he handed to Haiduk. 'This is the decree appointing you to your post. You will immediately be assigned bodyguards and will use a government terrapin, a German manufactured one rather than an American machine, and be provided with a government contact device of the highest category.'

He handed Haiduk a gadget manufactured by Kyiv's Artemida factory, which was not quite as sophisticated as the American communication device he already had. 'Set about the execution of your duties immediately. UMI is entirely at your disposal and you will direct them. The State Guard also requires controlling … if you can manage it. I adopted another resolution today and appointed Ruslan Foshchenko as Minister of Foreign Affairs. He is a promising lad. What do you make of that?'

'Thank you, Father,' Haiduk said, eschewing a reply about Foshchenko, 'I am deeply impressed. Thank you for the trust you have placed in me. May I go now?'

'Go, go. I will stay here for a while and work.'

Motrya, who was clearing away the crockery, looked stealthily at Haiduk as he donned his black coat and accepted the parade uniform from the hands of the adjutant.

'Is there anything else you wish for?' the hetman asked, 'say what it is now so there are no misunderstandings later.'

'I have two requests,' replied Haiduk.

'Say what they are,' responded the hetman.

'First, I will appoint my own team.'

'Certainly, that is understood completely. Let's move forward. And second?'

'Please give me the right, Your Excellency, to meet with you regularly and no less than once a week.'

'No question about that. Is there anything else?'

Haiduk hesitated, but decided to speak, 'Please give me the right to speak the truth to you, however painful it may be.'

'Don't be silly,' said the hetman, with unfeigned laughter. 'Do you think I don't know the truth? Do you know how many channels of information I have? You should see the information the State Guard is giving me. But if you read all this rubbish you would lose the will to live.'

'Information is not yet the same thing as truth,' Haiduk

said stubbornly.

'Okay. We will talk about this on another occasion. Goodbye.' The hetman opened the doors to the safe-house and, patting Haiduk amiably on the shoulder, asked, in a whisper, 'How much money did you earn on the arms deals? I have heard you have an account in Panama with sixty-million globos? Be more careful son, you have tangled with a nest of vipers. I am relying on you.'

Two bodyguards from the Georgian Brigade were already waiting for Haiduk in the forecourt. He handed one of them the dress uniform, but kept hold of the hetman's decree and the communication gadget.

31

2 May 2077
Secret
To all structures within the State Guard of Ukraine and all secret agents of the State Guard

In connection with a change in circumstances, we are recalling Operational Order No. 1377/2554 of 22 April 2077

Director of the State Guard of Ukraine, Yulii Merezhko

3 May 2077
10:00
Secret
To: President of the Confederation of States of North America, Andrew Van Lee

Sir
Our operational measures for the neutralisation of General Ihor Haiduk (Ukraine), who may be deployed by a person known

to you as the key witness in a matter involving the first lady, have been concluded unsuccessfully. Haiduk reached Ukrainian territory without sustaining any harm and, in spite of the warrant issued for him there, met with the hetman on Sunday 2 May. At 09:00 (Kyiv time) on Monday, the Ukrainian mass-media reported that the hetman has appointed Haiduk as his aide for national security and secretary of the national security council. This appointment transforms Haiduk into a key figure within Ukraine's national security sphere. The hetman also appointed the current Ukrainian ambassador in Washington, Ruslan Foshchenko, to the post of Minister of Foreign Affairs. Both I. P. Haiduk and R. V. Foshchenko are senior resident intelligence agents, representing the interests of different groups in the Ukrainian establishment. (Look at the reports on I. P. Haiduk and R. V. Foshchenko.)

A positive outcome is the temporary absence of leadership for Ukrainian intelligence on Confederation territory. A negative consequence is our uncertainty concerning the true positions of I. P. Haiduk and R. V. Foshchenko regarding the Confederation and the Horde. Equally negative is the temporary lack of knowledge regarding the goals of the hetman within the geo-political game on which he has embarked along with the rejuvenated leadership of the Ukrainian State.

Admiral Stanley Fisher

3 May 2077
11:30
Secret
To be delivered personally to the Director of the Central Security Service of the Confederation, Admiral Stanley Fisher

Dear Stanley
Thank you for the information. As a result of the timely measures

that were implemented, Fiery Sara has now rejected the idea of giving an interview and presenting her terrible accusations. With regard to Major General Haiduk, it is necessary to utilise intelligence methods to understand his true goals in this matter. I think that in his current rank he will not dare to engage in hostile activities towards the federation and damage the strategic partnership between our nations. Find all his weak points, wife, children, lover, friends etc, which could be used to pressure him in the event of any attempt by him to attack the White House and the first lady. Remember that the president must never be a cuckold and the first lady and senator must never be suspected of being a whore.

Andrew

32

At 08:30 on Monday, Yulii Yulianovych Merezhko was the first person to enter Haiduk's official office in the left wing of the hetman's palace above the Dnipro. He was accompanied by an aide, bearing in his arms a large, rectangular object wrapped in grey paper. Merezhko was wearing the black and silver dress uniform of a general in Ukraine's Corps of Gendarmerie, and a star glittering with diamonds on his tie. He also wore the obligatory Cossack sabre. In truth, the sabre had been shortened due to Merezhko's short stature and resembled a dagger. However, his vindictive personality and the capacity of his precise, computer-level memory compelled caution from those who wished to reduce the stature of this man of already reduced stature. Smiling delightedly, Merezhko opened his arms wide, like a fisherman exaggerating the size of a fish, 'My dear Ihorok, I am glad, boundlessly happy for you.' Merezhko rose to stand tiptoe in an attempt to kiss Ihor on the lips. This unpleasant habit of his was another source of mockery in the ruling circles of the state. 'I always believed in you from the time of the Bucharest campaign. Do you remember how you captured that Romanian General and we interrogated him together?' warbled Merezhko.

Haiduk invited him to sit at the long conference table, but Merezhko refused, 'I anticipate, Ihorok, fruitful cooperation between us and our offices alike. We only have one Ukraine and one hetman. It is necessary for us now, as never before, to be together. When is the sitting of the National Security Council?'

'Well, to begin with, I have to prepare it,' said Ihor, avoiding a direct reply.

'What is its theme?' Merezhko enquired. He had a large, heavy head, and his piercing, pale blue eyes radiated calm and confidence.

'The Newpeople and the Deathchristians,' said Haiduk.

'What, what?'

'I am joking. The hetman will determine the theme and he hasn't decided yet.'

'Of course, of course,' Merezhko said thoughtfully. 'Do these psychos who announced they have found the body of Christ really interest you?'

'I'm not occupied with religious matters.'

'I can give you some information about them, but I don't have time to spare now. I have an operative meeting at 09:30. I have brought you a little souvenir. Vasya, bring it here,' Merezhko ordered his aide.

The grey paper was unwrapped and Haiduk saw a wonderfully high-quality photograph in an attractive gold frame; it was of a smiling Haiduk with Bozhena and the Zundapp. He had just started the engine and Bozhena was sitting in the sidecar, delighted they were finally approaching Kyiv and she would soon see her brother. The shadow of the professor who had sold them the motorcycle fell across the blurred background where the advertising for the market glimmered.

'Well, how do you like that?' Merezhko asked with satisfaction. 'Who is that girl? Your daughter? She works at the Friedman firm?'

Seeing the expression on Haiduk's face, Merezhko made yet another attempt to kiss him on the lips. Then, bowing in farewell, he left an aroma of lilac eau de Cologne in his wake.

Haiduk summoned his aide, UMI Major Hryhoriy Nevinchanyi, and instructed him to check if the frame contained any bugs.

33

4 May 2077
Restricted to the Secretary of the NSC of Ukraine and Aide to the Hetman of Ukraine for National Security, Major General I. P. Haiduk

Dear Ihor Petrovych
My sincere congratulations once again on your high-level appointment, I am convinced that you will make a worthy contribution to the business of strengthening the national security of Ukraine. However, the main reason I am writing is that yesterday I formed the impression that the so-called 'Deathchristians' had engaged your interest. On my instructions, an agent of the State Guard, code-named 'Joan', composed a little analytical report on this sect, which I have attached to this letter. (One Copy)

Respectfully, Yulii Merezhko
Director of the State Guard of Ukraine

Deathchristians
Analytical Report
The first intelligence agency reports regarding the existence of a

secret sect, the so-called Deathchristians, began in 2071.

Kyiv's Pechersk-Lavra monastery has become the centre of their activity and their spiritual leader is the fanatic Shaman Sygismund Sansyzbayev, who originates from the terrain of the Horde and appeared in Kyiv in 2068. He pronounced himself a Christian arch-monk, although he continues to live in the Muslim manner, having three wives and secretly visiting the mosque at Batii-Hrad.

During 2071-2073 the fundamentals of the so-called teaching of Sansyzbayev developed regarding the earthly death of Jesus Christ. Utilising specially selected remains, found in one of the remote caves at Lavra, for his maverick goals, the self-appointed O. Kalerii (Sansyzbayev) began, with the support of the intelligence structures and agents of influence of the Horde, an active propaganda campaign to advertise his 'revelations' and new 'religious doctrine'. Meanwhile, in 2074, the State Guard succeeded in obtaining a portion of the tissues of the relics being presented in the capacity of the 'Body of Christ'. By a process of complex genetic, bio-chemical and radioisotope analysis conducted in the SRI of the State Guard, they succeeded in establishing, with absolute certainty, that the body of Christ belongs to an unknown man aged 50-55, who lived in the middle of the XVII century and had died from wound-related traumas incurred during one of the national liberation struggles of the Ukrainian people. X-Ray research of the body showed the presence of fractured tibia bones; Christ's leg was not broken when he perished. Perhaps the body is that of one of the Cossack Chiefs who led a devout, Christian life and was therefore honoured by burial in the caves at Lavra.

The objective, scientific conclusions regarding the so-called 'Body of Christ' were completely ignored by Sansyzbayev and his fanatical devotees. Furthermore, the results of the research were not published in the mass-media. This engendered a mass of rumours and speculations, allowing Sansyzbayev the possibility of disputing the scientific conclusions and simultaneously commissioning, from various charlatans at alternative para-scientific centre, support for his 'discovery'.

However, it is not particularly striking that such a controversialist has emerged and permitted himself to indulge in sacrilege regarding the canons of Christian teaching. Similar episodes have occurred before. The most impressive and socially dangerous effect of Sansyzbayev's 'discovery' is the fact that, from 2075 onwards, the teachings of the Deathchristians began to acquire serious support among both religious circles and the wider community, both in our country and in several foreign states. No rational arguments from the adepts of 'classical' Christian teaching are being taken into account.

Furthermore, Sansyzbayev and his devotees, utilising the support of certain leaders, have, by criminal methods, seized the sacred Orthodox Church of Kyiv Pechersk-Lavra. They overcame the resistance of the monks and destroyed, according to some sources, those who argued against them, and terrified others into compliance. They thus transformed Lavra into a Deathchristian stronghold.

The Deathchristians movement is distinguished by its aggressiveness, its uncompromising tendency towards violence, its doctrinaire quality, and the absence of any doubts regarding the veracity of its teaching. It has already become a factor causing serious division in society, which has begun to separate into Deathchristians and Risenchristians. According to the preliminary estimates of the State Guard's Sociological Service, the Deathchristians movement is supported by 18.6% of Ukraine's population and the figure is growing.

The sect's ideologue has emerged as the publicist of the Movement for Four Freedoms, Arch-Monk Borisogleb Chikirisov, the former cleric at the Semygradsky Cathedral of the Byzantine Patriarchate.

I regard the transition of the Deathchristians from

a marginal, divisive religious sect to a large, well-organised social and political movement as dangerous. This development merits the immediate involvement of the competent organs of the state. There may be unforeseen consequences for the state in lieu of the potential for hatred and fanaticism implicit in the Newpeople/Deathchristian ideology. The current de-Christianisation of Ukraine is far more dangerous than that which occurred in France during the revolutionary terror.

Christ has Risen.
Agent Joan

4 May 2077
Washington DC
His Excellency, the Advisor to the President (Hetman) of Ukraine on National Security Issues, Secretary of the NSC, Major General Ihor Haiduk

Sir
It is with great pleasure, and on the instructions of the President of the Confederation of States of North America, Andrew Van Lee, that I wish to congratulate you on your promotion to a high-level position. When recollecting our good relationship in Washington DC I am persuaded that we will be able to cooperate fruitfully on behalf of the strategic partnership between our nations.

Ever Yours
Admiral Stanley Fisher
Director of the Central Security Service of the Confederation and Presidential Aide

34

The windows of Haiduk's office, like those of the hetman's, looked out on the Dnipro. He could step through them onto a modestly proportioned terrace suspended over the cliffs, gulp the cold air and look out at the nameless island in the midst of the huge watery expanse. The island seemed bereft of life and consisted of white sand, stunted willows and an old, empty shack nailed together from, now rotting, planks by an anonymous fisherman. However, this structure, which was in fact erected from heat and cold resistant plastic deceptively fashioned to resemble wood, concealed the eyes and ears of the UMI radar and antennae with satellite connections. A subterranean facility belonging to UMI, which had been constructed at the same time as the hetman's palace, was located underneath the island. A special directorate of Kyiv's metro construction firm had built an underground line from Kyiv to Borshchykha, and the hetman could travel its length in a comfortable, high-speed capsule in twenty minutes. Another line, which ran under the Dnipro, had been created for the State Guard and linked the island with the left and right banks. This line allowed UMI to dispatch special units from camps on the left bank to the right bank of Ukraine and Kyiv. The area under the island contained the control centre for Ukraine's military missions in one hundred and ninety-six countries and other contingents of UMI, numbering sixty-thousand soldiers and officers.

Haiduk was extremely surprised when he acquired this information, having gained access to the highest category of state secrets. Apart from Haiduk, this level of access was enjoyed by only the hetman, General Clerk, Chief Military Otaman, the Director of the State Guard and, of course, members of the Aeropagus. Haiduk liked the metaphorical division of the special services into three landscape features. There was the 'Island', the State Guard, and the 'Forest', the foreign information service of the State Guard, which was based in the woods by Chabany Farm. Finally, there was the 'Mountain', the special division under the hetman, on Pecherska Mount at 11 Bankova Street. The headquarters of Kyiv's military district had once been based there, and the administrations of the first, forgotten presidents of Ukraine. The officers of the State Guard had a saying, 'The mountain leads in the forest, the forest is not visible for the trees, and the island fetches water in buckets full of holes to put out the fire.'

A long-standing, profound enmity and rivalry existed between military intelligence and the State Guard with its police and corps of gendarmes. Haiduk strove to explain this rationally, persuading his friends that the entirety of the issue was due to the poor organisation of the State Guard and its intelligence service. The more modern structure of UMI's subdivisions was, in his opinion, far more able to conduct intelligence operations. He recollected his friend Viktor Bezpalii, who had rejected a transfer to the State Guard, even though they had guaranteed him the rank of general, a high salary and promising career development. 'A true military intelligence operative never becomes a policeman,' Bezpalii had said proudly, rejecting the offer from Merezhko's deputy. The deputy had flown to Washington specially to persuade Bezpalii to take up the post of head of the State Guard's Foreign Intelligence Service.

As he recollected Bezpalii, Haiduk left the terrace because of the freezing air. Snow lay on the island and both the banks of the Dnipro and the spring melt-water in the reservoir seemed black.

Haiduk summoned his aide, Hryhoriy Nevinchanyi, who entered the room with a cunning smile. He was an older man, pleasantly plump from the many functions he attended with his numberless friends. However, he never allowed himself to refuse to participate in an operation. At present, he was wearing Israeli desert camouflage. Nevinchanyi had recently returned from Haifa, where the capital of Israel had moved temporarily after Iranian nuclear strikes against Tel Aviv and the western part of Jerusalem.

'Hryhoriy Ivanovych, what have you heard concerning the murder of Bezpalii?' Haiduk asked in an official tone, even though he greatly liked Nevinchanyi. During the Romanian campaign Hryhoriy had been young Lieutenant Haiduk's mentor. On one occasion, when they were in the outskirts of Bucharest, he had saved Ihor's life when he had spotted a Romanian sniper aiming at him. At that time he was an officer in an intelligence brigade. Nevinchanyi took out the sniper with a shot from a rocket-propelled grenade.

'And what would I know when the State Guard is dealing with the investigation,' Hryhoriy said, screwing up his eyes, 'our men with the military attaché in Washington have been pushed out of it.'

Merezhko again, thought Haiduk and said aloud, 'What will we do?'

'Fly,' said Nevinchanyi, and he really did fly, almost injuring his big, half-bald head on a chandelier, which swayed and chimed menacingly after the collision. Haiduk froze in surprise. 'Bloody thing, I can't control it,' cried Nevinchanyi, guiltily gathering himself into a horizontal position, as if executing a swallow dive, and banging his head against the wall where a portrait of the hetman hung. A small apparatus was attached to Nevinchanyi's belt, adjacent to the Israeli Micro-TAR-22 automatic pistol. Hryhoriy twisted the small arm on the device hither and thither, as if he were the owner of a model plane, and manoeuvred himself by remote control. He hung helplessly above Haiduk's table, not knowing how to assume a vertical position.

'Excuse me Ihor Petrovych, I got hold of this in Israel. Or, more accurately, I swapped it for a Chornobyl-30 anti-radiation suit. They are beginning to equip their special services with them. When they showed this in training it was like a hurricane. They were flying around like Ninjas.'

At last something in the apparatus worked and Nevinchanyi fell heavily to the floor. 'I have a bit of an idea regarding Bezpalii,' said Hryhoriy. 'We need to involve AMAN. One of our people works there, David Beylin. He's a sound chap. He brought his family here before the nuclear strikes. If you permit it …'

'I permit it,' said Haiduk. He was accustomed to Hryhoriy's various idiosyncrasies and the idea of a 'flying special services squad' was greatly to his liking. 'And how many such … apparatuses could you obtain for us?'

'A batch of ten at the most; there's a great deficit of them there. And you will help with the anti-radiation suits?'

'I'll help,' Haiduk promised.

'I have brought you a proposition for a special group that will work under you. Here is the list.' He handed Haiduk a computer fob, 'Everything is here, their characteristics, biographies, video records of military operations and training. There are ten men in all, and they can fly.' His naive, pale blue eyes glittered.

'Thank you, I will study it carefully,' said Haiduk.

'Ihor Petrovych, we received an invitation for you from Mintimer Basmanov half an hour ago. He wants to make your acquaintance.'

'Basmanov?'

'Yes, I advise you to accept the invitation. Even His Excellency sees Basmanov regularly.'

'Where do I need to go?'

'It's not far from here.' Nevinchanyi walked over to a large computer screen to display a map to Haiduk. 'This is in Chernihiv territory at the juncture of Ukraine, Russia and Belarus.' The outlines of Chernihiv territory appeared on the screen. Nevinchanyi guided the cursor to the north-east of Horodnya, deviating away from the M-13. The cursor halted at the River Tetiva and a large, forested area. He then drew a gleaming circle around Horodnya, Mena, Semenivka, Koryukivka and then into Russian territory, seizing a huge area within the circle. 'This is his domain.'

'I'll go there,' Haiduk decided. He dialled the hetman's number on a gadget.

'Your Excellency, I request your permission to take a trip to see Basmanov.'

'What does he need?' the hetman enquired with dissatisfaction.

'I don't know. But he's invited me.'

'Go. Only be careful. Pass yourself off as a greenhorn. You don't know anything yet, you have only just taken up your duties. Come to me with a report after the journey.'

'I hear you,' said Haiduk, switching off the communication gadget for the higher echelons of the UMCFS. He issued an order to Nevinchanyi, 'Prepare a terrapin for tomorrow. You are going with me, but leave this flying apparatus behind. Okay, there is one more thing. Please hang the photograph presented to me by Merezhko in the relaxation room.'

'I hear you,' laughed Nevinchanyi, 'there's no need to offend Yulii Yulianovych. Let it hang there. I have checked it and the bloody thing is clean.'

'Excuse me, Hryhoriy Ivanovych, I forgot. Could you find out about Agent Joan in Merezhko's bureau? I would like to make his acquaintance.'

35

THE HAIDUK FILE
9 May 2077
Top Secret (One Copy)
For the Aide to the Hetman of Ukraine for National Security
Secretary of the NSC of Ukraine, Major General I. P. Haiduk

Operational character report on Mintimer Basmanov, a citizen
of Ukraine, Russia, Belarus, the Union of States of the Horde,
Switzerland and China, and a Muscovite boyar.

He is a member of both the Aeropagus of Ukraine
and the Secret World Council, whose capital is in Chyngiz-
Saray. He is also Prince of Chernihiv and Tsar of Voronezh,
Ryazan, Stalingrad, Khan of Ulan-bator and Aral, and Chief
of the Order of the Warriors of Light, the Sacred Priests and
Guardians. Basmanov was born in 2010 in Moscow. His parents
are unknown and he was born homeless.

He became a criminal in-law when he was 18 and
was imprisoned, on more than one occasion, in the camps of
Perm, Ust-Tobolsk and Mordovia, and in prisons for especially
dangerous criminals in Vladimir and Stalingrad. He personally
killed eight prisoners-cellmates with a knife, and his record
includes the rape of women and boys from a children's home.

In 2030, as his biographers write, 'a vision came to
Basmanov'. One night, while he was in a single cell on death
row, he saw the spirit of Jesus. The spirit told Basmanov that,
in reality, Jesus had not risen from the dead after the crucifixion
but had died. He instructed Basmanov to announce the truth
of Christ's death to the world, to bury his body and establish
a new religious teaching. The spirit radiated such a brilliant
light that the prison guards sounded the alarm because they
thought Basmanov was making an escape. When the special
team reached Basmanov's cell, the guards were amazed to see

the chains in which he had been fettered had disappeared and Basmanov was on his knees before his bed, praying and paying no attention to anyone.

They say that from that moment Basmanov changed fundamentally. He became gentle and devout, he organised a Sunday School for prisoners, urging them to join the Order of the Warriors of Light, the Sacred Priests and the Guardians. He spread a rumour that he was the distant successor of Boyaryn Oleksiy Basmanov (sixteenth century), one of the founders of the repressive machinery of Ivan the Terrible, who subsequently ordered his murder. Basmanov's own repressive guardians, operating under the slogan 'fight crime', murdered half the prisoners and almost all the guards, seizing control of the prison, which was declared the 'Sacred Home of the Guardians'. In place of an icon depicting Christ, they hung up a portrait of Ivan the Terrible with the inscription, 'Everyone on whom the suspicion of the sovereign falls will be subject to torture. This will cleanse the spirit from darkness and multiply the light'.

Basmanov was freed in 2039 after intense pressure from the liberal Moscow intelligentsia and Stalingrad's human rights activists. He was then pronounced a saint.

Squadrons of Basmanov's Guardians organised into motorised rifle and tank brigades and embarked on the capture of an array of former Russian imperial territories. They launched punitive measures against corrupt officials, police, militia and ordinary criminals, decapitating them, severing arms and branding their foreheads, depending on their level of guilt. Basmanov's movement, which historians call 'The Great Cleansing of Russia', was supported enthusiastically by 78.2% of the population. Basmanov and his military, to a great extent, caused the collapse of the centralised Russian State, leading to the seizure of large areas of its territory by the Celestial People's Democratic Empire and the Horde.

During the Ukrainian-Romanian war (2048-2052)

when Bukovyna and the land in the Black Sea area of Odesa was occupied, Basmanov provided military assistance to General K. D. Makhun, the current hetman of Ukraine. Three motorised rifle units, along with the tank army of Makhun, launched an abrupt raid on Bucharest. Basmanov's units, the Ivan the Terrible, Protopope Avakuma and Stalin brigades were granted three days for the pillaging of Bucharest. As a reward for his outstanding contribution to Ukraine's victory, Basmanov was granted rule over Chernihiv territory.

According to rough estimates, Basmanov owns half a million serfs on the territories that belong to him. He cultivates female prostitutes and male gladiators on special farms, and sells them. They are transported primarily to the Horde and Celestial Empire (for more detail, see annexes I-VII).

Hetman K. D. Makhun, taking into account Basmanov's military power and role in assisting Ukraine, appointed him to the Aeropagus of Ukraine in 2067. In 2068 Basmanov formed the Movement for Four Freedoms, an apolitical mass-movement.

The basis of Basmanov's ideology incorporated the principles already formulated by him in 2037, during his incarceration in Stalingrad prison. He laid out these principles in his book *My Encounter With Christ and the Struggle for Popular Freedom*, written in the cell for the condemned. They are as follows:

1. The freedom of the state from separatism:
There are no, and may be no, nations, tribes, ethnic minorities and autonomous creations on Russian soil. There is just the YeDRON (the acronym for the Unified Statehood of Russian People), which is created by a state in the name of state-level goals and state unity. The state not only has the right but is obliged to savagely extirpate all manifestations of separatism. This is supported by 56.9% of society.

2. The freedom of the leaders of the Unified Statehood of the Russian People from any judicial norms and international obligations in pursuit of the construction of the state. Everything in the name of the state, everything for the state:

Everyone who resists the will of the leaders of the state or expresses doubt regarding their policies is an enemy of the state and subject to destruction. The more savage the repression of the enemies of the state, their family and friends, the stronger the state will be. This view is supported by 63.3% of the community.

3. The freedom of society from criminals:

All criminals must be branded and compelled to sit in prisons or concentration camps, and those whose limbs are severed or tongues cut out or eyes gouged out must be incarcerated in disabled residences, which are simultaneously prisons. This is supported within the range of 78-85%, dependent on the region.

4. The freedom of choice of citizens:

Every citizen has the right to independently decide who is an enemy of the state and a criminal and utilise measures to extirpate criminality. The freedom to punish foes is the greatest of the social freedoms in the history of humanity. This view is supported by 89.3% of the community.

Basmanov writes in his book, 'There will be no second coming of Christ. The central reality of the twenty-first century will be the coming of the all-punishing, all-merciful state wherein the principles of the Movement for Four Freedoms will be embodied'.

Notwithstanding his extreme anti-Ukrainian views - 'There never was such a nation and there never will be', is a quote from the book - he did not support the aggression of EnROS against Ukraine, conducted under the guise of the defence of the gas transport system against Ukrainian-American nationalists (2068-2070). The opposition of Basmanov to the Russian-Ukrainian war - 'We, the YeDRON are obligated not to wage war on ourselves,' he announced - led to civil war in Russia, the collapse of Moscow, and the separation of territories into a small, North-European province (St Petersburg) and zone of influence of the Horde. The ferocious anti-semitism of Basmanov and his personal friendship with Kara-Khan, the brutal dictator of the Horde, have led to the World Government of Globalists, the Locarno Club, pronouncing Basmanov an enemy of humanity and the Organisation for Global Security. They offered a reward of one billion globos for his head.

Basmanov, utilising his close relations with the hetman, is insisting on the fastest possible unification of Ukraine with the Horde, where it would have the legal status of the 'Kyiv-Dnipro Ulus'. He has promised Makhun the title of Khan, but a decision has to be made during the summit of the USH in Kyiv (Batii-Hrad) in December 2077.

He leads an ascetic life, neither drinking nor smoking, and is raising forty male orphans. He has created a museum of Ivan the Terrible and the Guardians and is captivated by the music of Pyotr Tchaikovsky and the art of Ilya Glazunov.

Analyst Maximilian-VI

36

They flew in the morning as a dry May snow fell, silvering the black exterior of the terrapin by which Nevinchanyi was waiting for Haiduk. He was freezing in his dark green UMI dress uniform and was therefore dancing on the cement runway on which the military helicopters and VTOL bombers of the hetman's personal guard were parked.

Nevinchanyi and Haiduk sat in the passenger seats of the terrapin. It was a small, five-seater vehicle, not allocated for military operations, although it was armed with four air-to-surface rockets, two machine guns and one 22 mm aviation cannon. The pilot and the onboard mechanic of the terrapin studied the computer map of the route and checked the control systems. It was warm inside the aircraft and Nevinchanyi discarded his coat. He carried his inseparable adjunct, the Micro TAR-22 automatic pistol, in a holster under his left arm.

Haiduk saw the German manufactured BMW terrapin for the first time; the well-designed interior space, the VIP comfort and the attention to detail. However, American military and police terrapins were far more powerful and well armed. Haiduk recollected his impression when he first saw the FAV-T1x (Flying Armoured Vehicle-Turtle I) at the Raytheon company test centre in Kansas. It was a huge flying saucer, similar to an ordinary terrapin, opaquely black without visible portholes or anything to indicate it was armed. Its enigmatic and opaque exterior enchanted him.

The Americans began by testing the defensive capabilities of the terrapin. Shots from canons and anti-tank rocket apparatuses were fired at the vehicle. The terrapin concealed itself behind a wall of powerful explosions, which had seemingly shattered it like an eggshell. However, after the fountains of soil had again fallen to the ground and the smoke had dispersed, everyone at the testing ground saw the black silhouette of the undamaged military aircraft. Haiduk was only granted the honour of observing the secret trials because he had proposed a swap with the Americans. He offered them the innovative water-hydrogen powered engines, manufactured by the Zaporizhia based Sich Motors, in exchange for the supply of some terrapins for Ukraine's armed forces.

This mutually beneficial transaction was personally sanctioned by Hetman Makhun and President Van Lee. The hetman, as a former tank driver, enthusiastically viewed the documentary film of the technical, tactical and military qualities of the terrapins, which represented another leap forward in the arms race. They combined the characteristics of a tank, armoured transporter, helicopter and amphibious vehicle. Makhun had observed them with a sinking heart and some self-pity because, alas, it was not he who would have to wage war in these machines nor see how the terrapins flew rapidly over the earth at a height of one to two metres. They soared, where necessary, to between twenty to fifty metres, maintaining intensive, destructive fire, piercing the defences of the opposition and sowing panic in rear positions and control centres. The hetman had fully endorsed Haiduk's deal and awarded him the rank of colonel in 2070.

The first five military terrapins transferred from the Confederation's European bases to Kyiv led to a breakthrough in Ukraine's war with EnROS. After terrapins made several strikes in the district of Vyshhorod, the A. Denikin volunteer reserve army of EnROS was destroyed and the Russian corporation subsequently evacuated its forces from Kyiv, Zhytomyr and Khmelnytskyi.

The terrapin in which Haiduk and Nevinchanyi were sitting flew at a low height over the Desna. A few stunted and snow-covered spruces clung to the river, imbuing the scene with the feeling that Christmas was approaching. Haiduk reflected on the Lancaster-27 and how he had flown low over the Atlantic under fire from the Karakorum MOP. An eternity seemed to have passed since then. He recollected Bozhena's warm hand resting on his hip and smelled the fragrance of her closely shorn hair.

'I have a request for you, Hryhoriy Ivanovych. Find out what happened to that girl ... Bozhena ... the one in the photograph. I will give you her location,' he said

'I hear you,' said Hryhoriy.

They flew onwards in silence while the pilot talked with the commanders of a surface-to-air missile unit located on the border of Basmanov's domain, and then to the control tower to request permission to land.

A group of Basmanov's armed guards met them on the runway where the terrapin had landed. The Guardians each wore grey wolf's-head caps, complete with fanged jaws, and long, black kaftans fastened with wide, red belts. Each of them held an automatic IZh-107, capable of firing powerful grenades, and sticking out from behind each of their shoulders were satellite antennae styled to resemble brooms.

The senior Guardian, whose nose had been sliced off at some point, looked at Nevinchanyi and said, menacingly, 'The *Khokhol* stays here.'

'No,' said Haiduk firmly, 'either he comes with me or I fly back to where I came from.'

The senior Guardian raised his palm to his mouth and Haiduk saw that his fingers had been cut off. He bandied a few words with someone and reluctantly agreed. The guests were seated in a golf cart, the senior Guardian at the wheel and the other Guardians running alongside and breathing heavily. Haiduk reflected that, from the side, this cavalcade would resemble a hungry wolf pack pursuing its prey. They travelled down a central alley, which was hedged on both sides with birch trees, pale and gently swaying. The black lenticels in their bark resembled the sad eyes of those suffering ones buried in this unfortunate soil.

Basmanov's palace was a forty-five storey structure, with columns, tower and spires, in the style of a 1950s Moscow high-rise building. They saw, to the front of the palace, the monument to Ivan the Terrible in the post-modern style, flamboyant and painted in various hues as lurid as the Cathedral of Saint Basil on Red Square. The Tsar, in the royal cap of Vladimir Monomakh, had a black beard, a yellow face and red cheeks, and it looked as if the day's frost was nipping at him too. The emperor was smiling delightedly and wearing a red, black and green striped robe. His hands held an axe smeared with bright red paint. Its blade was embedded in a block and was dark crimson with coagulated blood. Only the wolves raising their heads, who ringed the emperor and his chopping block, were dull; an inauspicious grey colour, the colour of a soldier's greatcoat.

The sun suddenly broke through the clouds and the monument glittered, all its colours were playing in the light. Is this all just an apparition? Haiduk thought, was I really in Washington not so long ago? Why have I returned to this horrible country of deranged wolves?

They entered the enormous vestibule of the palace, which was decorated with pink, Italian marble and expensive, terracotta-hued Chinese stone. A butler, wearing a white wig and an equally archaic gold jacket, white tights and slightly raised-heeled Venetian slipper-style shoes tied with pink ribbon, welcomed them.

'His Holiness will receive you in ten minutes,' he said. He used English for the last three words and continued in the same language, 'He's praying now.'

'Great,' replied Haiduk.

While they waited, a pianist, on a white grand piano, and a female harpist played music from Swan Lake. A bell sounded and the butler looked anxiously at Nevinchanyi as he spoke in English, 'I'm sorry, but screening has shown that this man has a gun.' He addressed his next words to Nevinchanyi, 'You have to leave your gun.'

Hryhoriy, who knew no language apart from Ukrainian, looked at Haiduk.

'Weapons must be left here,' Haiduk interpreted.

'No way, they might destroy it. But I would be better staying here anyway. Well, by God Ihor Petrovych, talk with Basmanov on your own. My presence isn't needed and the less I know the better I sleep. Bugger it.'

'Okay, stay here.' Haiduk followed in the wake of the

butler.

Basmanov received Haiduk in a dazzlingly white marble and gold, circular hall, which was situated in the main tower. An artificial light cascaded in from the roof at the top of the building and filled the space with a solar, pale blue haze. Basmanov was sitting on a tall throne, inlaid with gold and decorated with dark red rubies. Near Basmanov's feet, on the steps under the throne, a ten year old child was sitting with a gold wreath on his head. Basmanov was a grand, boney, old fellow with a long, grey beard and grey tresses protruding from under an aristocratic cap of beaver fur. He was dressed in white and in his right hand he held a long axe-cum-stick. It would have been hard for him to decapitate someone with this tool, but entirely possible to shear off someone's fingers.

The butler guided Haiduk to the place allocated for audiences with Basmanov, two metres from the throne. Haiduk, as required by protocol, bowed his head respectfully and said, 'Thank you, Your Highness, for the honour of being here …'

'Varrava, fetch an armchair for the guest,' Basmanov instructed. 'Sit down, you don't have to stand,' he said, addressing Haiduk as an equal and in a Ukrainian that sounded just a little strange and reminiscent of Belarusian, 'I am glad to see you.'

Perhaps he was using a particular variant of Ukrainian, Haiduk thought, one local to Chernihiv.

'I wanted to make your acquaintance,' continued Basmanov, in the throaty bass of a committed smoker, 'because I was involved in your appointment. The hetman very strongly requested that I agreed to your candidacy … This was a compromise because I had recommended the hetman appoint Ruslan Foshchenko to the post of Minister of Foreign Affairs and he was hesitating.'

'Thank you for the support,' said Haiduk, again bowing his head politely.

'I have heard much about you,' said Basmanov, looking intensely at Haiduk. His gaze was piercing, although his faded Boyaryn's eyes were masked by his grey eyebrows. Haiduk, striving not to divert his gaze from Basmanov, felt the alarming aura that radiated from him, as if from a famished wolf seeking some prey to sustain life. 'It seems to me that you are a rational person and not given to this bogus theory of a separate Ukrainian nation. This was part of the garbage of the twentieth century, all these ideas of Lenin and Woodrow Wilson regarding the self-determination of nations.'

Haiduk listened to Basmanov in silence.

'I will be honest with you.' Basmanov stared piercingly at Haiduk again. 'A time of great historic decisions is coming. Makhun is too old and foolish to understand this. He still plays around in Ukraine, surrounding himself with the idiotic decorations of a patriarchal past, without understanding that Ukraine has already ceased to exist. All the hetmans, all the presidents, all those who governed Ukraine were traitors. Why? Because the idea of Ukraine itself was treasonous from the beginning to the end. Ukraine is a myth, a fiction of separatists, a creation of Polish, Vatican, German and American agents for the purpose of splitting apart and degrading the Great Russian people. And we are obliged,' he continued in his strange accented Ukrainian, 'to finish with this historic injustice. Much will depend on you … Do you understand this?'

'I am afraid you overestimate my scope for action,' Haiduk said placidly. 'I am new to the post and inexperienced.'

'This is Nikolka,' Basmanov said, disregarding Haiduk's words and nodding at the boy who was deeply immersed in a computer game, 'he will be the next Russian Tsar, Nikolai the Third. Isn't that true, Nikolka?'

'It's true,' replied the boy confidently, without looking away from the screen, and added, 'Danzig, is that a Russian town?'

'Of course,' said Basmanov, thinking for a moment before returning to his favourite theme.

'What lessons has the twenty-first century given us? The first lesson: All forms of national statehood from the time of the eighteenth century have been revealed as unsustainable. National states are dying before our eyes. Look at France, Spain, Germany. What will survive? Large empires not based on nationality, not divided into ethnically defined scraps. You lived in America, did you not see that it has become one of the leading countries, where they are all independent of their nationality and religion? So it is the same with China, India … Russia, Ukraine, Belarus and Kazakhstan; they only have a chance of survival by creating a powerful Slavic-Turkic Empire. The Horde is giving us this chance. An empire that will compel the world to tremble at its power and greatness.' Basmanov fell silent for a moment, touched the slender neck of the future Russian Tsar, and continued, 'The second lesson: In the twenty-first century, people themselves have fundamentally changed. They really are Newpeople, as some theorists now call them. An ever greater and greater mass of people support the principles of the Movement for Four Freedoms, formulated by me. This is the principle of empire and the highest form of statehood. This is the principle of a state people, comprising honourable, disciplined, free and responsible citizens. I ask you therefore to think carefully and break with Ukraine, even more so, given that the country has almost disappeared from the map of Europe. On the eve of the summit of the Union of States of the Horde in Batii-Hrad we are duty bound to accept a decision for the liquidation of the Ukrainian people and state. We will have another state and another, united Russian people - The YeDRON.'

Basmanov tapped his staff three times and it seemed to Haiduk as if some pigeons, startled by the sharp knocking, flew off the upper part of the tower.

'And what will happen to the legally elected hetman?' Haiduk asked, feigning naivety.

'The hetman is appointed by the Aeropagus, that is me. Your job is to prepare the hetman for the inevitable change. You are an intelligent person and I anticipate that you will find a dignified way to extricate him. Your future depends on this. If you make the correct choice, you will secure a glittering career in the new empire. And pertinently, what nationality are your parents?'

'My mother is Polish and my father was Ukrainian.'

'How can the hetman be Ukrainian when his ancestry, which we have examined, is full of Russians, with some Jews and Lithuanians?'

'He considers himself Ukrainian.'

'And I consider myself a Mongol,' said Basmanov and angrily thudded his staff on the floor. 'We are all one people, remember this.'

The butler appeared next to Haiduk and gave a signal that the audience was concluded. Haiduk bowed deeply before Basmanov and began to step backwards as the butler had instructed him to do. He heard Basmanov's voice making a sound like a soft moan and turned his eyes to meet the gaze of the old Boyaryn, whose eyes were full of suffering, 'If you knew how they beat me … now all my bones ache …'

'Who … who beat you?' Haiduk did not understand.

'The guards in Stalingrad prison. I was young and wanted freedom.' Tears rolled down the burning cheeks of Basmanov. 'I wanted to taste semolina with butter … You must go, go. I am relying on you.'

Haiduk heard the old voice whispering behind him for a long time as he exited the hall, but could not make out the words.

On the way back, Hryhoriy Nevinchanyi told him enthusiastically about how the guards had taken him to the training hall for gladiators. Basmanov's heroes, armed with shields, a little bigger than tennis rackets, and short knives, had fought with a rotund brown bear, which had nearly bitten a young warrior to death before being shot with a tranquilliser dart.

Haiduk was silent, lingering among his sombre thoughts, understanding that, independently of his will, he had become a hostage in a game that was global in scope and yet more terrifying and dangerous on that account. Its participants, the hetman, Basmanov, Merezhko, Friedman, Stanley Fisher, Foshchenko, Andrew Van Lee, and many others had already cast their lots and were trying to draw him in some way to their side, compelling him to execute some role necessary for them in a drama with only one closing scene - the death of the hero and the triumph of criminals. How could an insider survive in these circumstances when he knew so many terrible secrets?

With the help of a miniature videocamera fitted in the medal 'For Service to the Homeland', which adorned his dress uniform, Haiduk had recorded his conversation with Basmanov. He decided not to hand over the recording to the hetman and instead restrict him to a general account of the conversation. However, he was compelled to add the recording to his archive.

37

20 May 2077
Top Secret
To be delivered personally to His Excellency Ivan Ovramovych Kreyda, Member of the Aeropagus of Ukraine, Warlord of Kyiv, Cherkassy, Makhnograd, Poltava, Podilia, Count of Luxembourg, President and Executive Director of the Central Energy and Industrial Territory, Governor of Slobozhanshchyna, General Co-ordinator of the internet of Kyiv-Rus, Chancellor and full member of USRAN (Ukrainian Section of the

Russian Academy of Sciences), Honorary Doctor at the Kara-Khan Academy of Human Rights (at Chyngiz-Saray, part of the Horde), Vice-President of SUKA (the East Ukrainian Communist Association), General Prosecutor of Ukraine Marshall of Jurisprudence

Your Excellency

With regard to your enquiry of 15 May 2077, No. 001375, I report that, notwithstanding the high-level state appointment of Major General I. P. Haiduk, achieved as the result of a compromise between Hetman Makhun, Boyaryn Basmanov and Baron Friedman, the State Guard regards all the accusations against I. P. Haiduk of treason and espionage for the Confederation of States of North America and the illegal financial operations connected with the arms trade (see addenda 1-11) as being in force. However, in connection with the circumstances that have arisen, the matter has been added to the ranks of, so-called, frozen cases These are, in effect, legal bombs that can be immediately detonated in the event of changes in the political situation. As you know, the State Guard is in working contact with our American colleagues, but, unfortunately, their attempts to reach a final outcome in the Haiduk case have been unsuccessful. The State Guard continues its surveillance of Haiduk through its agent network in UMI. I want to draw your attention, Your Excellency, to the fact that Haiduk arrived in Ukraine accompanied by Confederation citizen Bozhena O'Connell, who came ostensibly to visit her brother, Askold O'Connell. He works at the Feofania-Pyrohovo ZEK-116. We have established surveillance over these people and will inform you of the results of our observations. Please provide the official permission of the General Prosecutor of Ukraine (GPU) to conduct operational measures and searches regarding I. P. Haiduk, in order to prepare his case for reactivation as soon as the appropriate moment arrives.

In my view, the main danger I. P. Haiduk presents for the state political structure of Ukraine lies not in the formal/legal crimes of which he is accused but elsewhere. It lies in the pride and ambition that burn in the heart of this young and indisputably talented person. Having spent twenty years in another society, he has imbibed a philosophy alien to us, along with the idea of constructing society on the duplicitous liberal principles of democracy and the rule of law. I. P. Haiduk is becoming a huge threat to the Ukrainian State and the political traditions of our people. There are serious grounds to believe that I. P. Haiduk has, in his possession, information dangerous in the extreme to the Aeropagus, and the military and political leadership of Ukraine. He may utilise this information at the most undesirable time, resulting in the destabilisation of society, with catastrophic consequences. (See addenda 13-14 - the reports of agent 'Imperator' regarding the 'Haiduk File'.) Glory to Ukraine!

I bow before you
Yours truly Yulii Merezhko - Director of the State Guard of Ukraine

38

An Israeli intelligence services major, David Beylin, travelled to Washington at the end of May. His trip to the Confederation capital followed Haiduk's conversation with the head of AMAN, Major General Amos Levi, who had been a good friend of Haiduk's since their student days at MIT. Their conversation was conducted through the Israeli military satellite, 'Yeshurun', whose channels were inaccessible to the radio-electronic intelligence services of the Horde. David Beylin had been cooperating with Haiduk for a long time and would own responsibility for the 'closure' of some issues after the extraordinary events that occurred in Washington in April. Haiduk and Levi agreed that after his visit to Washington, Beylin would travel to Kyiv for a few days, and then to Haifa. They did not discuss the details because they trusted one another and it seemed that Amos Levi understood the essence of the problem. He immediately agreed to release Beylin without regard to the critical situation that had arisen in his country.

Tel Aviv and part of Jerusalem had been incinerated by Iranian nuclear warheads. Israel, surrounded on all sides by the Army of the Warriors of Allah, had been betrayed by its allies during the 'Nuclear Munich' conference on the Middle East, which was held in Cyprus.

Israel subsequently announced zero-hour, a time of mortal danger to its existence, a time of revenge and anger. The country had created a defensive zone around itself, with a number of nuclear explosions, which ranged from the Sinai Desert to the Golan Heights and the green valley on the border with Lebanon. A high level of radiation was sustained within this zone, which prevented the tanks and infantry of the Islamist army uniting to destroy the remains of the Israeli State.

David Beylin, accompanied by six soldiers of sub-division 262, the intelligence services of staff headquarters, went through the crossing point at Rafa to the Sinai Peninsular. He travelled in a battle-scarred 'Sara' armoured vehicle, which still enjoyed robust protection against radiation and was built using a Merka-8 heavy tank as its base. All seven men were dressed in Chornobyl-30 anti-radiation suits of Ukrainian manufacture. The readings on the Geiger counter swung from five to one hundred roentgen per hour.

A long, yellow ribbon of radioactive desert sand swirled in the wake of the vehicle. Their route lay along the Mediterranean coast, which offered an enthralling view of the piercingly blue, yet absolutely dead, sea. The road was strewn with the degraded remnants of wagons and fuel tankers, incinerated tanks and their blasted turrets. In the Al Arisha district they saw the heaps of carbonised bodies, the dead soldiers of the Egyptian Desert Foxes Division. The air, heated to 300°C, contained a terrible stench which made their driver/ mechanic feel faint. The air purification system in their radiation suits did not dispel the repellent aroma. On reaching Ramanah, which had been previously destroyed by the nuclear explosions, they turned north to Peloziyska Bay, where an Israeli navy submarine awaited them. Their subsequent route lay through Malta and Spain, then via aeroplane to Mexico. From there they would travel to El-Paso in Texas and on to Washington in an armoured jeep belonging to the intelligence directorate of the Confederation's Ministry of Defence (IDMD).

At 18:00 on Friday 28 May, an elegant, light-haired gentleman entered the bar of the Hilton Washington Hotel, which was situated near Dupont Circle. He was what is commonly called a handsome man and his appearance evoked trust in females of all ages. This was David Beylin, who had inherited from his Kyivan parents not only his pale, girlish lashes and innocent childlike smile but also the general aura of someone on whom one could rely.

He noted the solitary young woman, melancholically sipping her cocktail, sitting close to where the bar joined the wall, so that no one could sit to the left of her. Beylin gently touched the exposed skin of her back and she winced, startled as she turned to him.

'Hello Nicole,' said Beylin, as he smiled softly.

'Hello,' she replied automatically and winced again. 'Is it really you David?'

'It's me.'

'What about the war, the atomic bombs? It's so terrible … have you been here for a while?'

'Shall we have a drink?' he suggested, swiftly mounting

the high stool to Nicole Cohen's right.

She was the technical manager of the bureau that Haiduk had directed until recently. Beylin ordered two double scotches, taking his without ice, and kissed Nicole's earlobe in a way that used to work well on her. He sensed she found this pleasant and remembered those previous kisses.

Beylin told her he had come to Washington to conclude a deal for the supply of arms to an unnamed party. The weapons had been ordered last winter, but delivery had been held up after the senate adopted the resolution to impose a moratorium on the supply of all categories of arms to the Middle East. However, lawyers acting for the Israeli government had established that the Senate's prohibition did not have retrospective force in this instance. The problem lay only with supplying the arms to a blockaded Israel. Haiduk had agreed with the Antey Aviation Company that the arms would be transported from Greece in a large Antonov cargo plane.

Beylin had been a frequent guest of Haiduk's bureau, so Nicole shared all the recent news with him. All the bureau's staff had been called in for questioning regarding the murder of Viktor Bezpalii and Haiduk's disappearance. Subsequently, as if to order, the questioning ceased and the bureau renewed its operations. The acting director, Kostiantyn Slisarenko, had begun drinking heavily and had subsequently been dispatched to a psychiatric unit. Karl Thomson had resigned, so the sole remaining staff member was Nicole Cohen. Kyiv was silent and had not sent any new staff, and she was unable to decide any commercial or political issues. There were no meetings, she sat on her own in the bureau's offices, and almost no one telephoned. The silence was stressful for her.

The more whisky they drank, the closer they pressed against each other. David furtively licked the enticing neck of sweetly plump Nicole, and, as she had done before, she placed her palm on his knee and it began a hesitant, but entirely purposeful, ascent.

'My room number is three, one, three,' whispered David, 'come in ten minutes.'

'OK,' said Nicole delightedly.

The bar was already full of visitors wanting to pass their weekend in a cool place. The heavy humidity of a hot day in Washington occupied the street outside. Beylin turned his back to the surveillance camera, having managed to avoid allowing it a clear shot of his face while he drank whisky with Nicole. He passed through the crowd and went to the third floor. Ten minutes later there was a very gentle knock. He opened the door and drew Nicole into the room. He hung the 'Do Not Disturb' sign outside, locked and chained the door, and only then began to methodically undress her. The newest model of Micro-TAR automatic pistol was under his pillow, with an encrypted block on its firing control mechanism and a silencer. The drawer of his cabinet contained a Confederation navy dagger.

Nicole sighed, even as she first touched his hardness. She thought about how wonderful he was and part of her wanted to have his children. Then they were immersed in the darkness and dozed for a short while. When they returned to the reality of Washington in 2077, darkness had not yet fallen on the city, which was bathed in the long light of a spring evening.

'Where are your family?' Nicole asked, subconsciously anticipating an answer about their possible terrible fate, which would give her the right to suggest he stayed with her rather than return to certain death.

'Everything is fine with them. They are in Kyiv.'

'How many children do you have? Two?'

'Three,' he said reluctantly, for this conversation was breaking with the scenario he had planned.

'And if I have got pregnant today … you wouldn't be against it?'

He rose, put on a white coat, got onto the bed and knelt

while he looked at Nicole. 'I wouldn't be against it. But I also wouldn't be against it if you told me the whole truth.'

'What truth?' Nicole's face blanched to the whiteness of linen, making her black hair seem still blacker.

David extracted the marine dagger, 'You will tell me now, or else …'

'You will kill me?' Nicole smiled, still unable to believe what was happening.

'No, worse than that.'

He brutally splayed her fleshy legs and stuck the dagger upright in the bed in between them.

'Tell me,' he said impatiently, 'who do you work for and what do you know about the murder of Bezpalii? Tell me everything. Don't even think about lying. I know a great deal about you. We have yet to talk about your personal role in supplying low-quality weapons when my country is being drowned in blood.'

'What? What?' She trembled in fear, as if sick with fever, and her hand tried to protect that place where she sensed the cold of the dagger's bladed edge, but he plucked it away, leaving her exposed.

'Speak. I don't have any time.' The expression on his face frightened her more than the dagger.

'I … worked for the Central Security Service …'

'What a revelation!' He made a 'hmm' sound in an ironic show of surprise. 'Who would have doubted it. Carry on.' He moved the dagger to refresh Nicole's memory.

'I gave them the information they demanded from me. Copies of documents, audio recordings …'

'Is that everything?'

'That's everything.'

Beylin moved the dagger again. It was really hurting her now. 'I'll clarify things for you, baby. In a few minutes, if you haven't started talking, I'll stab this dagger into you and everything that makes you happy. And you will never have children. I will give you a narcotic, you will sleep, and if you don't die from blood loss, you will wake up in the morning of no use to anyone. You have compromised yourself as an agent. You can see there is a videocamera planted on the television. There will be a report for your bosses.' He squeezed her rotund face with his hard hand, 'So get started.'

She finally understood that this wasn't a joke. 'I slept with Viktor Bezpalii.'

'Did you carry on the same with him too?'

'No, this is totally different. He loved me and swore he wanted to get married. Can't you take this away?' She touched the blade with her finger, its steel glittering a few millimetres away from her.

'No. Continue,' Beylin ordered.

'Bezpalii told me that he hated Haiduk and that he worked for the State Guard and against Haiduk.'

'Carry on.'

'He said that Haiduk had gathered compromising material on the entirety of Ukraine's elite and its publication would be a bombshell. Haiduk is smart, oh so smart, but foolish. He trusted Bezpalii and Bezpalii was just waiting for Haiduk to reveal the hiding place of the materials to him. But he never did.'

'And who killed Bezpalii? Is that part of your information submission, bitch?'

'No,' said Nicole, weeping. 'I loved him. We had arranged that right after we had handed in Haiduk and received the money they promised, we would go to the Bahamas and get married ...'

'Who killed Bezpalii?' Beylin asked, flicking the dagger again.

'I overheard a conversation between two CSS officers .'

'When you were in the sack?'

'By chance. There is a version that Haiduk was protected by the first lady and her assistant, Martha Jefferson, and that the president hated him. The CSS had contacts with Ukrainian Special Services, who also wanted to dispose of Haiduk. I also heard a rumour that Martha Jefferson was helped by Ukrainian nationalists from URA.'

'What is URA?'

'The Ukrainian Revolutionary Army. Some Confederation citizens have joined their ranks. Maybe they got rid of Bezpalii, having realised that he would eventually destroy Haiduk … However, I don't know anything. Let me go.'

He took a red and white capsule from the pocket of the white coat and pressed it to Nicole's lips. 'Swallow. And don't even think about trying to fool me. You will sleep. The room has been paid for three days in advance, including breakfasts. If you are smart, you will tell no one of our conversation. You will continue to work for the CSS. A new boss for the bureau will arrive soon. You will not sleep with him.'

'Why not?' Nicole asked, as her guileless coquettishness was aroused.

'Because he's impotent,' snarled Beylin. 'So, listen to him and tell him everything you hear.'

He picked up the knife as he said, 'Baby, that's enough for today.' The capsule sent her to sleep.

39

5 June 2077
Secret (One Copy)
To the adviser to the Hetman of Ukraine on National Security Issues, Secretary of the NSC, Major General I. P. Haiduk

Operational Report
A UMI investigative group in the CSNA has examined the

circumstances around the Ukrainian-American Bureau for Scientific and Technological Exchange on 21 April 2077. These resulted in the director, Major General I. P. Haiduk, being compelled to flee the territory of the Confederation due to the threat to his life and the murder of his deputy, Bezpalii, on the same day. These events effectively led to the suspension of the bureau's operations in significant areas of Ukrainian-American cooperation, including collaboration in the sphere of defence and national security. The investigation yielded the following results:

1. The events of 21 April 2077 illustrate differing tendencies in the struggle among the higher echelons of power in the Confederation government regarding Ukraine. One group, led by the president of the CSNA, Andrew Van Lee, wishes to reach a geo-political compromise with the Celestial Empire and the Union of States of the Horde in order to divide the world into spheres of influence. This group is fully prepared to surrender Ukraine to the sphere of influence of these aforementioned supra-state unions and allow the liquidation of our state. The Ukrainian based allies of Andrew Van Lee and his group in this matter are Aeropagus members M. N. Basmanov and I. O. Kreyda. The executive instrument of their will is the director of the State Guard, Yu. Merezhko. He collaborates in the implementation of this plan with Confederation CSS Director, Admiral Stanley Fisher, and Ukrainian Foreign Affairs Minister, R. V. Foshchenko. The latter openly lobbies for the interests of the Horde on the international arena.

2. The group, which argues for a true strategic partnership between our countries, includes the First Lady of the Confederation, Senator Shirley Van Lee, her assistant Martha Jefferson (she is of Ukrainian origin), the head of the Committee for Foreign Security Issues in the Confederation, Senator Paul Andersen, the Confederation Minister of Defence, Oliver Brown, and highly placed individuals in the Pentagon, CSS,

NSC, State Department and other structures. In our view, it cannot be excluded that the first lady, as an influential senator, has her own political plans and ambitions, which run counter to the views of President Andrew Van Lee.

3 The main factor complicating the internal political situation in the Confederation is the stand off between Vice-President Sara Lou Lane on the one hand and the president and first lady on the other. A version of events is circulating in Washington intelligence circles to the effect that members of Sara Lou Lane's family were taken hostage in order to block her attempt to press accusations of treason against the first lady. These involved the intimate relationship between Shirley MacDowell and I. P. Haiduk that occurred 20 years ago. A rumour is circulating that agents of President Van Lee's Special Services seized her family and introduced a powerful toxin into their bodies, which can be swiftly activated and result in their deaths if Sara Lou Lane breaks her promise to remain silent regarding these accusations.

4 It has been established that the threat to Haiduk's life came personally from President Andrew Van Lee and a significant role may have been played by personal factors here, including masculine lust and jealousy. His close circle, including Stanley Fisher, A. Joseph, W. Crawford and others, were also involved. They may not have conspired directly with high-ranking Ukrainian officials. However, at the very least they had a secret agreement with Yu. Merezhko, R. V. Foshchenko, and others. A detailed list of the Ukrainian functionaries active in this matter is enclosed.

5 It has been reliably established that I. P. Haiduk's representative, deputy director of the Bureau UMI, Bezpalii, was a State Guard agent of many years standing and worked under the alias 'Imperator' while remaining under the direct control of Yu. Merezhko and R. V. Foshchenko.

6. The identity of Bezpalii's killer is still unknown. A large calibre, 12.7 mm, M-650 American sniper rifle was found

at the location of the shooting, with five of the seven bullets, which its magazine originally contained, remaining. No other traces or evidence of whoever might be a participant or the commissioner of the murder have been found.

7. The incident with the Bureau led to collateral damage. After I. P. Haiduk's departure from Washington on 21 April 2077, his girlfriend, Linda Kenworthy, disappeared without a trace. Nicole Cohen, an employee of the bureau, (translator, technical manager) was found dead in a Washington Hotel on 29 May 2077. The perpetrator of these crimes is unknown.

8. It remains unclear, and it is yet to be established, what role Hetman Kuzma-Danylo Makhun and Lieutenant General Klynkevych played in this affair. An analysis is still continuing.

Conclusions:

1. There is the threat of a collapse in Ukrainian-American strategic cooperation as a result of the political intrigues in the centre of these countries and external geo-political pressure, which may worsen Ukraine's national security.

2. The threat to the life of I. P. Haiduk continues to exist (see conclusion 1 above regarding the reasons for this).

3. The bureau's operations must be revived as swiftly as possible.

Analyst Maximilian-IV

40

After the blizzards and frosts of May, summer in Kyiv began abruptly within the space of a single day on Thursday 10 June. The temperature of the air, borne from the Sahara, rose to 32°C in the night and continued to increase. The town was gripped in a dense, hot zone, which baked the brick and concrete walls of buildings. It lapped up the remaining islets of snow instantaneously and penetrated apartments. Hundreds of thousands of air conditioners were switched on simultaneously, requiring the activation of the reserve energy source of the Chyhyryn nuclear reactor. Shelters opened in the town for old and disabled people who could not endure the heat, and fountains and pools were put into operation for the children. The last surviving chestnut trees on the side of the Khreschatyk, which were not scorched ruins, between the conservatory and the building housing the Universal Agricultural Market, where the Besarabsky Market was once situated, sprouted their first buds.

Haiduk had moved from the safe apartment to his former old apartment in the thirty-storey building between Instytutka and Bankova streets; his mother remained in the old parental apartment on Tolstoho Square. He woke at dawn due to the unusual heat that streamed through the open doors of the twenty-ninth floor balcony. He stepped through them and onto the balcony from where he had a panoramic view of the old part of Kyiv, Podil, the Dnipro and Trukhaniy Island. The cries of children travelled to him from far below, along with the warbling of sparrows from some unseen place, and the scraping of garbage containers, which, after the long winter, were finally being moved by the Green Clean Company.

The children's voices awoke painful memories within him. He had acquired this apartment after his marriage in 2060, and his daughter, Krystyna, whom he had not seen since 2062 when he separated from his wife, was born here. Lara had married a Japanese dentist not long after their separation and emigrated to Canada. She had stopped Haiduk from seeing his daughter. UMI agents would, from time to time, send Haiduk photographs of her. She was a beautiful, dark-haired girl.

A signal rang from his government gadget and a message appeared on its screen to the effect that the Hetman of Ukraine expected to see him at 10:00 in his palace. They were expecting the arrival of an official delegation from the Union of

States of the Horde. Haiduk would have to meet the delegation and participate in the negotiations. He sighed, perhaps from his recollections or maybe just the banal reminder of the negotiations. He recalled the preparations for the arrival of the delegation. Analysts at UMI and the NSC had developed an array of reports and materials outlining positions for the hetman, and also produced a set of talking points for the negotiations. The Ministry of Foreign Affairs, the State Guard, the hetman's special division, and the ministries of defence and the economy had all prepared their materials. However, Haiduk did not know what ideas and plans were contained in this material because the hetman governed by the tried and tested method of Caesar. He personally gathered all the papers together, studied them himself and adopted a decision. Makhun often astonished his subordinates with the unpredictable and paradoxical nature of his resolutions. Haiduk began to suspect that the hetman, before adopting a decision, agreed it with another party unknown to Haiduk.

He was having a swift, cold shower when his other, American, gadget rang. Haiduk leaped out of the shower cubicle, almost slipped, and left a wet trail on the parquet. He ran to the writing table and picked up the gadget.

'I'm listening.'

He heard an unknown, female voice say, 'Mr Haiduk, Mr Haiduk,' and fall silent.

'Speak,' said Haiduk irritably, 'I'm listening. I don't have much time.'

'Mr Haiduk, it's me ... Bozhena. Can you hear me?'

'Bozhena? You are surely going to be rich, as they say, for I didn't recognise you.'

'Maybe I should ring you at another time?'

'No, say what you have to say. Has something happened?' He had waited for this phone call for so long that he was agitated on hearing Bozhena's voice.

162

'No, everything is okay. I want to invite you to visit me and my brother. I live with him and his family in ZEK-116 in Feofania-Pyrohovo.'

'I know the place,' he said, thinking what an idiotic profession he had in knowing everything about everyone. Nevinchanyi had already reported to him where and in what conditions Bozhena lived.

'Lesi Ukrayinky Lane,' said Bozhena, and her voice seemed to him to ring as clearly as this birdsong summer morning. 'We'll expect you at 10:00 on Sunday.'

'I will definitely be there,' promised Haiduk thinking, unless a snare slips over my head before then.

'I am looking forward to seeing you. Bye-bye,' she said in English.

'Bye-bye,' he replied, gently touching the red indicator on the gadget and ending the call. This was the first time someone had rung him on the gadget since it had been presented to him in the White House.

The orderly and his bodyguards were already waiting for Haiduk outside the door of his apartment. Exiting from the yard and onto Bankova Street, Haiduk and his entourage headed for a sombre, grey building where the hetman's special division was based. Haiduk took the lift from the bottom floor, which was halfway to being in the basement, and descended to the subterranean station. The orderly informed him that the hetman was staying in the palace tonight and Haiduk would therefore have to travel to him via the hetman's capsule.

Haiduk took his seat in the hetman's luxury coupe; it reminded him of the first lady's limousine in which he had fled the White House with Bozhena. The bodyguards took their seat in the rear of the capsule. Haiduk switched on his laptop, which contained secret reports from the territory occupied by the Horde. The driver gave a short but powerful blast of the horn, akin to that of a metro train, and the capsule headed swiftly for the banks of the Dnipro and Mount Borshchykha.

Haiduk had dressed in a light cream major general's uniform because of the heat. The outfit was completed with a baseball-style military cap with the UMI cockade, a star and a gold leaf on the peak. The jacket was adorned with the red-green aiguillettes of the intelligence directorate, and his perfectly ironed trousers were ornamented with two crimson stripes. As he stood on the square by the hetman's palace he felt completely comfortable. The wind from the Dnipro did not feel as hot as that in the city. Haiduk was in an elevated mood in spite of the oppressive circumstances of the visit.

The platoon of honour guards were roasting in heavy *zhupans* as they gripped the barrels of their replica German storm automatic, NK-MR 7/12 rifles. Two years ago the State Guard had exposed a conspiracy against the hetman, which would have seen him shot during a formal parade in honour of a state visit from the President of the Far Eastern Russo-Japanese Republic, Ivan Popov-Imanaki-San. The commissioners of this crime were not uncovered, but those who would have implemented it were thrown out of a plane five thousand metres above the Black Sea. The use of real weapons in parades had subsequently been prohibited.

At precisely 10:00, a large landing-terrapin, a model manufactured by the Horde's Uralvahonzavod plant at Nizhny Tagil, hung over the square. Haiduk knew from intelligence sources that the armed forces of the Horde were equipped with nineteen of these terrapins, painted the same green as military tanks, and their sides were adorned with the Horde's black stars. The reports indicated that the Horde had problems supplying them with fuel. The chemical plant in Stalingrad that manufactured the fuel was staffed mainly by Russians and had suffered a number of acts of sabotage, which seriously affected supplies. The green terrapin with its black stars and white ID number 052-4040 on the side, touched down gently on the concrete. The hetman's orchestra played a fanfare, signalling to everyone to snap to attention. The drumsticks struck the Cossack *tulumbasy* drums, the hatch of the terrapin opened easily and a staircase descended from the interior of the craft. The commander of the honour guard, in a blue cloth *zhupan*, baggy crimson Cossack pants and a fur Cossack hat, with a red rim, suffered with the heat and sweated profusely as he flourished his sabre in salute.

After a few minutes a stockily built warrior appeared on the top step. He wore glittering bronze-coloured armour, similar to the bulletproof suits of special forces. On his head he wore a steel helmet topped with a sharp spike, a gold arrow shape ran down the bridge of his nose, and two red fox-tails hung down from the rear of his headwear. The warrior held the huge white flag of the Horde, which was decorated with thirty-five black stars symbolising the number of states and state unions that had, either voluntarily or as a result of subjugation, joined the USH. The warrior descended the stairs majestically and stood with the flag flapping in the wind from the Dnipro. Everyone awaited the emergence of the delegation.

'Bloody hell, what a scarecrow,' Nevinchanyi swore characteristically, in a loud 'whisper'.

'Button it,' barked Haiduk, and headed forwards to welcome the plenipotentiaries of the Horde.

They were three in number, their leader was called Mohammad Bek, a dark-bearded, tanned Arab, in a snow-white turban adorned with a diamond pendant. He was deputy to the leader of the Horde, Kara-Khan, and bore the special title of Bekler-bek, meaning the second person in the state. He was dressed in a long, black leather coat with a silver belt, from which a curved Iranian sabre, a *shemshyr*, hung. Mohammad Bek was accompanied by the Horde's Foreign Affairs Secretary, Ahdzhi Hyundyuz; a big-bellied, heavy-set fellow with a red dyed beard and a neck sprouting strongly from his torso. The third member of the delegation was a 'citizen of Slavic appearance', as they designated such subjects on the Horde's terrain. Haiduk recognised him unmistakably as a former cellmate of Basmanov's at the Stalingrad prison; his name was Khlyshchov. In official documents he was referred to as the political adviser to Kara-Khan on national and religious issues, Vizier Vadym Khlyshchenko-Khlyshchov. An entrancing young Mongol girl, called Altantsetsen, accompanied them, she was the *Zolototulka*, the delegation's official dragoman or interpreter.

The hetman received the delegation in the Ceremonial Hall of Military Glory, decorated with the flags of the Cossack brigades and military units of Ukraine, including the dark blue and gold embroidered pennant of the Cossack Space Military Force. The hall also displayed examples of Cossack weapons from the past; sabres, pistols, muskets, small cannons, Degtyarev machine guns and the MG-42 used by OUN-UPA units. The chief military relic of the hall was the T-100-UM Sickle tank of Kharkiv manufacture, with a powerful 152 mm calibre cannon. General K. D. Makhun had commanded the attack during the Ukrainian-Romanian wars from the command chamber inside the body of this tank; its turret was too small to accommodate any of its crew. Instead of attacking in a predictable, operational direction, the military of the South Ukrainian front, commanded by Makhun, had delivered a double blow against Romania, one element of which ran along the line of Izmail-Reni-Halats-Breyla-Buzeu-Ploeshti. They had simultaneously conducted an unanticipated landing operation at Konstanets and, via Chernovode-Feteshti, had penetrated the suburbs of Bucharest. The attack compelled the Romanians to capitulate and sign a peace treaty, under which Ukraine received the Moldavian-Trans-Dniester Republic. Several pictures and tableau depicted the feat of the Bucharest operation and compared it to the triumphant battles of Bohdan Khmelnytsky.

The table for the negotiations was situated not far from the historic tank and its cannon stared silently at the members of the delegation. The hetman viewed this as a successful psychological ploy, but this old relic made no impression whatsoever on the delegation from the Horde. UMI knew the methods of anti-tank combat within the Horde's armoury, including anti-tank rockets, an example of which was the Sverdlo lightweight, mobile rocket with powerful amour piercing heads, which would have reduced the T-100 tanks to heaps of hole-riddled scrap iron. UMI had long been interested in the agricultural machinery construction factory in Kazan, where rockets of this type were manufactured. However, only ideologically committed Tatars worked at the factory and every attempt by UMI agents to penetrate it was in vain. It was much easier for them to work with Russians.

The delegation had brought the hetman luxurious gifts: Sable fur, a Syrian sabre of rare beauty with a gold hilt, and a crow-black Arabian stallion, which they barely managed to get out of the terrapin to the enthusiastic bellows of photographers and TV reporters. The horse sniffed suspiciously at the hot air from the Dnipro and then neighed, happily breathing into himself the unfamiliar fragrance of water and grass, and a waft of air from his native Sahara.

The whole event resembled an operatic tale with stage-prop weapons and theatrical costumes. The story concluded when the delegation took their places at the negotiating table. The guests sat with their backs to where examples of weaponry hung. Mohammad Bek was in the centre and the interpreter, Altantsetsen, sat to his left. Haiduk was stunned by her beauty. Khlyshchenko sat to her left and Andzhi Hyundyuz filled the armchair to the right of the Bekler-bek.

The hetman briefly welcomed them to the meeting. Haiduk realised with satisfaction that Makhun had used his text which, while talking about the felicitations of peace and the good-neighbourly relations between Ukraine and the Steppe, did not even mention the USH summit at Batii-Hrad.

Mohammad Bek spoke next, 'Allah, the all powerful and compassionate,' the head of the delegation clasped his hands in prayer as he spoke, 'let him send his grace on this ancient Tatar land where the traces of our ancestors yet remain and where the memory of Batu Khan still lives. The Sun of the East, the Black Star of the Earth, Kara-Khan, sends his greeting and blessing to the greatest warrior of Eurasia, the defender of the people, Chief of Ukraine, Hetman Makhun. Let Allah preserve his rule. Allahu Akbar.' He gave a majestic signature to the ruddy-bearded Turk to continue.

Ahdzhi Hyundyuz smiled sweetly and, grooming his beard with his fingers, began to speak, 'The strategic situation in the world demands immediate action. The Horde, as a peace-loving power, which stands up for the right of people to free development, may no longer just observe passively when the powers of evil and darkness, globalists from the so-called world government and aggressive atlanticists, conduct an undeclared war against the Horde, undermining the sacred right of people to propagate their faith.'

The hetman, who was dressed in an attractive *vyshyvanka*, embroidered with red and black flowers, twitched nervously. Haiduk, who was sitting on Makhun's right, understood this gesture of impatience and anger.

The interpreter, a young UMI Captain named Dima Mochalkin, sat to the hetman's left. He was a fair-haired genius who resembled a typical Swede and had a thorough knowledge of twelve languages, ranging from Hebrew to Chinese, Arab and Greek. He quietly interpreted the addresses of the speakers as he spoke into the hetman's ear. Alongside him sat Ruslan Foshchenko, who smiled as he looked at the delegation, like a little girl who had seen an enticing doll. Double dimples appeared on the cheeks of the minister of foreign affairs, and

168

the varied colours of his two odd eyes became more noticeable.

Basmanov had received Foshchenko into his presence recently and promised that, in the event of Ukraine joining the Horde, he would become the Great Khan of the 'Kyiv-Dnipro Ulus' and receive a diamond star to hang from his neck.

An unpleasant pause ensued, during which Vitold Klynkevych, who was sitting behind the hetman and recording the discussions, raised his head inquisitively.

'Hold on,' the hetman interrupted the silent pause irritably, 'what are you talking about in concrete terms?'

'We are talking about the following,' Mohammad Bek plunged in brutally as the diamond pendant on his turban glittered. The sun had now risen high above the Dnipro and its rays blinded the guests who were sitting opposite the panoramic glass wall offering a view of the river and the left bank from beyond which the Horde was pushing into Ukraine. The hetman signalled for the blind to be lowered, so the delegation would feel comfortable.

Mohammed Bek continued drily, 'We are making demands that, firstly, before the beginning of the summit of the USH in Batii-Hrad, which must take place on 21 December, on the birthday of the Sun of the East, the incomparable Kara-Khan, Ukraine will cease to exist as a geo-political entity and become the Great Kyiv-Dnipro Ulus of the Horde and the thirty-sixth black star on our sacred banner. Before 1 December you, as Hetman of Ukraine, will pronounce the self-liquidation of your state, which is of no use to anyone. If you fulfil our first demand you will become a great Khan and receive a charter to rule the Kyiv-Dnipro Ulus, retaining all privileges and honours. The Sun of the East, the Great Kara-Khan, will hang around your neck … a black diamond star, the highest insignia of the Horde.'

Haiduk thought it would be more like a noose.

The hetman flushed and the colour of his skin started to

match that of the red flowers on his *vyshyvanka*.

'The second demand - Today we are developing a draft treaty for the incorporation of Ukraine within the constitution of the Horde. We are appointing a temporary governor, Vizier Vadym Khlyshchenko-Khlyshchov, with whom, as of today, you will agree all your decisions.' Former convict, Khlyshchov, on whose brow a mark glittered like a purple flower, inclined his head in a statesmanlike fashion. 'Thirdly - As of today, you are obliged to provide access for our representatives, who travelled here with us, to your rocket, chemical-fuel and electronic-machine construction industries, so that we have guarantees that no one will even think of sabotage or using high-precision weapons against the Horde. Your Magic Nine is of particular interest to us.'

'Is that everything?' asked the hetman, who was now almost black, like the flowers on his shirt. 'And you have not forgotten Ukrainian wheat and maize?'

'No, we haven't forgotten it,' Hyundyuz said, scratching his dyed beard as if he were plagued by scabies. 'Only uniting with the Horde will save you from the plundering of your reserves of foodstuffs. Within the conditions of the current global food crisis, food requisition squads have been formed in Eurasia, Europe, and even Africa, for the purpose of seizing Ukrainian grain and meat. The Horde will guarantee you stability for the development of rural agriculture and protection from the seizure of Kyiv-Dnipro Ulus's riches.'

'It's relevant to add,' Khlyshchenko-Khlyshchov said in Ukrainian, surprising his hosts, 'I, the governor of Kyiv-Dnipro-Ulus, guarantee all the fraternal people of Ukrainian territory free national development and peace and harmony between religions. The Horde is the most tolerant supra-state in the world.'

Haiduk had provided the hetman with a special report regarding the tolerance of the Horde, which included terrifying figures and facts. Countries and towns that offered resistance were destroyed with particular savagery. The conquerors showed no mercy to women, small children or the elderly and infirm. Those who surrendered voluntarily underwent a process of political purges, mass repressions and deportations, which had become the usual practice of the Horde.

This movement, which had begun in Mongolia, Kazakhstan and certain regions of Russia, swept tsunami-like through the countries of Central Asia, the large areas of the Urals and Western Siberia, and blazed along the Volga from Astrakhan to the Tatar and Bashkyr lands and Moscow region. It seized the North Caucasus and began to sweep the Don Steppe to the Eastern boundaries of Ukraine. The union between the Horde and Turkey, which was brimming with hatred for treacherous Europe and confused Judeo-Christian values became a turning point in world history, because in that country's wake a host of other countries joined the new empire ... Pakistan, Afghanistan, Iran, Syria, Lebanon, Iraq and Egypt, Algeria, Morocco, and later Albania and Kosovo.

The last to fall was Saudi Arabia when, during the course of a popular revolution, two hundred and forty-nine heirs of the Saudi dynasty were slain. This resulted in the cessation of oil supplies to Europe and America from Saudi Arabia, Iran and Iraq. Turkey had established in the International Court of Justice in The Hague that Russia had grossly violated the terms of the Paris Treaty of 1856, regarding the neutrality of the Black Sea, which was signed after defeat in the Crimean War.

Having won the court case, the Turks seized Sevastopol, which was also claimed by Greece. An autonomous Turkic-Tatar State was proclaimed on a triangular area of the Peninsula between Bakhchysarai, Sevastopol, which had been renamed Akhtiyar, and Foros. The Khan Devlet Geray Army Brigade was created for the defence of the new statelet, which was a de-facto protectorate of the Horde. Ethnic cleansing and mass

Islamisation were inflicted on the territories subjugated by the Horde.

The hetman proposed a short break to discuss the proposals and the emissaries agreed politely. Four members of the Ukrainian party remained in the room, the hetman, Haiduk, Foshchenko and Klynkevych.

'What will we do?' Haiduk had never seen the hetman so confused.

'I think,' said Foshchenko, with a know-it-all smile, 'that we cannot withstand this. Let's be realists. A completely new geo-political situation has emerged and we are obliged to come to terms with it.'

'Don't twist things with your fucking diplomatic politesse, speak in concrete terms. What should I do?' The hetman sighed in an almost despairing fashion.

Foshchenko smiled, as if he knew all the answers to all the questions, and said evasively, 'Well, we must certainly make some concessions today and promise something … only we must not leave this … Khlyshchov to be governor. He's a criminal type. But it's for you to decide.' Foshchenko already saw Khlyshchov as a potential competitor.

'Me, it's all for me. If it were something good, all of you here would want in on it. But if it's bad, you tell the hetman to decide for you. Why was I not warned that an ultimatum would be presented to me?'

'We did warn you,' said Haiduk. 'All the documents were given to Klynkevych.

'Vitold, where is the warning?'

'I will check. It seemed that we had everything in its place.' Klynkevych anxiously began to gather his papers into a leather folder which bore the hetman's monogram.

'And you, Ihor? What do you think?' the hetman addressed Haiduk.

'Do not make any concessions, for if you do, we will all

perish, you first, along with Ukraine.

'But tomorrow they will begin advancing. The Horde's tank armies are already concentrated on the Don.'

'They won't advance,' said Haiduk assuredly, 'they still need some months to transfer supplies and munitions to these forces. In addition, there is intelligence that Kara-Khan is terminally ill and a furore is already commencing over who will be his successor. Mohammad Bek wants, at any cost, to bring him the head of Ukraine on a platter. In which case he will certainly be that successor. If he does not do so, his chances of becoming the Khan's heir will be drastically reduced. A serious conflict will then commence. Turkey, Pakistan and Saudi Arabia all claim the right to Kara-Khan's place. This gives us time. We must immediately conduct negotiations with the Confederation of States of North America and the Organisation for Global Security. They are our natural allies. The loss of Ukraine for them means the loss of half of Europe. Finally, we must speak with the Celestial Empire. I don't think they are enraptured with the global ambitions of the Horde. It is necessary to consider all the possibilities and not to give up.'

'This is just an empty fanfare,' Foshchenko sharply disputed Haiduk's words. 'It seems that worthy Ihor Petrovych throws us the provocative idea of worsening our relations with a dangerous enemy who may avenge themselves on us all at any minute. That's not how international politics is done. It is necessary to make compromises. We're not ready for a confrontation.'

'Great,' the hetman said as he frowned. 'Go and drink coffee. I will stay here and think it through myself.'

Haiduk exited the building and entered the interior courtyard of the palace where a powerful fountain of blue Dnipro water, purified and cold, played in a white marble basin and cooled the air on hot days. He saw the sturdy warrior who had now discarded his bronze armour and dressed in a traditional Mongol tunic. The warrior sat on the marble rim around the fountain, rolled up his sleeve, lowered his bare, muscular arm into the cool water and drank it from his palm. A blissful expression sketched itself gently on the wet face of the Steppe soldier. The baking sun, the pure water, the sultry air and the splashes of the fountain that reached the young Mongol, created an unseen harmony.

Suddenly, from the shadowy concrete cloister where the delegation stood, a dark figure emerged and his arm moved quickly in a downward motion, while his curved sabre flashed in the sun. The Mongol warrior's arm, severed at the elbow, sank into the water, leaving a bright crimson trail in its wake. Haiduk and Dima Mochalkin ran towards the unfortunate man, who, not understanding what had happened, waved the stump of his arm and moaned with childlike anguish. Haiduk removed his belt and tightly bound the warrior's arm above where his elbow had been, and from whence blood now splashed out of the smoothly severed flesh and bone. Mohammad Bek, casting a few imprecations aimed at the unhappy warrior, returned to the delegation and wiped the edge of his sabre with a kerchief.

'He said that this boy had infringed the law of Genghis Khan, which forbids the lowering of a hand into the water. The law only allows you to gather water to drink by hand using a pot,' explained Dima.

The hetman's bodyguards caught the severed arm as it washed around the basin and dispatched the young Mongol to the transplant centre so his severed limb could be reattached.

The negotiations were renewed after a very short interval. The hetman announced that in order to answer the fundamental demands of the Horde he had to call a joint sitting of Ukraine's Aeropagus and National Security Council, which could be no earlier than September or October. He would need to study all the relevant international agreements in advance of the meeting, to enable the bodies to adopt the best resolution possible. He emphasised that good relations with the Horde were the number one priority for Ukraine. He was convinced they would reach a compromise.

At the end of the negotiations Mohammad Bek asked to be allowed to remain with the hetman for a one to one, twenty-minute meeting, with the interpreter, Dima Mochalkin, also present. Altantsetsen had gone to the clinic because the warrior with the severed arm was her lover.

Haiduk knew by the evening of that day what the two leaders had discussed in the shadow of the T-100-UM tank. Mohammad Bek enquired about Haiduk's role in Ukrainian affairs of state and strongly recommended that the hetman rid himself of him, this American CSS agent, an enemy of the hetman and all Ukraine.

41

11 June 2077
Official report of the UNIAN news agency

On 10 June 2077, his Excellency, the Hetman of Ukraine, General K. D. Makhun, led negotiations with a delegation of representatives from the Union of States of the Horde, led by the first deputy of the popular leader of the Horde, Mohammad Bek. The negotiations concerned important issues for the bi-lateral political and economic relations between Ukraine and the Horde. The parties agreed to develop bi-lateral relations in the spirit of respect for international agreements and new vectors within the global geo-political situation. The negotiations were conducted in the traditional warm and friendly atmosphere characteristic of the relations between the people of Ukraine and the Horde, and will soon be continued.

The delegation from the Horde visited Mount Batyieva in Kyiv and placed flowers on the spot where, according to legend, the tent of Khan Batii had once stood. A meeting also took place between the delegation and Arch-Monk Kalerii (S. Sansyzbayev) of Pechersk-Lavra monastery. The monk told the guests of the most recent discoveries of Eurasian academics in the sphere of Christian theology and the debunking of the mendacious Judeo-Christian legend of Christ's resurrection. The delegation subsequently returned to Chyngiz-Saray.

42

The iron gates, painted with blue lions and crimson roosters, creaked open and the UMI jeep, with Hryhoriy Nevinchanyi at the wheel, entered the territory of ZEK-116 Feofania-Pyrohovo. Haiduk ordered his guards not to accompany them and his loyal Georgian cavalry men remained in the shadow of the concrete defensive wall, which separated the district highway from ZEK-116. The Zone of Ethnic Consolidation (ZEK) was an epoch-making invention from the former leader of MUDA (the Marxist Ukrainian-Democratic Association) and currently the general prosecutor of the UCMFD, Ivan Ovramovych Kreyda.

Subsequently, a small 'k' in parentheses was added to the title of the organisation, in honour of Kreyda. Having become the monopoly theorist in the national question, I. O. Kreyda invented an ingenious method for resolving all disputes and conflicts regarding ethnic development. In response to the demands of the indigenous Ukrainians, whose protests concerning national oppression sounded ever more frequently at MUDA (k) congresses, he compelled the Aeropagus and Sejm to adopt a law.

The legislation required that all lovers of Ukrainian language, history and traditions were granted a pocket of land where they were permitted to settle entire families. Within these settlements they were allowed to work in rural agriculture and engage in traditional crafts, fishing and beekeeping, and

176

to procreate and die. Parochial schools were attached to the churches erected by the Zekivtsi, the inhabitants of these settlements, where children were taught literacy and accounting. There were no newspapers or televisions in the ZEKs, but they could chat and pray in Ukrainian as much as they wished. The zones were closely protected by the gendarmerie of the State Guard with the intention, as Merezhko explained, of preserving the tranquillity of their inhabitants and not permitting would-be pillagers.

The inhabitants of the ZEKs had the right to emerge from them into the 'outside world' once a year with the agreement of the special administration (AdZEK), for a period of no longer than one week, and only if there were valid reasons. Attempts to flee and remain permanently at large in the 'outside world' were severely punished. In addition to Ukrainian, there existed, in significantly lower quantities, Polish, Jewish, Greek, Gagauz and other ZEKs.

Leaving the jeep in the internal car park, where there were no other vehicles, and passing through another checkpoint, Haiduk and Nevinchanyi stepped onto a narrow pathway through a wheat field, which was golden in the unusually hot sunshine. They paused and stood for a while when they reached a hill top from which an idyllic prospect was revealed. The view resembled pictures produced by nineteenth century Ukrainian artists; pastures and tranquil paddocks, ponds, white church towers, windmills and village paths lined with poplars. Nevinchanyi, on seeing this unearthly view, paused and bellowed, 'What wonderful air here Ihor Petrovych. You could bale it like hay.'

Haiduk said nothing in reply, for anguish and an incomprehensible longing for something forever lost gripped his heart. This was a new feeling for him. As an urbanised and cosmopolitan individual, Haiduk had no sentimentality regarding rural life and its slow and, as it seemed to him, primitive rhythms governed, not by technology and means of communication but by the rotation of the earth around the sun.

They went further in silence and heard music in the distance, snatches of a *hopak* to the rhythm of tambourines. As they drew closer, Haiduk and Nevinchanyi saw village dancers on the square before the church. Little children, there were many children, in absurd straw hats danced and raised a dust cloud, which evoked happy laughter from their parents and grandparents, who were also vigorously stamping their boots to the rhythm of the music. The square was packed with wagons, as if it were market day. Sturdy youths faced girls, who bashfully sat on the wagons. They tensed and laughed as they slapped away the insolent hands of the youths who were dragging them to the dance. However, from time to time, resistance broke and a new pair were thrown into the whirl of the *hopak*.

The local drunks thronged out of the inn opposite the church. They were mainly older men and they stumbled into the dance to flaunt their choreographic talents. It looked like a scene from an old film, but this theatrical festivity, in the style of Sorochynskyi Fair, seemed to be a spontaneous outpouring of popular desire; though Haiduk could not believe it.

The crowd on the square paid no heed to the new arrivals. Haiduk's eyes had not seen so many young beauties flushed with health and enticing to the gaze of a single man for a long time, perhaps since his Venezuelan sojourn. One of these beauties waved her hand invitingly at Haiduk, as if calling him to her, and he felt morose. These young, attractive women would have no time for him. He looked around in order to see who she was addressing. Nevinchanyi was downing a glass with the drunken visitors at the inn and no one was behind Haiduk. The girl continued to wave her hand and, pushing her way through the throng, approached him.

'How do you do, Mister General,' the bonnie girl said

in English, smiling widely and adding, 'great to see you here.'

'Good God,' he said, finally realising who had approached him. It was Bozhena, but no trace remained of the torture, illnesses, bruises or fear. A tall, young woman stood before him, glowing with natural beauty and health. Her hair, auburn with an ashen play of colours, was woven into a tight plait, and her grey eyes glittered happily in her sunburned face. He noted that her snub nose showed absolutely no traces of being broken and deformed; Haiduk could not believe his eyes that this was the same person whose life he had saved by dragging her from the fragments of the Lancaster-27. 'Bozhena … what has happened to you?'

'This is my brother, Askold, you must get acquainted with him,' Bozhena said, ignoring his question.

A muscular man, sunburned almost to blackness, approached them. By contrast with the other inhabitants of the village, who wore *vyshyvankas*, he was dressed in a white football jersey adorned with a drawing of an old Cossack in blue Cossack trousers or *sharovary*, before whom knelt a young Cossack, probably his son, in red *sharovary*. The inscription below them, in English, read 'Ukrainian volunteers against Moskal aggression'. Below that, the shirt read 'Sons of Ukraine' in Ukrainian, before reverting to English, 'Cleveland, Ohio, Post 24'. Askold, on whose shoulders sat his mischievous, three-year old son, Yarema, shook Haiduk's hand amicably. A strongly built, pregnant young woman emerged from the crowd, drawing a young, weeping, five-year old girl after her. It was Lykera, Bozhena's sister-in-law.

'Good Lord Askold and Bozhena, why are you standing here in this dust cloud? Invite the guests to the house,' she said, smiling widely. The little girl, Bozhena's niece, ceased crying and looked at Haiduk with her blue eyes.

Askold's house stood not far from the square and was thatched with fresh sheaves of straw and beautifully white washed. The building retained within itself some ancient, probably even Scythian, fragrance because various kinds of herbs hung from the rafters, and in the corner, beneath the icons, stood a woven basket filled with rye grain. The house was ruled by an extremely pure, cool, ideal sense of orderliness, in spite of the mischievous boy and his sister. The simple, home-made furniture, benches and beds were draped with woollen rugs.

'Come into the garden,' Lykera invited them.

A table, set for the holiday festivities, stood beneath the cherry trees in the cool orchard. Its chief adornment was a huge wheat loaf with ornamented images of ears of grain and pine cones moulded into its crust. The loaf was decorated with little birds, fashioned from white dough. There were also small jugs of baked milk pudding with appetising skins floating on top, plates with jellied meat, jars of honey, butter, home-made sausages, cheeses and eggs.

Nevinchanyi extracted gifts from his bag; two bottles of Champagne, Armenian cognac, Finnish vodka, Scotch whisky, a jar of black caviar, Brazilian coffee, a pineapple, and Swiss chocolate sweets. Askold looked at the gifts but said nothing, simply transferring the lot to a small table under a canopy near the summer kitchen, which opened into the orchard.

A young priest, wearing a black cassock, with a small pine cross on his breast, entered the yard. He was short, with long, light brown hair and an attentive, kind gaze. He looked at Haiduk as if he knew him. 'This is Father Ivan, the rector of our church.' Askold introduced his guest.

Finally, everyone sat at the table, the children fell quiet and Father Ivan said Grace. Haiduk automatically crossed himself without thinking about the prayer. Father Ivan stretched out his hands to Askold and Lykera, who sat alongside him, and they stretched out their hands to their guests. Bozhena gave her left hand to Haiduk and he squeezed the warm palm of little

Mykhailina. They all bowed their heads and a silence fell, which was only ruptured by the sudden breeze passing through the leaves and playing some incomprehensible short melody.

'Please help yourselves to that which God has sent to us.' Lykera invited them.

Askold began to slice the loaf and give it to his guests. Nevinchanyi cast a tragic glance at Haiduk, sending him a signal - Look what we have got into Major General, these people don't indulge in alcohol, like Mormons and other sectarians. And they look normal.

They have a far better appearance than normal, Haiduk replied in his thoughts. Then he listened attentively to Askold's story about his life.

'In the beginning I worked as a potter, selling my pots on the markets. When I met Lykera,' he said, looking tenderly at his wife, 'I realised that this was not proper work for a young man. We acquired some land, not much, only four hectares. Our relatives in Cleveland gave us the money. Well, thus, bit by bit, we built it up … now we have six cows and bulls with which we plough ... three horses, and swine, geese, hens …'

'How do you manage all this?' Nevinchanyi asked.

'We do the main work ourselves … Well, Bozhena helped us in spring … but when we have a lot on we hire two or three workers without land of their own.'

Askold bore little resemblance to Bozhena. In America Haiduk would have ascribed him to the ranks of the Latinos; he was a sunburned, dark-eyed muscular man.

'And imagine,' continued Askold O'Connell, the son of a descendant of Irish rebels and a Ukrainian woman, 'the soil of these Ukrainian ZEKs has become the most fertile ground in Ukraine. The fertility levels here are three times higher than the average for the whole country.'

'Don't they tax you heavily?' Haiduk asked.

'No, they have definitely adopted a law not to tax the

ZEKs. We also earn money through selling honey, milk, meat and handicrafts.'

They only lack gambling, thought Haiduk, recollecting the Native American reservations.

'I want to talk to you in private,' whispered Bozhena during Askold's speech.

'Okay,' he said, squeezing her palm and feeling her fingers twitch gently in reply.

Mykola, the blacksmith, joined them half way through lunch. He was a wiry fellow who threw his weight onto his right leg as he walked and was known to all by the soubriquet 'Crooked Mykola'. He was a little in his cups and talked loudly and sharply. On meeting the guests from Kyiv he asked Haiduk, 'And where do you work? Are you a businessman?'

'No, I am a major general,' Haiduk laughed.

'Oh, a major general,' said Mykola delightedly. 'I am seeing a real live major general for the first time in my life. So tell me, Mr Major General, are you ready?'

'For what?'

'For the great cull.'

'Calm down Mykola,' said Askold, trying to put the brakes on the blacksmith's advance.

Lykera took the children into the house, accompanied by Bozhena, to put them to bed. The men remained on their own. Crooked Mykola did not sit at the table, on which there was no *horilka*, but limped around it, shouting about what bothered him, 'I could be calmed if someone gave me a glassful, that would be all it would take. No more trouble from Mykola … but how do we calm down other people? You don't know Major General that at our forge, and also at other ZEKs, we are fashioning weapons, knives, axes, sickles, we may make some other serious stuff too.'

'What has happened?'

'What's happened?' Mykola paused. 'Haven't you heard?

Though we haven't got television here, we know. The Horde is heading for us, Muscovites and Mongols and all kinds. They need our bread. Askold doesn't believe it. He works on the earth and has become a *kurkul*,' he said, using the Stalinist era word for a supposedly wealthy peasant. 'And they will come and strip the *kurkul* of his goods and send him to Siberia. They will pity no one. They want to destroy us … And this shit. Our hetman does nothing to save the remnants of Ukraine.'

'Mykola, Mykola, what's this nonsense you are jabbering?' Askold said in fear. 'Let's go, I'll get you a glass. Look how much good stuff we've been gifted.' He rose from the table and headed for the summer kitchen with Mykola; Nevinchanyi eagerly joined them. Haiduk remained alone with the priest.

'Pity,' said Father Ivan, nodding his head towards Mykola. 'He lost his leg in the war with EnROS. He doesn't love the Muscovites. But there is some truth in what he says.'

'And what is that truth?' Haiduk asked with interest.

'The truth in his words is that there is now a huge potential in the people for an outpouring of hatred. The Khmelnytsky and Haidamak uprisings will seem like children's games compared to that which is approaching. They all hate everyone and everything: the rich, oligarchs, the state, the hetman, the State Guard, Jews, Russians, Chinese, Uzbeks … The Deathchristians hate the Risenchristians, the inhabitants of ZEKs hate people who live in towns. All of them together are afraid of the Horde. Sometimes despair grips you when you barge against this wall of hatred …'

'And it seemed to me you were so happy here. This holiday … so pure.'

'Well, it really is like that here. Our people are basically good, but are they brimming with Christian faith?' the priest said thoughtfully. 'Today we commemorate the birthday of the sacred martyr, Isaakii Dolmatsky. You know the saying about when Isaakii follows Feodosia, vipers crawl out of every possible hole.'

'No,' Haiduk laughed, 'it's the first time I've heard it. There are things which, thank God, even Ukrainian Military Intelligence doesn't know.'

'Today the snakes and vipers are coiling together to engender new vipers … but we are not talking about that but about Isaakii, whose name means laughter, to laugh. He was renowned for exposing the Arian Heresy. We lack such as him today, for the Deathchristians are the new Arians; only much more frightening.'

'Arians … is that something similar to racial Aryans?' asked Haiduk.

'No, Arians are followers of the Orthodox priest Arius of Byzantine. He lived in the fourth century and asserted that Christ, as the Son of God, is lower than God the Father, that He is subject to God. As if God were akin to the hetman and you, as a major general, were subordinate to him.'

'Well, isn't that so?'

'Ah, you have got caught on the hook of Arianism,' laughed Father Ivan. 'This is a very simple hierarchical concept and very easily adopted in military feudal states such as ours. In reality it's much more paradoxical. Christ is God and equal to God the Father and the Holy Spirit. Christ came to the earth as God and was resurrected after death as God. His power lies in his experiencing of all the suffering that is the lot of each human being; contempt, hatred, depression, bodily suffering and the fear of death. However, along with all this He remains God. There was only one moment, tragic, terrifying and incomprehensible, which is often subject to dispute. You remember how in the moment of his death, Jesus cried "Eli Eli lama sabachthani?" That is, my God, my God, why hast thou forsaken me?'

Father Ivan was silent, as if recollecting Golgotha. Haiduk also thought about that remote and yet somehow close history. If Christ was God, would He have permitted himself to be mocked so? Would he really have feared death?

'What do you think of that modern sect, the Deathchristians?' asked Haiduk.

'It is a mortal danger, not only for our state but for all humanity, a special op. for the murder of Christianity. Good will be outlawed once and for all. Finally, I have written about this, perhaps you have read my work on this Sir Major General?'

'So it's you, Agent Joan?'

'I wasn't and never will be anyone's agent,' Father Ivan replied placidly but firmly, 'I may only be an agent of Christ. They asked me to give a consultation and I complied. It was the State Guard who asked me.'

'And who in your opinion is directing this special op?' Haiduk asked with interest.

'I only know that it's not Chykyrysov or Sansyzbayev. They are just the props holding up the guns. A total criminalisation of the world is underway, the banditisation of society; the destruction of all moral impediments. But the main thing is the fear of God is diminishing. The forces of evil have united to destroy faith in and fear of God and Christianity. They are transforming people into beasts. They teach people to think that there is no God and Christ is just an ordinary mortal. However, human civilisation cannot be sustained just on laws upheld by the police on the same principles as regulate the flow of traffic. Civilisation is based on faith, fear and self-restraint. As to whom all this benefits, you can see yourself. Are you, Sir Major General, religious?'

'I don't know,' said Haiduk, faltering and ashamed either to eschew a reply or crack jokes beneath the attentive gaze of Father Ivan. 'Probably not; I am distant from the church.'

'It's not about being in church. We are not in the church, the church is in us,' the priest said gently. 'The time will come when faith will make its abode in your soul. Permit me to bless you.'

Haiduk silently bowed his head and the priest made the sign of the cross over him.

The women returned, because the children were now asleep, and Askold and Nevinchanyi dragged the drunken blacksmith, Mykola, from the yard. Lykera decanted warm borshch into clay bowls and the meal resumed. Bozhena sat opposite Haiduk, trying not to meet his gaze. What has happened? Haiduk thought. I must speak with her. Have I done something wrong?

After a further course, comprising hot buckwheat and home-made sausage, they started singing. Lykera began with a low contralto and Hryhoriy Nevinchanyi, blooming after fraternising with Crooked Mykola, provided the baritone accompaniment. Father Ivan and Askold subsequently picked up the song; only Haiduk and Bozhena held back.

'Oh whose is that horse that stands with a white mane … to my liking is one lass alone,' Lykera and Nevinchanyi led out the anguished melody. Haiduk did not know the words and could not sing, but wondered why Bozhena did not sing?

At that moment, when the song transported Haiduk back in time to the land's remote past, he glimpsed a drone. It was concealed in an old pear tree among the bare branches and was twice the size of the Washington drone. He recognised the grey, steel sphere as a bomber from the Hawk range, manufactured at the Artemida plant in Kyiv.

Haiduk quietly approached the table covered with UMI gifts as if nothing had happened. Nevinchanyi had left the bag, in which they had brought the gifts, on the bench. Turning his back to the drone, Haiduk groped in the bag for his Clipper pistol with its small Osa homing rockets. On Monday they had undertaken some shooting in the field with the Clipper. This experimental weapon, which Nevinchanyi had acquired directly from the Zhytomyr KB, was greatly to Haiduk's liking.

He fired from behind the pillar, which held up the roof of the summer kitchen. The singing from the group around the table was loud and ardent enough so that no one heard the shot.

The Osa, which left a barely perceptible smoke trail, followed an illogical trajectory, rising high into the sky and then, as swiftly as a black kite, fell onto the desiccated tree where the drone hung. The pilotless killer drone clearly had not anticipated an attack and flew with some delay to where Lesi Ukrayinky Lane ended and O'Connell's fields began. It exploded one hundred yards away from Askold's orchard and fragments fell to the earth in a rain of fire. I hope it doesn't cause a conflagration, thought Haiduk.

The party singing around the table saw the flash of fire.

'What's that?' Father Ivan asked.

'Probably a firework,' replied Askold. 'The children are setting them off.'

Nevinchanyi looked inquisitively at Haiduk, who had already returned to the table, but said nothing.

The day expired, brimming with shadows and the first stars ventured into the firmament. Haiduk and Nevinchanyi began to make their farewells. Askold, Father Ivan and Bozhena decided to accompany their guests to the checkpoint.

As they left, Haiduk, lagging behind, remained alone with Bozhena. 'You wanted to talk …'

'Well, it would be a long conversation. Let's save it for another time.' She looked into his face and he felt that the topic of this deferred conversation would be something very significant.

They continued in silence and then he took her hand and a crazy idea flew into his head, 'Do you want to leave this place?' he asked, not looking at her.

She squeezed his hand tightly, 'I want to.'

'You could leave with me. We can go now.'

'No, no I can't now,' Bozhena said fearfully.

'When?'
'In a few days.'
'Okay.'
'But it's not that simple,' she said quietly. 'Understand this, we are prisoners and they won't let me go easily.'

'We will settle this,' said Haiduk angrily. 'While it's in my power to do so.' He yearned to lay his hand on her hair and was barely able to restrain himself.

Father Ivan gave the guests his blessing for their journey. The State Guard officer at the checkpoint snapped to attention on seeing the major general. When they exited onto the district road Haiduk said to Nevinchanyi, 'Please summon the manager of the Artemida factory to see me on Tuesday. Their products are antiquated, twice as heavy and three times slower than the American drones.'

43

16 June 2077
Top Secret (One Copy)
To be delivered personally to His Excellency General Kuzma-Danylo Makhun
Report

I would never have dared to write this report were it not for two factors: The position I occupy at your behest and your agreement to listen to me when unusual circumstances demand it.

My experience of working in the higher echelons of power is yet of extremely limited duration and I would have refrained from personal opinions and recommendations were it not for the mortal danger that threatens our state, our people and you personally. Immediately after you appointed me to the post of your adviser on issues of national security, I called together a special analytical group with experts from UMI, the State Guard, staff headquarters and relevant think-tanks. These individuals worked to a strict schedule and deadline for twelve to fourteen hours a day, without a break, to prepare a special report on 'The State of Affairs in Our Country', which is enclosed with this letter. I venture to summarise the main ideas in the report and present them for your consideration.

The electoral campaign of 2078 provides you with a unique chance either to enter Ukrainian history as a true reformer and statesman or, forgive me, as yet another loser, during whose period in authority the Ukrainian State may cease to exist. I will stipulate the five reasons why this is the case:

1. The geo-political situation in the world, which has changed drastically as a consequence of the collapse of the Russian State and the passage of the greater part of its territory and natural resources to the control of the Horde, the Celestial Empire and, in part, to Japan. Our security situation is worsening rapidly insofar as a fourth world war will inevitably flare up and inflict terrible casualties. The world's economic potential will be ruined amid chaos and the destruction of an array of states, including Ukraine. The global crisis is being engendered by the aggression and ideological implacability of the Horde and the instability of the Organisation for Global Security, which, in reality, is divided into three groups of states, a weakening in the global position of the Confederation of States of North America, and the uncertainty regarding the position of the Celestial People's Democratic Empire.

2. The regional situation of Ukraine - Following successive victories in the Ukrainian-Romanian (2048-2052) and Ukrainian-Moscow (2068-2070) wars, achieved under your leadership, the regional situation of Ukraine has, over the past two years, deteriorated significantly. We have not become members of any global/regional organisations; let's recollect the

propositions from Poland and Greece to join EllaPol, the Union of States of the Northern and Southern Seas, and our desire not to join the European section of the OGS or become an ally of the American Confederation etc. We have become a 'black hole' in security, an enticing potential victim for both our close and our more remote neighbours. The collapse of Russia resulted in the substantial danger of the incursion of millions of economic and political migrants into Ukraine, and the destruction of our food stocks. On the other hand, there was an increasing danger of the mass flight of Ukrainian citizens into Europe, whose borders, as a result of the Muslim uprising, are practically transparent.

3. The situation within the state - It should be recognised that the attempt by yourself and your predecessor to establish a Ukrainian Cossack Feudal State has failed utterly. The project itself has totally collapsed and been exposed as archaic and inappropriate for the reality of the twenty-first century. The divisions, and indeed the open hostility between different regions with opposing geo-political preferences, have strengthened. As a result, the separatist movement for the creation of a WUS (West Ukrainian State) that would join EllaPol has become dangerously powerful. In the east of the country, a Donetsk-Ukrainian Republic (DUR) has practically been formed. There is no point talking about Crimea, this territory has practically been lost. International experience teaches that the loss by a state of as little as one kilometre of sovereign territory leads to its collapse. In a world of predators we may, on any given day, abruptly become a victim. The military administration has been exposed as an ineffective means of governing civil society and been transformed into a fruitful source of corruption and nepotism. The emergence of numerous private military formations belonging to members of the Aeropagus and the Archons, and armed with the most modern categories of weaponry, is an extreme danger to the state at a time when

190

the armed forces of Ukraine are inadequately financed, poorly armed and suffering from low morale; this is particularly alarming. There is an increased potential for a loss of faith on the part of the people in the state and its leaders. The level of support for the state has fallen to 15.6%, and support for the current hetman to 8.4%. There has been a sharp increase in the percentage of people who might deploy force against the organs of the state, to 41.2% of the adult population. This is particularly high among younger people, from 15 to 25 years of age, 73.8%. Above and hereafter, we are providing data from secret surveys conducted by the State Guard's special sociology centre.

4. The political situation - A substantial majority of citizens reject the oligarchical system. The unusually negative view of the state and its leadership has been caused by establishing serfdom over a significant portion of the population, according to the law drafted by Friedman-Kreyda-Basmanov, regarding welfare subsidies for citizens and allocating them to a place of residency and work. Anger is fomenting among the people because of a game that has become widespread among the children of oligarchs. During the evening, young marauders organise races around the streets of various towns and cities, and the one who has collided with and killed the largest number of innocent bystanders is declared the winner. The level of hatred towards oligarchs is growing to a critical mass. The most detested are Aeropagus members Basmanov, with a loathing index of 42.1%, Friedman (94.7%), and Kreyda (67.3%). Against this backdrop, trust in Indira Holembiyevska is increasing (54.2%), as it is towards the new radical leader of the LUK, the League of Ustym Karmelyuk, Vasyl Kapran (75.8%). In the event of more or less fair elections being held, these people will come to power.

5. General population problems - The division of society into the Deathchristians and the Risenchristians has significantly

worsened the moral climate in Ukraine. The Ukrainian people have been denuded of their main spiritual acquisition - the Christian faith. The inactivity of the state in this sphere is criminal and inexcusable on any grounds.

Proposals:

1. Internal Politics - Taking into account the lack of political leadership in the country and the gradual destruction of statehood, you should take upon yourself complete responsibility for Ukraine. The constitution, at their desire, grants the hetman the full power and authority to do so. Do so and announce that your aims are:

- The liquidation of the oligarchic-feudal construction of state power in Ukraine as a system that is inappropriate for the realities at the end of the twenty-first century;

- the liquidation of the ineffective military form of government;

- the establishment of a presidential-parliamentary form of government;

- the holding of democratic elections at all levels, including presidential;

- the liquidation of the archaic form of the five chamber system of the Sejm, and the unconditional liquidation of the Aeropagus and the system of Archons;

- the presentation of your candidacy for the presidency;

- the return of a free mass-media and fundamental human rights, along with the unconditional maintenance of order and discipline of the state;

- the liquidation of all the ZEKs and the system of inflicting serfdom on the people to members of the Aeropagus and the Archons;

- the harsh and determined liquidation of the Deathchristians' sect and the proclamation of a state programme for the renewal of Christian values.

2. In the international sphere:

- We must immediately undertake negotiations with the OGS and the Confederation of States of North America with the aim of creating a union of democratic states to oppose the aggression of the Horde.

- In connection with the collapse of Russia into separate parts, the liquidation of the Empire of the Double-Headed Eagle and its subjugation by other geo-political entities, we should consider the following questions:

a) The possible renaming of Ukraine and the return to the historic name of Rus. The country's new name could be Rus-Ukraine.

b) The issue of transferring the remains of the nuclear arsenal of the Empire of Double-Headed Eagle to Ukraine.

c) The possibility of Ukraine occupying Russia's former place on the UN security council and in all international structures where Russia occupied a powerful position.

d) Announcing a doctrine for the defence of the Russian and Belarusian populations of Rus-Ukraine from subjugation to the Horde. All these objectives will be fulfilled on Ukraine's terms in order to avoid a repetition of the ancient Russian project for the subjugation and destruction of Ukraine. Kyiv must be the capital of the new state.

In order to realise these and other historic tasks, the following steps must be taken:

1. The creation of a Committee for the Salvation of Ukraine (CSU) consisting of nine or ten reliable and authoritative people under the leadership of the hetman, and the introduction of a state of emergency.

2. The preparation of a temporary Ukrainian constitution implemented via a decree from the hetman.

3. The announcement of the mobilisation of the armed forces and bringing rocket complexes with high-precision weapons into battle-readiness.

4. Reach agreement with the OGS about basing some units of strategic strike aircraft and bombers on our territory to strengthen the defensive potential of our state and as a demonstration of military capability against the growing menace from the Horde.
5. Utilise the human reserves of the Ukrainian people currently incarcerated in the ZEKs, to strengthen the patriotic potential of the state in the armed forces, security and administrative organs etc.
6. To end any discrimination against persons of Ukrainian nationality on the grounds of language, religion and other characteristics, and renew the constitutional norms of Ukrainian statehood.
7. The internment (temporary until their level of guilt before the state is established) of those who led and are leading the state to ruin by working on behalf of forces hostile to Ukraine. (A list of those who must be arrested will be handed to the Hetman of Ukraine in the event of his agreeing to large scale measures.)
The operation will be assigned the code name The Angels of the Abyss.

Respectfully, Ihor Haiduk
Adviser to the Hetman of Ukraine on National Security Issues, Secretary of the NSC, Director of UMI, Major General in the Armed Forces of Ukraine

Part 3

CONSPIRACY

44

June 16 was marked by a national holiday, the Day of the Ukrainian Goddess. This year Ksenya, a world-renowned writer and philosopher who owned the boxes of happiness network, was chosen for the role. The boxes were mobile booths on automobile chassis situated in all the towns and cities of Ukraine. At these facilities any man could, for a comparatively low price of one to ten globos, receive various sexual services from trafficked women. The booths, which were situated adjacent to schools or universities and adorned with a fiery neon sign spelling out XENYA, were exceptionally popular. The young males frequenting these received a 50% discount.

The hetman would sanctify today's festivities with his presence, as required. Haiduk was unable to refuse the invitation, which came in the form of a mini tablet incorporating a film biography and the text of Ksenya's various works. A ticket for two people was attached to the invitation, along with instructions on the dress code and a schedule for the conduct of the festivities.

Haiduk, with military punctuality, took his seat at 18:00 in a box at the opera and ballet theatre, which, happily, had not been damaged by military action during the EnROS invasion. His mother refused to attend the festivities and said that the tart was certainly not among the ranks of goddesses.

The theatre was brimming with the beau-monde. The seats before the stage below Haiduk's box glittered with diamonds and gold epaulettes, light flared off opera glasses inlaid with mother of pearl, and communication gadgets sparkled as they recorded every moment of the celebration.

This grand state affair began with welcoming smiles, amicable handshakes, jealous or triumphant glances, and brief disputes between those accustomed to deciding their affairs during such gatherings. All this happened under the sombre silence of the bodyguards, whose vigilant glances drilled into the crowd. Haiduk felt isolated and superfluous in this literal Vanity Fair, as if he had flown in from another epoch. To his relief the lights dimmed and Ukraine's leading voice, the baritone of television broadcasting, Myron Shvayky, who moonlighted as the Bishop of Fastiv District, roared like the announcer at the beginning of a world-title boxing match, 'His … Excellency … the H-e-e-e-tman of Ukrrra-yi-i ne … please stand!'

The projectors illuminated the figure of K. D. Makhun and his wife in the royal box. The hetman was wearing a bright red *zhupan*. Natalia Havrilivna was wearing a dark red suit, and gold and emeralds glittered on her left lapel; it was a filigree butterfly brooch, the supposed gift from the First Lady of the Confederation of North American States.

The combined orchestra of the garrison and the opera theatre struck up the national anthem and the choir, which was standing on the fifth level of balconies around the theatre, picked up the melody. Only a few knew the words of the anthem and it was apparent how mechanically and uncoordinatedly the state officials opened their mouths and how irritated they were by the words, 'Our foes will perish like dew in the sun.' The enemies were, in reality, thugs from competing gangs rather than the almost kindly 'foes' of the anthem, and would only be silenced by flame-throwers, targeted fire, lasers, or being thrown from a helicopter five thousand metres above the sea. There was no point waiting for them to perish like dew in the sunshine.

'The Goddess of Ukraine,' pronounced Myron Shvayky rapturously. 'Today we crown a great Ukrainian writer of genius and world-renowned philosopher, an activist in the global women's movement Femina, Lady Ksenya … who has just celebrated her one-hundredth birthday.'

A storm of applause resounded through the auditorium. A curtain, embroidered in gold with the hammer and sickle of those happy communist times, rose and the spectators saw a huge chair, with steps leading up to it, at the centre of the stage. Ksenya appeared at the top of the steps to the accompaniment of the crowd's ovations. She was a tiny, old lady dressed in a mini skirt. The centenarian was lifted by the elbows, to the point where she was almost airborne, by two enormous strippers from the men's troupe 'Boys' Peace'. They carefully planted her in the chair and stood at either side, demonstrating their powerful muscular bodies, which were covered only by narrow thongs. The celebration of Ukrainian culture and spirituality commenced.

Ksenya was wearing the transplanted face of a girl who had died in a car accident and her artificial black hair was cut short. She vivaciously blew air kisses on all sides. The hetman's favourite speechwriter, Professor Nykyfor Salyvon of the Academy of Literature and Arts, entered the stage. He was a short man with a dense mane of poetically tangled grey hair, who sang in a delicate fluting tenor, 'Oh Hutsul lass, Ksenya ... I will call to you on the mountain horn ... you in the entire world alone ... I will tell of my love.'

Someone quietly approached Haiduk's box and sat almost inaudibly behind him. Haiduk turned his head and looked intently at the stranger, but did not recognise him. He saw only the glitter of Pince-nez. A wide-brimmed, black hat engulfed the unknown man's face in shadow. The stranger followed the events on stage and the crowd attentively, and paid no heed to Haiduk. He was irritated by the presence of a stranger behind him. It even occurred to him to think about telephoning the head of his bodyguards, Tengiz, to ask who it was sitting to his rear. However, he dismissed the thought because no one could be here by chance on this particular evening.

'Is this display to your liking?' the stranger asked quietly. 'Is this the summit of the Ukrainian people's culture? If that's true, then it has no right to exist.'

'Who are you?' Haiduk asked.

'I'm Friedman. Rafael Friedman.'

'Haiduk,' the major general introduced himself.

'I know, I know, Ihor Petrovych,' Friedman assured him. 'I know a lot about you. In fact, I gather that you know something about me. Isn't that so?'

'Only within the framework of official information,' Haiduk replied drily.

'I have wanted to make your acquaintance for a long time,' Friedman said, removing his hat. 'It's hot in here.' He wiped his perspiring forehead with his palm and Haiduk saw that the hat had concealed a black skull cap. 'Maybe we could have dinner together? There is a not too bad restaurant, not far from here, by the Golden Gates. As for this nightmarish display ...' Friedman said, waving his hand contemptuously at the stage, 'it's not worth our precious time.'

'Okay,' agreed Haiduk. He really was repelled by what he saw; the old woman was from time to time kissing the bodyguard's bodies. Salyvon continued to elaborate his sweet roulades in honour of the centenarian Goddess.

They exited into the empty corridors where six of Friedman's bodyguards were waiting, wearing black hats and long, black overcoats like their boss. Haiduk's two Georgian cavalrymen were also there. They were led to a separate room in the basement of the restaurant, which was empty apart from them, where they were welcomed by the owner, an elderly Japanese man. Friedman exchanged some words with him and, after a ceremonial bow, he departed.

Friedman and Haiduk drank warm sake from porcelain cups. The businessman had a youthful, tender, timid appearance, with soft, almost pulchritudinous skin on his face. His dark eyes cast a kind gaze over his grey beard and black moustache. He spoke quietly, with a somewhat unusual accent, and listened to Haiduk while attentively bowing his head in agreement.

Toulouse Lautrec, thought Haiduk suddenly. That's who he reminds me of, although he is far from being a dwarf. Why? Was his head too big? Was it the Pince-nez? However, he shows no symptoms of alcoholism or syphilis. Toulouse Lautrec would be a lovely codename for an agent.

'That which is underway at the moment in the opera house is a global ignominy, the final end of that which was once called culture,' Friedman continued to develop his theme.

'There are similar phenomena in every culture or mass-culture,' responded Haiduk, adding, 'but it's quite another matter as to whether you need to base state politics on these things.'

'This is not state politics, but the hetman's personal PR. It's vital to him that, at the end of the evening, when that … that … bitch … receives the Golden Goddess she warbles, Glory to the hetman!' Friedman again replaced his hat and his face became shadowy and obscure.

'You don't love everything Ukrainian, that's understood,' said Haiduk, 'but what do you love?'

'A lot of it I do love,' said Friedman, his glasses glittering. 'Here is an example of what I like:

'Do the waves of the Southern Buh River know how they abused you, Mother?' Friedman declaimed his version of the verse with barely restrained and genuine pain.
'Do the windmills among the pastures know how your heart sickens with agony?
Neither the poplar nor the willow disperse your sadness and your troubled thoughts
Does God still walk with his flowering staff among hills with their

mantles of light and dark?'

'Wonderful,' said Haiduk sincerely. 'Who is it?'

'Do you like it? It's Paul Celan, my favourite poet. He transformed Chernivtsi into the capital of world poetry. I provided money for the Paul Celan memorial complex, opened the institute that bears his name, and sponsor a European poetry festival in Chernivtsi. His parents were killed by fascists in 1943. The same as mine in 2048. I will never forgive this,' he sighed.

'I understand your pain and I sympathise. However, you must surely know that during the temporary occupation of Bukovyna almost three hundred Ukrainians served in the securitade punishment groups. The overwhelming majority of the criminals have been caught and punished. And over ten thousand young Ukrainians perished in the battle against the Romanian occupiers. Is there a difference? Finally, Zeyev Zhabotynskyi said that a normal nation has the right to have its idiots and criminals.'

'Let's leave it,' said Friedman, lifting a further cup of sake.

'However, as with any official person, you may not have any other reaction. Statistics do not help in these instances. Certainly my father was a friend to the people of Chernivtsi, a favourite among all Ukrainians. And Mother ... she gave her soul to her pupils, among whom were thousands of Ukrainians. But I don't understand this. Your people are afflicted by a gene of hatred for all incomers. You accuse everyone but yourselves of responsibility for your misfortunes. You are affected by a gene of envy too, like a cancerous tumour. No people can survive such a combination of genes, it will not create a state. Your people are doomed.'

'Where are you heading with this? Would you rather see the Romanians or the Horde in this land?' Haiduk replied, barely restraining his growing anger; it must be the gene of

200

hatred he reflected. However, he pleaded inwardly with himself for understanding that he was being deliberately provoked. One rash move could be fatal.

'Don't get het up, Major General,' said Friedman placidly. 'I'm not as warped as you think. This is my native soil, I love its songs, its traditions, and its women.' He laughed. 'However, whether we want it or not, a sad end is approaching. The collapse of Russia brings the inexorable death of Ukraine ever closer. I anticipate that you are not some deranged Ukrainian nationalist and understand that Ukraine and Russia are like Siamese twins. They are a sole organism with the same blood and a shared destiny. So you Ukrainians are doomed also.'

They were silent, laboriously eating the exhibits from the rich collection of sushi proposed to them by the elderly Japanese man. The oppressively hot evening and the heavy theme of their discussion did not encourage their appetites. He, at any moment, might sit in his gold Rolls Royce terrapin and head for his Locarno, thought Haiduk, and his serfs and millions of other serfs will remain here and become the slaves of the Horde.

'Is there no way out?' Haiduk asked.

'There is always a way out.' Friedman summoned the Japanese man because he wanted to have an angry word with him about something. The Japanese man bowed profoundly and swiftly gathered the porcelain dish with its collection of sushi. 'It is necessary for us to think not about Ukraine on its own but about the Judeo-Christian civilisation of the West in its entirety. If you accept this as a fundamental starting point for our discussions we will propose a genuine action plan and a personal role for you within the global game.' Friedman left the table and nervously passed around the room, as if seeking video cameras placed therein by the Horde. However, it was known that this restaurant, which belonged to Friedman, was 'clean' and all of UMI's attempts to install secret surveillance apparatus had been in vain.

His legs really are too short for a skull of that size, Haiduk thought.

Friedman finally sat opposite Haiduk again, staring attentively into his face with those gentle gold, dark eyes and softly laid his palm on the major general's cheek.

Fuck you, Haiduk cursed him in this thoughts.

Friedman, as if he had heard Haiduk's curses, took away his hand and began to speak quietly; his words minted as precisely as fresh currency, 'I officially address a proposition to you in the name of the World Government in Locarno. Firstly, that you organise a military coup and lead Ukraine. It doesn't matter what you call yourself. You can be the hetman, though that name has wearied everyone now, president, chancellor, chief, marshall, manager of the state or military dictator. The main thing is that you, along with UMI Special Forces Airborne Units of the Ministry of Defence and certain police units, such as the Military Gendarmerie, take all state power into your hands. Secondly, during the summit of the Organisation for Global Security scheduled for Athens, EllaPol, in July, you will undertake negotiations for the immediate entry of Ukraine into the OGS and the conduct of joint military operations against the Horde. Thirdly, UMI Special Forces will liquidate Basmanov and his Guardians as traitors to the fatherland and agents of the Horde. Fourthly, taking into account your respectful stance towards the state of Israel, which we value greatly, you will conduct a special operation to purge Crimea of Crimean-Tatar separatists and allies of the Horde. You will support the relocation to Crimea of a portion of its population, armed forces and state institutions in order to create a national homeland for the Jewish people situated in the Peninsula; for it to exist as an autonomous part of the Ukrainian State. Fifthly, in the event of your agreement, the World Government will provide you
202

with financial assistance to the sum of one trillion globos. We will also secure the modernisation of Ukraine's ageing industrial sector, investing therein a sum of no less than five to six trillion ameros and provide for the supply of modern weapons systems to the Ukrainian armed forces. In exchange, you will, as high commander of Ukraine, take your military to the boundary of the Volga, in the area of Stalingrad, in order to destroy the main force of the Horde and prevent their further advance into Eastern Europe. The sixth and final point; my private wish. In the event of our successfully arranging an amicable relationship, you will provide me with the entirety of your secret archive with all its compromising materials. For, however cynical we may be, it is not necessary to make certain dirty pages of our biographies the property of history, is it not so, Major General?' He raised the cup to his lips and licked a drop of the warm Japanese home-brewed liquor with the tip of his pink tongue. 'In the event of your agreement I will travel with you to Locarno where we will sign a secret pact. You have two weeks to reply. I advise you to agree. We will be in touch.'

Friedman left the table and bowed politely. His bodyguards entered the cellar and surrounded the boss in a tight ring as he left. Haiduk remained motionless for a while and then rose heavily and headed for the exit. He did not know that a scandalous event had occurred at the theatre of opera and ballet, as a result of which both the first and second national channels, 'The Good News Channel' and 'The Bad News Channel' as they were popularly known, had to cease transmission.

The ceremony in honour of Ksenya was nearing its end. The strippers reminded the old lady of the ritual phrase 'Glory to the hetman', which she had to pronounce to all Ukraine, after which the megaphones would roar to stimulate the crowd to join them - 'Het-man! Hetman!' However, a full-chested, dark-complexioned young woman in a long embroidered dress with a garland of flowers in her dark hair had leaped unexpectedly onto the stage. It was Indira Holembiyevska. She bellowed into the microphone, 'Shame on this old bitch! Shame! Hetman out! Out with the hetman. Out! Out!'

What most impressed those present was the discovery of traitors among these, the select and elect, the celebrities of the state, who took up the slogan and cried, 'Shame! Out! Hetman out!' The picture disappeared from the television screens and the curtain lowered. When the lights were switched back on the hetman and his wife were no longer in the royal box.

45

THE HAIDUK FILE
2 December 2076
Secret
Special report of the military attaché of Ukraine in the Empire of the Double-Headed Eagle (Russia), Colonel A. Semyglazov, regarding the events of 28-30 November 2076 in Moscow

I will not submit a detailed analysis of the pre-conditions that led to the events of 28-30 November 2076 in Moscow, which came to be called the 'Bloody Kurban-Bayrami'. Rather, I will lay out the main facts. The report is compiled on the basis of personal observation, information from television bulletins, newspaper reports and the testimony of UMI agents in the Russian Ministry of State Security.

The 28-30 November 2076 saw the celebration of the traditional Muslim holiday Eid Al Adha (Kurban-Bayrami). The festival is widely celebrated in the Muslim world. Rams, goats, cows or camels are commonly used. Kurban-Bayrami has been widely celebrated in Moscow and in other Russian towns for the past seventy years. The routes, number of participants, points where the sacrifices were to be slaughtered, the locations where

204

the hides were to be transferred, the disposition of the kitchens for preparation of the meat, the sanitary procedures required for such an event: all this was agreed with the management of the Moscow police department and the responsible structures of the Russian ministry of state security.

The Forum of Muslims of Russia was scheduled to open simultaneously in the CPR (Congress of the People of Russia) Palace, Red Square, in the former state department store building, on 29 November. Between 550,000 and 600,000 people were due to take part in the events, according to the material submitted by the organisers of the festivities. However, in reality, according to various estimates, the number of participants already exceeded one million on the first day. These were mainly men aged between twenty and fifty years. As is now understood, an operation to gather together, in Moscow, significant contingents of people from the Russian regions, the Caucasus, Central Asia, Turkey, Iran and other countries had in fact commenced a month in advance of the main events.

The complicity of the Moscow police checkpoints had been bought with large bribes, so the real totals of those coming to the capital were either not calculated or were incomplete. The participants of the events were concentrated in workers' hostels, schools, empty hospitals and private apartments. They did not venture onto the street to avoid drawing the premature attention of the authorities.

The fighters were simultaneously supplied with arms in this period. According to incomplete data from the Russian Ministry of Peace Keeping Operations, during November 2076, 200,000 more than the average figure of IZh-107 automatics were sold. The data for other weapons was 12,000 large calibre machine guns, 3,500 mortars and 22,000 portable attack rockets. The director of logistics at the Ministry of Peace Keeping Operations, General R. Abarinov, who bore personal responsibility for allowing the sale of such quantities of arms and munitions, fled to Thailand, along with his family, the day before Kurban-Bayrami.

On 28 November, after morning prayers, five columns, numbering in total up to one million people, advanced along the Zhukov highway and Kutozov, Lenin, Putin, and Stalin avenues. The end point of the route taken by the columns, as agreed with the authorities, was the Volkhonka and Prechystenska riverside area, at the Church of Christ the Saviour, where for several years both Orthodox and Muslim services had been held. Kropotynska Metro Station and other stations around the perimeter of the church and the Kremlin had been closed in advance. The crowd marched along with heavy TATA3-6500 wagons, bearing the thousands of sacrificial rams. The movement of traffic in Moscow was totally paralysed and the attempts of the traffic police to ensure at least some order on the roads were in vain.

Rather too late, the surveillance helicopters and terrapins of the Moscow directorate of the state security ministry noted that a number of these so-called 'celebrants of sacrifice' were working, as we now know, to a precise plan. They headed for the Church of Christ the Saviour and pushed along Arbat to Aleksandr's Orchard, concentrating in the area of Red Square and the CPR Palace. They also occupied positions on the riverside area by the Kremlin and had effectively encircled the complex when the leader of the Moscow Garrison, Okhlobystov, realised this it was too late. The location where the L. Beria Fifth Armoured Tank Division of the State Security Ministry was situated had already been blockaded by squadrons of fighters. The insurrectionaries were provided with vital assistance by Boyaryn Basmanov, who ordered his brigades to remain neutral.

The crowd, which was directed by unknown fighters, who knew neither the geography of Moscow nor the Russian language and operated in accord with instructions and maps of the town, disarmed law-enforcement forces during

206

their manoeuvre. They mercilessly killed serving police and gendarmes in the event of even the least resistance. By midday on 28 November reports had been received regarding the killing of fifty-four and wounding of one hundred and seventeen staff of the law-enforcement agencies.

At 14:00 the lighting went down in Moscow and, within the wintry twilight, the city was transformed into a dark island of terror punctuated by fires, around which huddled groups of cold men waiting in anticipation of a slice of hot, cooked meat. Under cover of darkness criminal gangs began to roam, seizing warehouses with stocks of alcohol, plundering and burning shops, stealing electrical goods, arms, jewellery and food. A tragic incident occurred at 16:15 when a group of Muslims, who were concealed in the grounds of the Krasnyi Oktyabr factory, emerged onto Barsenyevskyi Lane. At the point where it becomes the Barsenyevska embankment, they attempted to cross the river on a thin crust of ice and reach the Prechystenska embankment. The ice could not bear the weight of hundreds of people and cracked, as a result of which eighty men drowned.

During the night, the attempts of Marshall Okhlobystov to contact the commanders of the Felix Dzerzhinsky Third Guard Army of State Security failed to achieve any positive result. The army's commander, Mukhitdinov, reported he would not wage war on peaceful citizens who were entitled to mark a religious holiday. Marshall Okhlobystov flew to the Kremlin where he proposed to his imperial majesty and general secretary of the MARS (Marxist Association of Russian Stalinists) Party, Comrade Kyryll, the second Medunov monarch of all the Russians, to flee the Kremlin before it was too late. However, the monarch refused and said he would remain with his people to the end. A sharp discussion then ensued between Marshall Okhlobystov and the monarch, accompanied by an uncensored lexicon of abuse. (A record of the conversation as transcribed by an agent is attached.)

The Forum of Muslim People held a meeting, which commenced on 29 November 2076 in the CPR Palace on Red Square at 10:00, in the presence of a huge gathering of the world's mass-media. The forum announced the liquidation of the Empire of the Double-Headed Eagle as a 'subject of international law and geo-political reality'. The announcement was made in the name of justice for the oppressed Muslim, Buddhist and Christian people of Russia. Simultaneously, the crowd of demonstrators completely blocked the Kremlin from all sides. The columns of demonstrators suddenly produced green Islamic and red Turkish flags, along with the black stars on white banners denoting the Horde. The inscriptions on their placards, seemingly written by the same hand, called for an end to discrimination against Muslims. The other slogans on these placards were 'Hand Over Empty Orthodox Churches', 'Let Us Not Forget 1552', 'Russia, the Prison of Muslim People', 'Let the Great Chief of all the Muslims in the World, Kara-Khan, live', and 'The Horde, the Faithful Protector of All the Oppressed Muslims in the World'.

The events of 2076 in Moscow testify to the detailed preparation undertaken by the diversionary-propaganda structures of the Horde and, possibly, the Celestial People's Democratic Empire (China) for the liquidation of Russia. The role of the Western world in the 'November Revolution' of 2076 requires further study. The final strains of this global drama, which millions of Russians watched with terror after being betrayed and abandoned by their own leaders, began at 11:00 when a crowd of well-armed fighters began to storm the Kremlin. Marshall Okhlobystov shot himself in his Kremlin office at 12:25. The Spaska and Nikolska towers were attacked, from the direction of Red Square, with anti-tank rockets, which destroyed the sturdy oak, steel-plated and barred gates. From the western side, a special battering ram tank smashed the gate and barricade of the Troyitska Tower. A mass of people swarmed through the gap and attacked. Simultaneously, along the uninterrupted Kremlin wall that runs eastwards to the Kremlin embankment, a huge explosion demolished the Troyitska Tower. The attackers penetrated the territory of the fortress through the gap and captured the Great Kremlin (Imperial) Palace, the main residence of Kyryl, the second Medunov. The ninety-two year old monarch, who was born in Germany in the twentieth century and suffered from Parkinson's Disease, was staying in the Granovyta Palace. He was borne carefully on people's arms, along with the throne, to the main cathedral square, placed in the imperial helicopter and transported in an unknown direction. The Imperial Standard was simultaneously lowered.

At 14:00 on 29 November, the heretofore little known deputy of Kara-Khan, the so-called Bekler-bek, Mohammad Bek, appeared on every Russian TV screen. He announced the fall of the Russian Empire and stated that the new authorities had been sanctified with the Black Star of the Horde and renewed the disrupted historical tradition of Russia's inclusion within the Turkic family of people. He provided assurances to the Slavic people of Russia regarding the security of their democratic freedoms and religious rights. Mohammad Bek simultaneously announced the establishment of Sharia law across the entirety of Russian territory. He advised women to wear Hijabs and Islamic dress. Mohammad Bek also suggested that Muscovites should temporarily abandon the city and relocate to rural areas due to the new authority being unable to secure supplies of water, electricity, gas and victuals.

The announcement by the new governor of Moscow sowed panic among the local population. A flood of refugees in old cars (new ones had been confiscated by the new government), wagons and home-made carts, laden with their valuable possessions, began to leave Moscow. On 1 December 2076 Moscow was half-empty and violence, plunder and lawlessness reigned in its streets and buildings. Representatives of foreign embassies and missions were invited to the Kremlin, where the temporary Command of the Islamic Commonwealth of Nations (ISCOM) was located. They were advised either to leave the territory of the USH or to travel to Suzdal, which the new authorities had granted the status of an autonomous Russian Province (Ulus). For my part, fulfilling a directive of central government, I will be returning to Kyiv on 5 December 2076.

46

The second hour of the night had already passed and Haiduk was still sitting with the hetman in the relaxation chamber, which neighboured Makhun's office in the hetman's palace. It was a beautiful room with ceiling-high panelling of red wood, divided into functional zones. There was a library with a writing desk for the mentally demanding work required of the unchangeable leader of the nation, a quiet sleeping area, and a kitchen with a dining area and a large dining table at which Haiduk and the hetman were sitting. The table was adorned with three bottles of Black Label whisky; half of which had already been drunk. It was also laden with a silver ice bucket, two crystalline vases for black caviar, a gift from the Horde, red caviar, a gift from the king of Norway, rural butter from Lisovody village in Khmelnychynna, where K. D. Makhun was born, and the best wheat loaf in all Ukraine, brought back from ZEK-116. All the food products had undergone a special examination at the laboratory of the hetman's special division, to detect if they contained dioxin, radioactive materials or any other poisons. The majority of dairy and meat products for the hetman's table were produced at a special agro-farm in the Sonyachnyi Shliakh, or Solar Path. In those ancient, bright communist times this was the Leninskyi Shliakh, Leninist Path, district collective farm, which had served the upper echelons of the Ukrainian Soviet Republic's elite. The hetman's logistical needs were secured by the Hrechkosii Brigade, which bore a special medal for its Cossack Glory, adorned with its emblem of a sickle with ears of grain.

'Do you think that this … this … this crazy, ragged creature … is necessary for me?' The hetman continued his bitter, two-hour monologue. 'But she is the only person they read in this country. No one else! Pour out some more.'

Haiduk had heard that the hetman drank people under the table, but this was the first time he had taken part in one of these sessions. His own glass, with its fat bottom, was ever more laden with ice cubs, which the dark brown liquid adhered to and immediately turned yellow. The hetman drank his whisky neat.

Some years ago Makhun had undergone a liver transplant at the clinic of the Johns Hopkins University in Baltimore. Only Haiduk knew about this because he had arranged the surgery and, along with Natalia Havrilivna and some close family members, had not left the patient's bedside. They managed to avoid any media coverage because the press's attention was directed to an island in the Bahamas where the hetman was supposedly relaxing on vacation. His role was successfully played by a double, Matvii Hryshko, an actor of the Bilotserkivsky Music and Drama Theatre. He was suited to the role because, like the hetman, he was a noted drinker, womaniser, gambler and braggart. He was awarded the title of people's artist after this Bahaman role. The paparazzi had not been allowed to get nearer than two to three hundred metres to the villa where the hetman's double rested.

'Oh for some reason she really irritates me,' the hetman grieved. 'That bitch Indira! If it weren't for me … I doubt she would have seen the Aeropagus … It was me who hauled her to the top. Have you ever seen the like? Arranging such a spectacle and sullying me before all the country …'

'They managed to cut off the TV Broadcast,' Haiduk reminded him.

'How do you know? You weren't there. Where were you?' the hetman enquired suspiciously. 'Do you think I don't know?'

'I was with Friedman. I couldn't bear to watch that old …'

'Crazy witch,' whispered the hetman. 'But, just so you know, she was once hot.' The leader of the nation laughed. 'Well, cheers!' They clinked their glasses.

Haiduk hoped that the hetman might have forgotten about Friedman.

'What do you have in common with that bloody Jew, Friedman? What is it with you, Ihor, don't you know he is weaving a conspiracy against me?'

'I'm not playing a part in any conspiracy,' said Haiduk firmly, 'and I won't betray you.'

'Ihor, son … I know that you are a person of honour.' The emotional and drunk hetman lumbered over to kiss Ihor. Backing away again, the hetman, without any unnecessary toast or clinking of glasses, eagerly drank the whisky. He grabbed a spoonful of black caviar and ate before falling into a long silence, as if wary of broaching a dangerous topic. He finally began speaking, 'I read it very attentively three times.' He looked at Haiduk with absolutely sober evaluating eyes. 'What do you want?'

'What do I want?' Haiduk said in confusion. 'Well, isn't that clear? I wrote about it all, everything depends on you.'

'Well you, Ihor, are stupid,' the hetman shook his head bitterly. 'Everything depends on you. Stupid? Naive? Or extremely cunning?' He paused to break off a chunk from the ZEK loaf and put it in his mouth. Then Makhun sniffed heavily and audibly. 'I promoted you … in spite of all the bad things Merezhko wrote about you. Keep an eye on him. He is your mortal enemy … but I spat on him. I wanted to have you recognised …'

'Recognised as what?' Haiduk asked.

'As my successor.'

'Do you even think …'

'Don't say anything,' the hetman said. 'You are like a son to me. You are the only one I trust. You are worthy to become Hetman of Ukraine. But you won't be.' He paused waiting for Ihor to ask why? Haiduk remained silent so the hetman continued. 'Because you … are a Jew.'

'And perhaps I am … Chinese?' Haiduk said as he laughed.

The hetman angrily struck his fist against the table, making the vases of caviar chime and rattling the cubes in the ice bucket. 'Shut up! Don't fool around. You are not a Jew by origin, but in spirit. You are of a different blood group to us. They will never let you come to power, remember that. They will use you, but they will never allow that. Do you know what the patronage service is?'

'It is people who bring cartridges closer to firearms,' Haiduk explained the term while barely restraining his anger, playing on the Ukrainian word for cartridges, patrony.

'That's close. It's the service of those who serve; various experts, academics, advisers, traitors. In a word, smart-arses. Power is not your element, for you do not understand its most important aspect. Nothing depends on those in power. They are like a puppet show; people see them dance on the strings and never see the puppet master. You are very clever, you remember many figures and know various theories. I love you for it.' He rose heavily and headed for the library section, extracting some papers from a drawer in the writing desk, then returned and placed them on the table. It was Haiduk's report scribbled over with various characters, exclamation marks and questions. The hetman's inimitable handwriting was easy to recognise.

'Do you think I'm an idiotic martinet? That I don't know about what you have written? That I don't understand the situation? And that you have come and in two months understood everything and revealed the truth to an old fool? Pour out some more.'

'Maybe we've had enough?'

'Pour it out,' the hetman ordered him savagely. 'I know my limits.' Sweat streamed down his face and he wiped his forehead with a starched napkin.

Haiduk only thought about one thing, whether he could make it to his office, fall onto the couch and deal with the blow the alcohol would deal him soon by taking painkillers. He understood that, compared to the hetman, he was a pitiful intellectual, incapable of these serious, manly discussions, and prayed to God that this binge would end. He cursed himself for writing that idiotic memorandum, which was unnecessary both for this play actor and whoever ruled Ukraine. They would sooner perish along with the country than change.

'I love my country no less than you, and maybe even more, for you know nothing about this cursed place. This isn't the same as Washington was for you.' Haiduk heard the hetman, who had just opened the third bottle. Makhun spoke quietly, carefully laying out the words that arose from the depths of his subconscious, disjointed, illogical, and possibly sincere. His manner was that of a person accustomed to cheating and deceiving others. The filters of his conscious mind transformed this torrent into an orderly monologue. The hetman dropped his voice to a whisper to ask, 'Have you heard who the Grey Prince is?'

Haiduk shrugged his shoulders.

'You are a poor spy then, and your UMI is a crappy intelligence agency, if you do not know who the Grey Prince is. And all your 'so-called' files are worthless. Who, in your opinion, rules Ukraine?'

'The Aeropagus,' Haiduk replied unthinkingly. 'The Archons. The Oligarchs.'

'Your Aeropagus, Archons and Oligarchs are so much shit, as is the hetman. We are just counters here, marionettes from the puppet theatre. The whole country is divided under three brigades, the central, the eastern and the western. The Grey Prince stands at the head of these brigades. This profoundly secret conspiratorial structure was formed in the forties, that is the nineteen forties. The first prince was Stalin, a criminal-in-law who handed the Soviet Union over to the control of international brigades. These are the red brigades - the party, the black brigades - the Cheka and the grey brigades - crime bosses. Throughout society, in state institutions, enterprises, in the army and diplomatic corps, in military and police forces and scientific institutions, representatives of these brigades were appointed in addition to the official leadership. No issue could be decided without their knowledge and agreement. When the Soviet Union collapsed, the red brigades, and to a degree the black brigades, perished. However, the system remained. The grey, criminal brigades gathered all the powers to themselves. After Stalin, the princes, with some exceptions, did not occupy the supposedly leading positions in society, they were not presidents, monarchs or emirs. They descended into the darkness, they descended into the basement, the underground. However, this did not diminish their power; on the contrary, it became easier for them to control the country without taking public obligations upon themselves, and not answering to anyone for crimes or mistaken decisions. But they controlled, and they still control with utter harshness, the life of the country and all its strategic and personnel decisions. Assholes like me are just necessary for them as decoration. The representatives of the grey brigade are everywhere; in your dear UMI and in the State Guard, in the hetman's administration, and in the services of each member of the Aeropagus. And above all of them stands the Grey Prince. And I, Hetman of Ukraine, do whatever he says; or else.' Makhun drew the edge of his hand sharply across his throat.

Haiduk was impressed and listened to the hetman, as if Makhun were narrating the plot of a thriller. He understood simultaneously that the old general was speaking the truth.

'You think that President Federico-Garcia Kostiuk perished so simply?' asked the hetman, gulping the last measure of whisky. 'You figure that he was killed by Friedman? You are mistaken. The Grey Prince's people brought down his helicopter with a Hrim Nebesny missile when he was flying over the Volyn forest. The funeral was fittingly ceremonious … So take this memorandum away and show it to no one if you want to live.' He returned the document to Haiduk. 'However, some things are in my power. I have agreed with my friend, Andrew Van Lee, that in a few days you will fly to Greece as my special representative at the summit of the Organisation for Global Security. We need to reach an immediate agreement with them regarding some joint actions. The Grey Prince isn't opposed.'

'Who is he?' Haiduk could not refrain from asking.

'Eh,' the hetman's drunken smile emerged, 'if you come to know a lot you will die early.' Then he tapped his finger on the table and barely audibly said, 'His representative is there.'

Directly below the office of the hetman, the room belonging to the right hand of the leader of the nation was situated. The general clerk of the Ukrainian Cossack Military Feudal State, Lieutenant General Vitold Klynkevych … the untiring official was not sleeping at this moment. Without switching on the light he sat quietly in a special room packed with electronic equipment and listened attentively to the drunken miasma of his leader. Klynkevych was exceptionally perturbed by the mention of the Grey Prince and the Grey Brigades. Whoever announced such secrets to strangers, people

216

who were not part of the inner circle, would be sentenced to death. Unfortunately, the young lieutenant general, the hope of the hetman and Ukraine, despite nervously tugging the right hand end of his moustache, was unable to hear the last words. Some thudding sound of unknown origin, perhaps a glass tapping on the surface of the table, had obscured them. The scrape of chairs being pushed back, the diminishing, drunken voices of the hetman and Haiduk as they moved away from the microphone in the table marked the end of a drinking session that had all the signs of being a conspiracy against the state.

Haiduk was barely able to stumble to his office as he gripped the walls, and by some miracle did not vomit onto his desk. Nevertheless, he managed to phone the duty commander and ask which of his colleagues was still at their place of work. He received a very precise reply, His Excellency Lieutenant General Vitold Klynkevych.

47

Haiduk slept for three hours, passing through drunken nocturnal nightmares and falling into an abyss on the couch in the grey dusk of the office, hanging between night and morning. He recollected the night with Linda Kenworthy and the CSS Drone, before waking at 06:30 with a horrible headache. Even the two tablets he had swallowed at 05:00 could not move it.

He decided to go for a swim in the Dnipro to revive himself and left the building through the service entrance, which was located on the eastern slope of Mount Borshchykha, and ran into the coolness of the park that circled the lower terrace of the hetman's palace. The path was carefully laid with red and yellow bricks, and led to a small bay with a sandy beach. One hundred metres to his right, nearer to the central part of the palace, a pontoon jetty oscillated on the water. A number of yachts belonging to the hetman and his colleagues were moored there.

The sun had risen above the left bank, but had not yet reddened the white silhouettes of the yachts; the light was sickly and dulled by the morning fog above the Dnipro and covered the islands like a curtain of smoke. Swiftly undressing, Haiduk threw himself into the water, which seemed extremely cold. He did a front crawl for two hundred metres to warm himself and ventured beyond the permitted area for swimming; the edge of which was marked by buoys. This irritated the lifeguard, who was on the brink of alerting the guard boat to pursue the transgressor, but just in time Haiduk made a sharp turn and dived down into the water. Switching to breaststroke, he swam fifteen metres under the water and again caused consternation at the observation point. He kept his eyes open while submerged in a red miasma, which was the true colour of the Dnipro's water. It occurred to him that after such a heavy drinking session, immersion in this cold, murky water might cause a shock to his system, which would significantly simplify the life of many people in the drama where he was compelled to play a part for which he had no desire. He broke onto the surface, ardently gulped the air and, feeling completely awake, noted that someone was standing near his clothes on the bank, waving their hand welcomingly. It was Lieutenant General Klynkevych. He was dressed in white shorts and a black T-shirt adorned with an image of Makhun and bearing the slogan 'I love the hetman'.

'Hey, you scared me when you plunged below the surface Ihor Petrovych. Is everything okay with you?'

'The water is really cold.' Haiduk rubbed his body vigorously with a towel adorned with a map of Florida.

'God is with you, Ihor Petrovych … it's twenty degrees and warm. I bathe here every day … you were probably working late? You look tired.'

'I was undertaking the hetman's work,' Haiduk replied sombrely. 'More to the point, Sir Vitold, military intelligence has gone on the trail of a crime boss with the pseudonym of The Grey Prince. Have you ever heard that name, The Grey Prince?'

Klynkevych undressed and raised his arms with relish, as if praying to the sun. 'No,' he replied distractedly, as if the question were not directed to him. 'And what's he known for, if it's not secret, this Grey Prince of yours?'

'He sold MX-Air Cleaner-124 rockets to the Horde, along with the KhARS missile guidance system.'

'It's the first time I've heard about this. As the head of the committee for arms sales, I would have to know. Are you sure that your glorious counter-intelligence agents haven't got mixed up?'

'No,' confirmed Haiduk with a sincere and amicable smile, 'they may have got mixed up. They might, you understand, have mixed up fridges with rockets and the Horde with the islands of Capo Verde.'

Haiduk finished drying himself, dressed and soon began to feel much better. He saluted the lieutenant general, said, 'Good day to you,' and ascended back up the slope with an easy stride as he felt Klynkevych's gaze upon him. The lieutenant general had surprised the lifeguard because, although he undressed, he did not enter the water as he usually did every morning.

Haiduk was wearing a summer camouflage uniform, woven from threads with self-regulating air-conditioning that made it easier for him to bear the Kyiv heat. He headed into the city where, at 11:00, he was scheduled to meet the General Prosecutor of Ukraine and Marshall of Jurisprudence, Ivan Ovramovych Kreyda. On reaching the underground station at Bankova, Haiduk did not head upwards but passed along the subterranean side passage to the classic Kyiv art-nouveau structure, the building with the chimeras. He descended from there to the Zholdak-Franko Theatre where Nevinchanyi was waiting for him, along with the manager of the investigative operations directory of military counter-intelligence at the State Guard, Colonel Palii. The three men sat on a bench near to the fountain. Its roar would hamper any attempt to hear and the wind occasionally sprinkled the bench and the asphalt with drops of water. After fifteen minutes the men left and the operatives of the State Guard, who were monitoring proceedings with a surveillance camera, were unable to establish the theme of their conversation.

Thanks to the blinding sun, the images were unclear because the contrast of shadow and radiance rendered the faces into black ovals, and the lip-readers could not decipher what had been said. The sensitive microphones only picked up the roar of water.

After ten minutes, Haiduk entered the premises of the GPU, which was situated between Bohdan Khmelnytsky Square and Mykhailivska. This had once been the site of the Prisutstvennoe-mesto, a building housing Tsarist-era state institutions, distinguished by its terrible pre-revolutionary architecture. The present structure now housed the prison, the so-called SIZO, the investigative unit of the police, the gendarmerie division, popularly known as Merezhko's viper's nest, and the GPU premises. This building, or more accurately the right to retain or demolish it, had been the subject of a struggle conducted over many years. However, I. O. Kreyda triumphed, not in his role as General Prosecutor of Ukraine but as the general co-ordinator of internet security on state territory. Kreyda succeeded in convincing the Aeropagus and the hetman that there was no better location for censoring the various information streams and preventing the least desirable, from the point of view of civic calm, ideas, thoughts and provocative calls from entering circulation.

The design for the new building was commissioned from the best Berlin based architect, Rolf Nagel. He situated twenty-two storeys of the Justice Building, predominantly occupied by prisons, underground. The twenty storeys situated on the surface were in the form of a black Zeppelin, the facade was largely perspex, that had docked temporarily on these ancient hills. Not surprisingly, Rolf Nagel named his creation Zeppelin and explained that a scenario had been discovered in the documents of the Third Reich, according to which Adolf Hitler would have arrived ceremonially in Kyiv in 1941 on a Zeppelin that would have docked in Bohdan Khmelnytsky Square.

The people of Kyiv, however, developed their own legend around the building. It was said that if the mooring cables, which seemingly attached the Zeppelin to the ground, were cut, it would soar into the sky and fly far away. They called it the *dyryzhaba* or Zeppelin toad.

Having passed through the required procedure of DNA examination and retinal scanning, Haiduk was invited into a vast hall. It resembled an airport terminal. Black models of strange flying machines and Zeppelins from the past hung in the upper recesses of the factory-style structures. The aviation history display ranged from the Wright Brothers' airplane and the Hindenburg airship, to the French space-capable Mirage interceptor and bomber. Haiduk raised his head and felt the remnants of a dull pain and a slight dizziness.

'General! General! Get yourself here quickly, the *halushky* will get cold.'

He saw, at the end of the hall, a bald man in the dark blue uniform of the general prosecutor. The meeting table was covered with embroidered cloths on which bowls of victuals steamed. Kreyda squeezed his hand and cautioned him, 'I'm Ivan Ovramovych, not Abramovych.'

'I know,' laughed Haiduk. He had heard that Kreyda's greatest enemy would be whoever referred to him as Abramovych, and suspected him of having foreign rather than rural, Slavic roots.

'Please be seated at the table,' said Kreyda, bustling hospitably. 'Maybe we could have a drink?'

'What are you up to, Ivan Ovramovych,' Haiduk asked, genuinely horrified at this fuss, 'I can hardly bare to watch?'

Kreyda sat at the table and thrust a red serviette into the collar of his white shirt. 'Help yourself. These are my favourite buckwheat *halushky*. It's ours, Ukrainian and rural. And this is wild boar meat. And here we have a very special desert, *halushka* with pineapple. It is, so to speak, Ukrainian in form, tropical in content.'

The buckwheat *halushky* flavoured with bacon were wondrously tasty and Haiduk felt famished. He almost felt well disposed towards Kreyda, as if the latter were a hospitable peasant farmer offering him bread and salt. The prosecutor was known behind his back as the 'Poltavian Halushka' in a jibe at his affected fondness for the cuisine of his home province.

'Our people are imbued with genius,' said Kreyda thoughtfully, 'with their immortal victuals and cuisine, borshch, salo with garlic, *halushky*, compote ... The diet creates the best culinary basis in the world for balanced human development. It includes everything, anti-oxidants, vitamins, the portfolio of necessary amino acids, anti-sclerotic substances ... Eat, eat. If it were up to me I would make the *halushka* rather than the tryzub the state emblem of Ukraine. Do you know that in the Kyiv-Rus State the tryzub was used to brand horses?'

'What are you talking about?' Haiduk asked, and, although appalled, moved onto the *halushky* with meat, 'it's the first time I've heard that.'

'The main secret to *halushky* is the percentage of salt in the water in which they are boiled. I sponsor a special Poltavian scientific research centre known as HaV, or *halushka* and *varenyky*, where they undertake serious research.' Kreyda inhaled the aroma of bacon with relish. 'So what request do you have for me?'

'I have a double request for you,' said Haiduk, extracting two accurately folded papers from the left pocket of his jacket. 'First, the problems under consideration at the next sitting of the National Security Council; we are anticipating your active participation and propositions … The second request is personal.'

Kreyda, relishing the dessert *halushky* stuffed with pineapples, put on his large, round glasses and swiftly studied the second, private document. It was a request to release a citizen of the Confederation of States of North America, Bozhena O'Connell, from ZEK-116. The grounds for her release were an oral statement from O'Connell and a petition from the Aide to the First Lady of America, M. Jefferson. The paper also gave a characterisation of colonist B. O'Connell's typical behaviour, provided by AdZEK.

'My dear friend,' said Kreyda, looking pityingly at Haiduk with his large, round, cunningly dark eyes, 'request whatever you like, but not this. We could lose the ZEKs like this. I can do nothing. The law is the law. She voluntarily signed a request to inhabit the ZEK. No one compelled her to do so. What kind of a general prosecutor would I be if I broke the law? So please understand me.' He straightened the diamond-encrusted marshall's star that adorned his black tie, and his bald pate glittered.

'What is it with you Ivan Ovramovych? I understand you as no one else does. I too am faced with a dilemma. My colleague, the director of the Swiss counter-intelligence directorate, Maurice Schweinsteiger, has contacted me. They have caught a Ukrainian citizen, Vladislav Maksymovych Kreyda, red-handed with a huge consignment of Afghan narcotics. The drugs underwent additional purification at a Poltava scientific research centre and were released on the European market under the name Halloween.'

The glittering lights on Ivan Obramovych's pate faded.

'Schweinsteiger wants to spread news of this matter throughout all of Europe. A special TV programme has been prepared incorporating Vladislav's admission of guilt and the exact secret addresses, passwords and surnames of those involved in this transaction. The authorities may close their bank accounts. However ...'

'However?' repeated Kreyda, as if enchanted.

'There are various possibilities. A Swiss intelligence agent was recently detained in Kyiv. He was gathering information on the newest, secret products of a Ukrainian chocolate manufacturer for a Swiss manufacturer, with the intention of organising sabotage. I would be able to propose an exchange to Maurice, who is an old friend - His agent for ... Kreyda. However, I cannot do it. The law is the law.'

Haiduk stretched out his hand to collect the paper with the request for Bozhena's release, but Kreyda did not hand it to him. 'Wait, I need to think. Are you sure that your friend will be willing to make the exchange?'

'I am absolutely certain because this agent is his distant relative. This is an extremely sensitive episode for Maurice.'

'Oh well,' Kreyda said, writing one word on the paper and signing it. 'Although this other Kreyda has no connection to me, not even from the same family, the reputation of the state may suffer. I strongly request you to make a deal with your Swiss contact.'

The submission for Bozhena was now adorned with his handwriting. It read 'Release, and was signed and dated I. O. Kreyda, 24 June 2077.'

While drinking cold compote Haiduk reached an agreement with Kreyda regarding the further strengthening of cooperation between the agencies. Kreyda's black writing desk stood not far from where they were lunching. It was there he signed death sentences, which had been re-instigated

224

from 2066 onwards after the murder of Ukrainian President Federico Garcia Kostiuk. The process of signing death sentences was broadcast by Kreyda's television channel, popularly known as 'The Bad News Channel'. This outlet broadcast obituaries, natural disasters and crime documentaries. 'The Good News' channel, which belonged to Friedman, broadcast soap operas, celebrity weddings, Ukrainian operettas, song and dance marathons, a high-fashion show, comedians from Odesa, and Californian pornography.

The sociologists were amazed because, in opposition to all the rules of logic, the ratings of Kreyda's channel were higher than that of Friedman's. Kreyda had been granted special permission from the parliament to broadcast the literal execution of death sentences. However, parliament imposed an array of restrictions on the broadcast. The programme, called 'The Power of the Law', could only be transmitted at midnight on Fridays and only viewers aged eighteen and above were permitted to watch the transmission. The entire country held its breath as it gazed at the gallows erected in the KNN studio and the noose that was hung around the necks of the victims.

On exiting from the dark, cold rooms of the 'Black Zeppelin', Haiduk felt momentarily happy as he glimpsed the dome of Mykhailivska Cathedral, and inhaled the hot Kyiv air. The thermometer on the Intercontinental Hotel building, which also belonged to Kreyda, indicated that it was 43°C.

Hryhoriy Nevinchanyi was waiting for him in the jeep. On taking his seat in the vehicle, Haiduk issued a brief order, 'Head for Feofania-Pyrohovo.'

They descended into a tunnel of fast moving traffic, which exited onto the Dnipro riverside area, and headed swiftly in the direction of ZEK-116.

48

22 June 2077
Secret
To the adviser to the Hetman of Ukraine on National Security Issues, Secretary of the NSC, Major General I. P. Haiduk
Analytical Report

This report concerns the situation that has emerged on the eve of the summit for member countries of the Organisation for Global Security (OGS). The conference, which is scheduled to be held on 5-7 July 2077 in the vicinity of Athens, on the Greek Island of Evia, will certainly become, in the opinion of global analysts, the defining event of the twenty-first century. The summit will certainly affect the destiny of the geo-political system, which is changing fundamentally before our very eyes. The collapse of Russia and its disappearance from the world map has become the most significant event of the last third of the twenty-first century. It has shifted the global balance of power. The Horde has increased its strength by seizing a larger part of Russia's territory and its military-industrial potential, including its nuclear capacity.

The present situation is characterised by the pretensions of the USH states to world dominance, the confusion among the member countries of the OGS, and the sharp decline in the power and influence of the Confederation of States of North America. These are all the subject of great concern among the democratic countries, which have sharply reduced in number since the middle of last century.

The possible resolutions that may be adopted, in the opinion of UMI's agents and analysts, at the summit are as follows:

1. A decision on the part of the Confederation of States of North

America to enter the conflict around the Arctic and deliver several preventative nuclear strikes to the command centres and facilities of the Horde's Air and Space Forces, without a formal declaration of war.

2. The transformation of EllaPol (the Union of Northern and Southern Sea States, comprising part of Greece, Bulgaria, Romania, Hungary, Slovakia, Poland and Lithuania) into a central element of the OGS, whose role will be to arrest the onslaught of the Horde. The Horde's goal is to end western Europe and unify the Islamic enclaves on the territory of Germany, France and Spain. It is anticipated that a resolution will be adopted at the summit regarding basing Revenger XI tactical missiles on EllaPol territory. The resolution would also require the transfer of two military units to the Ukrainian border, each unit would have one hundred of these vehicles and be equipped with FAV-TX 3 terrapins, with the goal of actively opposing the aggressive plans of the Horde.

3. The OGS intends to propose immediate membership to Ukraine, along with the signature of a treaty for friendship, peace and co-operation, incorporating a secret protocol for its union with EllaPol, the Scandinavian Pact and the Black Sea Christian Commonwealth. The protocol will also require the mobilisation of Ukraine's armed forces and its defence industry, in preparation for a peacekeeping operation against the USH.

4. The information acquired by our agents, which requires further evaluation, is that on Canadian territory, in the town of Churchill, a new category of weaponry, whose characteristics are as yet unknown, is being manufactured in conditions of absolute secrecy.

Senior Analyst Maximilian-VIII

49

The liberation of Bozhena occurred in a pedestrian fashion. She was handed to Haiduk in a room at the checkpoint as if she were a commonplace item. The protection officer and the elder of ZEK-116 had composed a formal statement enacting the transfer of 'trainee' Bozhena O'Connell, born 2051 in the state of Illinois, with no health concerns. She was being given into the hands of UCMFS citizen I. P. Haiduk, born in 2027 and currently residing in Kyiv. The document was adorned with four signatures, those of Bozhena, Haiduk, the elder, and the AdZEK representative, and the date stamp, still wet, indicated that it was Thursday 24 June 2077 at 15:00. Askold and Lykera did not attend the ceremony.

The protection officer's German Shepherd sniffed Bozhena and her big linen bag embroidered with blue flowers. The dog, smelling something untoward, leaped up and began to beat the bag with its paws.

'It's only bread,' said Bozhena alarmed.

'Sorry,' said the officer, throwing up his hands, 'it's just procedure. We are checking for drugs. Get back Mukhtar,' he ordered the dog. 'You may come this way, we don't have to open the bag.'

Bozhena silently and detachedly took her seat in the jeep, like she had once taken her seat in the Cadillac. Only when they were near to the Mormon church, and she saw the angel with his trumpet shining in the sun, did she speak reproachfully, 'I was afraid you had forgotten me.'

'Forgive me, I couldn't get you out earlier.'

'No, you must forgive me for being an idiot.'

He took Bozhena to his apartment and showed her to her room. He had allocated her the bedroom. He gave her some money to go shopping and assigned one of the guards to assist her. Once he had sorted out Bozhena he went to the island in order to determine the conduct of the operation UMI had to undertake during the OGS summit. He returned late, after 22:00, to find Bozhena curled up asleep in an armchair in the living room. A bottle of rural milk from Askold O'Connell's farm stood on the coffee table, along with a sliced loaf on a breadboard; the produce of ZEK-116's good agricultural husbandry. Two chunky, ceramic cups for the milk were waiting to accompany this vegetarian supper.

Bozhena was wearing Haiduk's white dressing gown, which she had taken from the bathroom, her auburn plait lay over its collar like a handful of autumnal grass. A profound sleep had fallen on her, and in the twilight of the room her peaceful face wore an untroubled, childlike expression. Haiduk again barely restrained himself from touching her hair. Quietly, without switching on the light, he took off his uniform in the study and dressed in a white shirt, bearing the UMI logo, and light shorts, before tiptoeing back into the living room where Bozhena slept sweetly.

The doors of the balcony were open. Haiduk stepped through them and, entering an altitude where the wind from the Dnipro dispersed the stagnant, hot air, leaned against the railing. The panorama of the ancient city opened before him in the failing twilight of one of the longest days of the year. This was really not the same town remembered by his generation of Kyivans. The Dnipro precisely divided this ten-million strong metropolis into two cities, Kyiv-East and Kyiv-West.

The ugly barracks of Kyiv-East lay along the left bank of the river. It provided a refuge for the streams of unfortunate Eurasian immigrant workers who had been compelled to abandon their homes due to war, drought and famine. It was there, in Kyiv-East, that commercial and craft centres, operated by emigrants from India, Pakistan, Vietnam, and the Asian area of Russia, developed. The indigenous Kyivans, who continued to inhabit Darnytsya and Bereznyaky, were divided from the new waves of immigration by crossing points, walls and armed guards. The bridges and crossings were kept under close surveillance by a special section of the State Guard. They only allowed these undesirable foreigners the most limited access to Western Kyiv.

However, the western part of Kyiv had not managed to eschew substantial changes. The flames of the advertising dragons of Podil, which had been transformed into the city's China Town, glittered far below Haiduk. Under a special agreement between the governments of Ukraine and the Celestial People's Democratic Empire, the Chinese were not subject to the restrictions at the Dnipro crossings. The Chinese had constructed a nano-technology manufacturing complex, Kurenivtka, and had brought thousands of Chinese workers and their families to work at the plants. They had opened the Deng Xiaoping Sino-Ukrainian University of High Technology. The land and facilities of Batyieva Hill were almost completely purchased by representatives of the Horde. The German settlement lay to the west of the Borshchahivka district; the Friedrich Ebert University and Energy Research Centre had been established in this area.

Haiduk sighed as he imagined how hard it must be for Merezhko and Kreyda to sustain even a modicum of order in a city divided between dozens of ethnic bands, who controlled the narcotics trade, brothels, casinos and questionable banks that engaged in money laundering. However, his thoughts suddenly turned to his own affairs. What was to be done with Bozhena, whom he liked so much and who had evoked such an aching desire in him, but … how long might she live with him? Did she want to live with him? And what would the hetman say, along with all those monsters in his entourage, when they discovered she had served in the Mars Legion, the special forces created by the President of the Confederation for the conduct of surface and space-based intelligence operations? In addition,

230

Bozhena was entangled in some dark history and had incurred the wrath of her commanders. She might become, if she had not already done so, a victim of twofold blackmail from the State Guard and Confederation military counter-intelligence. The prison on the Mansfield Military Airbase, which had been relocated from Guantanamo Bay, belonged to military counter-intelligence and it was there that the criminals most dangerous to the state were incarcerated. As he gazed into the endless, glittering sea of lights that was Kyiv-West, Haiduk reflected on the situation into which he had fallen as a result of this woman and his weakness.

He suddenly felt someone nudge him lightly in the back. Haiduk flinched in fear, imagining that he was about to be thrown from his twenty-ninth storey balcony, and rapidly looked to his rear. Bozhena was standing behind him and laughing.

'I was scared,' he said, feeling how his heart pounded in his chest.

'Never stand so close to the edge of a balcony. Especially when you are in the vicinity of strangers. Do you want some supper?'

'I'm so famished I could eat a whole bull.'

They returned to the room but did not switch on the lights.

'I don't eat meat,' Bozhena informed him.

'What about fish?'

'I'll eat that.'

'I have some smoked eel. Do you fancy that?'

'No thanks,' said Bozhena, pouring some warm milk into the mugs and handing him a slice of bread.

He swallowed the milk, which preserved the distant and vivid fragrance of his childhood when Ihor had gone to visit his father's sister, Aunt Olya. She had lived in a village near Uman and had given him just this kind of milk.

'What happened to you in the ZEK?' he asked. 'Was it a bad place for you? Did they victimise you?'

She adjusted her plaits and pulled her robe tighter, as if acting out the concealment of her secrets from him. 'I'll tell you about it another time. No one bothered me. Everything was great … too great, but I suffered in ways I couldn't say. I was expecting something terrible to happen all the time. After a week I understood that this limited village life was not for me. I had the impression time had stopped and I was living in the thirteenth century on some farmstead that had been forgotten by everyone. It felt as if riders, dressed as black crusaders or some such, were galloping past; that somewhere far away cities were burning and battles raging and I was there and did nothing, not understanding any of it.' She lapsed into silence, poured more milk and ate a little slice of bread, squeezing the soft crumbs off her boyish fingers, as if gathering them to feed the birds.

In the darkness, which had finally fallen, her facial expression was invisible and it seemed to Haiduk as if she were meditating with closed eyes.

'It's weird,' she said, moving a little, 'but when I was on Mars, I just sat for an entire year on our base. I had the same feeling, chrono-collapse, the collapse of time …' She suddenly changed the theme. 'I was convinced that while you were standing on the balcony, you were thinking about what to do with me?'

'Yes, I was,' he replied.

'I had a chat with Aunt Martha. She promised that in a few days our embassy would collect me from here and I would return to … I don't know where … perhaps to Washington.'

'Where are you in a hurry to get to?' Haiduk asked, in conflict with all the logical rules he tried to live by. 'Live here for as long as you like. If you don't want to live here, I have another apartment. You would be on your own there.' Then he said what he only dared to say in the darkness, 'I like you and I really want you to stay.'

She didn't reply immediately. 'I like you as well, and it scares me.'

'Do you have a husband?' he asked.

'No, but I am not a free agent.'

Who among us is free? Haiduk thought.

'I'm not free in a sense other than what you think,' said Bozhena, as if reading his thoughts, 'but I need time. Unfortunately men are always in a rush.'

He took her hand, kissed the tips of her fingers and, as if afraid of his own gesture, released her. 'I'm not in a rush to get anywhere anyway. Stay with me and we will see what happens.'

'You will have problems. As far as I understand, your leadership has no great love of America …'

'They don't love anyone. Not even themselves …' He yawned. 'We must sleep now. I am really tired.'

The hands of the huge clock on the Black Zeppelin showed it was midnight. Bozhena rose and he felt her breath and caught the fragrance of her hair. This was the best chance he would have to kiss or embrace her, but something restrained him. She swiftly left the living room and quietly closed the doors of the bedroom behind her. He unfolded the settee in his office, made it up as a bed and lay down quickly, but could not sleep. Anguish and hopelessness reigned over his soul, confusing his thoughts and any logical constructions he might put on things. The deadline for his reply to Friedman was inexorably approaching. Haiduk had decided to utter a firm 'no' in response to the offer. Agreeing to participate in the conspiracy automatically meant a death sentence for him. However, uncritical trust in the hetman and blind adherence to the officer's code of honour appeared laughable in these conditions, when the Deathchristians and criminals were transforming the country into a veritable Gulag. But could Haiduk and the dozen or so intelligence officers who were loyal to him prevent this from happening? If so, how?

Not knowing the answer he switched his train of thought to Bozhena. Haiduk recollected her words about the thirteenth century, the black riders and the crusades. He yearned to go to her in the bedroom, to lay quietly beside her, to embrace her and understand whatever it was that tortured her. He wanted still more for her to understand his troubles.

He had begun to drift off, collating in his imagination the brutal images of reality, the illusory phantasmagoria of Bozhena's life on Mars, the flight of the Lancaster, the naked, blood-soaked nursing sister he had dragged out of the operating theatre ... then he heard the sharp ringing of his American gadget. It was after 03:00.

Haiduk heard an unfamiliar, masculine voice which, precisely and as indifferently as if it were an ordinary event, reported that today, on the 24 June 2077 at 18:00, in the White House, while receiving a Mexican delegation, the President of the Confederation of States of North America, Andrew Van Lee, had been assassinated. The Vice-President of the Confederation, Sara Lou Lane, had been arrested on the orders of General Prosecutor Enrico Pekenya. She was accused of treason and preparing the assassination of the president. Under a senate resolution, the role of temporary, acting president of the Confederation was allocated to the president's widow, Senator Shirley Van Lee, who took her oath in the Oval Office. The screen of the gadget monotonously repeated images of the White House, a photograph of the president in a black frame, Fiery Sara, Shirley Van Lee and the state emblem of the Confederation.

He grabbed the Ukrainian government communication gadget and contacted the hetman, who due to another hangover could not at first understand what had happened. While Haiduk was still explaining to him Bozhena entered the study and approached him. 'I know everything, my auntie has just phoned me. I'm scared. Hold me,' she said.

He embraced her and felt how her body trembled as he pressed against her while talking with the hetman. He also trembled as the air conditioner, which he had switched on for the night, wafted air that was too cold over him.

50

25 June 2077
10:00 Washington
Secret
Adviser to the Hetman of Ukraine on National Security Issues, Major General I. P. Haiduk
Operational Report

The events that have unfolded in Washington shocked diplomatic circles. It transpires that during a meeting between the President of the Confederation, Andrew Van Lee, and the overall commander of the Anti-Drugs Task Forces of Mexico (ADTF), General Ramon Fernandez, in the Oval Office, the latter's deputy launched himself at Van Lee at 18:00, and murdered him instantaneously. The Deputy General, Porfirio Sapaterro, who is a former Mexican martial arts champion, broke the president's neck.

At 19:18 it was announced that Sara Lou Lane had been arrested on charges of conspiracy to undertake a coup and seize power. The murder of the president, General Porfirio Sapaterro admitted, was, as the allegations suggested, undertaken in collaboration with Sara Lou Lane. The videotaped confession of the general was transmitted on CNN at 19:35.

At 19:45, the Senate of the Confederation unanimously confirmed Senator Shirley Van Lee acting President of the Confederation of States of North America following the withdrawal of their candidacies from consideration by the Speaker of the Senate and the Secretary of State.

A state of emergency was announced within the Confederation at 20:20, along with the introduction of censorship of the mass-media and the disconnection of the civilian mobile network. According to UMI's intelligence sources, a classic military coup has occurred in Washington. At its head stands the widow of the Confederation President, Shirley Van Lee, along with her aide, Martha Jefferson, who, according to some sources, might become the Vice-President of the CSNA, the Defence Minister, Oliver Brown, and the head of the Committee for Foreign Affairs in the Confederation senate, Senator Paul Anderson. According to rumour, Anderson has already been appointed Director of the Central Security Service of the Confederation. The fate of his predecessor, Admiral Stanley Fisher, is currently unknown.

During the night, at 23:00, the acting president addressed the nation. She expressed a high opinion of the life and work of her husband, which were dedicated to ensuring that the Confederation flourished and strengthening peace and global security. She called on the citizens of the Confederation to unite around the heritage of Andrew Van Lee during these tragic days. Madame President vowed to continue the work of her husband and condemned, in the strongest terms, the organisers of his assassination. 'Behind this act,' announced Shirley Van Lee, 'stand not only former Vice-President Sara Lou Lane and her husband, with his sordid business activities, but powerful Mexican drug cartels who have set themselves the task of seizing power on the North American continent and fundamentally changing the internal and external policies of the CSNA. They aim to conspire with the Horde to acquire free access to the drug market in Afghanistan.'

The complete text of Shirley Van Lee's speech is attached.

The situation in Washington DC, as in other large American and Canadian cities, remains predominantly calm at present. Military units have surrounded the White House and the building housing the CSNA congress. Terrapins and armoured transporters have appeared on the central streets of the capital and other large cities. Military helicopters are patrolling the air space above cities and flights by civilian passenger aircraft have been suspended for an indefinite period. Only the CNN channel is distributing official information, along with broadcasts of West Side Story and Gone with the Wind.

At 08:00 on 25 June 2077, ambassadors from member countries of the Organisation for Global Security visited the White House and offered the recognition of Shirley Van Lee as acting president of the Confederation; they offered her their support for her actions to combat the forces of aggression and oppression, and the division of the world by criminal powers. Unconfirmed information is being circulated regarding a revolt against the Mexican government led by Jose Sapaterro, the brother of President Van Lee's murderer. He is, according to the military attaché of Ukraine in Mexico, the director of one of the most powerful drug cartels in Mexico, which is situated in the city of Ciudad Juárez on the Texan border.

According to the attaché, shots have been heard in the capital, Mexico City, and a ferocious battle is raging near the presidential residence at Los Pinos. They inform us that a one hundred thousand strong crowd has gathered at El Zocalo, the central square in the city, and it is enthusiastically supporting the revolution and Mexico's exit from the Confederation. Jose Sapaterro addressed the crowd from the central balcony and, striking the bell of freedom, commenced the traditional Grito de Dolores of Mexican Presidents, a prayer for the country. He announced Mexico's independence from the Yankee occupational regime. The crowd greeted the lowering of the Confederation's flag and the raising of the largest (thirty by twelve metre) state flag of Mexico, on the flagpole at El Zocalo, with huge enthusiasm. Revolutionary radio stations broadcast anti-American slogans.

The murderer of the Confederation President, General Porfirio Sapaterro, was declared a national hero. A number of significantly successful actions by the rebels have been reported, which may represent a serious threat to the existence of the Confederation and weaken the resistance of North America to the forces of the Horde. We will immediately inform the centre regarding any further changes to the situation.

The Military Attaché of Ukraine in the CSNA, Colonel S. Orlyanko

51

On the evening of Friday 25 June, at 18:00, the hetman called an extraordinary sitting of the Council of National Security for the purpose of discussing the external and internal situations of Ukraine. Throughout the day Haiduk, anxious and suffering from lack of sleep, acquainted himself with encrypted messages from diplomats and intelligence agents in various countries, and the views of the world press regarding the events in the CSNA. He chased up NSC analysts, who were preparing reports and draft documents, and telephoned members of parliament. He concluded agreements regarding various technical details connected to the arrival and protection of such a large quantity of 'big fish' and worked on the text of the hetman's speech. He ignored Nykyfor Salyvon, the hetman's irreplaceable speechwriter, on this occasion, on the grounds of the exceptional secrecy of the issue under discussion.

Seven members of the Aeropagus arrived for the sitting, along with twelve Archons, the owners of the geographical areas of the state. The country's lands were divided into territories, its energy, industrial, agrarian and intellectual power, and its human resources, which were the property of these owners.

238

The list of those invited included some senators and heads of parliamentary committees, ministers and Cossack Otamans, including Lieutenant General Klynkevych.

Haiduk ordered that a detailed list of those present be compiled, which was to omit no one, not even the technical clerks, along with details of their biography and personal characteristics. He anticipated that the Grey Prince would somehow worm his way into the attendees.

The sitting was held in the situational room in the hetman's palace. This chamber, which was hidden deep underground within the ample mass of Mount Borshchykha, was reminiscent of a mission control for space rockets. There were countless monitors, huge computerised maps of the world and Ukraine, remote controls and other decorative gewgaws that created a great impression on people lacking competency in such matters. This description applied to most of the participants of the meeting.

The hetman appeared, wearing a black *zhupan* as befitted his mood; he was sombre and had dark areas under his eyes. With a commanding gesture he ordered everyone to sit. Then, as if in disgust, he picked up some papers between his thumb and index finger and looked angrily at those present. 'What is this? I ask you. What is this? Sir Merezhko and Sir Kreyda, have you been working so hard that this crap has appeared on my computer? Switch on your monitors,' he ordered, 'and read.'

A text was illuminated on the screens of the participants:

The Scenario of the twenty-first century
THE PEOPLE HAVE THE RIGHT

The words were accompanied by a photograph of two men hanging from a long branch, while below them thronged a delighted, tumultuous mob. The photograph was signed Lynch Law and the text was simple and unadorned:

- There will not be enough charter flights for you all.
- The crimes of the so-called elite against the workers are grounds for the organisation of open popular tribunals and public punishment against these untouchable monsters.
- Our demands are the return of the land stolen from the people by them, including its forests, woods, rivers, beaches, parks, sanatoriums and factories, not to mention equitable pay, liberty and the future.
- The return of the possessions stolen from the masses will be realised through the verdicts of popular tribunals. The main instruments for implementing these verdicts will be the axe, fire, knife, rifle, rope and bomb. The verdicts will be final and not subject to appeal.
- The popular tribunal has unanimously affirmed the severest punishment possible for the degenerate hetman, the members of the Aeropagus, the Archons and their henchmen. The sentence will, with certainty, be executed.
- Open season has now been declared against the enemies of Ukraine.

The League of Ustym Kameliuk - LUK
June 2077

'Have you read it?' yelled the hetman. 'Are you satisfied? This affects all of you; all, without exception. This is a declaration of war. They killed the president in America, while in Ukraine they threaten to murder the hetman and the upper echelon of power. And there are those among you who are delighted by this, who incite the people to illegal activities. There are those who do not understand that they are sawing off the branch on which they, themselves are seated. I demand that the law enforcement agencies immediately find these criminals who are threatening murder and aiming to de-stabilise the state and destroy what we have gained, our independence!'

Merezhko and Kreyda bowed their heads, carefully making a note of something, as if the hetman had informed them of the names, known only to him, addresses and codes used by the crooks and hackers who had penetrated the brain of the state.

As a technocrat, a disciplined and military person, it was unpleasant for Haiduk to realise that utter chaos reigned in the state. He recollected Crooked Mykola, the blacksmith and resident of ZEK-116, with his Haidamak-revolutionary hatred for all lords and foreigners. The text which the hetman had cited with such anger contained something arrogantly childlike and therefore just and true.

The hetman calmed down and gave a speech following the scenario prepared by Haiduk. He proposed to immediately express, on behalf of the state, regret for the tragic loss of President Van Lee, while sending a telegram to the acting President of the Confederation, Shirley Van Lee. The telegram would emphasise the desire to strengthen and develop the strategic partnership between Ukraine and the CSNA. The third point of his proposals was particularly significant. It called for the adoption of a resolution for Ukraine to request immediate entry to the Organisation for Global Security and active military cooperation with the OGS to oppose the aggression of the Horde.

Haiduk reflected that this was the first attempt to align Ukraine geo-politically since a gang of inept bandits had seized power at the beginning of the twenty-first century and announced its 'neutral status', turning the state into a black hole of European security. The hetman was making an attempt to correct this historic mistake and save the country from ultimately perishing. A sombre silence reigned in the hall, for no one dared be the first to speak.

Finally Indira Holembiyevska rose and, tidying her long, dark hair with the fingers of both hands, said, 'All of you know my view of the hetman. However, in this instance, I welcome his words and support him. It has long been necessary to do this, cease being "Asiope" and become a European country. I support this measure.' She was endowed with a deep, musical voice which moved many of those present. It seemed to them as if Indira were speaking personally to each of them. Haiduk saw for the first time, at close hand, the favourite of millions, 'Indi' as she was popularly known.

Boyaryn Mintimer Basmanov angrily pounded his staff and without rising from his throne, which had been carried into the situation room by his Guardians, hoarsely threw in his view, 'I am categorically against it. Uniting now with this Judeo-Christian pack of predators in its last agony is a crime and a betrayal of the YeDRON. I warn the hetman personally that you will bear personal responsibility for actions directed against our natural allies, our Slav-Muslim brothers.'

The hetman bore himself as if nothing had happened, not even blinking an eye, and astonishing Haiduk more than a little with his wise statesmanship and patience.

'Who else wants to speak?' asked K. D. Makhun.

Friedman rose, but did not remove his black hat before he spoke, 'I congratulate Your Excellency on taking such a wise step. The decision of Your Majesty will enter world history, for only by locating itself within the OGS can Ukraine rebuff the onslaught of the Horde and save Europe. Just as Kyiv-Rus saved Europe in the thirteenth century, draining the power of the Horde of Batii and the Golden Horde. I support this decision and within the scope of my modest possibilities will work for its realisation.'

The Minister of Foreign Affairs of Ukraine, Ruslan Foshchenko, demonstrated his marvellous diplomatic geo-political balance. He proposed a daring project for Ukraine's simultaneous entry to two organisations, the Union of States of the Horde and the Organisation for Global Security. This would, in his view, guarantee Ukraine that neither of these powerful blocks would intervene in its affairs. Haiduk looked with contempt at the dimples on Foshchenko's well-feed cheeks, imagining how Ukraine would be transformed by the combined power of both blocks into a blood-soaked field, a no-man's land where people could be murdered with impunity and new arms systems might be tested. Foshchenko's proposal was not even discussed.

The results of the Aeropagus vote, six to one in favour of joining the OGS, satisfied the hetman. The chance of entering world history at the gentle touch of Friedman's hand gratified the heart of the old captain.

The National Security Council confirmed Haiduk's authority to act as the hetman's personal representative at the summit of member states of the OGS in Athens. This caused consternation on the part of Foshchenko, but the NSC gave no heed to his concerns.

A resolution was also adopted which demanded the severest punishment for members of LUK, URA and others that incited hatred between different national and social groups, and destabilised the situation in the state.

The hetman, giddy with the support of the Aeropagus, concluded by reading aloud a decree which honoured M. Basmanov, R. Friedman and I. Kreyda with the Golden Mace adorned medal of the order of Bohdan Khmelnytsky. The decree likewise promoted Klynkevych to General and Haiduk to Lieutenant General. Although this unexpected promotion should have gratified Haiduk's self love, he listened sombrely to the hetman's greetings. He knew that this was payment for his silence, for agreeing to retract his letter, with its naively idiotic proposals for reforming the established order, to the hetman. The order of this state, rotten and denuded of hope. Its structure had been totally determined by the majority of people in this room and they would permit no changes.

The hetman invited everyone to supper in the banquet hall, which was decorated with frescoes on the theme of the life and the historic battles of Kyiv-Rus. Haiduk, feeling a sharp pang of loneliness, accepted the congratulations of the participants in the meeting, all the generals, counts, barons and other rulers of Ukraine. He cursed himself inwardly for his opportunism, his martinet-style military discipline, and envied the unknown authors of the letter that had appeared on the hetman's computer. Haiduk sat at the edge of the table, not far from the exit, so he could flee at the first opportunity. He thought of how Bozhena had pressed against him when she was trembling during the night.

'Ihor Petrovych, I want to make your acquaintance,' Indira Holembiyevska stood before him, smiling welcomingly. He stood and she proffered him a hand, which he kissed. 'I congratulate you on your promotion and wish you success in Athens. A lot depends on you,' she said, not releasing his hand. She appeared younger in close proximity than she did on the television screen, notwithstanding her full figure, and wore a long, black dress with a daringly revealing neckline.

Indira was the mother of four children. She was born in Kyiv-East, in a left bank district of poor barrack-style dwellings inhabited by emigrants from Asia. An area of wretchedly poor shops and squalid markets. The area was controlled by Vietnamese, Thai, Chinese and Korean street-gangs. Her mother was a refugee from the Punjab, who washed dishes in a Chinese restaurant. Her father was a poor serf from Brovary, who found employment in the Darnytsva computer repair workshop. The workshop began to flourish, thanks to Bohdan Holembiyevsky's facility for electronics, and extended its operations to the right bank area of Kyiv-West. On obtaining the right to travel freely to the right bank, Holembiyevsky arranged a place for the dark and beautiful Indi at the Bilyi Slon cyber-chess school. She performed brilliantly and graduated with a gold medal. Her parents expended all their savings to give her the best education possible.

Young Indi's political activism began in the most blighted districts of Kyiv-East with the organisation of mutual funds for women from India, Pakistan and Bangladesh. These provided micro-credit to working women, allowing them to develop small workshops, canteens and cooperatives. The young leader of the black and minority ethnic community was soon elected to the regional council of Kyiv-East. She became renowned for her fiery speeches in defence of immigrants and was elected to parliament. Every other aspect of her career was generated by her blazing energy, her imagination, and the teamwork of her political consultants. Millions of people began chanting her name at political meetings.

'Goodbye, Lieutenant General, and please, let's meet up sometime.' She finally withdrew her warm hand and, tidying her dark hair, headed for the exit, accompanied by two muscular bodyguards. Her forehead was marked with the crimson circle of the Bindi at the top of the bridge of her nose where her brows met.

The fresco beneath which Haiduk sat as he quaffed *horilka* depicted Princess Olha and her vengeance on the Slavic tribe of the Drevlians who had slain her husband. When she had received a gift of doves, one from every dwelling, from the hated town where they had lived, she ordered that clumps of straw be tied to the birds and set on fire when they were freed. The fresco showed the birds bearing fire as they returned home, setting their native dwelling on fire. Olha was wearing dark robes and the light cast by the flames shone on her face. Something about her reminded Haiduk of Indira Holembiyevska, whose Ukrainian surname, which echoed the word for dove, fitted her, for she was, he thought, the dove of peace.

52

Haiduk returned home in the middle of the night when it was almost 02:00 and Bozhena was asleep. He changed his clothes and went to the kitchen, switched on the light and extracted a bottle of whisky from the closet. He also opened the fridge and selected some home-made Kamyanets Podilsky sausage, smoked to the point of blackness, which Nevinchanyi had brought back for him. He filled his plate with onion, cucumber and tomato, and sliced some bread. He felt hungry, lonely and frustrated. He poured out a glass of whisky and silently uttered a toast in his thoughts, cheers, two-star fucking lieutenant general. He gulped the bitter liquid, which immediately soothed his spirit. Haiduk considered the ineffective sitting of the NSC, a parody of a genuine statesman-like, responsible discussion of burning problems, the lack of desire on the part of that pack of traitors to contradict the hetman at present, the unexpected death of President Van Lee, and the new president, Shirley Van Lee. Had he really loved her once or was all of it just nonsense? After the second slug of whisky everything receded significantly into the distance, becoming a mirage, a chimera akin to the blue-winged butterfly he had seen once in the aquarium on the island.

He went to bed and slept immediately, falling into a darkness, as if someone had just flicked a switch, and woke when something tickled his nose. It was Bozhena's hair, she had lain alongside him, filling his body with a soothing warmth. He felt her hair carefully, tracing her nose and lips with his finger, which she kissed.

'Mr General, are you drunk?' she asked, her voice quivering with laughter.

'Yes, I am,' he replied, kissing her nose.

'What's the occasion?' she asked. 'Have you conquered the Horde?'

'I have conquered my fear of the Horde. Don't you want

to eat?'

'No. Auntie Martha sends you her greetings and says that you can meet Shirley in Athens.'

'Hang on, we didn't agree this.'

She took his hand from her breasts, rolled onto her back and placed it on her stomach so his palm nestled against the soft, short hair of her pubis. 'Just lay there calmly as you are now,' she whispered, 'don't hurry.'

He froze, tensed and held his left hand on her stomach, and felt a wave of heat surge through his fingers. For a moment he turned off his consciousness, becoming a part of that warm field that billowed between him and Bozhena. Then he realised he was falling down as Bozhena slipped off the settee, laughing and drawing him onto the rug with her. When he recovered, he was dazzled by the light where Bozhena lay because her naked body seemed to glow, as if radiating a soft fluorescence from a hidden light source. He could not recollect when he had undressed her. Haiduk felt that he had never seen anything more miraculous or beautiful. This was a mystical event, this illumination, a rarity even for a woman who had visited Mars, such a thing as may happen only once in a person's lifetime.

He leaned over and began kissing her body, but when he tried to enter her she cried in pain and wept. Turning onto her belly she sobbed bitterly and, confused, he smoothed her hair, not knowing how to calm her.

53

27 June 2077
Secret
To: His Excellency the Hetman of Ukraine General Kuzma-Danylo Makhun

Your Excellency
I recommend for your consideration, a recording of the

words spoken by a citizen of the Confederation of States of North America, Bozhena O'Connell (born in 2051), who has embarked on an intimate relationship with your majesty's adviser on national security issues, Lieutenant General I. P. Haiduk. The recording, which was made on the night of 26 June 2077 in I. P. Haiduk's apartment, has not only private but also public interest and affects the state. It illustrates, in my view, how dangerous this relationship may become in the event of its further development.

All the recorded words of I. P. Haiduk have been deleted from the text in accord with Hetman Decree UH-088/2068 regarding the non-audio surveillance of civil servants of the highest rank.

Director of the State Guard of Ukraine - Yulii Merezhko.
Hetman's decision to acquaint I. O. Kreyda and V. Klynkevych with the material.

Text of the recording:
'So, this is what they did to me. They inserted a thick wire into my vagina and passed an electric current through it. It was unbelievably painful, I screamed out. Then they passed an electric current through my head, and tried to drown me in a bath. I blacked out and dreamed only of one thing - death. This all happened on the Mansfield Airbase where I stopped with you, do you remember? (…) They accused me of breaking the Confederation law about public morals and the healthy development of the nation. Under this law, sexual relations between a man and a woman are only permitted if the age difference between them is no greater than twenty years. How old are you? Fifty? And I am twenty-six. According to this law we are criminals, your age is four years above the permitted limit. And if you reach ninety years you only have the right to love women no younger than seventy. (…) The authors of this law

had supposedly noble ideas: these crazed neoconservatives and theologians wanted to bring back biblical times when families had seven or eight children, when there weren't so many openly gay people, so many break ups and new relationships between older and younger men and women (…) Have you really never heard about this law? Well, because it failed right from the start it could not, a priori, be implemented. They added a load of addenda, amendments and reservations, a load of legal hooks, and the law was stillborn. But … the thing was that the government of the Confederation used this law against me and Dick Stone. Have you heard that name, Dick Stone? (…) Yes, yes it's him. In his time known all over the world as a hero of the Confederation and humanity. The first person who stepped onto the surface of Mars in 2053, about the time I was born. Do you remember his first words? "I am that earthly stone from which we will begin building a new Mars." He was the same age as you are now, fifty, when he became the first ambassador of humanity on Mars. You would have been twenty-six then and you probably well remember what happened on the earth after the successful return of the American expedition to Mars. When I was at college I wrote a historical research paper on this theme and studied all the video and print sources. There was nobody on earth more popular than Dick Stone. A three star general, the director of NASA's Martian programmes, the manager of the first military space base on Mars. He was awarded the title of Star of Humanity from the hand of the general secretary of the UN, dozens of honours from various countries … streets and squares on every continent were named Stone in his honour … an avalanche of glory had fallen on him … however, he survived all this. It didn't break him. Later in his life he told me that when he was on Mars he realised something which changed his views of life, death and so-called glory … Try to do that once more … only gently. Yes. Yes! Yes!!! (…) I was so afraid that I would never, never feel this … (…) In seventy-five I was sent, as a young analyst in the Mars legion, to the Phoenix Base. The commander was Dick Stone. I was twenty-four, he was seventy-two. He had already fallen out of favour, for some reason they didn't love him in Washington and being on Mars was an honourable exile for Dick. The base was old, its operational life would have to end in a few years, and the mines for the extraction of strategic metals were located far away from us at the Mariner Base. There were seven of us, four men and three women. We lived in those squalid cisterns that are called modules. I remember the crackle of the meteorites landing on them. (…) I was so scared. At first they paid absurdly good money and I am now rich. You wouldn't believe how crazily beautiful the colours of the sky are when the sun rises. There are pinks, reds, and a violet nimbus around the sun itself. There is nothing in existence more beautiful in this world. (…) Yes, I was in love with Dick. There was no one closer to me in the whole world … no, not because he was a hero and a world star, although perhaps this played a part and flattered my ego, but this was not the main thing. My duties included securing analytical information for Dick Stone and executing his directives (…). Within a few months I was madly in love with him and he with me. He had a large family back on earth, a wife whom he loved, but earthly rules didn't apply on Mars … I only had Auntie Martha and Askold, I was free and had no obligations to anyone. Yes, just here … how good that feels (…) Of course they all knew about it. But everyone had their own plans, their own contracts; no one wanted to interfere in any one else's business, particularly that of the base commander. However, in seventy-six, Major William Crawford arrived as a replacement for one of the officers. His nickname is 'Butcher Bill'. Do you remember that we met him before we came to Kyiv (…) He immediately cast his eyes at me and for him that meant he had to get his claws into me. During one of his repeated attempts to fuck me I kicked him, probably broke

250

his balls (laughs). Not long after that a commission came from the Central Security Service to examine me and Dick Stone. The accusations were terrible (indistinguishable whisper). Have you ever heard about this? (…) Do they bug your flat? (…) Don't be so sure of yourself. They arrested us and took us back to earth. The last time I saw Dick was when we were in chains and red jump suits, like the last prisoners being taken out of the ship's brig. (weeps) (…) They took me to the Mansfield Airbase and Dick to the most terrible military prison in the state of Utah. The whole case was framed as a violation of the law on public morals. But what really bothered them was something else … what happened (indistinguishable whisper). Did you never hear about this? (…) I understood that if I gave up Dick and admitted that I knew the whole story they would kill me immediately and Dick as well (…) I don't know. They told me that Dick had admitted everything and denounced me, but I don't believe that. I loved him. (weeps) I wanted to have a child with him … but after the torture I can't have children. (weeps) Excuse me, I shouldn't be saying this when things are so good with you. (…) Martha told me that Dick Stone died and they buried him quietly at Arlington Cemetery (weeps) with no honours and no reports in the press. America's best son, who was only killed because he didn't want to hand over (indistinguishable), they crippled me … and you like a country like that? (…) But your country is no better. (…) You would have seen what goes on in the ZEK, how people are afraid to say a word out of place … they are scared of squealers, the elders, the administration. They are scared and they hate them. You know what they say about your beloved hetman, this fool from the operettas. (…) Okay, okay, I won't. Put your hand here. Lower. Yes. How good that feels, Jesus, as if I am alive again.'

54

The huge, old pine, a child of Stalin's long-ago five year plans, hung above the lake and gripped the edge of a hillock occupied by an ant hill. A portion of the grey roots, twisted like wire cables, hung in the air and promised the tree a death by hunger. Directly below the hillock, on a little sandy beach, Haiduk and Bozhena were alone together. The lake, which belonged to the vast water system of the Dnipro, seemed empty. There were no structures on the opposite bank, which was overgrown with oak. There were no shrieks from holidaymakers or fat, middle-aged ladies in electric-blue swimsuits washing greasy saucepans or sooted kettles in the water. There were no fishermen in boats to be seen on the water-lily overgrown inlets. There were no inquisitive citizens or noisy tourists at the lake because it was surrounded by barbed wire and an inscription on a sign to the effect that it was a 'Forbidden Zone'. This was the training camp of UMI special forces, where elite units, such as Hrim and Blyskavka, trained in the quietest and most effective ways of destroying people and overcoming water damage. Other skills acquired here included the conduct of storm operations at night, undertaking lightning attacks and parachuting from terrapins.

However, a hetman decree had pronounced the last Sunday of June an official holiday for airborne and special forces. The majority of troops were granted two-days leave and only a small number of them remained on duty. That was why the Rohulka, as this lake had long been known, now belonged to silence, fir trees, oaks and the sun.

For a long time they did not release their embrace of each other, then they threw themselves into the water, trying to find some cool current in its warm, wide expanse. They sunbathed, inhaled the rich air, redolent of fir trees, and succumbed again to their embraces, feeling like this was the happiest day of their lives and such days would be no more. They waited for a long time for the broth to be ready. Haiduk breathed on the logs, which barely glimmered, and wafted sparks on his face, tasting the deep, bitter flavour of smoke. Bozhena pressed against him, her bright eyes glittering with tears from happiness, or the fumes. Sipping the salted broth, she told him that which she had not managed to tell him the night when she was whispering crazy secrets about the Martian expedition into his ear. He had laughed as she whispered, because she tickled his ear, and he did not understand what she was talking about.

During Bozhena's Martian trip, when old Dick Stone had almost gone crazy with happiness, there was one time when a sandstorm had begun and the red tornado tried, with all its fury, to destroy the modules of the Phoenix Base, and depression seized all its personnel. Dick had embraced her, like Haiduk was embracing her now, and then the old astronaut shared with her a secret known only to him. During the first expedition to the Red Planet, Stone and two other astronauts had found a warehouse with the Martian weaponry that had caused the civilisation of the planet to perish. This weaponry destroyed water.

'Water?' Haiduk did not understand and set aside the bowl with the, as yet, too hot broth as he spoke.

'Water,' confirmed Bozhena. 'Judging by everything he knew, it was thanks to this weaponry that the Martian hydrosphere disappeared. This happened, probably, instantaneously or the surface of Mars would not have retained its dry river beds, canyons and the banks of reservoirs with an almost intact appearance.'

'And what happened later?'

'Later? Eek, this is disgusting,' said Bozhena, pouring away the broth, 'you've messed that up. I told you not to salt it so much. What's up with you, are you in love?'

'Don't deflect us onto trivial matters,' he said, kissing

her.

'Then his fellow astronauts perished on Mars and Stone told no one of that cave where they had found the stock of weaponry. He was afraid these arms might be used on earth. Imagine if this lake disappeared and left just a deep black hole, then the Dnipro and Mississippi and then the seas and oceans ... Let's go into the water ...'

When they were in the lake she embraced him and continued. 'However, the rumour of some terrible Martian weaponry got out. Maybe one of the astronauts managed to tell someone about it before they died ... or Crawford managed to sniff something ... or Stone had said something to his family or friends after he had returned from the expedition. Those who tortured me at the Mansfield Airbase were only interested in that weapon. They knew almost nothing about it, its characteristics or the principles of its construction. "What do you know about the weaponry?" they asked. "And where on Mars is it concealed?" '

'And do you know?' Haiduk plunged and, grabbing Bozhena's legs, tried to tickle her heels. Bozhena began to beat the water with her arms, like a bird taking off, and laughed. She slipped out of his embrace and pushed her face close to him. Her eyes appeared white, only the small dots of her pupils defined her gaze. Bubbles streamed from her nose and mouth and her auburn hair strayed in all directions.

She nodded firmly, 'Yes, I know.'

They burst onto the surface in yells and laughter and lay on their backs, undulating gently on the waves, in the shadow of the fir trees. Then they silently stepped back onto the sand and dressed.

A point from some secret report about the manufacture of new weapons at Churchill, Canada, drifted through Haiduk's mind. It was completely possible, however, that this project had no connection to Mars.

55

THE HAIDUK FILE
23 June 2077
Top Secret (One Copy)
To the Adviser to the Hetman of Ukraine on National Security Issues, Secretary of the NSC of Ukraine - Lieutenant General I. P. Haiduk

Operational character report on Ivan Ovramovych Kreyda, citizen of Ukraine, member of the Aeropagus of Ukraine, Warlord of Kyiv, Cherkassy, Makhnograd, Poltava, Podil, Count of Luxembourg, President and Executive Director of the Central Energy-Industrial Territory, Governor of Slobozhanshchyna, General Co-ordinator of the Kyiv-Rus Internet Network, Chancellor and Full Member of the Ukrainian and Russian Academy of Sciences, Honorary Doctor at the Kara-Khan Human Rights Academy (Chyngiz-Saray), President of SUKA, General Prosecutor of Ukraine, Marshall of Jurisprudence, owner of the 'Bad News' channel, presenter of the 'Power of the Law' programme.

Kreyda was born on 13 March 2017 in Poltava and completed a course for rural accountants; he then attended catering college and specialised in making *halushky*. He embarked on his first business at the age of 15, when he purchased a dumpling manufacturing machine at Kemerovo (Russia) and converted it for the production of *halushky* and *varenyky*. Not wishing to pay tax, Kreyda opened an underground workshop for the manufacture of *halushky* at the pig farm owned by his father, Ovram Musiyovych Kreyda. He employed fifteen Vietnamese workers, who lived on the farm in inhuman conditions.

Being distinguished with renowned gifts in the area of illegal business, the HaV firm has been one of the five most profitable companies in Ukraine since 2038. For the first time in the history of Ukrainian *halushky* and *varenyky* manufacture, he embarked on the production of alcoholic and narcotic variations of these foodstuffs - the so-called 'Jolly *Halushky*' and '*Halushky* Fantasy'. These varieties were hugely popular among the youth, and *varenyky* with cognac and liqueurs became a novelty on the provisions markets of Ukraine and Europe.

In 2040 Kreyda's personal fortune was assessed as one billion ameros, and the equity in his HaV firm had peaked at a high level on the London Stock Exchange. During this period his competitors disappeared one by one. They were murdered, vanished without a trace, or imprisoned. The journalist, Yu. Andronov, who researched Kreyda's criminal operations was killed by employees of the Poltava police force's criminal investigation unit. His manuscript disappeared without a trace. UMI's experts have succeeded, with great difficulty, in using the remains of the shattered computer to recreate the text of the manuscript (see annexes I-VII).

Having monopolised Ukraine's large-scale commercial manufacture of *halushky* and *varenyky* in 2043, I. O. Kreyda decided to occupy himself with politics. Transferring the ownership of his HaV firm to his older brother, Petro Kreyda, I. O. Kreyda, who had already bought a graduate diploma for the Judicial Faculty of the Kremenchuk Higher School of the State Guard (then the Interior Ministry Forces) founded the Marxist Ukrainian Democratic Association (MUDA). He stood for parliament in the name of this party and, after being elected, was appointed as head of the committee for the development of Ukraine's energy and industrial sectors. From 2046 to 2070 he was a permanent member of the parliament, initially in the Commons, then in the Employers' Chamber and, from 2054, a member of the Senate. Utilising the money earned from the sale of *halushky* and *varenyky*, I. O. Kreyda, via corporate raids undertaken by the legal firm, Tsezar, which he owns, seized the industrial and energy complex of the central area - twelve nuclear and thirty-two thermo-electric stations. This manoeuvre allowed him to become one of the largest exporters of electricity to Europe. I. O. Kreyda subsequently purchased a steel plant in Luxembourg and immediately built the largest casino in Europe at the site, opening therein a special room for suicides, with a complete selection of the implements clients would require to take their own life. The Supreme Court of Human Rights in Europe recognised the entitlement of Kreyda to organise these services on European territory. The popularity of these facilities, which began to appear on the territory of North America and China, stimulated one hundred and thirty-two series of the 'Terminal' television series, filmed with funds provided by I. O. Kreyda.

He is regarded as a theorist of the Ukrainian question and has published numerous works. His books unite elements of Marxist and Nazi doctrines, with the newer approach of neo-market theory, which views the individual as a market product.

He has promulgated a theory based on defending the population from information, which undermines trust in the fairness of the state structure of Ukraine and the permanence of the existing order. He heads a corporation for the defence of the internet from the ruinous influence of liberal, democratic ideas.

Kreyda has developed a theory of the positive influence of 'Bad News' on society, arguing that information about catastrophes, deaths and scenes of violence compels the citizen to evaluate the reality of their life and take delight in their existence in everyday mundanity, however unpleasant it may be - see I. O. Kreyda's book *Taming Society* (2072). After the publication of his work, *The Death Sentence as the Highest Form of State Liberty* (2068) he was appointed General Prosecutor of Ukraine and awarded the title Marshall of Jurisprudence.

In 2070 he organised the USRAS (the Ukrainian Section of the Russian Academy of Sciences), becoming its professor and chancellor. He facilitated the transfer to Kyiv of the fundamental elements of the Russian Academy of Sciences, and its full and corresponding members are allocated a monthly ration of *halushky* and *varenyky*. The research of USRAS has found that ethnic Ukrainians are Sub-Russians and are distinguished by certain regressive characteristics from Full-Russians. Kreyda's research on this theme contained in the text *From Sub-Russians to Full-Russians: problems and perspectives* (2073) is considered the last word in state policy on the national question.

Thanks to his personal connections with the punitive organs of the Horde, he has free access to sources of narcotics supply from Afghanistan. These substances, after undergoing the necessary processing at the scientific research chemistry centre operating under the roof of the HaV company, are distributed in the West via the 'Terminal' network of I. O. Kreyda. The distribution and transport of depressive and suicide stimulating narcotics, particularly 'Halloween', undertaken outside Ukraine, is directed by Kreyda's nephew, V. M. Kreyda. According to intelligence sources, V. M. Kreyda has established a close relationship with one of the most powerful Mexican drug cartels headed by Jose Sapaterro. There is also unconfirmed information regarding the cooperation between I. O. Kreyda and the NOP pharmaceutical company, which belongs to the husband of Confederation Vice-President Sara Lou Lane. UMI analysts also draw attention to the fact that I. O. Kreyda, exploiting the economic difficulties of Greece, purchased the island of Karpathos in the Aegean Sea (its new name is Kreydos). It is now practically impossible to gain access to the territory of the island. The Sich-77 satellite has recorded intensive construction work on the island, the character of which is not understood. In May this year a UMI agent, with the code name 'Poseidon', succeeded in penetrating the island in the guise of a builder (see his report, addenda VIII-IX).

I. O. Kreyda is married with three children and is an

exemplary family man. He loves Ukrainian folk music and plays the accordion and tambourine. He has one of the best collections of Ukrainian icons and paintings of the baroque era.

Senior Analyst Maximilian-IV

56

On 2 July, on the eve of his flight to Athens, Haiduk gathered a council of UMI's executive leaders, which was held on the island in what was known as the 'Submarine Kingdom'. The reinforced glass of a huge aquarium served for one of the walls of this subterranean chamber, which was theoretically impossible to bug. The wall revealed the magic sub-aqueous world of the Red Sea. Fish of an unearthly beauty, decanting all the colours of the rainbow, swam among coral reefs in the transparent sunlight-infused water. They seemed like toys rather than living things. Hryhoriy Nevinchanyi, as manager of M-Division, which secured UMI's material and technical needs, was exceptionally proud of this window into another, happier, paradisiacal and unreachable world. The idea of an aquarium and its realisation alike belonged to him.

Haiduk's deputies appeared at the meeting; the director of his office, the bosses of nine directorates and six services, the commanders of the Hrim and Blyskavka special units, and Dmytro Mochalkin, the interpreter. The only absentees were the commanders of the Muslim special groups. The senior analysts of UMI, the numerous Maximilians, who Haiduk particularly valued, also attended. The new manager of the second scientific and technical directorate, which until recently had been led by Haiduk, had not yet been appointed.

The manager of the first directorate, which was responsible for global strategic analysis and prognoses, Colonel Kyreyko, wearing a white suit and his unchanging bow tie, bore more resemblance to a professor of law at Harvard University's Kyiv branch than a soldier. He was, as always, cautious; as if afraid that his prognoses might be realised and result in irreversible changes in world history. He discussed the possible decisions that might be taken at the OGS summit in Athens and their effect on the course of global events. He even compared the summit with the Yalta Conference attended by Churchill, Roosevelt and Stalin in 1944.

Haiduk looked at the officers, who were lost in concentration within their laptop screens, and asked himself who among them represented the all powerful Grey Prince? Who were the members of the Grey Brigades that tormented this unfortunate country? He knew all who had gathered here today, they were the brain and soul of a military intelligence service. He would be able to vouch for each of them. Would be able to and would do so were it not for the dark fissures of the human spirit.

It was not in vain that the consultant psychoanalyst of UMI, Professor Weber, spoke of the three levels of human consciousness. There was the human, the most fragile and flimsy, the avian, and then the lowest, the still undestroyed crocodilian. This reptilian element of the psyche would transform the most spiritually and morally developed being into a merciless predator who would look unblinkingly on their prey, wait for a moment to pounce, then tear and carve them up. Then, having barely cleaned their fangs from fresh blood, they would play to the television cameras and declaim about patriotism and service to the country.

Haiduk recollected Viktor Bezpalii, who had seemed honest and above board, but had for some reason become a traitor. He sighed heavily and compelled himself to return his attention to the council. The manager of the sixth directorate, which was responsible for special operations, Colonel Semyhlazov, a former military attaché in Moscow, complained about N-Division (responsible for illegal operations). They had not prepared false documents for the Turkish group. He also berated E-Division (special electronic operations) because Major Stryhun's merry hackers had not given the commander of the Greek group the codes necessary for the conduct of the operation.

Notwithstanding the discussion of particular technical details, the core of Operation Achilles Heel and its end goal was not revealed. Haiduk took personal responsibility for the conduct of this operation and had not cleared it with the hetman or the State Guard. In the event of failure, a death sentence awaited him, and in the event of victory ... He did not know what he would do.

After the council, he invited them all to stay to celebrate his new rank. Hryhoriy Nevinchanyi transformed the meeting room into a banqueting hall. The manager of the seventh directorate, the agent networks, approached Haiduk. Colonel Nazarovna was an unremarkable looking, middle-aged woman. She whispered to him that they had received a report from Agent Poseidon confirming that preparations for the operation were fully complete.

Haiduk greatly respected this quiet woman, who gave the appearance of being naive and narrow minded, but who was distinguished by a deeply analytical intelligence and a brilliant facility for recruiting agents. She was renowned for the occasion when, as UMI's resident in Europe and working for a bogus firm in Brussels, she entered the men's room of the OGS. The Deputy of the Commander of the Mediterranean Section of the OGS Forces, French Admiral Jean Duval, was washing his hands in there and she managed to recruit him in four minutes by showing the confused naval officer some photos and handing him a packet of 50,000 globos. It was Jean Duval who was now assisting UMI to conduct this operation in the Aegean Sea.

Nevinchanyi fetched a huge, crystal flower vase, threw

in the general's stars and began to fill the huge goblet with nine big black bottles of Crimean 'champagne'. After the tedium of the official, congratulatory speeches, addresses were given by Major General Ivanyshyn, Haiduk's first deputy, and Colonel Tsekhansky, who was the manager of the directorate for operational tactical intelligence. Then there was such celebration that within half an hour the vase was empty except for a little foam whispering alongside the general's stars.

Haiduk was moved when Dima Mochalkin presented him with a volume of Paul Celan's poems. He opened the book at random and read:

It's falling, Mother, snow in Ukraine …
The Saviour's crown, a thread of suffering …
My tears will no longer meet you.
All becomes a proud muteness …
What would have become of me, Mother, wakening or wound -
If I too had vanished in the snows of Ukraine?

Which one of you is betraying me? Haiduk thought, looking, as if for the first time, with new eyes at the officers who greeted him; just as sincerely as his colleagues at the bureau in Washington had greeted him on his birthday. Viktor Bezpalii, Kostya Slisarenko, Carl Thompson and Nicole Cohen - Which of you will stay with me to the end? Haiduk asked himself, saving the most important question for the last moments of his internal interrogation, and am I ready to travel to the end of this road?

A humorous moment accompanied the consumption of coffee and Kyiv torte. A grey-black shark appeared from nowhere and made the little fish flee like a flock of frightened birds and hide among the coral reefs. The shark, flying from the depths of the aquarium, struck its head against the glass and opened its maw to display rows of sharp fangs. Even the well-trained intelligence officers flinched momentarily, discomforted by this sudden attack. Nevinchanyi's guffaws dispelled the tension as they realised this was yet another prank from the veteran intelligence officer. He had installed an electronic model to remind his officer colleagues of the dangers that stalked them at every turn, so they did not lower their guard ... Even on this hot summer day, sultry lethargy did not penetrate here, twenty metres below ground.

When they had dispersed and Nevinchanyi and Dima Mochalkin were clearing away the aftermath of the festivities, Haiduk requested that David Beylin be brought to see him. Beylin was currently based on the island awaiting further orders from AMAN and UMI.

Haiduk loathed July, which had become for him the most dangerous month of the year. It was the month when his father had died, the Third World War had commenced, and storm squads of EnROS troops had attacked Kyiv. The world's greatest catastrophes were all scheduled for July. The deadline for his reply to Friedman would expire in two days, and in July, in Athens, the fate of Ukraine would be determined. Would the country, like Russia, be dismembered by the geo-political butchers and, like a stripped carcass, be thrown to the birds by its treacherous rulers.

Beylin entered and blinked his auburn lashes inquiringly.

'David, you are the only one I can say this to,' Haiduk paused, as if hesitating and wondering whether to trust this man whose parents had worked with his own father at the Antonov factory. He decided, finally, to make his request, 'In the event of some ... emergency situation ... I ask you to please take my mother to Poland.' He sent an encoded signal with Marek Horol's Polish address and all the necessary email contacts for this task to Beylin's gadget.

David was in no way surprised by Haiduk's request. On the contrary, he understood immediately and examined the information; he did not ask any unnecessary questions.

'And just one more thing,' Haiduk said, 'please help Bozhena O'Connell if needs be. This girl, an American, lives with me.'

The next batch of information was dispatched to Beylin's gadget.

'I will do everything you ask. May I go now?' David squeezed Haiduk's hand tightly as they shook hands in farewell and, retaining his grip for a few seconds, said, 'I didn't murder that girl ... Nicole Cohen. I gave her a narcotic. They framed me.'

When he was on his own Haiduk sat motionlessly for a long time, looking at the calendar and studying the schedule for July; the plan of a future as yet illegible to everyone. He thought that it was not a fake shark, who had peered through the aquarium glass, but the Grey Prince come to overlook his demesne.

57

The summit in Athens was held eighty kilometres from the heavily built-up Greek capital, with its toxic smog. The Greek government could not guarantee the security of the heads of forty-seven states and governments, the numerous members of delegations, their protection units and journalists in Athens. The citizens of this city below the mountains were plagued with heat, along with water and fuel shortages and permanent crises. They had no desire to leave even the leadership of their own country in peace and regularly arranged riots and revolutions. It had therefore been decided that this summit of the leaders of states within the Organisation for Global Security, from the Confederation of States of North America to Australia, would be held on the Island of Euboea. The island, which was located near the shores of Attica, resembled a long fish warming itself in the clement waters near a familiar rocky coast. The authorities had decided to divide the island, which was firmly yoked to the continent by bridges over the Euripus Strait, into two sections. The north section, which was left untouched, and the south section, from the town of Chalcis to the Kolpos Bay, which was handed over to the authority of the OGS and transformed into a closed zone. This section had undergone a thorough overhaul in preparation for an event of this magnitude; a new road network was constructed, tunnels excavated, an OGS palace was built, along with fifty separate residences, a bespoke airport and five sea terminals. The area was guarded by twelve thousand OGS police and troops.

Haiduk flew to the island of Euboea on 4 July, along with Ukraine's Chief Military Otaman, the Defence Minister, Lieutenant Colonel Petro Ivanovych Pryadko, and members of the delegation, including various aides and experts. They flew in the hetman's AN-270, the hold of which held containers designed to be habitable for human beings while resembling ordinary cargo carriers. A special forces unit consisting of fifteen people hid in these vessels. The troops had been assigned to participate in Operation Achilles Heel. Two military terrapins were already located in the area of Avlos village, where the residence of the Ukrainian delegation was situated. The containers, which, according to the official itemisation, contained food, water and equipment for the needs of the delegation, were delivered there.

The divine, dry heat of Greece wafted softly over Haiduk and his subordinates as they left the plane. The herbs and grass surrounding the landing strip filled the air with countless aromas. A high, craggy mountain, bathed in blue and rose tones, which marbled its form, pierced the sky not far from the airport. It was pleasant and easy to breathe in this balmy air, notwithstanding the temperature of 45°C. Having passed through the border, the larger part of the delegation went to the Avlos residence. Haiduk, Hryhoriy Nevinchanyi, Dima

Mochalkin and the head of the protection unit, Tengiz, took an open-top electronic jeep. It was pale blue, displayed the symbols of the OGS and was reminiscent of the Willis jeep from World War Two. They headed for the village of Eretria near where the palace of the OGS was constructed on the shore.

They were not allowed on the main road, which was reserved for VIPs, and this compelled them to travel by the side roads. Haiduk turned his attention to how the defence of this section of the island was organised. At every ten metres along the sides of the main road, which was constructed above the sea, stood gendarmes from the united OGS police force. They wore white Kevlar helmets and dark grey, bullet-proof vests, and held M-32 laser-assisted, automatic rifles. Helicopters hovered above the road with snipers, their legs dangling in the air, scanning for potential terrorists, which meant anyone without a special badge emitting an authorisation signal. The signal code changed automatically every four hours.

Haiduk noted that the system of defence appeared very showy. However, the Kevlar helmets, bullet-proof vests and ineffective M-32 automatics were long out of date. UMI's special units were armed with far superior weapons. Simultaneously, he reflected, with some relief, that such showy activity from the defence units on the western coast of the island would make it far easier to conduct Operation Achilles Heel on the eastern shore where the Ukrainian delegation was situated.

After they had travelled eight kilometres from Eretria, the new arrivals from Kyiv saw a dazzlingly white palace, executed in an unusual architectural style, in the foothills of the mountains. The building resembled a huge seashell, fashioned from white and pink marble. It was surrounded by four towers, white as snow, with dark blue and crimson domes, like fragmentary portions of Greek Orthodox cathedrals. The towers resembled the four compass points on the emblem of the OGS.

A nervous atmosphere reigned in the secretariat of the summit. Young diplomats bustled around with stony faces and gave the impression of being very busy; secretaries ran from one end of the hall to the other. They were in Greek chitons and lightened the atmosphere in a room filled with sombre male bigwigs in black coats and generals in blue, green and yellow uniforms. Haiduk and his subordinates were looking at the dark-haired Grecian secretaries when a fair-haired American approached, smiled amicably and greeted them. It was the aide to Martha Jefferson, who Shirley Van Lee had appointed national security adviser three days previously. Defence Minister Oliver Brown had become acting vice-president.

'Do you remember me?' Martha's aide said, smiling broadly. 'I accompanied you in the limousine. Mrs Jefferson is waiting for you. Please come with me.'

They went to an adjoining hall, divided into rows of cabins, where bi-lateral delegation meetings were being held. Leaving Nevinchanyi and Mochalkin in the main hall, Haiduk stepped into a cabin, which bore more than a passing resemblance to a movie actor's trailer. Martha Jefferson was waiting for him. She seemed thinner and more faded since the time when they had last met, but her eyes, the dark cherries of her eyes, lush and intoxicating, shone as youthfully as in Washington. The comical grey plaits he remembered were nowhere to be seen.

After Haiduk had closed the door, Martha approached him and kissed him twice, looking into his face. He knew what her first question would be, but remained silent. They sat at the meeting table and Martha laid her hands on its cold aluminium surface, hands that were far older than her eyes.

'Where is Bozhena?' she asked.

'She didn't come with me.'

'You left her at the residence?' Martha did not understand him correctly.

'No, she remained in Kyiv.'

'In Kyiv?' Martha asked, nervously flexing her fingers like a pianist warming up before a concert. 'What's up, is she ill? What has happened? She didn't say anything to me.'

Haiduk remained silent.

'Just tell me the truth,' Martha Jefferson asked him plaintively. 'We had certainly agreed, you promised ...'

'I love Bozhena,' said Haiduk firmly, as if someone were arguing with him.

Martha Jefferson looked at him as if he were deranged.

'I love her and she loves me. She has decided to remain in Kyiv.'

'But we had agreed,' said Martha, her fingers tracing mechanical circles on the table's silver surface. 'How has this happened? I have no one apart from her. Understand this, she wanted to get out of Ukraine and asked me to help. And now ...'

Haiduk could bear it no longer and laid his heavy hand over Martha's fingers. 'Forgive me for not warning you. I didn't stop her from coming, on the contrary, I tried to persuade her to come with me. It is such an occasion ... but, honestly speaking, I'm glad she stayed behind.'

Martha took her hands from the table and, as if the conversation had not happened, crossed out some part of herself and in a dry, estranged voice said, 'In the name of the President of the Confederation, Mrs Shirley Van Lee, I wish to hand you the preliminary agreed proposals of the OGS for the leadership of Ukraine.' She handed him a memory stick; it was tiny, yet it bore so much information. The pale blue exterior was adorned with the emblem of the Organisation for Global Security. 'The president has scheduled your meeting for the day after tomorrow at 17:00, for half an hour. At 18:00 she will be flying back to Washington. She anticipates that you will study the document and be able to provide, if not a final answer, an expression of the acceptability or unacceptability of these

268

proposals. However, time demands swift decisions.'

'As you understand, I do not have the authority to make decisions. However, I promise that, as soon as possible, I will acquaint the leadership of Ukraine with the proposals of the OGS.' Haiduk felt as if he spoke with an alien voice.

Martha Jefferson rose from the table, followed by Haiduk, who stood for a moment with his head lowered and tried not to meet the gaze of this woman in her official suit of dark grey linen. He noticed some ancient coral beads, dark with time, hanging lower down on her wrinkled neck. Bozhena had told him the tale of this necklace, which had been borne to the States, having been taken from a village in Volyn in 1942.

He was deafened for a moment. A powerful system to block audio surveillance had begun to operate in the cabin and Martha's words reached him through the pounding of heavy electric impulses.

'If you loved her, you would get her out of Ukraine as quickly as possible. You and Bozhena are at risk because you are playing with fire. Unfortunately, Mr Haiduk,' she ceased using his first name, 'you bring grief to women. Shirley had to marry that yellow douche bag because she was pregnant by you … and that poor Puerto Rican … what was she called … Linda, died for no reason at all … and now Bozhena.' She threw open the doors of the cabin as if to assure herself they were not being eavesdropped and saw that there was no one standing outside.

58

4 July 2077
16:00
Containing the highest category of state secrets. To be delivered immediately and personally to His Excellency, the Hetman of Ukraine, General Kuzma-Danylo Makhun.

The Adviser to the President of the Confederation on National Security issues, M. Jefferson, has handed official proposals from the Organisation for Global Security to our representative, for the Ukrainian leadership's consideration. (See the annexes for the full text.) The following of the document's main provisions require attention:

1. In the event of the UMCS leadership's agreement, Ukraine will be fast-tracked to acceptance in the OGS.
2. The Confederation of States of North America is prepared to relocate ten batteries of the tactical Revenger XI missile from the territories of Germany, Czech Republic, Poland and Romania to Ukraine, and two squadrons of F-160 fighter bombers, with appropriate personnel and the associated repair and maintenance infrastructure.
3. Romania categorically refuses to participate in any military assistance programme, insisting on the return of Bukovyna and Trans Dniester, and Moldova's exit from Ukraine's sphere of influence.
4. Poland has agreed to situate the Lech Wałęsa Rapid Reaction Force, consisting of five air-mobile brigades, on West Ukrainian soil.
5. Fortress Berlin proposes the Self-Security Police Force to bring order to the rear of the army.
6. The OGS (particularly the CSNA) proposes to issue a significant credit line (up to five hundred billion ameros) for the modernisation of Ukraine's military defence complex and equipping its armed forces with the most modern weapons systems.

The conditions presented by the OGS are as follows:
A legitimate decision from Ukraine on the basis of parliamentary law regarding its accession to the OGS (due within six days);
- the liquidation of Horde agents in the leadership structures of

the state, including the armed forces, State Guard and UMI. A list of enemy agents will be provided to Ukraine immediately following formal accession to the OGS;
- the signature of a secret treaty with the OGS regarding the securing of Ukrainian food produce for OGS countries, and the granting of access of the OGS logistics committee to the resources of the 'Magic Nine'.
- The democratisation of Ukraine and liquidation of the feudal oligarchic system of government (to be implemented in phases).

I await your answers I. P. Haiduk

59

The formal opening of the OGS summit was held the following day. A rectangular table, which would have filled a football pitch, had been set up in the huge marble meeting hall. The delegations of forty-seven countries' heads of state and governments, ministers of defence and foreign affairs took their seats around it, along with numerous military, economic and financial experts and intelligence and counter-intelligence representatives.

Haiduk and Pryadko, with their rights as observers, had been planted in a far corner, along with the delegations from Kurdistan and Equatorial Africa. The delegations took their places in a half light, assisted by young women with flashlights. However, the area in the centre of the hall was dazzlingly illuminated. The floodlit OGS emblem squatted on the floor, a blue square with the white contours of the globe of the world and four black and white-arrowed compass points. When all the delegates had taken their places, the emblem disappeared and the hall rang with the powerful, troubling music of Evangel Dionisos, a Greek composer of international renown who had authored the opera ballet Marathon. A group of young women in white tunics appeared on the podium, to be joined by children in brightly hued costumes, and they all swirled in a happy circle. A text glowed on four massive screens:

In 490 BC Eretria, on whose soil our summit is held, was a happy and free territory.

The troubled melody transformed into the harsh piercing signal that portended war. The participants of the summit flinched involuntarily when sinister black figures swooped low over them with a rustle of fabric. These aviators descended on the carefree dancers like modern day special forces dropping onto the ground from terrapins. The choir sang or perhaps shrieked a dissonant tragic cacophony, akin to women and children beseeching assistance. A new text appeared on the screen:

The invading forces of Persian Emperor Darius seized Eretria and burned it to the ground before beginning their advance towards the coastal area near the town of Marathon.

Greek youths in gold-coloured helmets and white chitons, with round, red shields and long spears lined up for battle, while the warriors of Darius's imperial army swirled in a black flock. Two pieces of contrasting music echoed in the hall of the OGS. The masterfully composed work of Evangel Dionisos, the ancient Greek melody of liberty, of the mountains and sea, played on sweetly sounding bouzouki, the melody of Sirtos, of the ancient dance where this civilisation began. This was followed by the vicious, primitive music of the dark invaders, composed of clashing swords and screaming horses. The stupefying clash of tympanum sounding like a whiplash.

The dark figures raised their bows and fired into the sun, which appeared to rise above those in the hall, and the silver sheaf of arrows flew to meet the solar light. The battle began, accompanied by a new text on the screens:

On 12 September 490 BC the battle, near Marathon, which would become one of the ten most significant in history, commenced. This was a clash of two civilisations wherein the fate of both Europe and democracy was decided. Sparta refused to assist Athens, which placed the Greek army under a potentially fatal threat. The Greeks chose the best tactic they could under the circumstances; a preventative hand-to-hand battle in the centre and attacks on the flanks.

A spiralling battle swirled over the stage, the white chitons turned red, and the black figures of the Persians became the colour of clotted blood. The whirlwind of battle gradually slowed and the soldiers fell onto the scorched soil. Finally, all had fallen save for one Greek youth borne above the field of battle to the mourning song of the choir. Women in purple, brown and grey robes stepped onto the field of blood, seeking their brothers and their fiancés.

Darkness gradually fell over the field of battle and the summit's participants focused their attention on the youth, who flew over the hall, conquering the distance from Marathon to Athens. Finally, he descended on the earth and ran, gasping and falling from fatigue. Entering the empty space in the centre of the still-darkened hall, the Marathon runner barely overcame the last few metres. He headed for the central part of the table where the heads of the states who had founded the OGS were sitting. These states were the Confederation of States of North America, the British Commonwealth of Nations, Japan, Fortress Berlin, EllaPol, India, the Scandinavian Pact, Argentina, the Protestant States of Europe, the Black Sea Christian Commonwealth, New Zealand and Australia.

Only when the Marathon runner had reached the head of the table with his remaining strength did the lights flare brilliantly into life. The runner hoarsely uttered the one word they awaited from him, 'Victory! Victory!'

The solemn chords of the OGS anthem sounded, the music and words had been composed specially for the summit, and everyone rose to their feet. The OGS emblem shone again at the spot where the battle of civilisations had swirled over so recently. The young runner stood before the meeting table and stretched out his hand to the president of the Confederation, Shirley Van Lee. It was as if he had dedicated the victory to her personally and had borne here the precious gift of history.

Haiduk did not take his eyes off Shirley. She was wearing black because the funeral of her husband had occurred two days ago. The expression on her face was invisible, obscured by the black veil hanging from the small hat that was shading her face. Her visage was lost in shadows, even on the large screens.

The president of Greece, Stavros Venizelos, spoke in the name of the hosts. He announced that the lessons of Marathon must not be forgotten if Europe's ancient civilisation was not to be destroyed by a merciless enemy.

Shirley Van Lee spoke next and began by saying, 'It is hard for me to speak after the personal tragedy I have survived and which has so deeply affected the citizens of the Confederation and our friends. However, as president of the Confederation, I bear the highest responsibility for global peace and security, and this compels me to forget my personal grief and return to the affairs of the life, or indeed death, of our Union of Democratic States. No, I have not made a mistake. We are talking about our common destiny, the destiny of our countries and our values, the fate of our children.'

Haiduk's heart ached at this rhetorical flourish of 'our children'.

'We are dealing with the most serious challenge of the twenty-first century,' Shirley continued, her voice not sounding as sonorous as it always had. Her service chip monotonously dictated the words of the speech to her and she repeated the words, drafted by Martha Jefferson, in a monotone, 'Today, this wonderful performance, for which I sincerely thank the President of Greece, reminds us once more of the importance of our unity as we face the threat of aggression. Sparta came too late with its assistance to Athens. However, today our free nations are obliged to unite before the menace from those dark forces that bring subjugation, ruin and death. We must remember the lessons of history when free nations united in the struggle against Nazism and Communism and triumphed. We have, for a long time, too long a time, made concessions to the aggressors. We have tried to find compromises and sought for a peaceful existence. However, coyotes will never become vegetarians and hyenas will not renounce carrion. The Horde has gone too far. Its forces ruined Russia, which was our strategic partner in Eurasia. This Horde stands near the gates of Ukraine, seeking to immerse Europe in a flood of darkness and transform the islands of the Islamic population in Germany, France and Spain into a united archipelago of Islamic fundamentalism. Within the last few days the Horde took an unprecedented step, they exploited the murder of President Van Lee, and the shock caused by this crime, and concluded a treaty with the so-called revolutionary government of Mexico, headed by the drugs baron Jose Sapaterro. They commenced supplying arms to the insurrectionaries with the aim of destroying the Confederation. However, the aggressor had miscalculated. The skirmishes of the American legion with the narco-rebels in the states of Texas, New Mexico, Arizona and California demonstrate the rapidly growing unity of the American people. The heroic actions of the legion, the glorious, brilliant victories over these criminals, have aroused the enthusiastic support of our whole society. They have strengthened the resolve of the American people for the global battle with the aggressors we face. I inform you that, with the unanimous support of the Congress of the Confederation, I have taken a decision to situate three military combat space stations (CSS) in a geo-stationary orbit. The George Washington, Harry Truman and Ronald Reagan stations are equipped with the latest weapons systems and defensive equipment. These space analogues of sea-going aircraft carriers are the foundation of America's unconquerable power. The process of assembling the stations from items delivered into orbit by the Confederation and an array of member states of the OGS has commenced. The crew of the stations will include, not only the citizens of the Confederation but also citizens of our ally states. I have also issued an order to bring our military bases on the moon and Mars to full battle readiness. We will be able, at any moment, to deploy nuclear missiles, laser, gravitational, energy, computer and other new categories of weaponry against the aggressor. I call on all member states of the OGS to display unity in this time of mortal struggle with the foe. I call on the governments of those countries that are not members of the OGS, who already feel the breath of those dark predators, to join our organisation and participate in the common struggle. I call on the government of the Celestial People's Democratic Empire to demonstrate wisdom, preserve neutrality, and not to side with the aggressor. However, let neither our enemies nor those who hesitate have any illusions, if global war commences we will ultimately triumph. And the world will be told of our victory, not by the dying wounded citizen of Marathon, Pheidippides, but by two billion warriors of light, the immortal warriors of democracy, progress and peace.'

Shirley Van Lee's final words were accompanied by an ovation, after which an interval for negotiations was announced.

Haiduk and Pryadko headed for the hall with the rows of cabins where they were due to meet with the Polish representatives. At exactly 12:00 Przemysław Rosiak, Minister of Poland's National Defence, entered the cabin, along with General Krzysztof Samsonovych, Commander in Chief of the United Military of EllaPol. Rosiak, the young, elegant son of the Mayor of Chicago, embraced Haiduk and slapped him on the back as he said, 'How are you, old pal?' He had maintained a close working relationship with Haiduk's bureau in Washington.

General Samsonovych was adorned with a proud moustache, like General Piłsudski, and conducted himself in a more restrained manner. He saluted the Ukrainians, bowed his bald head and clicked his heels. The general was acquainted with neither Pryadko nor Haiduk.

The Polish had brought them the draft of a secret agreement regarding military cooperation between the armed forces of Ukraine and EllaPol. They let the Ukrainians know that their military had now been joined by the Norwegian Arctic Unit and the Swedish Airborne Army, who were prepared for war in the Polar areas. Rosiak frankly acknowledged that the Southern Black Sea flank was of great concern to them. Neither Romania nor Bulgaria could oppose Turkey's dominance of the sea. Greece, after the seizure of its former island, Chios, by the Turks, was concentrating its forces exclusively on the Aegean Sea. General Samsonovych was predominantly silent, he stroked his moustache and did not interrupt the two defence ministers. Pryadko handed the Polish a list of the arms and equipment required by Ukraine. Haiduk looked with sympathy at this son of the village, who had grown up in Khmelnychyna and become one of Ukraine's best staff officers, which resulted in him catching the hetman's attention during the war with EnROS.

In reply to Rosiak's question concerning the stance of his Ukrainian colleagues towards the OGS proposal to transfer Polish military forces to West Ukraine, Pryadko replied that this was a matter for the country's political leadership. Haiduk said that the plan might evoke a certain analogy with Stalin's 1939 proposal to move the Red Army to Polish territory in order to restrain Germany. The reaction of the Polish leadership had been sharply negative. General Samsonovych intervened at this point and said that in the given instance the historical analogy was bogus, the two events were distinguished by different circumstances and challenges. Rosiak advised them that in no circumstances were they considering a repetition of the tragic mistakes of the past. He spoke of his dream that one day he would see a united Polish, Ukrainian, Lithuanian State. 'Thirty-million Ukrainians, fifty-million Polish and fifteen-million Lithuanians, uniting their industrial potential and armed forces, would become a very influential part of Europe,' he suggested. Haiduk added to this fifteen-million Belarusians who were striving to build a democratic society.

Having agreed to remain in continuous contact, the delegations headed for lunch. Haiduk and Pryadko pushed their way to the bustling, noisy and democratic food hall, in other words the one where the cheap buffets with the national cuisines of OGS member countries were situated. There were also various styles of bars, little restaurants and quiet coffee houses.

After a prolonged search they found a free table for two. Around them thronged the participants of the summit, laughing, shouting, conversing, or silently munching salad; their chests adorned with third level access badges. Delegates with first and second level access were lunching in separate halls.

'What do you think about all of this, Petro Ivanovych?' Haiduk asked.

Pryadko thoughtfully drank his carrot juice. He squeezed a lemon into the glass and his hand curled around the rim so he did not splash the table. 'I recommend that you try a vitamin bomb,' he said. 'This is possibly the best kind of bomb in the world.' Then, unexpectedly he added, 'There will be war. They will burn us from both sides. We are not ready. We have lost Ukraine. The armed forces have, in reality, been destroyed by politicians. However, we need to salvage something, even its remnants. A swift preventative strike is needed. Everyone here will need to work for that,' he swept his eyes over the hall, 'particularly the strategic, space forces of the Confederation. But we mustn't let the Polish into West Ukraine because they will stay there, we must deploy them to the left bank into Kharkiv, Luhansk, and Rostov-on-Don.' He turned his attention to the glass again, seasoning the carrot juice with salt and pepper as if it were a Bloody Mary. Thinking for a moment, he raised his head, 'I will be frank. Everything depends on you, Ihor Petrovych. The army is relying on you.'

'On me?'

'Yes, only you are able to dispel this nightmare pervading the country. There is no one apart from you. The army will help. It does not have the strength just to sit by and watch this debacle …' He sighed and pushed his glass aside. 'We support you. Get started.'

Haiduk was extremely moved by the other man's honesty. He had previously been unaware of Pryadko's views; all his sources confirmed the utter professionalism of the Chief Military Otaman, but none spoke of his political position because he was exceptionally guarded. However, anguish pierced him. Various forces were propelling him towards a treasonous coup that, as they always did, would involve bloodshed. He recollected the coups in Russia, Spain, Greece, Iraq, Chile, Argentina, Poland, Germany, Serbia, Romania, China, Egypt, Indonesia, Nigeria, and in dozens of other countries. They unfolded in the same way everywhere, with murders, purges, arrests, fiery slogans proclaiming justice, a brief period of improvement and stabilisation behind which stood another stupid dictator, renewed mistakes and crimes, political repressions and corruption. A cursed and enchanted circle endlessly repeating itself. And why was he, a person now remote in essence from Ukraine, a person estranged from the country, obliged to take on himself all the responsibility for a new, possibly more savage, cycle of violence?

Haiduk swiftly ate his Caesar salad and drank his espresso in one gulp. He squeezed Pryadko's hand firmly as they shook hands in farewell, and went to the negotiation hall where Dima Mochalkin awaited him.

'Ihor Petrovych, do you like the air here?' Dima asked him.

'What?' Haiduk asked, as if sombrely. 'Is there a plan to lay a pipeline from Greece to Ukraine? To agitate the air of democracy?'

'No,' Dima laughed, 'I was in the sea, I swam for a while, then breathed this air and recollected Pythagoras. He said that the aroma of herbs and spices was a better offering to the Gods than the aroma of frying fat and therefore I …'

Haiduk's face remained sombre and motionless. 'What are you after?'

'The Russian delegation has asked to meet you.'

'The Russian?'

'Yes, they are here as guests. Give them some of your time.'

'Okay. Where are they?'

'They are waiting in the thirty-third cabin.'

When Haiduk and Dima entered the cabin, three officers in black naval uniform stood up. The senior of the delegation - his badge was inscribed Special Guest - was Rear Admiral Feoktysov. He was accompanied by Captain of the First Rank Syedov and Captain of the Second Rank Yuvzhenko. The guests presented themselves as members of the UOR, the Union of Officers of Russia. Rear Admiral Feoktysov stated that he had three nuclear submarines with strategic missiles from the northern fleet under his unified command. These included the fleet's flagship 'Moscow' and the 'Stalingrad' and 'Arzamas' submarines, each of which was commanded by one of his colleagues.

'Well now, Lieutenant General,' said the rear admiral; he was a thin, wiry man with grey, bristly hair, who for some reason looked not at Haiduk but at Dima Mochalkin, 'when those vampires, the leaders of Russia, betrayed our country, fraternised with infidels, sold our resources, made the vilest deals, we were sitting for years under the water, gradually earning ourselves leukaemia and thinking about how we served that great Russia that shat on us … but now we have realised what needs to be done and taken a decision. We request you to inform the government of Ukraine that we are ready to serve under their country's banner in the name … the name of revenge for our betrayed homeland, for humiliated faith, for the suffering of the Russian people. We are ready to unleash a nuclear missile strike of devastating power on the Horde. The crews of two other submarines have come from the Pacific Ocean to join us.'

'How many of you are there in all?' Haiduk asked, thinking about the desperate resolve of these people who had lost everything; their homes and families, their native soil. They were ready for any and every act at the behest of revenge.

'In all we have one thousand, six hundred officers and sailors, five submarines of the 999 Octopus design, and surface-going craft, which include a marine-repair base and hospital ship. Our armaments consist of thirty-seven operational tactical cruise missiles of the Harpoon class and twenty-six SS-60 M-Iks inter-continental ballistic missiles. The service life of the missiles has expired but, well, I think they will still fly.' The veins began to bulge on the rear admiral's pale, wrinkled face. 'We are presently on the surface. Our people are suffering from beriberi, the situation with provisions is chronically bad, our location is …'

'I know it,' said Haiduk. 'Our satellites monitor your position.'

'Lieutenant General,' said the rear admiral, finally looking at Haiduk. His eyes were a cold grey and his gaze was exhausted and fearful. 'We have offered our services to OGS intelligence operatives, but they don't trust us … they are afraid of us … that we will go over to the side of the Horde. And above all else … they don't know what to do with us.'

'I don't know what to do with you either.'

'Lieutenant General, let's be honest with each other,' said Feoktysov. 'We know that the leadership of our country behaved like pigs with regard to the relationship with the Ukrainian people. Responsibility for the last war between our countries lies completely on the conscience of the traitor Medunov and his entourage. We condemn that policy and are prepared to adopt a political declaration in the name of the UOR and renounce that approach. At the end of it all we have one mother, Kyiv-Rus. We should be together.'

'Mr Haiduk,' the second rank captain, Yuvzhenko, suddenly intervened. He was a muscular man who resembled a professional fighter and, by contrast with his superior officer, spoke Ukrainian. 'I am a Ukrainian myself, from Bila Tserkva. Don't trust him. He never refers to Ukrainians as anything other than *Khokhols*, traitors and Banderites. No fraternal friendliness will exist with such as him, but have consideration for the rear-admiral, who is in the third stage of leukaemia. We have arranged to leave him at a clinic in Athens. He is a courageous officer and a good commander. His family perished in Moscow during the bloody Kurban-Bayrami.'

'I very much regret that,' said Haiduk, 'please accept my condolences Rear Admiral.'

Rear Admiral Feoktysov sat silently while tears rolled down his cheeks, accumulating in the deepest wrinkles that gathered under his chin, and fell to the table. 'I had a son, much like your captain.' He pointed at Dima Mochalkin. 'He served in the Kremlin guard and perished when it was stormed … and later my wife and daughter …'

'If you want, Rear Admiral, we could take you to Kyiv and place you in a military hospital. Why would you stay in Athens?' Haiduk suggested. 'Regarding the use of the submarines, it's an interesting idea. I will support it and hope that the idea is also supported by the hetman. There is only one political condition - let us hear no more of older and younger brothers, Russia is not better than Ukraine. We are equals.'

After the meeting with the Russians Haiduk went to the beach. He sat by a chunky palm tree, switched on his American gadget and called Bozhena. Everything was fine in Kyiv. She was missing him, she had been to visit Maria Yuzefivna, and was learning how to cook borshch. She did not ask him about the summit or Martha Jefferson, and seemed totally carefree. Haiduk felt easier at heart after their call.

60

5 July 2077
Kyiv, 21:00 - Secret
To: I. P. Haiduk

His Excellency, the Hetman of Ukraine, awaits you on 7 July at 10:00 at a meeting of the Aeropagus and NSC, where the proposals of the OGS will be considered and a decision taken based on their merits. Do not make any reports or promises prior to the adoption of a resolution.
General Clerk, General Vitold Klynkevych

61

The island of Keaparos, now known as Kreydos, lay at a distance of one hundred and twenty-five kilometres from Euboea. It was formed from two high crags, united like Siamese twins by a narrow rock causeway. The Greek government had established a radar station on the eastern crag to alert them to a Turkish attack. The station's crew consisted of five men, technicians, engineers and electricians. They had a coastguard boat at their disposal and could go on unauthorised leave any time they wanted, if they left one person in charge. Kreyda, who had bought this island for a price that had proved impossible to establish, supported the radar station because it was in his interest.

The facility covered the island with a sleek electronic parasol, effectively concealing the secrets of Ivan Ovramovych from his too-inquisitive compatriots and foreign intelligence agents. However, in the protocol signed by I. O. Kreyda and the Greek electronic intelligence services, it was stipulated that the personnel of the station did not have the right to cross to the western crag and interfere in the private life on the island. This condition was embodied in the steel fence that bisected the stone umbilical cord linking the crags. It appeared to be an unconquerable barrier to human curiosity, jealousy, and any irrepressible urge to pry into your neighbours' secrets.

It transpired that a month before the events described, a happy-go-lucky Greek builder from Macedonia had appeared in the area belonging to Kreyda. He had made contact with the radar station crew, occasionally taking them to Piraeus, where he knew a few towns with a lively night life and attractive young women. His name was Vasylios and he was born in Ukraine, in the Steppe, near the Sea of Azov, into a family of local Greeks. He travelled with his parents to Greece when he was fifteen and then illegally returned to Kyiv where he graduated from the Military Intelligence Operatives' Academy. Vasylios also graduated from the faculty of computer technology at the Dresden Polytechnic Institute. However, he registered for work as a qualified builder at the labour exchange. He was able to gain the trust of the manager of the construction division at the Cypriot offshore Rosukrhellenic Bank. The firm was at that time engaged in construction work on the island of Kreydos.

Overnight on the fifth to the sixth of July, four employees of the radar station were held up in Piraeus because someone had stolen their boat and they could not return on time from their carousing. Meanwhile, Vasylios was enjoying his down-time with the remaining duty officer at the station. They were barbecuing lamb on the shore and drinking strong, red Demestina wine, which soon lulled the Greek officer to sleep. Vasylios carefully covered him with a warm sheep's wool blanket and entered the station. It was now 01:00 and three UMI terrapins were approaching the island. Their official flight path was from Euboea to Thessaloniki, where they would supposedly refuel before returning to Kyiv. The aircraft flew at an altitude of two metres above the surface of the sea, in a dead zone of radar coverage which Vasylios had just created.

The central directorate of the electronic intelligence service in Athens noted no suspicious movement in the Aegean Sea sector covered by the Kreydos station. The orientation point for the terrapins was the fire on which the unfortunate lamb was currently carbonising. The vehicles landed on a small, sandy beach. After talking it through with Vasylios, the marines ascended the stairs hewn into the rock. They bypassed the ally country's radar station and passed through an aperture in the steel fence onto the ground where I. O. Kreyda's domain began. His palace guards were knocked out by tranquilliser darts.

The building was modelled on a traditional Poltavan cottage, but the walls were of white marble. The roof was thatched with natural straw, and, near the barely lit house, swans glided on the black surface of an artificial pool. The special troops roused Nykodym, a village elder, from his bed. He was a muscular man with a profuse beard, reminiscent of an Orthodox priest. He was also Kreyda's personal representative and, according to Vasylios, displayed bestial savagery towards the hired builders. He would whip them for the slightest transgression.

Only two of the special troops, who were fluent in Greek, stayed and talked to him. They told him that the special squad for combatting narcotics had been alerted to the presence on the island of a transit point for Turkish narcotics. Nykodym initially created the impression he did not understand Greek. 'I am Ruso … Russiche,' he claimed. But when the barrel of an MR-50 pistol was thrust into his mouth he co-operated.

Nykodym agreed to open all the rooms to show the gentlemen there were no narcotics on the island. Then one of the troops entered the warm pool, opened the vents and began to empty the water. The swans, which ought to have been perturbed, did not fly away. It became apparent they were electronic toys and as the pond drained they drifted to the corner and became a heap of white rags. When the pool was completely empty, the special troops located the concealed doors in the underwater area and opened them. The commander of the unit pulled Nykodym down the steps hewed into the thick rock and compelled the old man to input the code to open the hefty bank-vault style doors. They led Nykodym back out of the pool and forced some sleeping tablets into him.

Then the boys from E-Division got to work. They were in the room housing the most secret servers, where powerful computers worked to an automatic regime with a resilience factor of 99.999%. Thanks to this room and the family of servers it contained, which was designated 'Impartiality', Ivan Ovramovych Kreyda had gained power over the majority of Ukrainian oligarchs and politicians, and also over influential state figures in Europe. Streams of information on the tangled and illegal machinations for the laundering of criminal money through Cypriot banks were flowing through the server.

The heart of the server was an ingenious programme, developed at Kreyda's request by the half-insane mathematician, Vasserman. In exchange for the creation of the programme, he had received the General Prosecutor's permission to forsake the Jewish ZEK-72 in Medzhybizh and travel to Israel. Unfortunately, the aircraft of the Mayberg and Company Airline on the Kyiv-Tel Aviv route was downed over Turkey by an individual self-guided missile. The Turks immediately accused the Kurds of the crime.

The hackers of UMI swiftly downloaded the information while taking the hard drives of the Orion X computers to be decrypted. The Greek part of Operation Achilles Heel was concluded at 03:00 and the terrapins set a course for Thessaloniki. Vasylios flew from the island, along with the special forces troops.

62

Two days before the events on the island of Kreydos, seven young Turkish playboys, who worked at the Slovyansky Bazar Company, specialising in supplying young, blond women from the markets of Russia, Ukraine, Belarus and Poland to the Istanbul central district, decided to take a short jaunt to the Aegean Sea. They flew from Istanbul to Ankara and then to Izmir. Then they travelled by minibus on the D-300 road to the small town of Cheshe, on the shores of the Aegean Sea, to stay at the dirty, three star Privato Hotel, where they drank the night away. They knew the border police would be interested in their arrival and would listen into their conversations in the hotels and bars. Certainly Chios, which had been seized at the beginning of the year by the Kemal Ataturk Second Turkish Army of Avengers, was in the zone of military operations and at the centre of OGS intelligence operatives' attention.

The following day the Turkish UMI group, which consisted of Crimean Tatars under the command of Captain Zaur Khamzyn, crossed the eight kilometre channel separating the occupied island from the Turkish coast and landed in Chios.

They saw the half-empty, ruined town, the scorched remains of the old market, which had once seethed with life, and the police checkpoints dividing the island into sectors. The red flag of Turkey, with its crescent moon and the black-starred banner of the Horde, fluttered everywhere, on two storey buildings of various hues, on piers, and on warehouses emitting the disgusting odour of rotting fish. The walls of buildings, fences and shop windows were graffitied with the phrase 'Remember 1822'.

The air conditioning in the commander's office was not working and the Turkish officers in there wore grass-green military shirts, darkening with sweat. The young playboys presented their accreditation from Ankara and Istanbul, and an official letter from the Slovyansky Bazar Company regarding its wish to revive the once glorious tourist facilities in Chios. The company planned to create a network of casinos and cabarets on the island. This idea was very much to the liking of the officers. They issued Zaur Khamzyn with a pass to travel to the island and helped him lease an old, green, bullet-hole-riddled bus, without a windscreen, at the bus station. The Greek driver, who was keen to earn some money, was equally reluctant to converse with them.

The rugged mountain road ascended to the village of Volissos, above which soared a summit dominated by a Genoese fortress. Its walls and towers looked particularly sombre in the translucent pale blue air with the giddy aroma of Jasmine. They were exhausted with the heat and the terrible road which had impeded them, so they only travelled forty kilometres in two hours. The Turks were subdued by the sight of a concentration camp for POWs, which was situated in the ancient amphitheatre. The Greek driver began to yell something angrily and wave his arms, but they did not understand him.

The bus stopped and they decided to have a quick nap under the shade of the orange trees. Only Zaur Khamzyn, an unnoticeable man with a grey aura and a lizard's agility, headed for the village. He met the local midwife there, an old lady called Khrysanfa, and had a long talk with her while going over the map of the route. Operation Achilles Heel had to be synchronised to the minute for both groups, commencing at 01:00.

Haiduk was co-ordinating their operation from the residence on Euboea. At midnight the Turkish group headed for the Genoese fortress. The night, sticky and hot, was filled with the chirruping of cicadas and the rustling of bushes through which the special troops penetrated. Earlier in the day, near the same grove of orange trees where they had rested, they had found some weapons, helmets, night-vision goggles and electronic apparatus stashed there for them by Greek partisans who operated on the island.

On reaching the fortress, the special troops located a huge tower with a break in the wall on the western side. Zaur raised his hand. It was 01:00. The voices of Haiduk and Major Sorkin, from the Greek group, sounded in his helmet, while the interior of the protective visor displayed information about the situation on Kreydos. When the Greek group began to approach Kreyda's domain, Captain Zaur Khamzyn hurled a stone into the centre of the tower. Blinding arc lights attached to the interior and exterior walls of the tower flared into life and gunshots sounded.

Zaur Khamzyn cried, 'Don't shoot, I am an officer of Milli Istihbarat Teskilati. Who is in charge here?'

The firing ceased and after a minute a military police officer appeared in the aperture in the wall and screwed up his eyes against the glare. Captain Khamzyn showed him the insignia of MIT, Turkey's national intelligence organisation; a half-moon against a circle, depicting the earth and its continents.

'What the hell are you doing here?' grumbled the officer irritably.

'We have intelligence that Greek partisans are hiding out here. Permit us to check.'

'There are no partisans here,' the tower's guard said stubbornly.

Khamzyn began to feel agitated because he saw on his display that his Greek colleagues had uncovered the secret entrance in the pool. Time was running out fast. Khamzyn pressed the MR-50 pistol with its silencer against the officer's groin and whispered, 'You Greek pig, I'll blast off your rancid balls right now. Show me what you are hiding here. I have an order from Saïd Gyundesh. Have you heard of him?'

'I have. I have,' burbled the military police officer. 'he's the director of MIT. But I have an order … Oy, that hurts … Sergeant, switch off the projectors and open the doors.'

The arc lights were extinguished and the doors into the tower opened. It was impossible to see how many people were protecting the structure. Khamzyn pressed a button on his gadget, sending an encoded signal which gave the order, 'Two of you come with me, the other four must stay outside. In the event of any difficulty, liquidate the guards.'

Pressing the barrel of the pistol to the back of the officer's head, Khamzyn descended with him into the cellar, followed warily by two of his special troops. It was colder down there because the air-conditioning was operating. Two military police were playing backgammon and two slept on bunk beds. Khamzyn counted a total of six sleeping places, which meant that in all there were eight or nine guards here. Those playing backgammon were amazed to see their commander being held at gunpoint by the intruders. One of them darted for an IZh-107 automatic, but after a muffled shot from Khamzyn, he tripped over a stool and blood gushed from his head.

'Sit quietly,' said Khamzyn. 'Whoever moves,' he pointed to the officer with a gunshot wound to his head. 'Open the doors.'

'I can't … I'm not authorised … I swear,' the military police officer pleaded.

Khamzyn unfastened the top buttons of the police officer's military jacket. He saw, hanging next to the dog tag dangling on the man's chest, a thing that resembled a flash drive and tore it off. He punched the code into the keypad and the door of the server room began to swing open freely. Some shots from sedative ampoules knocked out the officer and his three subordinates for the next twenty hours.

Haiduk's voice sounded in Khamzyn's helmet, asking with some anxiety what had happened and requesting him to report on the situation immediately. The computer experts who had accompanied Khamzyn were already dealing with the computers in the server room. It had become clear there was a direct cable connection between the Turkish coast, Chios and Kreydos. Haiduk had become aware of the server in the Genoese fortress through reports from the underground Greek organisation. There were assumptions made about the character of the server, but in truth no one knew what kind of information it gathered for Kreyda, or if Kreyda was working alone.

The special troops rigged the server chamber with explosive, closed the armoured doors and began to ascend the stairs to the tower. The muffled boom of the explosion echoed behind them. Khamzyn, who was at the rear, told Haiduk of the successful execution of the operation. At that moment he felt a terrible impact in his chest and a stupefying pain in his right arm. As he fell he saw, with amazement, his own hand, still gripping the pistol, on the ground and severed from him. He died without comprehending what had happened.

63

6 July 2077
16:00 Central European Time
Secret
To the Adviser to the President of the CSNA, M. Jefferson

In the early hours of 6 July, the Confederation spy satellite designated 'Inquisitive', which monitors the coastal regions of Greece and Turkey in the Aegean Sea area, recorded the flight of two terrapins. The aircraft travelled from the island of Euboea, where the OGS summit was taking place, to Kreydos, where they landed. The character of the operation in which the aircraft were involved is, as yet, not understood. A brief armed skirmish was simultaneously recorded in the north of Chios. This was, in all probability, an operation undertaken by the Greek partisans against the contingent of Turkish troops occupying the island. A more detailed explication and analysis will require some time.

I send these details with regard to the presence on Euboea of President Shirley Van Lee.

Paul Andersen, Director of the Central Security Service

64

The meeting between Haiduk and President Shirley Van Lee took place in the terminal of the new airport, constructed immediately prior to the OGS summit. In order to prevent terrorists from monitoring the travel schedule of state delegations, a plastic pavilion, resembling a vast tent, had been erected over the road. This invention had long been deployed at the UN during important international conferences. Haiduk and his comrades in the open-top, electronic jeep looked comical by contrast with the black, armoured limousines. However, due to his meeting with the President of the Confederation, which was confirmed by Shirley Van Lee's protocol and protection units, they allowed him to enter the security corridor for a ten minute interval when the road was free.

The plastic covering sweltered in the Greek midday sun and it seemed almost airless inside. Nevinchanyi wiped heavy globules of sweat from his forehead with a damp kerchief, Mochalkin said that he felt as if he had been stuffed into a basketball player's sweaty wool sock, and Tengiz sang a Georgian song to distract himself. Only Haiduk was subdued and silent, for even the preliminary data from the decrypted information on both servers, particularly the Turkish, called on - no, ordered - him to undertake a military coup and establish a temporary dictatorship in Ukraine. But what was the hetman's regime if it was not a military feudal dictatorship? He remembered someone's pithy aphorism, darkness destroys darkness. How would the darkness of Haiduk's rule be preferable to the murk it succeeded? In opposition to all his doubts and the suffering of his conscience, he began to compose the plan for a coup with military precision.

Operation Angels of the Abyss: goal - The collapse of the existing regime, means - The creation of a Committee for the Salvation of Ukraine, COSALU. Members - Haiduk, Pryadko … they would divide their responsibilities by sector … select the objects of attack, concentration of forces and means and seize the information centres …

He did not notice their journey to the terminal's underground garage. He took Dima Mochalkin with him to record the conversation. They were taken into a luxurious VIP hall. Eight marble Ionic columns surrounded the central oval-formed area, wherein sun-rays cascaded through the skylight above. The walls of the interior perimeter were adorned with purple cloth woven with a gold pattern depicting plant shapes. The marble-tiled floor tinged the shadows of everyone who stepped into the hall rose and pink, imbuing them with the sense they walked in heaven. A statue of Venus stood at the far end of the hall. This was not a marble copy of the Venus de Milo but a reworking of that original, a post-modern composition of ivory with gold plating. An antique, white armchair, which resembled a throne, stood at the centre of the hall. The organisers of the meeting had set up two rows of three chairs facing each other.

At 17:30 Shirley Van Lee entered wearing black; her inscrutable face was shaded with a veil. She did not offer her hand to Haiduk and merely gestured for everyone to sit. Martha Jefferson came with her, along with an unknown, dark-complexioned young man, probably the interpreter.

'Mr Haiduk, have you obtained a reply from Kyiv regarding our proposals?' Shirley asked.

'Kyiv has decided to join the OGS, however, there is, as yet, no detailed reply. Tomorrow there will be a meeting of the Aeropagus and the NSC, where a final resolution regarding the proposals will be adopted.'

'Mr Haiduk,' uttered Shirley wearily, 'I want to remind you that *we* are helping *you* and not the other way around. Time is passing and Ukraine still has not decided. According to our intelligence the Horde may commence its advance on Europe in August. If you do not fulfil our conditions, we will have no legal grounds for providing you with military or financial assistance.'

Martha Jefferson handed Shirley a note and the president raised her veil, scanned the note swiftly and covered her face again. In her black mourning clothes and on the stage of this marble hall, with its empurpled walls, she resembled the heroine of a Greek tragedy. There was something theatrical, an exaggerated pathos in her mourning. Haiduk felt her hard stare on him, even through the black mesh over her eyes.

'Let's get to the point,' she said. 'We have information that someone in the higher levels of Ukraine's leadership supported Sapaterro's conspiracy against the legitimate government of
294

Mexico and even supplied arms to the insurrectionaries. If these facts are confirmed, we will act without any hesitation and punish the guilty parties in accord with American law. However, it would be better if Ukraine itself revealed and punished this criminal. And finally, I request that you release Confederation citizen Bozhena O'Connell as swiftly as possible. She will be appointed to an extremely important position in the space force's command.' Shirley touched her left elbow with her right hand; just for a moment.

So that's what this is about, thought Haiduk. Bravo Shirley, that was a class punch.

President Van Lee, rose from the throne-resembling chair and they all followed suit.

'Protocol photo,' Martha reminded her.

'Excuse me, yes, yes, we must have one,' said Shirley, heading for the statue of Venus.

Haiduk and Dima stood to Shirley's right-hand side and Martha and the unknown youth to the left. Haiduk, standing close to her and inhaling the fragrance of her perfume, which was absolutely alien to him, felt a cold indifference to Shirley. She resembled that younger woman he had known in the past as much as the gilded, glamorous caricature of Venus resembled the true marble Goddess of Love. He thought now that he had never really known Shirley and, looking sideways at her, suddenly realised she was going grey.

'Cheese,' said the photographer, but Haiduk did not even make an attempt to smile.

A few minutes after the conclusion of the audience, a young woman from the protocol service came to Haiduk and Mochalkin with photographs. It appeared that only Dima was smiling with childlike delight. The rest looked sombrely into the camera, as if attending a funeral service.

'Who is that?' Haiduk pointed to the dark youth standing alongside Shirley.

'That's the president's son, Peter Van Lee, didn't you know? He's a handsome lad, isn't he? He looks like his father, Andrew Van Lee. Peter is a student at the Massachusetts Institute of Technology. They say the boy is brilliant.'

Part 4

COUP

65

The sitting of the Council of National Security, which was dedicated to the results of the summit in Athens, was conducted in the senate chamber rather than the hetman's palace. The senate was based in the multi-storeyed Sejm building, which stood on the Dnipro cliffs near the former Ukrainian parliament, Verkhovna Rada, building, which had been transformed into a museum of Ukrainian democracy.

Haiduk, who had returned to Kyiv at 03:00, immediately told Bozhena of Shirley Van Lee's demand that she return to Washington and take up an important position in the space force's command. Bozhena just shrugged her shoulders without answering.

After spending two hours in Bozhena's embraces Haiduk took a cold shower and drank a double espresso, which his old coffee machine sputtered out in drops, and sat down at his desk to prepare for the meeting. He realised that the OGS had presented Ukraine with harsh demands and it would not be easy to persuade the hetman and others to accept them. However, the OGS itself needed the support of Ukraine and this gave him some hope that an acceptable compromise might be found. Haiduk drafted a brief with the main provisions of the agreement between Ukraine and the OGS, which he expected to hand over to the hetman before the meeting. However, he could not do so because the hetman was engaged. He was delivering a speech before participants at the Council of Prison Workers and other corrective organs, and presenting state awards, including the Freedom Medal, to outstanding figures in the penitentiary service. The country had celebrated a state holiday on Sunday,

'Prisons' Day'.

Haiduk was forced to attend the meeting without having talked through the issues with the hetman. The loss of Zaur Khamzyn, one of UMI's best officers, had painfully affected Haiduk. He had ordered Colonel Semyhlazov to undertake a detailed investigation into the circumstances of the Turkish operation. He needed to know where and at what stage the fatal mistake had been allowed, and why. Perhaps treachery was involved?

Haiduk anticipated that he would have the opportunity to speak frankly with the hetman after the meeting and tell him about Operation Achilles Heel and the first results acquired following the download of information from the servers. However, a substantial amount of time would be required to completely de-code the information. Haiduk had therefore dispatched Mochalkin directly from Euboea to the German town of Giessen. Haiduk's old friend, Vasya Kostiuk, worked at the ancient Justus Liebig University in the faculty of artificial intelligence. He was the nephew of the former president, Federico Garcia Kostiuk, and one of the best computer experts in the world. In addition, he had invented a unique decryption apparatus. He and Mochalkin would be joined by the hackers from the Greek and Turkish groups in order that they might jointly de-code the records from the servers.

As he walked towards the Sejm building, along Shovkovychna, Haiduk smelled a stifling aroma. The Russian forests and peat were burning. The aroma was borne aloft from the north, obscuring the sun and generating the effect of an artificial twilight on the banks of the Dnipro, as if it were a solar eclipse. He gagged on the fumes and remembered the stories his father had told him, having been told them in turn by his father. For Kyivans, the tales of the radioactive cloud that had swarmed over Kyiv during the Chornobyl disaster still summoned up a pain in the throat and an unusual metallic taste.

Haiduk dressed in a lieutenant general's summer uniform of light cream for the meeting, rather than his usual comfortable camouflage. The hetman set great store by form and propriety. He managed to swop a few words with his deputy, General Ivanyshyn, who had provided him with secret reports regarding events in the world and Ukraine over the past three days. Ivanyshyn did not utter a word about the loss of Zaur Khamzyn. Perhaps he did not know.

Haiduk, in accord with protocol, sat at the presiding end of the table, to the right of the hetman's chair. The meeting hall of the senate was completely full, but also quiet. All the members of the Aeropagus were in attendance, apart from Holembiyevska, who was on an official visit to Warsaw. There were many unknown faces in the hall; the hetman had probably invited officials from the foreign affairs and defence ministries. They were all waiting for the hetman, who was running late.

Haiduk saw Friedman. The haulage magnate indifferently skated his gaze through his glittering pince-nez over Haiduk, as if the latter were merely an old wardrobe in the tedious surroundings of a drab office. Kreyda did not even notice Haiduk, he was immersed in some paperwork and occasionally made notes and signed items. And what is he signing? Haiduk though. Might they be death warrants? Today, immediately after the sitting of the NSC, I will hand in my resignation. I can't go on like this. No more conspiracies, no more coups, no more politics. Otherwise I will come to resemble this lot … I must get away from here before it is too late. I will go with Bozhena … but where? To Poland? To Canada? To Australia? The fourth world war will commence soon. Is it possible to flee from it? And what will my subordinates say? He was a coward, a deserter.

He noticed that everyone was suddenly standing and the hetman had arrived. He was wearing a bright red *zhupan* and the hetman's dagger in a gold sheath. General Vitold

Yaropolkovych Klynkevych followed in his wake, wearing a black *zhupan*, which gave him the semblance of a monk. Vitold handed a packet of papers to Makhun and sat to the left of the head of state, although this was not provided for by protocol. Haiduk glimpsed the defence minister, Pryadko, who was late and now carefully excusing himself, taking his place, afraid of incurring the wrath of the hetman. But the boss was in a placid mood.

'Dear comrades, ladies and gentlemen, friends,' the hetman said, commencing in an almost cordial fashion. 'Today, as never before, we need to be unified in thought and action and in a common prayer for Ukraine, our beautiful fatherland on whose ancient soil Indo-European civilisation was born. Here Cossack democracy arose as the highest form of government. A form that we are developing creatively today within the framework of a unique project, MORD, modified ritual democracy. Thanks to this project we have achieved a high level of societal consolidation, based on ancient Ukrainian values, the highest exemplar of which is our national hero, Taras Bulba.'

A few in the hall exchanged uncomprehending glances, where was the hetman going with this? I sense the hand of Nykyfor Salyvon, thought Haiduk with revulsion.

'Taras Bulba, who himself became the archip... archetype of the Ukrainian people, with his tender singing and his heroic and tragic soul, gave us an example of responsibility and sacrifice in the difficult moments of historical struggle. Let us recollect his severe but just verdict on his son, Andriy, a traitor to the fatherland and enemy of the people, who lay under the enchantment of a foreign agent when a potentially fatal danger hung over Ukraine.' The hetman's voice began to acquire an alarmed sound and those who knew him froze in passive foreboding of the approach of a ruinous hurricane. Within the framework, at the height of that modified, ritual

300

democracy that ran the country, death squads operated and mercilessly dealt with any dissenters. 'Therefore,' the hetman uttered ominously, his face growing pale and rendering his moustaches coal black by contrast; or perhaps that was entirely down to the Schwarzkopf dye, 'I inform the members of the NSC of the decision I have adopted. Ihor Petrovych Haiduk is to be removed from his post, stripped of his rank, and arrested. He is accused of treachery to Ukraine, preparing a coup, working with the agents of foreign intelligence agencies and having criminal relations with an agent from the Mars Legion, the space espionage service of the Confederation of States of North America. Mr Klynkevych, execute his arrest.'

Klynkevych and three guards threw themselves on Haiduk before the eyes of the frozen crowd in the hall, twisted his arms and handcuffed him. Klynkevych tore off Haiduk's epaulettes with such fury that he also ripped off the left arm of his jacket. Haiduk, for his part, noted that the unknown people he had seen in the hall were wearing identical grey suits. Merezhko ran these people. They surrounded the presidium table in a tight ring, drawing out heavy Kruk pistols, even though it was categorically forbidden to attend meetings in which the hetman participated while bearing arms. Haiduk managed to meet the hetman's glance. It seemed that Makhun looked in fear and terror at the wolf pack now ripping into his former favourite.

General Prosecutor Kreyda forced his way through the throng of State Guard agents to Haiduk and read out the decision of the GPU regarding his arrest and six months detention in severe isolation in order to conduct an objective investigation. Immediately after this a black hood was pulled over Haiduk's head. Now it's that solar eclipse, he thought, tasting something metallic in his mouth. It was the flavour of his own blood after a blow in the face had broken his nose. The beginning of his July had become a thing of glory.

66

7 July 2077

22:00

The official report from the Chancellery of the Hetman of Ukraine, for distribution on television channels and other means of mass communication:

Today, 7 July 2015, a regular meeting of the National Security Council was held, chaired by His Excellency, the Hetman of Ukraine, General Kuzma-Danylo Makhun. Pertinent questions regarding the strengthening of national security within the context of the international situation were discussed, along with the resolutions taken at the Organisation of Global Security member countries' summit in Athens. Analysing the situation that has arisen in connection with the sharpening confrontation between the states of the Horde and the Organisation for Global Security, the NSC adopted the only possible resolution. We will formally announce Ukraine's neutral status once more and address all countries in the world with a call to respect this decision. There is no doubt that the sovereign people of Ukraine support the decision of the NSC as evidence of the predictability, peaceable nature and consistency of the UCMFS's foreign policy. It is yet one more proof of the justness of the Ukrainian national idea embodied in the phrase, 'My house is at the end of the village,' or, 'We mind our own affairs'. This stance guaranteed our people peace and prosperity in the seventeenth, eighteenth, nineteenth, twentieth and twenty-first centuries.

The NSC expressed its conviction that the fire of global conflict would not touch the sacred territory of Ukraine and condemns any attempt to draw our state into dangerous alliances that run counter to the national interests of the country. The National Security Council made several staffing decisions:

Due to serious deficiencies in his work, I. P. Haiduk has been dismissed from his post as secretary of the NSC and adviser to the hetman on national security issues. The same reasons also underpin the dismissal of defence minister, Chief Military Otaman P. I. Pryadko.

General V. Klynkevych is appointed to the post of secretary of the NSC and adviser to the hetman on national security issues. The hetman will take upon himself personally the duties of Chief Military Otaman.

Major General M. P. Ivanyshyn is appointed director of Ukrainian Military Intelligence.

The sitting of the NSC demonstrated the immovable unity of Ukraine's leadership and its consolidation around the national leader, Hetman K. D. Makhun.

7 July 2077
18:00 Kyiv time
Secret
To the Adviser to the President of the Confederation on National Security issues, M. Jefferson

Today at 10:30, CSNA Citizen B. O'Connell telephoned the Embassy of the Confederation in Kyiv and informed us that some people had tried to forcibly enter the apartment she shares with her boyfriend, Lieutenant General Haiduk. Haiduk is the adviser to the Hetman of Ukraine on national security issues. The individuals who attempted to enter the premises identified themselves as agents of the secret police (State Guard) and stated that they had a warrant to detain B. O'Connell and search the apartment. B. O'Connell did not open the door to these unknown individuals and requested assistance from the embassy. I immediately dispatched an armoured transporter to the scene, along with the second secretary at the embassy,

Martin Husak, accompanied by four marines. As a result of the proactive work of the embassy's representatives, who threatened to deploy a high-powered laser weapon against the agents of the State Guard, we succeeded in extracting B.O'Connell from the blockaded apartment at 11:40. In spite of the threats and attempts to prevent our operations, we transported her to our embassy.

At 13:00, I was summoned by the Minister of Foreign Affairs of Ukraine, R. V. Foshchenko, who handed me a note of protest and in harsh, undiplomatic language condemned the actions of our embassy. He announced that B. O'Connell was accused of espionage, and Lieutenant General Haiduk of treason and espionage. Foshchenko informed me that Lieutenant General Haiduk had been arrested and dismissed from his positions. I informed him that Haiduk's case was an internal Ukrainian matter and the embassy would not become involved. However, we could not permit the arrest of a citizen of the Confederation without the provision of appropriate assurances that she would be guaranteed all her due rights, the participation of a lawyer, representation from our embassy and American journalists in the investigation and trial.

Foshchenko was visibly furious that we had succeeded in protecting B. O'Connell and warned me that such actions by the embassy harmed the strategic partnership between our countries just when we need unity to preserve peace and stability in Europe. He reported that Kyiv would not officially allow the departure of B. O'Connell from the grounds of the embassy. Minister Foshchenko also informed me that Ukraine had adopted a resolution confirming its neutral status and would refrain from participation in the OGS operations against the Horde. This will, of course, fundamentally alter the geo-political balance of forces in the region. I have the impression that significant events are occurring within the Ukrainian leadership, a manifestation of which is the removal of Lieutenant

General Haiduk from the political arena.

With regard to B. O'Connell, she refused my suggestion that she be evacuated from Kyiv via a 'back fire operation'. She requested to remain at the embassy until the question of Haiduk's fate at the hands of Ukraine is decided.

As I send this letter, the embassy is blockaded by Ukrainian police units, which allow no one to enter and let no one leave without being thoroughly checked.
I await your instructions.

The Ambassador of the Confederation of States of North America in Ukraine, John O'Sullivan

67

After being incarcerated for several hours in an iron box and being jolted around to the percussive racket of the vehicle and its engine, Haiduk was finally pushed into a windowless, concrete cell. At one point he had even thought that he was being taken to the Kharkiv-Eurasian International Prison called, with no apparent irony, The Friendship of the Peoples. Two wall-mounted ventilators, with inbuilt fans twisting lethargically, failed utterly to refresh the consistently warm and stifling air. After what seemed like a long interval of simply existing in the darkness, Haiduk screwed up his eyes and tried to work out where he had ended up. His wrists, only recently freed from the handcuffs, ached; his government communication gadget and his special forces watch had been confiscated. Luckily, his American communication gadget, solid proof for the authorities that he had sold out to the hated Americans, remained at home.

'Who are you?' asked a hoarse voice to his rear.

He looked around and saw a two-metre high, bald man, burly and flabby with drink, wearing a convict's striped shirt and pants.

'And who are you?' Haiduk asked, only to receive a blow to his face that made his nose bleed anew.

'Shut up,' barked the burly inmate. 'I ask the questions here. Who are you?'

'Lieutenant General Haiduk.'

'Here you are no one and your name means nothing. Remember that. Your number is one hundred and thirteen. Do you get it now? Who are you?'

'Lieutenant General Haiduk.' Haiduk was felled by a blow to the jaw and the convict began kicking him in the groin.

'Who are you I ask?'

'Number one hundred and thirteen.'

'That's correct,' said the convict with satisfaction. 'Get up. Take off those rags. All of them.' He contemptuously kicked the remains of the lieutenant general's uniform, pants, socks and shoes into the corner where the rubbish bin stood. 'Stand there,' the convict said, pointing to the opposite wall.

Picking up a hosepipe, he directed an icy jet of water at Haiduk until the latter was frozen to an oak-like solidity and ached right to his fingertips. The convict sat Haiduk, now frozen to the bone, on a metal stool, the legs of which were cemented to the floor, and began to shave his head. The trimmer he used did not really cut his hair as much as it plucked it out. Having completed the sanitary procedures, the burly convict threw some grey rags and rancid boots, with the bootlegs cut off, at Haiduk. 'Dress.'

There was a new, square patch containing a blue triangle with the number one hundred and thirteen sewn onto the left breast of the too small, too tight jacket, with the too short sleeves. Haiduk knew the blue triangle was used to identify the most dangerous agents of enemy intelligence during wartime.

Two guards, wearing black masks with eyeholes, and black lab-style coats, entered. They handcuffed Haiduk again, pulled a hood over his head, and led him along passageways, descending and ascending frequently. He lost one of his boots on the steps and one of the guards, putting it back onto his bare foot said, 'Lose it again bastard and we'll cut off your leg.' Haiduk sensed that he meant it.

A barred door clanged shut behind him and he was in a cell which measured one by two metres and was, he estimated, up to four metres high. A ventilator rotated in a circular aperture in the ceiling from which meagre, artificial light fell. A bed, bolted to the wall, and a metal lavatory were all it contained. The hatch in the door creaked open occasionally and someone's hand shoved a light, nano-plastic plate with a bowl of pea-coloured gruel into the cell. The surveillance cameras above him never shifted their lenses from Haiduk. There were no external indications of the passage of time, such as the passing of day into night, or instructions to go to bed or get up. No one responded to Haiduk's banging on the metal doors, painted army-tank green, or to his demands to provide him with a lawyer. Before long Haiduk lost all sense of time and was snared by the apparent collapse of time itself. Hallucinogens were probably mixed in with his food because he was persecuted by a number of terrible and realistic visions. He was continuously in the epicentre of some terrorist atrocity, somewhere in Pakistan or India, mired in a slurry of dismembered bodies and pooled blood, seeking Bozhena.

Haiduk remembered a special information report by an agent of UMI, concerning products developed at the suburban Moscow based Twentieth Anniversary of the NKVD pharma-technology plant. The plant had discovered a psychotropic drug that allowed information about any real event, ranging from sexual scenes to terrible air disasters or terrorist atrocities, to be introduced into the patient's delirium. The drug, in combination with narcotics, could induce a profound depression, resulting in suicide attempts, insuppressible fear or, if required, utter euphoria.

Finally, on the fifth or seventh day by his calculations, Haiduk was taken for interrogation to what was a spacious room, compared to his cell, with a sufficiency of artificial light and fresher air. They sat him at a table with his face towards a large window of mirrored glass, which concealed whoever was monitoring his interrogation. An individual in a GPU uniform, wearing a white hood with eyehole slits, entered the room. The Ukrainian Ku-Klux-Klan in action, thought Haiduk.

The man introduced himself as a counsellor of justice of the first rank, General Belyayev. Haiduk immediately recollected the 'Tandem of Belyayev-Chernyayev' described in text books for the conduct of interrogation. The Slavic names, referring to black and white, indicated that the tandem was simply the good-cop bad-cop interrogation technique.

Belyayev really did demonstrate a veneer of goodness, asking him how he felt and whether he had any complaints regarding the conditions of his incarceration. However, in response to the demand to see a lawyer, he showed Haiduk the relevant item in the penal code that forbade access to a lawyer. The article was aimed at protecting the secrecy of the investigation and applied to those accused of particularly heinous acts of treason. Belyayev sighed, as if apologising, and stated that Haiduk's American masters imposed the same restrictions on prisoners at the Mansfield Airbase and at a facility in Utah. He seemingly confided in Haiduk, the current suspect, that he had at one time worked in a prison in Utah and had great respect for America's proficiency in brain and soul-washing. He suggested that Haiduk voluntarily cooperate with the interrogators and provide sincere and honest answers to five questions. Haiduk's responses needed to be as detailed as possible, with names, facts, dates, and the sums of money concerned:

1. Who was the initiator of the conspiracy against the Hetman of Ukraine? Who was at its head? Who were the members of

the CSU (the Committee for the Salvation of Ukraine)? What was the organisational network of the plot? What date had the conspirators allocated for the coup?

2. When and how was Haiduk recruited by the Central Security Service of the Confederation, the espionage bureau of the OGS, MI-9 and the counter-intelligence department of Switzerland? What state secrets did Haiduk pass to the enemy? What sums was he paid in remuneration, and where was he holding them? What role did the agent of the space intelligence services of the Confederation, B. O'Connell, play in Haiduk's recruitment?

3. Who sanctioned the conduct of Operation Achilles Heel? What was its goal? What was achieved as a result of the operation? Why did Zaur Khamzyn die? Where were the hard drives with the information extracted from the servers?

4. Why did Haiduk murder Colonel Bezpalii and who assisted him with the killing?

5. On what grounds did Haiduk collect compromising material on the leaders of the state? Who sanctioned these actions, and where were the files stored?

'Of course,' Belyayev informed him in a kindly manner, 'you will be publicly accused of corruption and using your position for your personal aims, and causing the state massive financial losses. Our people love to read such stuff and place great faith in this kind of material. A television documentary has already been prepared about your overseas real-estate, along with a series of internet publications and newspaper articles about your use of state transport, your sale of advanced Ukrainian technology for millions of globos and your amoral sexual abuse of minors. After that, General, the gallows will seem like the best exit from the situation for you. We undertook a huge volume of work during the three days you were in the isolator. Hundreds of witnesses in your case were interrogated and dozens of your subordinates were arrested, along with members of your CSU.'

He turned to the mirrored window and snapped his fingers. Two guards in black uniforms dragged the blood-soaked, almost unconscious, General Pryadko into the room. The bruises around his eyes resembled a black carnival mask and spoke of the brain injury that would have occurred due to the violent abuse inflicted on him.

'Repeat again, Pryadko, what you know about the conspiracy and Haiduk's role,' Belyayev ordered him.

'Ihor ... Petrovych ... forgive me,' Pryadko's lips barely moved as he spoke. 'I told them all of it.'

'All of what?'

'All ... about our conspiracy ... They knew it all anyway.' Pryadko was dragged from the room.

Belyayev was satisfied with this scene and asked Haiduk delightedly, 'Well, what about that General? Shall we drill into the case? Don't drag it out ... I have some really aromatic Brazilian coffee ... write up your confession and we'll drink it together. Do you smoke? There are Cuban cigars too.'

'Fuck you,' said Haiduk. 'Did you get those cigars from Sapaterro? You are on the lists, remember that.'

Belyayev was startled by such impudence and grabbed his Ku Klux Klan hood as if he intended to tear it off so it did not impede his breathing in this moment of righteous anger. 'You ... you ... American prick ... are you threatening me? And I treated you ...' He waved his hand at the glass and yelled, 'Chernyayev ... get to work on this ...'

'Listen to me you clown,' said Haiduk, 'tell Kreyda to come here immediately. I have some bad news for him and if this scumbag does anything,' he nodded towards Chernyayev, who was wearing a black uniform and a correspondingly coloured hood, and was already rolling up his sleeves, 'the news for Kreyda will be even worse. Do you understand?'

'Yes, that's clear,' said Belyayev in confusion, and was gripped by the fear that he was being dragged into some

310

menacing and incomprehensible stand off which might cost him everything. It was certain that Ivan Ovramovych Kreyda was standing on the other side of the mirror and it was unclear if the threats of this American prick could be ignored? Belyayev (his real surname was Opryshko) decided to play for time and discuss what he should do with the general prosecutor himself. Haiduk was, in any case, unable to go anywhere and would remain in the clutches of the most just legal system in the world. He gestured to Chernyayev, whose real surname was Dzahoyev, to leave the room and, looking formally at the mirrored window, announced, 'We are taking a break. Give the suspect some water.'

Belyayev went into the neighbouring room to consult with Kreyda. Haiduk eagerly drank the warm, chlorinated water while being tortured by the thought of what had happened to Bozhena? Might they even bring her in front of him in an hour, for a face to face confrontation, in the same state as General Pryadko? Would Haiduk's blackmail work on Kreyda, who well understood the threat presented by the loss of the servers at Kreydos and Chios?

Unfortunately Kreyda did not waver. A decision was taken in the next room to ignore Haiduk's threats and he refused to meet him. They decided to destroy, utterly, Haiduk's will to resist and secure a quick and complete admission of his guilt.

Chernyayev entered the room with two assistants. Haiduk felt the blow of a rubber truncheon to his head and lost consciousness. When he recovered he was lying, fastened by an adhesive strap, on a table. They attached electrodes to his scrotum and delivered an agonising shock. Chernyayev utilised a special resistor to raise the charge of the current. The pain became unbearable, fire raged in the depth of his stomach, waves of convulsions swept over his body, and his brain seemed to be burning. Only one thought offered him salvation. He could admit everything and end the pain. He was ready to whisper to his tormentors that he acknowledged his guilt, all the crimes he had committed and those he had never committed, but his voice did not come. Haiduk lost consciousness.

'He's fucking shamming it,' said Kreyda. 'When he's slandering people he's a hero and when he has to answer for his actions he suddenly takes a trip to the other world.'

Kreyda sat at a little table, which stood adjacent to the mirrored window. He wrapped *halushky* in bacon and consumed them with relish, steaming up the window slightly. Eventually he had to wipe the glass with his hand for a better view of how the enemy of the Ukrainian Military Cossack Feudal State was being punished.

'Call a doctor and revive him,' Kreyda commanded. 'He's a shitty intellectual. Continue the interrogation. If necessary, press him all night until he cracks. I'll show him his Achilles Heel.'

'Got it,' said Belyayev snapping to attention.

68

12 July 2077
Washington 10:00
His Excellency Hetman of Ukraine K. D. Makhun

Sir

I am extremely concerned by the events that occurred in Kyiv on 7 July. I have in mind the attempt to arrest a citizen of the Confederation of States of North America, B. O'Connell, on an utterly false charge of espionage against Ukraine. B. O'Connell is an officer/analyst in the space command of the CSNA, who worked heroically as part of an expedition to Mars, and is absolutely unconnected to any espionage operations on the earth. I wait with some impatience for the return of B. O'Connell to Washington so she can continue her important mission.

With regard to the arrest of Lieutenant General Haiduk and the charges against him, I will break with the tradition of not commenting on the collaborative intelligence work of the Confederation.

I am officially informing you that a detailed examination has shown that Haiduk is not, and never was, an agent of any American intelligence service. Furthermore, we hold in great esteem his contribution to the development of the American-Ukrainian strategic partnership, particularly at a time when our mutual security interests compel us to be united. During our last meeting at the summit of the Organisation for Global Security in Athens on 6 July this year, Lieutenant General Haiduk informed me that Ukraine had taken a significant decision to join the OGS. This move would allow for the organisation of joint operations against the aggression of the Horde. How huge was the disappointment of summit participants when the very next day we learned Ukraine had suddenly adjusted its political course by 180 degrees and affirmed its neutral status.

The fate of such neutral states as Turkmenistan, Kuwait and the United Arab Emirates, all of whom became victims of aggression from the Horde, illustrates convincingly that neutral status can protect no state from their malignity.

In connection with the situation that has arisen, the Confederation of States of North America and its allies in the OGS have decided to immediately take the following steps:

1. To freeze the 100 billion ameros credit issued to Ukraine by the Global Reserve Fund.
2. To cease the supply to Ukraine of all categories of arms and high-tech goods; computers, communication technology and robot technology.
3. To cease the supply of high-class automobiles and premium-class terrapins for Ukrainian government functionaries, along

with other luxury items enjoyed by Ukraine's governing circles.
4. To freeze the accounts of representatives of Ukraine's governing elite in member countries of the OGS. (A list is appended.)
5. To seal the border between member countries of the OGS and Ukraine.
6. To block the Embassy of Ukraine in Washington until the issue of Bozhena O'Connell's freedom to leave Ukrainian soil is resolved.

In addition, we demand that you immediately launch an investigation into one of Ukraine's senior political leaders. (A report is attached.) This individual is suspected of supporting Sapaterro, the Mexican drugs baron, who headed an uprising against the Mexican government and is trying to ignite a civil war on the territories of several North American states.

We anticipate, Mr Hetman, that Ukraine, delays and hesitation notwithstanding, will join the family of democratic nations in the face of the threat to the very existence of this ancient European country.

Shirley MacDowell (Van Lee) President of the Confederation of States of North America

69

Makhun sat hunched over his writing desk for the second consecutive hour before the evening set in. He was thinking over the text of the message sent by President Shirley Van Lee. That bitch who had first turned the head of Haiduk then grabbed the slant by the balls and dragged him to the presidency before bumping him off. Now she had slithered into the Oval Office and was trying to lead the world and, in particular, independent Cossack Ukraine. He darkened with anger, longing to reply in the style of a letter from the Zaporizhian Cossacks to the Turkish

Sultan. Yes, let her know our peppery Ukrainian lexicon of abuse and be afraid. But, at the moment he was preparing to summon his personal speechwriter, Nykyfor Salyvon, to offer a worthy reply, a signal echoed on the most secret communications channel. Irritably he grabbed the receiver and, thinking that it was Vitold Klynkevych, yelled, 'What are you after fuck-wit? I'm busy.'

In reply he heard the quiet voice of Friedman with what, to him, was a sinister, strangely Indonesian, accent, 'Are you letting yourself carry on like this, you old moron? Do you want to be removed from your nest above your tankodrome of military hardware tomorrow?'

'Forgive me, my dear Rafa, I didn't think it was you. What has happened?'

'You are really asking what has happened? Just that now they have closed the border between Ukraine and the OGS and my caravans have halted. I am sustaining terrible losses for every minute they are idle. And you listened to that dumpling maker and picked a fight with America? With normal people who give you money? You little tank driving Napoleon,' he ranted.

'Rafa, Rafa, be afraid of God,' said the hetman placatingly.

'I am afraid of God. My own God. And you want all the computers to go down tomorrow. You will lose everything, you will disappear from the radar …'

'This isn't down to *halushka*,' said the hetman, daring to share his secret.

'Who then? Kara-Khan himself, who is dying right now in great agony?'

'No, the Grey Prince; it is his decree.'

Friedman fell silent as he digested this. Finally he spoke, 'It's a mistake. It is necessary to convince him of that …'

'He's angry at Haiduk because of something he did in Greece and is cutting off his Achilles Heel.'

'I spit on Haiduk. Let him do with him as needed. He is a traitor,' Friedman's words rang as clearly as freshly minted coins. 'However, the border must be opened and we must have friendly relations with Shirley Van Lee.'

After this conversation the hetman reconsidered his decision to summon Nykyfor Salyvon and again immersed himself in the president's letter. Communication channel one rang again. Aeropagus members, Klynkevych and, of course, the Grey Prince, were entitled to contact him on the line. On this occasion the hetman answered cautiously, 'You have my attention.'

He heard the low, sexually alluring voice of Indira Holembiyevska, 'What's this fiasco in Kyiv Mr Hetman?' Once, in better times, she had called him Kuzya affectionately. 'I am stuck in Warsaw. The border is closed and they won't let the plane depart. So what do I do, create a government here in exile? And what is it with you, do you want the Horde to be standing on Batyieva Hill tomorrow? Are you losing the plot or what?'

'Indi,' said the hetman kindly, like in those long ago days. 'Dirochko, don't get worked up ... it will all be okay. I am working on this now. Give the Polish my fraternal greeting. A big kiss.'

He put down the receiver, utterly satisfied with his diplomatic gifts, and immediately summoned Klynkevych and Merezhko. Fear and loathing rose in his gorge when he saw Vitold Yaropolkovych's delicate fingers, with their mother of pearl manicure, and recollected how he had torn the epaulettes off Haiduk's jacket. Merezhko, for some reason, did not slip towards him for a kiss as usual.

'Read this,' said the hetman, handing them the text of the missive from Shirley MacDowell. How swiftly she had renounced her spouse, he thought bitterly, as if he felt regret for Andrew Van Lee, whose body now rested at the Chinese cemetery in Vancouver, his home town.

'This is just mundane blackmail,' Klynkevych said, pushing the missive aside with indifference. 'In a couple of days they will have forgotten all their threats. Don't give in to this. These corrupt democrats only respect force, there is no leader among them of your standing. They will open the borders, issue credit and unblock the embassy. Study the examples of Hitler, Stalin and Kara-Khan, their resolution and consistency.'

'I heard that Kara-Khan is dying,' said the hetman.

Klynkevych was genuinely annoyed by this remark. 'It's a lie. Yesterday Chyngiz-Saray announced that the thirty-eighth wife of Kara-Khan has just become pregnant. Imagine what his tackle must be like. This will be his one hundred and forty-eighth child.'

Merezhko was more cautious. 'This cannot be ignored,' he said, handing the missive to the hetman. 'It is necessary to make a few trivial concessions while maintaining consistency on bigger strategic issues. For example, what use to us is Bozhena O'Connell? She is Martha Jefferson's niece. Give her the hell back. Rein in Kreyda a little, there is information that he is going over the top and may murder Haiduk. We still need Haiduk; he knows a lot. During the interrogation he has already threatened Kreyda that a bomb might soon explode …'

'What bomb?' asked the hetman in consternation.

'An information bomb, and we do not know what it contains. Therefore, we should play a subtler game with Haiduk and call off these butchers. Promise him something positive in exchange for cooperation with us …'

'Maybe you are right.' The hetman meditatively stroked the bald bronze pate of Churchill, thinking that this once ruddy-haired English lord had a far simpler task in governing his country. He had no one standing over him to hamper key decisions.

'And one more thing, Your Excellency,' Merezhko said,

drawing his argument to a conclusion. 'Haiduk is now in our hands and presents no threat to us. We are ready to ensure he is completely compromised and utterly destroyed whenever we want. However, only he can reveal who messed up things for you by forming an alliance with Sapaterro and supplying weapons. What are we, Russia? Why are we embroiling ourselves in America? Don't we have enough problems of our own?'

'No need to be so blunt,' Klynkevych said, shifting in his chair with dissatisfaction. 'This isn't proved. Perhaps it's a provocation by the Americans in order to scare us?'

Merezhko rose to his feet. 'Permission to leave, Your Excellency?'

'Go,' said the hetman, 'and keep me informed about Haiduk.'

'I hear you,' said Merezhko.

Shifting his gaze from the director of the State Guard, the hetman looked reproachfully at Klynkevych. 'He has a case. You fuckers set me up. Now I have to sit in this shit.' He irritably cast aside the missive from Shirley MacDowell, 'What did the search of Haiduk's flat give us? Was any evidence found of his participation in preparing a coup?'

'The flat was clean. But Pryadko gave evidence …'

'Pryadko, Pryadko,' the hetman sighed sorrowfully. 'He is a wonderful general, but a terrible coward. He plans operations brilliantly, but when the time arrives to launch the attack he goes to pieces.' He laughed, delighted at these fond old recollections and instructed Klynkevych to summon Kreyda to him immediately.

70

13 July 2077
10:00 Kyiv Time
Secret
To: Her Excellency, The President of the Confederation of States of North America

Dear President
Your last missive was met with great regard and understanding in Ukraine's governing circle. They regard you as an example of a politician amicably disposed to Ukraine, with an aspiration to strengthen the strategic partnership between our countries. I want, above all, to dispel a certain misunderstanding regarding the so-called 'suddenly adjusted … political course by 180 degrees'. I venture to assure you that no change in course has occurred. We interpret the conception of neutrality, not as a moribund dogma but as a flexible instrument of Ukraine's foreign policy in the current difficult international situation. Ukraine has not changed its principled position regarding collaboration with the OGS for the strengthening of peace and global security in the face of the aggressive preparations by the states of the Horde. Ukraine remains faithful to its duties as an ally. Within this context we again affirm our position as expressed by Lieutenant General Haiduk during his meeting with you in Athens.

In order to completely eliminate any unpleasant misunderstandings, I have adopted the following resolutions:

1. Ukraine is prepared to immediately revive the secret negotiations with the OGS regarding political, financial and technical military cooperation in the security sphere.
2. We are ready to examine EllaPol's proposal regarding entry to this organisation.
3. We are immediately ceasing the blockade of the Embassy

of the Confederation in Kyiv and guarantee the free transit of Confederation citizen Bozhena O'Connell from the grounds of the embassy and Ukraine.

4. We will ensure a just and transparent trial of citizen Haiduk and, notwithstanding the severity of the charges against him, are prepared to grant court access to American lawyers.

5. I have arranged for the creation of a commission to investigate the case of possible cooperation between a high-ranking Ukrainian official and the drugs baron and international criminal, Sapaterro. We will be grateful to the American party to this case for the provision of assistance to Ukrainian law enforcement agencies in this matter. In the event of the suspicions being confirmed, the criminal will be severely punished and, if necessary, handed over to the enforcement agencies of the Confederation.

I once again beseech you, Lady President, to repeal the measures deployed against Ukraine as swiftly as possible - points 1, 2, 3, 4, 5 and 6 of your letter.

With great respect
K. D. Makhun
Hetman of Ukraine

71

Haiduk, like someone suffering from a fever, was persecuted by a recurring nightmare. He tore off his own skin like a scuba diver's wet suit. It peeled away agonisingly and his exposed body was transformed into an anatomical maquette of crimson muscle and white tendon. He then picked up the cast off husk and searched it for a special tattoo, a special code that would indicate where his files were hidden, along with the information obtained during Operation Achilles Heel. He searched for, but could never find, the key on his own skin.

This vision was repeated dozens of times with variations. On one occasion Bozhena, doused with blood, helped him. On another occasion General Pryadko tore off his own skin and suggested they check it. His hide resembled a yellow rag and it had to be spread over the fence of Haiduk's Washington home and carefully searched, centimetre by centimetre, for that accursed code. Occasionally a drone flew up to them and circled. Haiduk, who was freezing without his skin, would try to shelter the place where the code had to be with his body. But there was no code; although Haiduk clearly remembered Bozhena sitting naked on his back, he felt her warm moistness between his shoulder blades as she tattooed a number on his inner thigh. On one occasion he dreamed that his skin, which was drying near a fire on the banks of the Rohulka, ignited, burned, darkened and crumbled to powdery black ash. Haiduk wept because he had become defenceless and pitiable, like a person without clothes, documents or an identification number; without a name, without a native soil where he might be remembered, and without a future. He wept long and despairingly until he awoke and it seemed to him that he was in a morgue. People bustled around him, probably the coroner and their staff, who were wearing some grey rags and carefully examined his body. He was convinced he had no skin, that it had disappeared, and this grieved him.

'Who are you?' an old man with a grey beard, who resembled the head coroner, asked him.

'I am one hundred and thirteen,' Haiduk said, barely able to breathe.

The greybeard laughed, 'Don't be afraid, we are on your side. Who are you?'

'I am one hundred and thirteen,' Haiduk said stubbornly. 'Where is my skin?'

'What, are you cold? Your skin is on you of course. It's horribly hot here, but cover yourself up.' The stranger threw a torn, quilted blanket onto the bed.

'Where am I?' Haiduk asked.

'You are in a cell for those sentenced to death,' the bearded man informed him cheerfully. 'But don't fret about it. It is temporary … What's up with you? Are you not feeling well? Maybe I should get you some water,' he said soothingly.

'No,' said Haiduk, raising himself up on the bed, 'I don't need anything. I will manage on my own.' He planted his feet in his shoes and drew the blanket over his shoulders, but lacked the strength to get up. His legs were shaking.

Haiduk counted his cellmates, there were five, two of whom lay supine on their beds without participating in the life of the cell. Two others squatted by the walls in a manner reminiscent of patients in old lunatic asylums. Only the vivacious man with the grey skipper's beard, who had shown concern for Haiduk, was on the go all the time. He chatted continuously, either with himself or with his silent cellmates. Haiduk remembered Merezhko's golden rule. The first cell mate who speaks to you is the stool pigeon.

'What are you doing here?' he asked the bearded man suspiciously.

'I am Professor Buraho. Have you heard of me?'

'No.'

'No one has heard of me,' said the professor in a tragic and lachrymose voice, as he sat himself in front of Haiduk. The aroma of an old dog wafted from him and it seemed to Haiduk that the professor had yellow, canine eyes. Buraho lowered his voice. 'Listen, number one hundred and thirteen, after tomorrow they are taking me to the gallows; and these two,' he nodded to the two prone prisoners, 'are being executed tonight. So listen to me carefully. I will entrust you with my secret, for there is no one else. I was the director of one of the largest Ukrainian-Russian-German research institutes. It was called Incomnazi. Have you heard that name?'

'No.'

'How is this possible? The day after tomorrow I will no longer exist and no one will know about this matter and my life.' He wanted to raise his arms skywards in a gesture of pathos, but the upper bunk hampered him. 'The institute for the study of Communism and Nazism and their rich, immortal legacy was one of the most important institutes in the state. It had branches in Moscow, Berlin, Munich, Vinnytsia, Magadan … yes… I'm not lying, even in Magadan. We had a logo, a white circle with a red star inside and at its centre a masterfully drawn, black swastika. When Communism and Nazism collapsed, humanity made a terrible mistake and decided, once and for all, to forget, to cross out of their memory all that was devised by Communism and Nazism. Oh, believe me number one hundred and thirteen.' Professor Buraho raised a grubby index finger and threatened some unseen entity with it for some time. 'Oh, believe me number one hundred and thirteen, this was a fatal mistake because Communism and Nazism alike had enriched world civilisation with unbelievable treasures, captivating discoveries and immortal technologies. Fortunately, people were found who understood that such treasures could not be lost, for it would be a crime against humanity. So, seventy years ago, communist and nazi ideologists held a meeting in Weimar and agreed on the creation of the institute. Of course, this was kept completely secret from the liberal-democratic governments, who consisted of imbeciles. So the institute worked and truly blossomed under my leadership … for my predecessors had studied fairly primitive things. Methods of killing people and physical torture … no, I wouldn't say it was wrong … don't think I am against that, Communazism made historic discoveries, true breakthroughs in that sphere. However, I enriched the themes of our science and broadened its horizons indefinitely. I shifted the emphasis from physical methods, all those shots in the back of the head, gas chambers, or torture with electric shocks were worthless.'

'Bullshit,' said Haiduk, thinking that all of this was worth some sort of attention from human civilisation if it wanted to exist even a little longer.

The professor's eyes burned with yellow flames in the shadow cast by the upper bunk. 'I opened two new divisions of Incomnazi. The department of death and torture was augmented with the department of fear and the laboratory of defamation of political opponents. ... So, where was I?'

'The new divisions of Incomnazi,' Haiduk reminded him.

'Yes, yes, Lenin created a thing of genius with the Cheka, the secret police. Polish romanticism, Jewish passion and blood-soaked Russian terrorism were all united in a single project. For the first time in history, the ChK-GPU-NKVD became not only a repressive police organ but a powerful generator of irrational fear. So, before people were arrested and killed they were already terrified. The will to resist had been burned out of them. They were ready to break and admit their guilt.'

'Well, so what?' Haiduk asked.

'How can you ask, "Well so what?" We began to study terror in its communist and nazi variants. How it was generated and propagated. We published the five-volume study, *The Anatomy of Terror*. We would not let this priceless legacy die. We discovered a veritable Atlantis of terror and returned it to humanity. There was no bigger bestseller than our *Anatomy*. Every state purchased copies of the book and it was studied in police academies across the world. Let's say there is a fear of making mistakes when writing an autobiography or filling in an application form. Fear of losing a transit pass and therefore one's life. Fear of not obtaining a confirmation of one's address. Fear for every word ever spoken ... How could all this be forgotten? The brightest talents of the most beauteous empires in the world worked on this. However, the most promising research

324

was undertaken by the laboratory of defamation. Portraits of Goebbels and Vyshinsky were hung on the walls. The academics studied the *Pravda* and *Völkischer Beobachter* newspapers; year after year and page by page. All these gains, all these discoveries of the Red Star and the Black Swastika were carefully recorded, systematised and published by us in *The Book of Defamation.*'

This paranoiac had begun to seriously annoy Haiduk and that was the first sign that his recovery process had begun.

Without waiting for an answer, Professor Buraho ploughed on with zest, 'The methods of defamation discovered by the communazis only truly revealed their potential now, in the epoch of global communication. If you had said once upon a time that Commissar Yezhov was a pederast or paedophile, it would have been heard by twelve or twenty-thousand people, and five thousand would have believed it. Today this would be heard by a minimum of two billion people and believed by one million. I revealed one of the fundamental laws of the world, the transit of the little, powerless word into a global phenomenon. This is Professor Buraho's law. Remember it.'

The doors of the cell creaked open and a guard stood on the threshold, dressed in a mouse-coloured, flannel lab coat, with no mask. He bellowed menacingly, 'Hey Buraho, motherfucker … you deviant psycho, always upsetting things. Time to leave this cell.'

Buraho jostled around, jumped up in fear and surprise, and banged his head on the iron frame of the upper bunk. He cast a farewell glance at Haiduk and exited, clasping his hands behind his back. The guard now looked at the prisoners squatting by the wall. 'Why are you sitting you lazy mothers? Someone was told to take the corpses out of the cell, so get on with it. Start with Pryadko.'

Haiduk's cellmates rose timorously and headed for one of the beds on which a corpse lay, grabbed the ends of the sheet, which almost tore with its weight, and dragged it to the door.

Haiduk wanted to help but the guard stopped him and when the prisoners had gone into the corridor said, 'You don't need to do this Ihor Petrovych. Hryhoriy says hello. You will be taken to the clinic.'

72

13 July 2077
Secret
Special Report of State Guard Agent, Codename Buraho

I met with the suspect, I. P. Haiduk, in the condemned cell at the moment he emerged from a terminal state and, not comprehending what had happened to him, he was completely frank and open. I asked him a series of questions to which I received the following answers:

Question: Who are you?
Answer: Marshall Haiduk, the Hetman of Ukraine and Dictator of the Grey Brigades.
Question: Who brought you here?
Answer: The criminal clique of Makhun-Kreyda who are afraid of having their crimes exposed before the Ukrainian people.
Question: What were you intending to do with Makhun-Kreyda in the event of victory?
Answer: An open trial would have been held and a just verdict pronounced: death on the gallows.
Question: Who was involved in the organisation of conspirators?
Answer: UMI, the Minister of Defence, the entire Ukrainian people.
Question: What was the goal of the coup?
Answer: The establishment of democratic dictatorship and liberal tyranny, the construction of a slave society in Ukraine.
Question: Who supports you?

Answer: The Confederation of States of North America, the Horde, the Celestial People's Democratic Empire, EllaPol and the County of Braunschweig.

Question: Who, apart from you, would be able to lead the Ukrainian State?

Answer: Vitold Yaropolkovych Klynkevych. After me he is the most worthy.

Master of Philosophy - Professor Buraho

Decision of Yu. Merezhko - to immediately acquaint His Excellency the Hetman of Ukraine and V. Klynkevych with this report.

73

Haiduk washed with relish in the hot water of the shower at the prison clinic and dressed in clean, pale blue pyjamas and thrust his feet into a pair of brand new slippers. They took him to an empty ward with four, neatly made beds. A small television, showing dancers swirling happily across the screen, hung on the wall; the sound was switched off. Haiduk realised these changes in his situation were not incidental, something extremely significant had occurred. Perhaps his threat to divulge the secrets of the islands of Chios and Kreydos had worked. Either that or other forces had become involved in the game, temporarily halting the zest of Belyayev, Chernyayev and those behind them. What did the greeting from Hryhoriy Nevinchanyi mean? He had definitely stayed in Greece after the OGS summit. His family had joined him and they had gone to the island of Rhodes for a holiday. If Hryhoriy had returned openly to Ukraine he would have been immediately arrested. Perhaps this was a provocation? How fortunate that no one in UMI, apart from Dima Mochalkin and the absolutely trustworthy hackers, knew about Giessen. Absolutely trustworthy … no one knew. He laughed bitterly, remembering how close he was to self-destruction, a step away from spilling everything.

A knock on the door of the ward almost made Haiduk laugh out loud. Two men entered. One was older, had three days' worth of black stubble, and wore the dressy uniform of some unknown organisation, modelled on the style of Emperor Napoleon Bonaparte's guard. It was adorned with gold epaulettes and rows of gold buttons on an old style, military greatcoat. The young man with him was wearing a white doctor's coat and reminded Haiduk, for some reason, of the young mechanic on the Lancaster-27, who had fired on the Karakorum platform.

The Napoleonic officer held a dark red folder with the monogram of the GPU. 'Are you citizen Ihor Petrovych Haiduk?'

'That's me.'

'General Prosecutor Ivan Ovramovych Kreyda has ordered the conduct of a special investigation into your case,' the functionary read out the words, 'as a result of which it has been established that during the inquiry gross violations of the European Charter of Prisoners' Rights occurred. Ivan Ovramovych Kreyda has punished the guilty, removed them from the investigation and requests that you excuse the injustice that has occurred. I represent the control-revisory directorate of the GPU.' The Napoleonic reviser raised the index finger of his right hand to his mouth, moistened it carefully and turned the page. He looked through the lenses of his spectacles at Haiduk and it seemed that he had seen those same eyes gazing through the eyeholes of the white hood worn by General Belyayev. The Napoleonic officer continued, 'Your charges are being re-examined. The charge of the homicide of Bezpalii is dismissed. A new formulation of the charges you face will be presented to you later. During the period of your treatment you are permitted to walk outside for half an hour in the fresh air

328

and use the library. You will also be granted the right to choose a lawyer.'

'And to have visitors?'

'That is not envisaged as yet,' the reviser replied drily as he closed the folder. 'That's all from me, commence the test doctor.' He turned away in a grandiose manner, displaying his massive derriere, topped by the gold buttons in the vent of his greatcoat, to the prisoner and exited the ward.

The doctor, asking the patient to call him Yura, seated Haiduk at a small table, which stood under the television. He attached sensory wires to the patient's body and switched on a small device, similar to a laptop, known as a UDA, Universal Diagnostic Apparatus. 'Let's have a look at what's going on with you.'

The indicators of Haiduk's condition, as they appeared on the screen, resembled a satellite image of a bombed area. Graphs and data, which Haiduk only understood partially, were displayed, but they all indicated a deviation from the norm. During the scan of internal organs Doctor Yura pointed out to Haiduk the results of trauma and haemorrhaging. The kidney and bladder had suffered markedly. Haiduk was already weary of this odyssey around his own body, but Yura urged him to look at the screen so he could understand how the way he felt was reflected in objective indicators.

Haiduk saw some words on the screen:

Be careful. They have changed their tactics, but the goal remains the same, to accuse you of crimes and destroy you. UMI is being routed, there are mass arrests. Hryhoriy is still at liberty, Bozhena is in the Embassy of the Confederation awaiting your release. Your mother is very anxious and has refused to leave. Undergo the treatment, regain your strength. We will keep you informed of the course of events. URA

'There are suspicious signs that your spine was damaged in this area,' said Yura.

'Yes, I feel pain there,' Haiduk confirmed, 'but it's not as bad now. Thank you doctor'.

Yura switched off the machine and dictated the regimen of treatment to the centre of patient control and monitoring. It included rehabilitative medication, vitamins and the introduction of stem cells into the affected area, which would require Haiduk to visit Yura's office daily.

74

15 July 2077
Secret
To: His Excellency, the Hetman of Ukraine, General Kuzma-Danylo Makhun

It is with great concern that I wish to inform you of the increasingly tense social, political and moral situation that has recently been observed in Ukraine. In particular, the so-called movement of Deathchristians, headed by Father Kalerii, Arch-monk Sygismund Sansyzbayev, at Pechersk-Lavra in Kyiv. The ideologist of the sect is Father Borisogleb Chikirisov, the right hand of Sansyzbayev. They have transformed into an aggressive, mass-political party that preaches violence, intolerance and disrespect for the law. It openly sets as its goal, the realisation of a political coup and the removal of you, Your Excellency, from power. The grounds are your participation in the televised Easter service and your address to the nation ending in the traditional Easter salutation 'Christ is Risen'. This illustrates for them that you belong to the Risenchristians.

Their sect has committed a series of hostile acts against the Risenchristians and has desecrated several churches by arson, seizure of the buildings, and defacing and mocking the icons.

Particularly dangerous and resonant was the seizure by the sect of a place sacred to Orthodoxy, the Pechersk-Lavra Monastery, which was harshly condemned by the patriarchs of various countries. In answer to such acts, a number of denominations in Ukraine have begun to organise and arm self-defence leagues. During the first half of 2077 the number of skirmishes involving arms, which arose on religious and political grounds, increased by 30.5% compared with the previous period. The number of people killed was eighty-seven, while three hundred and fifteen sustained trauma or wounds. (A list of the incidents is attached.)

The actions of the Deathchristians are causing great frustration among broad sections of the population and galvanising such radical nationalist organisations as LUK, URA and others. Slogans are spreading among the population, such as:

They stripped us of our language, our history and liberty, now they want to take our faith. All who are against them rise up now!
Defend Christ! - His second coming approaches!
The hetman is a Deathchristian
Death to the Antichrists and the Oligarchs

There exists the danger that a wide-scale front proffering armed resistance to the Deathchristians will develop, further drawing the country towards full-scale civil war. The State Guard is processing data that indicates the financial propaganda and armed support for the Deathchristians is provided by the Horde. Unless urgent action is taken, we will see religious war in combination with social excesses, pogroms, plundering the wealthy, and the destruction of the oligarchs and their property. This will lead swiftly to the collapse of the existing state, political and economic order of Ukraine and the total destruction of the political elite.

I propose:
- Organising a secret special op. for the destruction of the leadership of the Deathchristians and the liquidation of the party structures of the Movement for Four Freedoms - Operation Bartholomew Night
- To announce the Christian character of the Ukrainian State, the legitimate successor to the Byzantine Empire
- The prohibition within the boundaries of the state of all sects that dispute Christian dogma, along with the incorporation in the constitution of the tenet of Christ's resurrection; an example is provided in the Greek Constitution (article 3) which states that 'the ruling faith is the Eastern Orthodox religion of the Christian Church.'
- The head of state should be ordained as head of the Christian church in Ukraine; the Kyiv Pope.

Director of the State Guard of Ukraine
Yu. Merezhko

75

During the period from Thursday to Sunday, the would-be Kyiv Pope, K. D. Makhun, was unable to make a decision regarding the core of Merezhko's proposals. Although, previously, he had responded swiftly to policy suggestions, something had broken in the soul of the old commander after the last NSC sitting and the arrest of Haiduk. He did not regret his protege's fate; the hetman was convinced that his favourite really had planned to undertake a military coup and gather power into his own hands. Haiduk's memorandum had persuaded him of that fact. The last straw had come with the maverick Operation Achilles Heel, which was not sanctioned by the hetman. Haiduk had dealt a fatal blow to the fabric of the state, its highest leadership and the secrets carefully concealed from the plebs, incurring the wrath of the Grey Prince. The hetman had no choice, therefore, but to destroy this arrogant, dangerous, young upstart for whom the corporate interests of the Ukrainian elite were alien. The principle of combat at close range operated here, it was kill or be killed.

The hetman did not hesitate to pull the trigger. It was not the reproaches of conscience but something quite different that troubled his soul. He felt that after the arrest of Haiduk, who was now being tortured by Kreyda's people, which was quite normal with regard to the laws of the struggle for power, a sense of emptiness and aimlessness had infused his life. Perhaps this occurred after he had strictly instructed Natalia Havrilivna not to meet or talk on the telephone with Haiduk's mother. The bodyguard had picked up the receiver and told Maria Yuzefivna that her friend was not in Kyiv. What a cretin Haiduk must be to consciously ruin the brilliant career that I arranged for him, Makhun reflected. Why did he want to have my power? What did he lack? Did that bloody auburn-haired American incite Haiduk to treason? Were there other reasons? Perhaps Friedman, with his pathological hatred of Ukraine, had bought Haiduk, tempting him to destroy this state that I have worked so hard to build? he thought sadly.

He occasionally felt shame at having read out the text of that hirsute sycophant, Nykyfor Salyvon, comparing himself to Taras Bulba and Haiduk to Bulba's son, during the NSC sitting. What did they have in common, the brilliant hetman, creator of a new Ukrainian State, respected across the world, and that primitive bumpkin, Bulba? Perhaps it had been unnecessary to arrange this Hohol style spectacle at the NSC. Maybe it would have been better to arrest Haiduk and dispose of him so no one would have known what had happened to him?

He recollected the book from the special division's library, which had been labelled secret, *The Anatomy of Fear*. The authors had asserted that anonymous repressions engendered irrational fear in the population, strengthening the position of the government.

On Sunday 18 July, the hottest day of the year, when the temperature of the air reached 52°C, the hetman decided to take an excursion to Rohulka, his summer residence, with Natalia Havrilivna. It was one of twenty-six official residences he could have chosen. However, the allure of the Rohulka dacha lay in its proximity to the UMI training base. The entire perimeter was closely guarded by intelligence special forces, whom the hetman trusted more than his own protection unit.

Natalia Havrilivna lingered in the large glass orangery, which was beautified with sturdy coconut palms, before lunch. She tended to her favourite orchids as she basked in the gently harmonious tropical colours. The hetman sat with a glass of whisky in his cool office, from which a glass wall revealed an enchanting view of pine trees and a lake. The water was divided by a huge subterranean net into his area and the section where UMI officers engaged in training.

In addition to Merezhko's memorandum, the hetman took with him reports about the Deathchristians of whom he had previously heard almost nothing. He was amazed at the logic of their teachings and the force of their arguments. The report regarding the discovery of Christ's remains in a Kyiv cave was particularly to his liking. He could envisage the awesome volume of tourists this discovery would generate, thereby strengthening Ukraine's authority. On the other hand, he was perturbed, not at the prospect of civil war, for Merezhko was exaggerating, but of local skirmishes and terrorism destabilising the state. It would have been tempting to finish off the Deathchristians during the course of a single night, but the hetman understood they had powerful backing. Their main supporter was Basmanov, who could not be ignored.

He imagined the bishops at Sophia Cathedral dressing

him in gold vestments, and how brilliantly and sublimely the choir would sing. He lamented his weak grasp of Christian ritual that might hamper him. He was more interested in turbo-diesel tank engines and the calibre of self-propelled canons. Above all, he longed for a mechanism to maintain power over this country.

Swallowing the last of the whisky, he dozed sweetly. When Makhun opened his eyes he flinched with astonishment at seeing Klynkevych standing before his desk in a snow-white *zhupan*. 'What do you want?' he asked in surprise. 'Have I summoned you?'

'They summoned me, Father. They said that I should bring you this.' Vitold Yaropolkovych placed a paper in front of the hetman. 'Sign it.'

The hetman donned his spectacles, picked up the paper and began reading slowly and reluctantly. It was probably another request from one of Klynkevych's friends for a parcel of land with an allocation of serfs, he thought. However, the paper was on quite another theme:

To the members of the Aeropagus, the Archons, members of the Sejm, the Government, and the Cossack-military administration of Ukraine

I am informing you of my resignation from all my positions due to the state of my health, as of 18 July 2077. I recommend that you appoint General Vitold Yaropolkovych Klynkevych as Hetman of Ukraine.

K. D. Makhun
18 July 2077
12:00 Kyiv Time

'What's this?' the hetman asked. It seemed to him that he roared loudly, as a hetman should, like he had once shouted over the racket of tank engines, but his voice, in reality, sounded old, weak and confused.

Five or six men in grey suits, with identical piggish-snouted masks, entered the room and approached the writing desk. The hetman, by contrast with Haiduk, had nothing that could be dramatically torn off, except for the faded green sweatshirt from the tank academy.

'Sign it,' repeated Klynkevych, almost tenderly.

'You … you … sick bastard.'

'You abuse me,' said Klynkevych gently. 'I am your son and you know this. Sign.' He handed the hetman a golden peacock-feather quill, adorned with diamonds, a gift from General Mguanbo, the president of Sierra Leone. The hetman angrily cast it aside and it flashed through the air like a gilded fish.

'You, you … who are you to dictate to me? I am the Hetman of Ukraine. Guards! Arrest him!'

'The guards are here,' Klynkevych explained. 'And Lady Natalia is in safe hands. You have a choice. There are three options.'

The guard standing behind the hetman threw a silk chord around his neck and began to pull it tight. The old man began wheezing and his face had turned blue before Klynkevych gestured for the man to stop.

'The options are these,' he said, counting them off on his fingers. 'First option - You sign the paper and are guaranteed a tranquil old age, retaining completely all your honours. Do you understand? Option number two - You die after five minutes in the noose. You are pronounced a suicide, an alcoholic who took his life in a demented drunken fever. You will agree that the death of the supreme commander by the noose is shameful. Your name will disappear from history. And option number three.' Klynkevych reached into a cupboard where the hetman kept his stocks of whisky, and extracted a small trunk, fashioned from some red wood. He laid it on the table and opened the lid to reveal a heavy Colt Peace-maker on dark blue velvet. The 45 calibre gun was a copy of an 1872 gun, a gift from Confederation President Andrew Van Lee. Alongside the Colt, in special pouches, were six cartridges with gold bullets. 'This option consists of you writing a farewell note in which you stipulate the reason for your suicide is a fatal illness. You must not accuse any one of anything. You will depart this life like a soldier, with absolute fortitude. We will announce five days of mourning, you will have a state funeral, and Vasylkivska Street will be renamed Hetman Makhun Street. The academy for the tank military will bear your name. So make a choice. And Lady Natalia is still alive and healthy. I will give you three minutes.'

The silk garrotte again tightened around the hetman's neck, spittle oozed from the corners of his mouth and blood seeped from his eyes. The hetman was transformed into a pitiable, unremarkable, old man. So that's how this will end, he thought, before barely audibly managing to utter, 'I … have chosen …'

The garrotte slackened. The hetman's voice now rang out firmly and every word breathed of hatred and conviction, 'Listen to me, you fucking bastard. I raised you from shit and mud … dragged you out of prison … and took you to the top of government. But remember, you are no one and your name means nothing, you are impotent, for you are unable to take a decision alone. You are incapable of commanding a battalion, never mind Ukraine. You can listen to a criminal godfather or a brigadier, but you cannot command. You are nothing next to Haiduk, whom you slandered with such expertise. I will never sign anything.' He cast a glance onto the resignation letter wherein he would have appointed Klynkevych as the hetman. 'Give me a pen and paper, and leave …'

He picked up the Colt, opened the chamber and began to load the cartridges. The guards surrounded him tightly to prevent any foolishness from the old man. They did not want him to shoot the new leader of the nation. However, Klynkevych asked them all to leave and stayed on his own in the office with the hetman.

'Forgive me,' he said sombrely, 'do not be angry with me. I am guilty of nothing as far as you are concerned. Your time has simply come to an end. It's not my decision, the Grey Prince has ordered that it be so.'

'Just go son,' the hetman threw the words out without looking up, 'and may Christ forgive you.'

A monitor displaying the events in the hetman's office was in the next room. The guards watched it intently, their heavy police pistols were drawn and ready for anything. The hetman wrote his note, clicked back the loaded drum of the Colt, cocked the weapon and curled his finger around the trigger. He placed the muzzle against his temple at first and then his forehead, chin and chest. The right hand, which held the Colt Peacemaker, trembled. Finally, he opened his mouth and inserted the muzzle, which clattered against his teeth.

Klynkevych felt he was about to vomit just as the shot sounded, deafeningly. He ran into the office, caught his feet in the rug on the threshold and fell. When he got to his feet the guards were already bustling around the room. He darted towards the body and saw that the hetman was still alive. A huge hole gaped where his left cheek had been, and the blood was already darkening. Half his jaw had been destroyed by the shot and the left section of his moustache was a few scorched wisps of hair above the empty abyss of his mouth. The note floated in a pool of blood. The hetman moved the remains of his jaw as if he wanted to say something and blood sloped out of his mouth. He did not shift his gaze from Klynkevych. Vitold seized the note, which was warm with blood, and read, *The hell with everything. Natalia, I love you, Kuzma.*

'Oh you bitch, do you want to make idiots of us? Help

338

him!' Klynkevych ordered.

One of the guards raised the revolver from the floor and fitted it into the hetman's left hand; the right was now paralysed. The executor tightly held the gun in Kuzma's hand and lifted it to the old man's left temple before squeezing the trigger. Blood and brains sprayed the guard, who was propping up the hetman from the right. They all froze around the table on which lay the head, now shot twice, of General K. D. Makhun. The acrid aroma of the shot, bitter as ashes, hung in the air.

'Sir Hetman, remove your *zhupan*, it's covered in blood,' said the guard in charge of the death squad.

Klynkevych, who had begun to be overcome by nausea, did not realise at first that he was being addressed as Sir Hetman. However, in accord with protocol, the words should have been preceded by Your Excellency.

The summer holiday season in Ukraine began on the day the hetman died. Millions headed for the north of the country, anticipating they would find cool re-invigoratingly fresh air in the recesses of Volyn's and Chernihiv's forests and lakes.

76

To the multi-national people of the territory designated Ukraine.
ADDRESS

To the members of the Aeropagus, the Archons, members of the Sejm, the Government and the Cossack-military administration of Ukraine, it is with great sadness that we inform the citizens of the Ukrainian Military Cossack Feudal State that today, 18 July 2077, in the seventieth year of his life, the hetman passed away.

The hetman had been awarded the title Hero of Ukraine on three occasions. General Kuzma-Danylo Makhun was a glorious son of the multi-national territory designated Ukraine.

He departed life like a true soldier to avoid surrendering to an invidious enemy. While being aware of his terminal illness Hetman K. D. Makhun worked until the last minute, making decisions on issues vital to the existence of the state. Until the last moment, he gave his talent in the strategic and constructive service of our people. However, understanding the illness would triumph, the hetman dared to execute a courageous and soldierly act and departed this life.

While leading the state for a period of eleven years, K. D. Makhun absolutely rebuilt the structures of government. He harmonised relations between the military Cossack Otamans, businessmen, political and religious leaders, scientists and artists. His Excellency acquired great authority and respect from the international community with his peace initiatives, which were aimed at strengthening Eurasian security and bringing to life the Ukrainian nationalist ideal. The hetman was a distinguished academic and theoretician. He enriched both the theory and practice of popular rule with the MORD project for Modified Ritual Democracy. This system was successfully implemented, not only on the territory of Ukraine but in other countries who embarked on the path of constructing democracy, including Haiti, Sierra Leone, Libya, the Islamic Republic of Albania, Nauru, and the Republic of Chechnya.

Hetman Makhun was a true Cossack patriot who, with his spiritual qualities and intellect, was reminiscent of Hohol's colourful hero, Taras Bulba. His image will always remain in the memory of the people.

At the meeting of the government, held on 18 July 2077, the high leadership of Ukraine unanimously supported the candidacy of a faithful student of the hetman's, who will continue his work, a true Makhunite, V. Ya. Klynkevych, and elected him Hetman of Ukraine. The popular support for V. Ya. Klynkevych will be manifested in the form of a national democratic election on Wednesday 28 July. For the first time in the history of the state, the out-dated paper votes and ballot boxes will not be used. In order to make the process more convenient for the voters, it will be possible to vote by computers, communication gadgets and mobile phones. This will generate huge financial savings and allow the result to be immediately calculated on the central server of the electoral commission.

In order to perpetuate the memory of Hetman K. D. Makhun, a resolution has been adopted for the renaming of Vasylkivska Street as Hetman Makhun Street. Under the resolution, the village of Lisovody, where the hetman was born, will be renamed Makhun village, and the Tank Warfare Academy will also bear General Makhun's name. The Ukrainian Section of the Russian Academy of Sciences (USRAS) has been instructed to publish a scientific biography of Hetman Makhun and prepare a six-volume edition of his works for publication, his military orders, political decrees, speeches and greetings telegrams. Three days of mourning will take place. The body of the departed will lay in state in the pillared hall of the National Philharmonic for people to say farewell. The funeral will be held on the Avenue of Glory above the Dnipro.

77

On the evening of that day, Doctor Yura, who was on duty in the clinic, entered Haiduk's ward with the Universal Diagnostic Apparatus. It was apparent that something had troubled the doctor. As he attached the sensors of the UDA he became confused, on a few occasions, about the channels he needed to use, which had never happened before. Finally, the familiar schematics appeared on the screen with the images showing an improvement in Haiduk's condition.

'So, let's take a look here,' murmured Yura, as he tapped the keyboard.

Haiduk read:

The hetman died today. It is possible they killed him. Klynkevych has been appointed as the new hetman. You must flee at once or be murdered. Go to the doctor's office now.

URA

'Oh,' Doctor Yura said anxiously, 'I really don't like this. I am afraid that the haemorrhaging might have started up again. Does it hurt here?'

'A lot,' groaned Haiduk.

'Then let's go to the office. I will block off the internal haemorrhaging. Hold on to me.'

Yura placed Haiduk on an examination table in the office and moved a screen so that it concealed the prisoner from the surveillance camera. Surgical instruments clattered as Yura bustled around and gave Haiduk a soft mask of polypate, the latest creation of nano-technology. Haiduk pulled the mask over his head and Yura extracted a mirror from the drawer and held it.

'Oh, it really hurts,' yelled Haiduk, seeing how the mask had transformed him. 'Be careful.'

'Be strong Cossack one hundred and thirteen. You will be an Otaman,' Yura ordered him severely.

The mirror reflected the face of a bald man wearied with age, hard work and alcohol, bushy eye-browed and deeply lined. A typically average face that would be hard to recollect. Haiduk, still moaning because it really was painful, swapped his pyjamas for the grey dungarees of one of the mortuary workers. He hung a badge around his neck, which gave him third-level security under the prison system. Then he memorised the name of the man whose name he had adopted, Ivan Ostapenko. Doctor Yura gave him a silent sign that he must hurry.

'Doctor,' Haiduk asked piteously, 'what if it hurts again during the night?'

'I am finishing my shift, but I will hand you over to my colleague, Yevlogiy. He will give you injections as required. That's all for now, go.'

He led Haiduk through the dead zone in the surveillance system and pushed him into the corridor where a 'colleague', also dressed in grey, was waiting for him.

Haiduk's new workmate swore loudly, 'Vanya, you useless mother … what is it, have you been drinking on the job again? Come on, the dead are waiting on us.'

They entered the antechamber where the coroner worked. A sickening smell of viscera hung in the air. There were six bodies laid out on the table, but not all of them could be removed. A number of the bodies lacked proper documentation as yet, or the appropriate last rites. Only three corpses had been properly processed. The coroner, in the presence of the officer on duty, attached electrodes to the chests of the corpses, already sewn up after an examination, and released a high-voltage current. The deceased bodies went into convulsions. Haiduk approached the doors to the next room and quietly opened them to avoid seeing this grotesque spectacle. However, what he saw disturbed him still more. The naked, waxy-hued corpse of Hetman K. D. Makhun lay on the table. Haiduk recognised him because of the tattoos on his arms, which depicted various types of tanks. Some pathologist, professor or attendant stooped over Makhun's head, probably the morgue's beautician, fitting a prosthetic, a half mask, to the mangled left side of his face. The professor carefully groomed the whiskers of the artificial moustache which adorned the plastic half of the hetman's head.

Haiduk shut the door and closed his eyes. He felt an inexpressible regret mingled with shame for the old hetman, as if he had pried into something intimate and private, not intended for a stranger's eyes.

They packed the corpses that had undergone the electric purgation in black body bags, which were sealed by the duty officer. Then they stacked the bags, one on top of the other, on a trolley, and headed for the service lift. They were accompanied by a young turn-key dressed in black, who asked why Ivan was so miserable today.

'Don't ask,' said Vanya's colleague, 'he's not had his two hundred grammes of vodka yet, his head's on a round trip to hangover hell and his guts are empty.'

The turn-key dropped the subject.

The lift took a long time to ascend, but eventually they ended up in the garage where a lead-coloured prison van stood. His colleague pulled the trolley towards a white minibus, adorned with the inscription 'Fresh Vegetables without GMO'. They cast the bodies onto the floor of the vehicle and his colleague furtively shook Haiduk's hand and sat next to the driver. Haiduk hunkered down above the corpses. The turn-key clanged the doors at the back and shut, then slapped, the metal panel, as if it were a horse's rear, 'That's everything you freaks. Good riddance and get out.'

The van exited onto the street and into the night. Haiduk glimpsed Mykhailivska Cathedral through the gap in the door. He was once again afraid, unable to imagine that he had been incarcerated in the centre of Kyiv itself, in the depths of the Black Zeppelin, in the control of Ivan Ovramovych Kreyda.

The minibus slowly descended Mykhailivska Street to Independence Square and halted briefly at some traffic lights alongside the popular eatery, Puyzata Khata. Destitute Kyivans gathered for the free meals provided to beggars; the menu obligatorily included Kreyda's buckwheat *halushky*. Cheap, poisonous alcohol, which served as fuel for lorries, was also available. Here the Chinese sold narcotics, including the popular brand of Halloween.

Someone opened the door and proffered their hand to

Haiduk. There was no street lighting here and Haiduk did not recognise the stranger who dragged him through the crowd and into a side street where an electric Ford Scorpion, which had once belonged to UMI, was parked. The stranger sat at the wheel and turned the ignition; green and red lights flashed on the dashboard. He turned a smiling face towards Haiduk and said, 'Bloody hell, what has happened to you Ihor Petrovych? Is it or is it not you? Say something, a password of some kind.'

'Curse not the king, no not in thy thought; and curse not the rich in thy bedchamber: for a bird of the air shall carry the voice, and that which hath wings shall tell the matter,' declaimed Haiduk. These were the lines from Ecclesiastes, which were engraved in gold on the marble tablet in the vestibule of the Confederation Central Security Service's main building.

'No, that's not the way to go,' laughed Hryhoriy Nevinchanyi. 'Our slogan: Be afraid of no one, know everything and forget nothing.' He went to give Haiduk a greeting kiss on the cheek, in line with Ukrainian tradition, although the lieutenant general's polypate visage made his gorge rise.

Haiduk stopped him, 'Don't ruin the face. It's still needed. And remember this pearl of wisdom too: don't be afraid, don't expect, don't ask.'

They headed into the darkness of the night. In the well-lit, high-rise building housing the head directorate of the State Guard, Yulii Merezhko, held an emergency meeting with senior officers in the police and gendarmerie. They were considering how to strengthen security during the days of mourning for the hetman. But Merezhko was tortured by another more essential issue as far as he was concerned. Would Klynkevych leave him in post as the Director of the State Guard?

78

To simply lay supine on the warm earth, inhaling the fragrance of pears, decaying to a summer sweetness, strewn all around. To simply breathe and gaze, without thinking, into a sky where the warm winds from African deserts tumbled. To delight in the ants crawling on your hands, just to roam, to smell something on the body that yet ached. To forget everything that was and not even think about the future that is not. There is only relaxing beneath the pear trees, the deranged joy in survival, at having emerged from the rank and stifling basements to the surface. The joy in encountering a hay bale or cold water in an enamel bucket. To plunge in your head, drink as much as you like, and no one will grip your throat; you can raise your head, for no one will try to drown you, and no one will sear your bladder with an electric shock. You will not be injected with par-amnesiacs developed by American military psychopharmacologists. There will be no syringe to inject it between your toes where it would leave no traces.

Two years ago Haiduk had sent a description of this drug and some ampoules to UMI's central directorate. Now he had experienced the effects of the par-amnesiac himself. It paralysed the legs as if they were immersed in concrete and the paralysis spread higher, seizing the base of the spine and the lower torso. To be gripped by the terror of death from the paralysis of the respiratory muscles or remain motionless forever. A body bereft of strength, encased in concrete. An investigator would demand to know everything while holding a syringe with the antidote that would save the prisoner. Haiduk knew something the other suspects did not. The effects of the par-amnesiac were short lived and those people who did not surrender to uncontrolled panic, might retain their secrets.

Yearning filled him. Yearning to forget all this, to soar above this old timber building at the edge of the forest and soar further over the wetlands by the River Irpin. His dreams of birdlike flight did not extend beyond there. Haiduk had the bitter realisation that the feeling of freedom, which came to him so suddenly, had concluded just as swiftly. Something expired in his spirit. Simply to exist like a bird flying over the Irpin or some green lizard that effortlessly let its tail be torn off so it could be free … so easy to renew that which had been lost … it could not be thus for him.

After some moments of bliss, gifted to him by this morning, he returned to the human dimension. A thirst for vengeance began to fill him, flooding his conscience and driving out all other feelings. An ardour for a primitive, blood-soaked vengeance and a feeling of degradation and the heartache of the injustice he had known in his native country. He thought of being stuck in that rat hole, a few metres from Saint Sophia and the golden domes of Mykhailivska Cathedral, and adjacent to Desyatynna Church. What had happened to this soil, which had voluntarily relinquished freedom? What will happen to the people transformed into serfs and turn-keys?

Ringing as harshly as the news of some death, his voice broke into this pathetic turn in Haiduk's thoughts, 'What makes you, lieutenant general, depraved by a free life in America, a dumb martinet executing your orders, a careerist, blinded by the mirage of power, what makes you better than all the other jobs-worths who served this pack of traitors and bandits headed by the Grey Prince?'

The voice contained such unendurable truth that Haiduk was glad when Hryhoriy Nevinchanyi appeared with a litre jar of mead, from which someone had obviously already sipped. Hryhoriy laid an old mattress on the ground, with a torn sweater for his pillow, and lay alongside Haiduk, swatting the troublesome bees away. He had a hefty growth of beard, but the cunning gaze of his blue eyes remained unchanged.

Leaving his family in Greece, Nevinchanyi had returned illegally to Ukraine and, along with some UMI officers, had organised a group to break out Haiduk. They had spent five hundred thousand globos on bribing the prison guards, using

UMI's secret fund that had been set up with the proceeds of arms sales.

After Haiduk's arrest UMI was effectively destroyed. The main role in its dismemberment was played by Haiduk's former closest colleagues. This terrible trio comprised his deputy, Brigadier Ivanyshyn, and the manager of the first directorate, Semyhlazov, together with the director of the fourth division of operational-tactical intelligence, Tsekhansky. During meetings of the UMI leadership, personally presided over by one time Lieutenant General Klynkevych, these three not only distanced themselves from Haiduk but condemned the activities of their former boss. In particular, they deemed Operation Achilles Heel as unlawful, a crime which undermined the basis of national security. That's true enough agreed Haiduk mentally, as he listened to Nevinchanyi. The operation undermined the basis of security for the criminal gang controlling Ukraine.

Immediately after these meetings, the arrest of Haiduk's people began, based on a list drawn up by Ivanyshyn. Those who really were his people had swiftly evaluated the situation and gone into hiding. They were existing illegally, using false documents, prepared in advance by N-Division, polypate masks, safe apartments and other measures. Rumours circulated among UMI officers that the 'higher ups' wanted to liquidate military intelligence as a separate body and place it within the remit of the State Guard. This, although it was odd, made no impression on Haiduk.

Nevinchanyi concluded with some good news. Immediately after Haiduk's liberation, the plan for transferring his mother to a place of safety was implemented. David Beylin had dealt with the two makeweights who were keeping Maria Yuzefivna under surveillance, and taken her to the place that had been agreed; Nevinchanyi did not need to know the location. They had succeeded in making contact with Bozhena through Martin Husak, the second secretary at the Confederation. She was in the embassy complex on Kotsiubynskyi Street, in room 512 on the fifth storey of S-Building, where she was being guarded by CSS agents. Although the blockade of the embassy had been formally removed, the adjacent areas were in fact under the blanket control of the State Guard. It was impossible to leave the site without being detected by the agents, except perhaps in Ambassador G. O'Sullivan's limousine. However, it transpired he was not to be trusted and was the first to greet Klynkevych when he received the hetman's mace on 18 July. The ambassador was extremely dissatisfied with Bozhena's reluctance to return home and was not prepared to offer her any support whatsoever.

Having finished his monologue, Nevinchanyi asked whether Haiduk would agree to meet the representatives of the Ukrainian opposition in the underground?

'Yes,' agreed Haiduk without hesitation.

'Perhaps you will wear the mask?'

'No, they don't need to see the mask, let them see me.'

Haiduk overcame his pain and went to the building nearby, which belonged to a distant relative of Colonel Palii, the chief of the operational investigative division of military intelligence. Nevinchanyi telephoned someone and said that he was prepared to sell them honey at a low price.

While sitting at a large table in the parlour and drinking milk, Haiduk noticed a carriage pulled by two bay horses, adorned with ribbons, as if for a wedding, arrive. The carriage was covered with a dazzlingly white solar-protection roof. Hryhoriy met the visitors and said something to the coachman in the light-coloured, linen Cossack tunic of the kind known as a *chumarka*, and straw hat.

The coachman went down the slope of the little hillock on which the building was situated. Three people entered the parlour. Haiduk recognised one of them immediately, it was Father Ivan of ZEK-116. They embraced and Ivan blessed

Haiduk. 'I have heard about all the troubles fate has heaped on you. Don't let revenge cloud your heart.'

The second member of the trio was Vasyl Kapran, the head of the League of Ustym Karmeliuk. He was a young man with dark hair, cut in the shape of a bowl, and was wearing a Ukrainian *vyshyvanka* and baggy, grey Cossack pants. The third was a young woman, Olya Hudyma, who wore a blue and yellow ribbon in her golden hair; she had a child's full lips and a gaze as pure and transparent as a tear. Well, these are wonderful subversives, thought Haiduk, just some decorative, infantile youth guard against a pack of scuzz-balls equipped with subterranean prisons, torture chambers, secret agents and death squads.

'Lieutenant General,' said Father Ivan, 'we are grateful for the opportunity to meet with you, and even more delighted that, thanks to the concern of Our Lord Jesus Christ, you are at liberty …'

Kapran angrily struck his fist on the table, making the glasses of milk shake, and bellowed powerfully, 'There is no God. No God is watching over Ukraine, or if he exists he is dead and sees nothing and hears no one. If there is a God,' roared Kapran, as if at a political meeting, raising both hands upwards, 'could He be so indifferent and permit the abominations that occur on this land? There was a God over every country. The imperial God of the third Rome who sat on the double-headed eagle above Russia and looked down on the world. He sought for whom to invade, to destroy, to ruin. Now he is broken with his eagle, soon Ukraine will be seized. But the country will have perished before then. There is no universal God nor His will, there is only the human will, and evil. Evil that we must oppose with the will of our people, a will yet more evil and pitiless. Evil may only be vanquished by greater evil and blood by yet more blood.'

'The teachings of Christ are eternal Vasyl,' Father

Ivan disagreed with him mildly, as if disputing with an uncomprehending child. He was in the same black cassock he had worn in ZEK-116, and his right hand often touched the cross carved from cypress at his neck.

The head of the League of Ustym Karmeliuk reacted with a furious conviction, 'Only a vast spilling of blood can wash away the shame under which Ukraine lives. If they showed no mercy towards the hetman, one of their own people, who will they show mercy to? What use is the word of Christ here?' He waved his hand. 'We have approximately two hundred thousand fighters ready to come out and do battle right now. Popular tribunals have been formed. We have arms, but not enough of them.'

'And what is your programme?' Haiduk asked Kapran.

'Programme? Judge Lynch for the oligarchs. Ukraine for Ukrainians; free and independent.'

'And what about me, a half-Ukrainian-half-Polish man. Will you accept me in your Ukraine?'

'Lieutenant General, everything depends on how much of you is Ukrainian in your soul.'

'And what will be done with the guest workers who may support the liberation movement? Indira Holembiyevska may be able to unite them around the cause.'

'They will have to accept our values and not force their values on us,' Kapran replied with conviction, as if he had answered this question more than once.

'Well, okay. We'll overthrow the government. What will happen then? What kind of Ukraine will we build?' Haiduk asked and, without pause, added, 'presidential, parliamentary revolutionary-dictatorial? What kind of economy? State controlled? Capitalist? What shall we do about our debts? About administrative divisions? Corruption? The police?'

Kapran did not like this array of questions and replied sombrely, 'I did not think, Lieutenant General, that you would attach any significance to this kind of thing. It's just various kinds of formalities. Our task is to destroy the existing authorities. We have no time for theories. Don't you understand they are simply destroying us?'

'I get that.'

'Soon not even the name of Ukraine will remain. Olya conceived of an ingenious action called the last Ukrainian. Everyone who is not indifferent to our fate should imagine they are the last Ukrainian in the world. And take appropriate action so this does not happen.'

Father Ivan gently entered the discussion, 'Not only the last Ukrainian, but the last Christian … we have to unite the national and Christian movements. Ukraine without Christ, without God … it is the wild pagan field, the field of blood, violence and oblivion; Armageddon. Therefore we, the Christians, have created the union of the Resurrection of Christ and I have been elected as its head. Our slogan is 'A Resurrected Christ, A Resurrected Ukraine'. We are planning a peaceful action in defence of the teacher and his immortality, and against the Deathchristians.'

'How many of you are there?' Kapran asked.

'Several million. These are Christians of various denominations who believe in the Resurrection of Christ. We are the Risenchristians and we are against violence.'

Olya Hudyma, who had been listening impatiently to all that took place in the parlour, finally had her turn to speak. Haiduk had heard a little about this young woman whose father, Svyatopolk Hudyma, was a general in the gendarmerie corps. 'I am a member of the executive of the URA, the Ukrainian Revolutionary Army,' she introduced herself.

'I thank the URA for assisting with my liberation,' said Haiduk, laying his hand on his heart.

'I represent the internal organisation,' said Olya, 'but we have branches abroad, everywhere there are Ukrainians. In

352

the Confederation, mainly in Canada and America, in what was Russia, the EllaPol countries, Germany.' Olya continued with pride and without any inkling of how many analytical reports dedicated to URA Haiduk had read. 'We have undertaken a series of armed and propaganda actions. It was our people who liquidated the traitor Bezpalii in Washington.' She looked directly into Haiduk's face with her transparent, ice-cold gaze, anticipating some reaction, but he was silent. He did not like ecstatic revolutionaries of the kind he had encountered in Latin America and Africa. He was afraid because these failed poets, for some reason they all wrote verses, were frequently provocateurs. Compressing her lips in a capricious manner for a moment, Olya adopted a conspiratorial tone. 'Is this place bugged?'

Nevinchanyi, who had been dozing in the corner of the room below the icons, awoke, 'It's clean. The place has been checked.'

'So,' announced Olya solemnly, 'one of the divisions of URA is working on the creation of an atomic bomb. Two warheads have already been prepared, but we need the help of the army. Your help Lieutenant General. We need to transport the warheads, set them up properly and make all the necessary calculations ... the potential effect, the number of casualties, the character of the devastation they will cause. Will you help?'

'And where do you want to explode them?' Haiduk asked, barely restraining his anger, and understanding that this crazed girl was willing to set off a nuclear bomb anywhere, even in her own home.

'The targets have not yet been allocated. It wouldn't be a bad idea to blast Mount Batyieva apart during the summit of the Horde,' Olya explained coldly.

Haiduk remembered the words of Lesya Ukrayinka, which he had declaimed during a performance at his school one evening; 'Avengers take up my weapon and boldly go to war'. So here they were, the new emissaries of vengeance. They would blow Mount Batyieva sky high without pity or hesitation. And, simultaneously, the Baikove Cemetery would be hurled upwards with its ancestral bones, along with the Amosov Institute and its patients and doctors, the huge residential complex on Solomyanka; him, hiding in his safe apartment, and half of Kyiv.

Father Ivan rose nervously from the table, approached the icon and crossed himself; Nevinchanyi, so as not to hamper him, had moved to sit by the window. Then he drew close to Olya Hudyma, 'That would be an enormous sin before God and your people, woman. What do you want, a little Hiroshima, a little Seoul, a little Kashmir or Israel? I am opposed to such a revolution. I will be better off sitting in the catacombs with those who believe in Christ and love. I'm going.'

'You know what's best for you,' Olya threw out haughtily, turning red with anger or shame. She had the look of a schoolgirl whose essay had not been understood by the teacher. 'I might also go,' she added, getting out of her chair.

'Sit down all of you,' Haiduk ordered them authoritatively. 'Do you want to fight the foe or squabble among yourselves?'

He waited until Father Ivan and Olya had sat at the table and calmed down before continuing, 'There are only a few of us. We are divided. We still do not know what the new hetman will bring us. In all probability it will be far worse … it isn't some childish romantic game of revolution ahead of us but hard, dangerous work.' Pain gripped his head and he closed his eyes for a moment, rubbing his temples with his fingers. 'I have a few proposals. First, we agree to create a broad front for the liberation of Ukraine, the ULF, which everyone can join, from ultra-revolutionaries,' Olya sat with growing indifference, not looking at anyone, 'and peace loving Christians,' a shadow of discomfort passed over Father Ivan's face, 'fighters and professors. The ULF will have two wings, a legal and political wing, and

354

an underground wing, in the manner the Irish nationalists once operated. Indira Holembiyevska could head the political and legal wing, if you are agreed, or someone else. I want to head the military wing. My officers will conduct courses in conspiracy planning, deception, conducting military operations in urban surroundings, safeguarding secrets, organising networks of underground cells and similar activity. If we don't use them you will all end up stuck underground between Sophiyska and Mykhailivska squares. Secondly, no organisation joining the ULF will be obliged to change its structure, programme or method of operation. The ULF is a broad organisation whose programme must be very brief and developed by you all. Thirdly, we have a squad of soldier-hackers, military internet operatives, but we need additional forces to undertake telecommunications based military operations.'

'We have some people who can help out with that,' Olya responded.

'And us also,' Kapran informed him.

'So, that's okay,' Haiduk smiled for the first time. He suddenly liked these young people and their readiness to do battle. 'You can regard the front for the liberation of Ukraine as being established.'

The carriage with the solar protection roof came half an hour later. A certain Colonel Palii was the coachman. As they said their farewells Haiduk asked Olya, 'Do you write verses?'

She protruded her lips contemptuously and said, 'What kind of rubbish is this? I hate verses. I studied at a specialist school for physics and mathematics. I have heard much about you from my father. In fact it was he who told me about Agent Bezpalii.'

'An atomic bomb, are you serious?'

'Yes, the URA is a serious organisation. If you want we can show you the bomb.'

Are we really the last Ukrainians on the earth? Haiduk

wondered as he watched the carriage with its jaunty, nuptial appearance churn up coils of dust in its wake. The thought terrified him.

79

Secret
To the Adviser to the President of the CSNA on National Security issues, M. Jefferson

Dear Auntie Martha
I have already spent twenty days in the embassy without knowing what my role is here; whether I am a guest of honour or under arrest. Of course, I am boundlessly grateful to Ambassador O'Sullivan for everything he has done to save me, even risking serious conflict with the authorities here. That's quite something because their vindictive nature is as great as their willingness to sell out. Auntie, you can't imagine what I went through in those minutes when the bandits from the State Guard were breaking into the apartment and threatening to use gas grenades ... I was lucky to end up at the embassy of course, where I have my own room and am watched over everywhere. However, I also feel very unhappy knowing that Lieutenant General Haiduk, a person who has done so much for Ukraine, has been sitting in prison until recently, unjustly accused of treason. And accused by whom? The hetman, who it turns out was a sleazy traitor himself. I would really appreciate it if you could find it in your heart not to be angry with me. You are all I have in the world because I have almost nothing in common with Askold, even though he is my brother. I simply cannot leave Kyiv until the situation with Lieutenant General Haiduk is resolved. I really love him. He saved my life and I had such happy times with him that I forgot my ordeal on the Mansfield Airbase ... But when Lieutenant General Haiduk was arrested I was terrified,

imagining it would be a similar situation to what happened with Dick Stone. I even thought that maybe I am cursed and bring bad luck to whomever I love … Thank God Haiduk is free now, even if he is in danger. You can't imagine, Auntie, what goes on in this country. Both the television channels are controlled by the government and slander Haiduk night and day. Of course, they don't forget about me when they do that. Our diplomats tell me there are 'WANTED' posters for Haiduk throughout the city, promising a reward of one million globos for whoever gives him up. The television shows some old man who supposedly helped Haiduk escape; they are also searching for him. Overall, it is as if the authorities here have gone crazy since Haiduk absconded. They say that a whole group of people who are suspected of helping him escape have been arrested.

After Haiduk's escape and my refusal to go to Washington, the embassy had a downer on me. Ambassador O'Sullivan subjected me to a few unpleasant conversations and threatened that I would be forcibly deported. He strengthened the guard around my room and barred me from walking in the park in the grounds. He said that it was because State Guard snipers might take me out. And I have become aware that they want to renew the investigation of my 'Martian' case. William Crawford (Butcher Bill) is due to come to the embassy any day now in order to 'work on me'. I'd rather die than give in to that slime-ball … But I'd like to think about something pleasant. Haiduk is free and just the thought of that makes me happy. In my dreams I often see Washington in the fall … when the Indian summer blazes in all its glory. Do you remember, Auntie, how we used to go to the cathedral on Wisconsin Avenue? How we loved to stroll around the herb garden, sit in the stone gazebo and bask in the pink blooms of the magnolia. Do you remember the statue of the prodigal son embraced by his father? Well, sometimes I feel like the prodigal daughter and long to come back so you can hug me again. I remember the evergreen boxwood and that live oak with its small leaves … we loved to sit under it … the black fluffy seeds on the bright green grass. Lord, how long ago it was and what wonderful times we had.

Tears fill my eyes as I write. I have lost America, and Ukraine has been revealed as a huge mirage. Now, when I have to somehow swallow what Ukrainian life is, it seems to me that it is a country without hope, cursed by God. The natural environment is wonderful, the people are lovely, but the country's organism is ruined by some malicious virus. Moscow's contaminated blood has poisoned Ukraine for centuries, changing it irrevocably. I cannot live in this country where there are so many traitors, slaves and mutants, all heading for the vampires' ball. Our diaspora is so mistaken when they idealise Ukraine and long to return here. My dream is to get out of here with Haiduk and go somewhere, even to the ends of the earth, where we can lead a normal, quiet life.

Please excuse me Auntie for taking up your time, but I am swamped with so many memories and thoughts in my present situation, where I am like someone under arrest.

I love you, Bozhena

Sent via the closed channel on a CSNA government communication gadget on 27 July 2077 from the Embassy of the Confederation in Kyiv.

80

The preparations for the inauguration of the new Hetman of Ukraine, Vitold Klynkevych, began immediately after the body of his predecessor had been transported in a black body bag to the GPU morgue. Tyberii Kotyhoroshko, a senior lieutenant in the post-death squad and the best post-mortem beautician in the country, had worked on the body.

In the meantime, a state commission, headed by Ivan Ovramovych Kreyda, was established to deal with issues connected to the inauguration. A detailed programme of the festivities was developed and the main directions of the reforms the country anticipated were devised. A universal electronic election was held for the hetman on 28 July. As everyone expected, it demonstrated huge popular support for the candidacy of the young, handsome man. His political broadcasts were, after all, being transmitted day and night on the channels owned by Kreyda and Friedman. Stage coaches pulled by horses replaced buses and trolley buses in central Kyiv on Kreshchatyk, Hetman Khmelnytsky and Hetman Kostiuk streets, and on Eurasia, Kostelna, Tserkovna and Synagogalna avenues. The horses trotted along the freshly named Hetman Makhun Street, and on Stepan Bandera and Heroes of Stalinist Five-Year Plans streets. There were giant plasma screens everywhere, beaming out full-length portraits of Klynkevych and his new slogan, the three 'Aitches', hauteur, honour and humanity.

It was not surprising that by midday the hetman had received 99.99% of the votes. There were also incidents when the percentage of yes votes from the regional servers reached 110-120%. In such instances the wise heads of the electoral commissions shared the surplus of votes with colleagues, who, for technical reasons, had experienced failures in the vote count, with Klynkevych only receiving 92-94% of the ballots. The young hetman paid particularly attention to the vote in the embassies, and not without reason, their results reflected the reliability of the diplomatic corps. In countries where less than 95% of the electorate voted for the hetman, the ambassadors were immediately dismissed from their posts. In Nauru, where the ambassador voted with his wife, who was the embassy accountant, and their son, the consul, the son accidentally touched the wrong button on his gadget, which resulted in a 66.6% yes vote. Half an hour after the election, the ambassador and consul were fired. Luckily, the son was married to the daughter of a local tribal chief. Due to global warming all that remained of Nauru was a tiny scrap of territory not yet engulfed by the ocean; no planes or ships routinely visited the island, so the ambassador decided, with great satisfaction, to live out his days there until the sea completely overwhelmed the place.

Because there was no doubt in Klynkevych's victory, it was decided to conduct the inauguration on the day of the election, Wednesday 28 July 2077 at 18:00. A concert and sports hall was prepared. The structure was erected at the site where, alongside the M. S. Khrushchev stadium, the old palace of sport, which resembled a collective farm feed mill, had once stood.

Haiduk decided to witness this historic change of power, although Palii and Nevinchanyi tried to dissuade him from this dangerous idea. He obtained an invitation in the name of one Vasyl Semenovych Petrenko, a hero of labour, employed at the Bolshevik factory. Haiduk selected the best polypate mask for this role, the semblance of a staid intellectual with greying, dark brown hair, a well-sculpted nose and bright eyes. The disgraced lieutenant general had to apply special contact lenses to pass through the retinal control at checkpoints, and adhered thin membranes with false fingerprints to the fingertips of both hands. The papillary lines on the prints belonged to the real V. S. Petrenko, who was on holiday in Finland and taking a break from Kyiv's oppressive heat.

Haiduk asked Nevinchanyi to provide him with a baggy, grey suit that would lend him a resemblance to a State Guard agent. He was convinced that hundreds of these agents would be delegated to the inauguration because they were the country's most reliable citizens from the government's standpoint.

Tens of thousands of people were invited to the meeting. They waited in vast bustling lines before the five checkpoints, where State Guards kept close surveillance to prevent any ill

360

wishers from gaining access. Fingerprinting, retinal control, body scans, examinations of the microchips in the invites, and tests for explosive devices in clothing and shoes took place. The security was thoroughly well organised and greatly to Haiduk's liking.

A separate checkpoint operated for diplomats and foreign guests. The ambassador of the Confederation of States of North America, John O'Sullivan, was a squint-eyed, auburn-haired elephantine fellow, who weighed just under three hundred pounds. He arrived at the checkpoint at the same time as the special emissary of the Chief of the Horde, Chief Kara-Khan, Vizier Vadym Khlyshchenko-Khlyshchov. He was a skinny man; a convict tanned with the winds of the Steppe, who bore the perpetual brand of a felon on his brow. Both of them were dressed in black tuxedos with white bow ties. The two representatives of opposing parties bowed courteously to each other and were led into the VIP room. They were greeted there by the Minister of Foreign Affairs, Ruslan Foshchenko, who was beaming with happiness in a dark burgundy tuxedo and yellow bow tie. He was following the trends of Eurasian fashion.

There were no VIP halls allocated for the representatives of the people. Therefore, the plain folk, who the members of the Aeropagus and Archons referred to as the throng of the great unwashed, were on the first floor around the buffets. The disrespectful name arose because all kinds of cosmetics and deodorants were rationed through coupons and were very expensive. Everyone crowding around the buffets was allowed one free bottle of the artificial Chinese beer, Yantsy, or two bottles of China-Cola.

In order not to attract undue attention, Haiduk, like everyone else, bustled around the food and drink and listened to the colourful abuse the workers' representatives heaped on one another. He noticed a bustling, elderly man in front, who cleared a path to the beer with particularly sharp elbows as he bellowed, 'What are these buggers doing with the working people? They can't even supply us with proper beer; they give us this horse piss while swaddling themselves in gold. Do you know what a banquet is taking place on the fifth floor? There are barrels of black caviar, salmon, and French Cognac and what do we get? What kind of government is this? How long can we put up with it? They've bumped off the old moron and stuck a young idiot at our head. What's really going on?' The comedian looked around to see if there was any support for his brave speech, but the people around maintained a reserved silence, creating the impression they had not heard the stranger's words. They only wanted to grab a cold beer, sit in the stands and feel the stupefaction of brewed hops seep into their head so they would not know or hear any one. The majority of people standing in this line had either not voted, or pressed the red button for 'against'. However, en route from the server to the central commission the vote had been changed due to a modification of the system.

Haiduk had seen this jolly quasi-intellectual with his grey skipper's beard before, but could not remember where. The stranger grabbed a bottle of beer, stepped into the shadow of the columns and eagerly gulped the liquid. Some of it foamed onto his beard and his old tie of an indeterminate pea colour. Haiduk saw the yellow, canine gleam in the stranger's eyes and recognised Professor Buraho from the condemned cell. He thought that now would be the best moment to kill this *gnojek*. He could not think of a better term for the man than this vulgar Polish word. He could easily enter the press of people and, with one blow to the neck, liquidate Professor Buraho before blending back into the crowd. However, he decided not to ruin this festival of democracy for the young hetman. It would be better to bring Vitold Yaropolk another, more socially significant, gift.

He went to the huge, brilliantly lit and rather cold hall

and took his place on a high stand close to the front, where he would have a good view of the stage and the stalls. An array of four by five metre screens would display all the details of the coming ceremony to every spectator, however far away they were sitting. The stalls were situated below on the hockey pitch where the representatives of the enforcement agencies were sitting in a disciplined manner, in dark blue, dark green and dark brown rows. A separate area of seating was reserved for middling and small oligarchs, landowners, each of which had no fewer than ten thousand serfs, along with industrialists and merchants belonging to the first guild. There was separate seating for officials, members of the Sejm, representatives of the arts and sciences, and stars of film and television. In a special area, near to the, as yet, empty stage, the participants of a ceremonial meeting gave interviews, one after the other, against the backdrop of a portrait of the young hetman. Their enraptured faces beamed out from the screens from which could be heard phrases such as 'a happy day', 'the beginning of a new era', 'high hopes', 'popular support', 'peace, freedom and democracy' and 'a brilliant victory'.

Haiduk had a good view from above of how Indira Holembiyevska, wearing a long, black sari, passed along the wide, crimson rug laid in the passages between the stalls. She was accompanied by a security officer, who guided her to the seventh row to sit alongside the mayor of Kyiv, Krishna Singh, who was wearing a pink, formal turban. Nykyfor Salyvon ran hurriedly to the front and groomed his long, greying hair with his fingers in a nervous manner. He was the author of the inauguration scenario. Haiduk saw Ivanyshyn, his former deputy and now the director of the military intelligence division of the State Guard. He saw many people from that distant time, with its nightmarish veneer now consigned irrevocably to the past. They passed before him and awakened no emotion in his soul.

The guests were finally seated, leaving the red carpet between the stalls empty. A fanfare sounded from the orchestra, which combined all types of military, opera and ballet orchestras, along with Fima Mohylevsky's jazz band. The unique, most renowned bass voice of Ukraine, the voice of Myron Shvayky rang out; hundreds of decibels resonating in the lungs and hearts of the audience, 'Let us b-b-begin the official cer-r-remony of the inauguration of His Excellency, the leader of all the people of the territory of Ukraine, head of the Kyiv-Dnipro State, Sir Vitold Yaropolkovych Kly-y-ynkevych. I ask you all to stand.'

The name of Klynkevych's post was new, already the word hetman was discounted, and Ukraine's name had also been revised. However, the surprises were only just beginning. The young, sporty leader of the people appeared on the stage beaming, with teeth polished to a dazzling brilliance by his dentist. He wore a quasi-military-style jacket with an upright collar and gold epaulettes, red military britches and lacquered boots with glistering high legs.

The public, who had been holding its breath, realised that the hetman period of Ukrainian history was concluded and gave a standing ovation to the new master of the territory. The Grand Master of the Church of Christ's Death was invited onto the stage, along with his entourage and the members of the Higher Justice Congregation, led by Marshall Ivan Ovramovych Kreyda. A trio comprising Sygismund Sansyzbayev, Borisogleb Chikirisov and Abbess Sylfida moved along the red carpet, accompanied by the warriors of light, the Sacred Guardians. Sylfida was Mother Superior at the Convent of Mary Magdalen in Suzdal.

They all wore black cassocks and wolf-head caps with open-fanged maws. Sansyzbayev alone had augmented his outfit with a mantle the colour of fresh blood, reminiscent of the *zhupan* Makhun had worn on the day of Haiduk's arrest. The guards bore red banners on which the image of Christ was painted over with black paint. Instead of crosses, the Deathchristians wore heavy, gold, T-shaped pendants around their necks. These symbolised the crucifixion of Christ and, simultaneously, the word terminus for the end, death. Chikirisov bore, in his hands, a dish darkened by fire, on which lay a book blackened with the dust of time. It was the so-called Gospel of James the Grave Digger, the story of the true and irreversible death of Christ.

Kreyda strode behind him, accompanied by people in Napoleonic-style uniforms. Perhaps the officer who had visited Haiduk in the prison hospital was among their number. The procession ascended the stage. Klynkevych knelt before Sansyzbayev and, submissively bowing his head, beseeched him, 'Bless me, Your Holiness.'

Sansyzbayev carefully lowered his hefty palm and stubby, short fingers onto Klynkevych's head. He scrupulously avoided disturbing Vitold's perfectly pomaded hair, which had been groomed into individual tresses. Every minuscule detail was visible on the array of large television screens.

The priest of Death-christianity announced, 'In the name of that all-powerful dark energy that rules the world, I bless you, Your Excellency, who bears such labour for us, Head of the Kyiv-Dnipro State and I bless all your future acts as a statesman. We unite together in a prayer in the name of the triumph of the Movement for Four Freedoms that will bring your territory peace and prosperity. I now pronounce you Head of the Church of Christ's Death, the Grand Master, and humbly resign from the position myself as I make way for you.' Sansyzbayev shed the crimson mantle and draped it around the shoulders of Klynkevych. Then he hung the gold T around his neck.

'I hope,' continued Father Kalerii, whose round, Mongolian face was utterly bereft of any whiskers, 'that you, Your Excellency, unite in one person, spiritual and worldly power, that you will lead the struggle with Judeo-Christian heresy and the fantasy of the resurrection of Christ from the dead and lead our people onto the path of truth. I also hope that by your labours you will raise, in the Russian capital of Kyiv, a Mausoleum wherein the mortal body of Christ will rest. Christ has died, search for the truth within yourself.' He and his entourage placed the palms of their right hands against their foreheads. This was the gesture with which the Deathchristians had replaced the Christian tradition of crossing oneself. It signified that a person had to rely solely on their intellect, on a balanced evaluation, and not on the heart or the spirit.

Klynkevych repeated this gesture and rose from his knees. Borisogleb Chikirisov raised the dish with the gospel towards him and requested that he place his right hand on the black book. 'Repeat after me,' said Sansyzbayev. 'I swear allegiance before the face of the dark energy that governs the world …'

Klynkevych repeated the text word for word.

The Grey Prince must be here, thought Haiduk. He is definitely nearby. He and his generals are sitting in this hall and before the eyes of millions of viewers they are destroying an ancient country. But maybe the country is destroying itself by losing the will to live? He suddenly smelled again the repellent, nauseating aroma of rats in the prison cell.

'… I swear,' Sansyzbayev continued, 'to act in accord with the interests of the great Eurasian Union of People, formed during a thousand years of common history and foster the development of the territory I govern.'

The hall was engulfed in a deathly silence. It seemed to Haiduk as if all who were present suffered a collective paralysis that would lead to collective death. At that moment a whistle echoed in the hall and young voices bellowed from a distant spectator stand, 'Shame! Death to traitors! Glory to Ukraine!'

Immediately, one hundred or so people in light grey suits hurtled, like sprinters hearing the crack of a starting pistol, towards the stand. A brief skirmish ensued, but soon silence fell and after a minute the upper benches of that stand were gapingly empty. This unpleasant episode apparently made no impression on those on the stage. It was not seen by the television viewers because the inauguration was broadcast with a five minute time delay. The editors were able to cut out the unwanted audio-visual material. It seemed to Haiduk that the aura, programmed by the psycho-technologists of some mysterious and grandiose act taking place, had dissipated and everything became a little bustlingly agitated and prosaic.

Sansyzbayev and his wolf pack trampled the stage, not knowing what to do next. Kreyda, speaking hurriedly and garbling the words, read out the act pronouncing the election of Klynkevych as the nineteenth president of Ukraine. His words evoked a wave of doubts and conjectures in the audience. It was understood that Klynkevych was not a hetman. But what was he in reality? A king; he had been addressed as 'Your Majesty'? Was he a Chancellor or was he the manager of a territory? Or, as Kreyda had just announced, nothing other than the President of Ukraine? Disputes immediately began in the fifth row of the stalls, where constitutional and legal experts and lawyers sat, regarding the definition of Klynkevych's place in the power system of Ukraine.

Shvayka's voice boomed out and ended these squabbles, 'We invite the nineteenth president of the Kyiv-Dnipro State, leader of the people of the territory of Ukraine, Grand Master of the Church of Christ's Death, His Majesty Vitold Yaropolk Klynkevych to speak.'

The new leader of the country approached the gold inlaid lectern on the stage with an easy, athletic gait. He looked attentively at the auto-cue screens, struggling to see if they showed the inauguration speech he had written personally, soon after the murder of Hetman Makhun. Nykyfor Salyvon and his sickly-sweet, soppy, sentimental rhetoric could not be allowed to direct this historic affair. The text had been approved by the Grey Prince himself.

'I greet the people of the Kyiv-Dnipro State on this celebration of democracy and freedom.' The speakers at the back of the stalls welcomed this with a pre-recorded soundtrack of an ovation and yells of 'Glory'. 'As supreme commander I greet our gallant armed forces and law enforcement agencies with a new phase of internal consolidation and the strengthening of the defence potential of the country.' The black, blue, green, and brown rows of military and police bosses reacted stormily to these words. 'Greetings to all those of our faith and mind, all the brothers and sisters in the Church of Christ's Death, who prayed for me, beseeching the dark energy that governs the world that it might present me with this triumph.' He pressed the palm of his right hand against his forehead and remained silent for a moment before continuing, 'But that's enough rejoicing in the triumph of democracy and the dispelled illusion of prosperity that flourished under the previous leadership. We must acknowledge, frankly, that their policies placed the country on the edge of an abyss. Social demagogy, populism, empty promises, hypocrisy in internal and external politics destabilised the state and led to a drastic fall in its international authority. We must acknowledge,' Klynkevych's voice drew close to Shvayka's now in the strength of its dramatic modulation, 'that the attempt to create a Ukrainian Military Cossack Feudal State has completely collapsed, the project itself has been revealed as archaic and unfit for the realities of the twenty-first century. The military administration has shown its inability to effectively govern civil society and has mutated into a hotbed of corruption and cronyism. The potential for a loss of faith on the part of the people towards the state and its leaders has increased.'

Haiduk did not believe his ears. These were his words from the secret memorandum prepared for Makhun in June.

The hetman had sworn, as he handed the report back, that no one apart from him had read it.

'A primitive, rural nationalism of a provincial stamp was implanted in the state, instilling archaic traditions not in accord with the Eurasian spirit of our history,' Klynkevych continued. 'Therefore, I, by the power vested in me by the all powerful dark energy and the voters, adopt the following resolution, contained in decree number one, which I have signed today: Firstly, as of now, the country will be named the Kyiv-Dnipro State, eschewing the words 'Ukraine' and 'Ukrainian' as degrading to our national pride because they have the pejorative meaning of the edge, the wayside, the margins. Secondly, the blue and yellow state flag will be augmented with an inverted black star at its centre, the symbol of the Eurasian community to which our state belongs.'

The state flag was slowly lowered onto the stage, enriched with this new decorative element.

'Thirdly,' Klynkevych continued reading the decree. 'The state emblem, the gold trident of Prince Volodymyr, will also be enhanced with the black star. Fourthly, the federal state is transformed into a unitary state. This is aimed at realising a more vertical system of controlling the territory and simplifying fiscal policy. Fifthly, the five-chambered Sejm and Senate are hereby liquidated and all former deputies of this ineffective body, which is loathed by the people, lose their privileges and immunity. New elections to the National Assembly, the Parliament of the State, will be ordained by my separate decree and held in March 2078. The sixth point, the system of state power in the territory is reorganised. The obsolete Aeropagus is liquidated and replaced by the creation of the highest organ of state governance, the Directorate. The head of the Directorate is the president of the state, that is me. The composition of the Directorate will also include Ivan Ovramovych Kreyda, Mintimer Nykonovych Basmanov and Ruslan Vitaliyovych

Foshchenko. The Military Cossack administration will be replaced with the introduction of general governors of the provinces. The Cossack armed units are immediately disbanded and in their place punitive units of the Ministry of State Security and Internal Affairs, or the MSSIA, are established. The State Guard is liquidated as a separate organ and incorporated within the MSSIA. Ivan Ovramovych Kreyda is appointed to lead the new ministry. The seventh point, in order to reduce the risks in the sphere of national security and strengthen the sovereignty of the state, I have invited a limited military contingent from our ally, the Horde, onto the right bank territory of the state and into the Hero City of Kyiv. This force will assist with the maintenance of order and protecting our democratic gains.'

Haiduk saw the huge Confederation ambassador leap, with a swiftness that belied his weight, from the two seats he occupied on the third row. O'Sullivan unceremoniously barged aside colleagues in the diplomatic corps and headed for the exit while simultaneously talking into his mobile phone.

Right now would be the best time to crack the American cipher, thought Haiduk. They will send Washington the text of Klynkevych's announcement, which could become the key to deciphering the code; it could be done if Kreyda's most powerful computers were used. Unfortunately, I don't think the *halushka* dumpling manufacturer really understands what is happening.

Many people were now darting out of their places, shocked at the loss of their positions, immunity and privileges, and the destruction of their careers; above all, at the loss of the foundations of a state that had become familiar during the Kostiuk and Makhun periods. The first rows of the stalls swiftly emptied. However, only a few people noticed this peripheral turmoil because the end of the ceremony and an interval, which would be followed by a concert, was announced.

81

28 July 2077
20:00 Kyiv time
Secret
Urgent
To be immediately reported to the president and to the adviser to the President of the Confederation on national security issues, M. Jefferson

The newly elected President of Ukraine, V. Klynkevych, announced an unprecedented change in Ukraine's external political course today. The advancing occupation of the left bank of Ukraine and Kyiv by the Horde's military (the full text of Klynkevych's speech is attached) signifies a drastic change in the geo-political situation in Europe, drawing the Confederation and OGS towards inevitable military conflict with the states of the USH. We calculate that three days remain until the occupation of Kyiv. Taking into account the possible cessation of diplomatic relations between Washington and Kyiv and the potential seizure of the embassy by the forces of the Horde, I have issued a directive to prepare for evacuation. This includes a list of staff and family members who require evacuation in the first instance, the preparation of the archives for destruction, possible immediate destruction of codes and special apparatus, warning our contacts and information sources of the danger, and organising means of communication for use in extreme conditions etc.

Due to the emergency situation I urgently request that you now order the immediate evacuation of embassy personnel based in Kyiv. I await your instructions regarding the further actions required of the embassy.

The Ambassador of the Confederation of States of North America in Ukraine, John O'Sullivan

28 July 2077
20:00 Kyiv time
Top Secret
To His Excellency, the Bekler-bek of the Horde, General Mohammad Bek

Glory to Allah, the All Powerful and Compassionate, Glory to the Sun of the East, the Black Star of the Earth, His Majesty, Ruler of the People of the Horde and the World, Kara-Khan.

Bowing my head before you, I rush to report the announcement of the Great Khan of the Kyiv-Dnipro District, Klynkevych. He requests that the all-conquering liberating forces of the Horde occupy the eastern territories of the district and Batii-Hrad from 1 August 2077. (The text of his speech is attached.) After prolonged persuasion, vacillation and the presentation of new conditions, including financial, the young Khan finally agreed to a deal on the basis of territory in exchange for power and diamonds. Substantial assistance in finalising this deal was provided by Mullah Sansyzbayev, Boyaryn Basmanov and Minister Foshchenko. I congratulate you, Your Eminence, on your great personal triumph, on the triumph of the peaceful policies of the Horde.

In order to achieve the successful realisation of the plan to unify the entirety of the Steppe into a single Great Steppe, I propose the following measures:

1. The preparation of a list of all Jewish, Judeo-Liberal, and Judeo-Christian leaders, all Israeli agents of influence and all enemies of the Horde in Ukraine, for their immediate extermination. I inform you that I have issued an order to the Steppe intelligence network for the immediate arrest of Judeo-Imperialist traitor, Friedman, and alerted all border posts at the district concerning this directive.

2. The preparation of a list of the best premises in Batii-Hrad

for the accommodation of the officer corps of the Horde's liberating army.

3. I propose to transfer the diplomatic representation of the countries of the USH to Mykhailivska Square, to the building that once housed the Ministry of Foreign Affairs of former Ukraine.

4. I propose that we situate the headquarters of the liberating army of the Horde in the premises of the Sejm (parliament) of the district above the Dnipro.

5. I propose that the civilian administration of the occupied territory should be controlled by Mullah Sansyzbayev.

6. As the first steps, the preparation of a plan of measures for the requisition of grain stocks and other provisions, utilising the Horde's means of transport and vehicles belonging to the locals.

7. The selection of convenient locations for four or five concentration camps for military prisoners. I propose we deport Ukrainian nationalists to currently unpopulated desert areas on Horde territory.

Special Emissary of the Black Star of Humanity, Vizier Vadym Khlyshchenko-Khlyshchov

82

Haiduk mingled with the flood of functionaries who, stunned by the content of Klynkevych's speech, began to flee the hall without waiting for the concert. Passing through the dark alley that connected the building with Tolstoho Square, his heart ached when he saw the six-storey building on the left, where he had been born and where his mother had lived until recently. He reached Pushkinska Street, not far from the Nimetsky Dim, a building housing various German institutions, where Nevinchanyi was waiting for him in the Ford Scorpion.

Haiduk sat in the electronic vehicle and switched on

the portable tele-screen. The triumphal concert was due to commence. The vehicle turned left from Pushkinska Street onto Shevchenko Boulevard and headed west towards the few lingering crimson traces of sunset.

'What the fuck is going on?' Nevinchanyi sighed.

The advertisements for various processed foods ended and the country's main stage flickered onto the screen again. Haiduk saw the hall was full again because the seats abandoned by those functionaries who had fled were now replenished with people who were smiling happily. The camera focused on a line of people moving from the depths of the hall along the long, red carpet. Klynkevych led them, having swapped his outfit in the interval. The newly elected leader had shed the supreme commander's uniform and now wore a white tuxedo and red bow tie. A young beauty glided majestically next to him in a long white dress with an alluring diamond necklace around her soft, girlish neck. The face of this presidential companion seemed familiar to Haiduk.

'What, is he married?' he asked Nevinchanyi.

'It's the first I've heard if he is.'

Nevinchanyi looked for a moment at the television screen and realisation dawned on him, 'It's Motrya from the fourth directorate. Our Motrya, who went to serve the hetman. Well, bloody hell, she's given way to him.'

'Not given, but taken,' said Haiduk. 'This is called policy continuity and respect for tried and tested personnel.'

Klynkevych and his cute, snub-nosed companion were followed by Basmanov in his unchanging Boyar's cap, holding the boy Nikolai, Russia's future Tsar, by the hand. After them came Kreyda and his wife, and Foshchenko and the female boss of the foreign affairs ministry's protocol decorate. She was now a major in the State Guard, but Haiduk remembered her as the buxom secretary at Ukraine's Washington Embassy.

The upper echelons of the state and their companions

sat in the seventh row of the stalls and the concert began. The curtain rose and viewers saw the Grand Viennese Mozart Symphony Orchestra on the stage. One hundred and fifty of the world's best musicians guided by the American conductor, Jan Gontmacher. Haiduk thought that after the primitive folk concerts, involving lots of *sharovary* Cossack pants, from Makhun's era, the invite to such an orchestra was an accolade for Klynkevych.

'Dear Friends, we will begin the concert,' announced a sweet, female voice, which had replaced Shvaika's booming baritone. 'We will begin with a pleasant surprise. His majesty, the nineteenth president of the Kyiv-Dnipro State, leader of the people of the territory of Ukraine, Vitold-Yaropolk Klynkevych, is invited onto the stage.'

The young president leaped onto the stage with an easy feline grace and approached Jan Gontmacher. The American bowed deeply, shook Klynkevych's hand and led him to a black Steinway piano.

'There will be a performance of a concert for forte-piano and orchestra on the theme of an immortal work of folk art, which needs no recommendation or commentary,' the announcer's voice was brimming with happy roulades.

Jan Gontmacher positioned himself at the conductor's stand, tapped his baton severely, and gestured towards Klynkevych. The screen showed a close up of the new president's hands, with their long fingers and the mother of pearl glister of his nails. The glister flickered across the keyboard as the elegiac introductory passage of Chopin sounded. Haiduk found himself actually being pleased with Klynkevych, who knew English and could play Chopin brilliantly; so very different from Makhun.

Then, after the solemn opening notes of the overture struck, the melody of the *Murka* sounded on the piano. This hymn of the criminal underground echoed in the hall one hundred and fifty years after its music inspired Odesa's crooks, wet-jobbers, street thugs and their whores.

An ovation echoed around the hall, which on hearing the strains had sensed something kindred and dear to them. The music spoke of new times when no one need be ashamed of anything, when all that had held true in the previous epoch had been discarded ... when your own people came to power and criminal brigades sat in the hall and you sensed the unseen presence of the Grey Prince himself. The members of the brigades, hearing the familiar strains of the *Murka*, could already taste the infinite promise opening up before the territory. It would become the main transit point for the narcotics trade from Asia to Europe and America. They could supply the mini-submarines, manufactured in Kerch, to the drug barons of Colombia. They would extend and modernise the network of pornography television studios on the left bank, intensify money-laundering operations through Cyprus, Chios, Kreydos, and eventually the whole world.

Calls were now being made right from the concert hall to all the provinces of the territory, with instructions to prepare for the arrival of the Horde's liberating army. Fair-haired girls aged thirteen and upwards would be traded for narcotics and diamonds.

Haiduk extracted his communication gadget from the glove compartment and simply said, 'Let's begin,' into the mouthpiece.

The screen immediately glittered, as if a blizzard had commenced, and the strains of the *Murka* ceased. An image of Klynkevych's inspired face, transported by the music, his eyes half closed, appeared over the piano with the inscription:

HE IS A MURDERER

The black and white footage of the surveillance camera at Makhun's dacha appeared with Klynkevych's face deformed by hatred and his cry, 'Oh you bitch, do you want to make idiots of us? Help him!'

The terrible image of the hetman's face, blown open by gunshots, and blood-drenched eyes, which were brimming with suffering; the Colt, gripped by the strong fingers of the executioner, and the shot in the left temple ... Klynkevych wiping his bloodied hands on his white *zhupan* ... This grotesque kaleidoscope flickered before the eyes of millions of viewers, then the camera returned again to the hall where Klynkevych played the *Murka*. A new inscription appeared on the screen:

HE IS A TRAITOR AND MURDERER
GLORY TO UKRAINE! URA

The broadcast was suddenly cut off and the test card of the good news channel appeared on the screen.

'Good lass, Olya,' said Haiduk, switching off the monitor.

In front of them, near the polytechnic, they saw some police cars, with their lights flashing, blocking Peremohy Avenue. Nevinchanyi braked and asked, 'What should we do?'

'Just drive like you were doing,' said Haiduk. 'They're not for us.'

A number of cars were now accumulating by the police barrier, their horns sounding dementedly. Nevinchanyi approached close to the police cordon, 'What's going on chief? I am driving a surgeon to hospital for an emergency operation. Maybe you could let us through?'

The policeman, who was wearing shades, though dusk had long since fallen, peered into the car and said apologetically, 'Jesus, it's you. Excuse me. I thought I recognised you. You performed an operation on my wife. But I can't let you through. There's a bit of a problem going on there.'

He pointed at a large supermarket, which stood on the right-hand side of the avenue, one hundred metres from the police cordon. Dark, armoured, police assault vehicles and red and white fire engines clustered there. The upper storeys of the supermarket burned, illuminating the area around with a flickering crimson light. Dark figures could be seen bearing bags and boxes of cartons from the store. Shots rang out.

Nevinchanyi turned right into Starokyivska Street in order to cross the yards and alleys and break through to Dehtyarivska and then to Lukianivsky Market and the Artemida factory.

'That's how wars begin,' said Haiduk.

Nevinchanyi did not utter a word about what was happening. He was silent and looked into the black, empty streets of a city gripped by panic. They saw a few smaller stores being looted here and there.

'Do you know, Ihor Petrovych, how much those jackals stripped from us so we could have access to that recording?'

'How much?'

'Half a million ameros. They asked for it in globos, but we didn't give way. And they will sell ten copies to various CNNs and go to the Bahamas.'

'Hauteur, honour and humanity,' said Haiduk thoughtfully. 'Humiliation, slavery and occupation. We must immediately gather the co-ordinators of the Ukrainian Liberation Front. We can't imagine what lies ahead.'

They both fell silent, wrapped in their own thoughts.

83

29 July 2077
Address of the Ukrainian Liberation Front

Citizens of Ukraine
A group of criminal conspirators have murdered the legally elected Hetman of Ukraine, General K. D. Makhun. They have simultaneously undertaken a coup and seized power. The conspirators have executed the most heinous act of treason, destroying the sovereignty and violating the territorial integrity of Ukraine. They have surrendered the people and the state to the most malicious enemy, the Horde. Instead of the slogan promised by the traitor, Klynkevych, of hauteur, honour and humanity, the Ukrainian people have received humiliation, slavery and occupation. In these circumstances ULF calls on all citizens of Ukraine, irrespective of nationality, language, religion, or political views, to unite around our political and military wings.

We declare an uncompromising war on Klynkevych's criminal group. We have irrefutable evidence of his involvement in the murder of Hetman Makhun, which will be presented to court when the time comes for him to face justice. ULF is making public, secret material that testifies to the international illegal and corrupt activities of the criminal oligarchic state elite. This material will demonstrate to the Ukrainian people who exactly is thriving in our national misfortune.

We declare war on the feudal oligarchic system and on the serfdom imposed on millions of Ukrainians. We call for the people to struggle against the occupation of Ukraine by the forces of the Horde.

Citizens of Ukraine! The Horde has come to subjugate you and transform you and your children into slaves, and to plunder Ukraine. They will strip the natural resources of our soil and strategic raw materials, and take away grain, meat and dairy products. They will destroy the technological, agrarian and information potential of the country. It is necessary to organise local ULF committees and units to undertake defence and maintain order, to prevent the plundering of our stocks and the marauding and banditry that threaten Ukrainian towns and villages.

Prior to the arrival of the occupants, these committees and units must either conceal food stocks or hand them to the impoverished sections of the population.

We address the soldiers in Ukraine's armed forces. Your duty is to organise armed resistance against the advance of the Horde. You must destroy the invaders and refuse to execute the criminal orders of the high directorate. We call for the immediate organisation of partisan units and underground groups, for the creation of widespread civilian resistance to the occupants and their henchmen.

Citizens, do not obey the criminal orders of the occupying power and the treacherous regime of Klynkevych, Kreyda, Basmanov and Foshchenko. Remember, the occupants will be destroyed and collaborators will be punished.

People of Ukraine. In the terrible battles of the twentieth and twenty-first centuries, during years when you were severely tested, you created and defended your state, affirming your right to independence.

The creation of the Ukrainian Liberation Front marks the triumph of true democracy and is the first step towards the formation of a democratic government in an independent Ukraine. We are not a territory without a voice, we are not just a district of the Horde. We are a state that originated with Kyiv-Rus from the adoption of Christianity on the banks of the Dnipro.

We will never become pagans and Deathchristians. We will never renounce our faith in the resurrection of Christ and his second coming.

Everyone must join the struggle. Glory to Ukraine!

The Co-ordinating Committee of ULF

Part Five

OCCUPATION

84

The plan for Operation Tamerlane was prepared by the beginning of July 2077 and consisted of three phases. First, the seizure of the left bank of Ukraine and Kyiv by the Horde; second, the occupation of central Europe and connecting with the Balkans to assist Albania, Bosnia and the Kosovo-Macedonian Kingdom; third, the complete subjugation of all Europe, including its western area, with the remnants of France, Spain, and the Turkic-German republic, which had emerged in Bavaria.

Mohammad Bek, Kara-Khan's deputy and the Beklerbek, was appointed supreme commander of the liberating forces and simultaneously chief of general staff. He was a graduate of West Point and had been awarded a doctorate from the Prussian Higher Academy of Geo-politics. The brilliant and highly educated, four star general in the Jordanian Kingdom's army became renowned for his role in the so-called 'Great Fuel Battle' on the Arab Peninsula. In 2075 the Sun of the East and Black Star of the Earth, Kara-Khan, had ordered his forces to advance along the Russian border in the direction of Europe, to seize the fuel deposits in the Arctic and Siberian fields. He declared Russia a failed-state, which was true when the ruinous policies of Russia's rulers and its demographic catastrophe were taken into account.

Using the UN Security Council resolution concerning Russia, Mohammad Bek proposed the idea of declaring part of Siberia and its fuel and forestry reserves a World Heritage site. The area would then not belong legally to any state, especially a failed one. He then led the Horde's military onto the disputed territory. He had crafted the plan for destroying the remains of Russian statehood during the events of the bloody Kurban-Bayrami of November 2076. The renowned strategist and military commander was awarded the title of first deputy to Kara-Khan for this achievement. He received the highest insignia of the Horde from the hands of the chief himself, a black star fashioned from a twenty-carat diamond.

The detailed planning of Operation Tamerlane commenced in April 2077. Mohammad Bek gathered together the most talented officers to draft the operation. They included generals from the defunct general staff of the Russian armed forces, German lecturers from the Prussian higher school of geopolitics, and Pakistani, Iranian and Turkish military officers. An international intelligence unit (IIU) was created under Mohammad Bek's headquarters. The unit established a well-resourced scientific research centre devoted to the study of Ukraine as the first target in Operation Tamerlane. The unit thoroughly analysed Ukrainian history, particularly the reasons for the collapse of Kyiv-Rus, the defeats of Cossack uprisings and the failure to establish a strong Ukrainian statehood. Another vector of their research was the study of contemporary state-political life in Ukraine, particularly its weak spots and vulnerable areas. A third, no less significant, area of research was the psychological characteristics of Ukrainians; such attributes as their corruptibility and capacity for betrayal, their inability to unite, and the absence of a firm sense of nationhood. The centre was directed by a Russian intelligence officer and specialist in Ukraine, Colonel Kornilov-Kyseliov, whose code name was KaKa. He had defected to the Horde after the events of 2076 and handed the riches of Russia's special services archive, detailing centuries of exploiting Ukraine, to his new masters.

The first phase of Operation Tamerlane envisaged a military advance along six lines, with strikes being delivered in the event of resistance:

1. Orel — Zheleznovodsk — Hlukhiv — Bakhmach— Nizhyn — Brovary — Kyiv;
2. Belgorod — Kharkiv — Poltava — Cherkasy;
3. Millerovo — Luhansk — Donetsk — Dnipropetrovsk;
4. Kamensk — Shakhtynsk — Krasnodon — Makiyivka — Donetsk;
5. Dzhankoy — Melitopol— Zaporizhia;
6. Perekopsk — Armyansk — Kherson — Mykolayiv— Odesa.

The forces of the Horde, deployed for the operation, comprised four assault armies consisting of up to 40% ethnic Russians. They were strictly controlled by Islamic commissars and counter-intelligence operatives. Initially they were concentrated at Stalingrad, then from June onwards they were gradually relocated to Kalach-on-Don. Thereafter they were broken into four groups and relocated to their starting positions. The transfer of the military forces was undertaken in conditions of absolute secrecy, utilising the freight wagon convoys of the Friedman firm. The wagons transported arms to the Horde from Ukraine and, in order not to return empty, transferred soldiers from the Horde to the Ukrainian border, which allowed Friedman a double profit. Two assault groups for Odesa and Zaporizhia were consolidated in Crimea, which still formally belonged to Ukraine. The Peninsula had declared its union with Russia on two occasions. However, in reality, it was in the hands of Turkey, which supported the Crimean State, with its capital in Bakhchysarai. Turkey organised the transport by ferry of military and arms to Crimea under the guise of young Turks taking their summer vacation.

UMI knew in general terms about the plan to occupy Ukraine, but did not have the full picture. The alarm signals sent by Haiduk to the hetman were blocked by Klynkevych. A mole working within the UMI allowed the Horde to arrest some of Haiduk's loyal agents. The Horde's own intelligence network had grown exponentially from early 2077. Agents of influence operated virtually in the open, working against the state in parliament, government agencies and mass-media.

The Deathchristians project had proven particularly successful, utterly sundering apart a society already rife with discord, sowing strife among families, citizens and groups of people with once shared views. Having invested large sums in the purchase of Sansyzbayev and his people, Mohammad Bek knew that when the great triumph over Ukraine and Europe came, this man and his sect would be of no use to the Horde. He despised and detested this Mongol-Kazakh apostate. He and his mob would be liquidated.

During his evening meditations and prayers, the general reflected on the terrible weaponry devised by Christ; benevolence. The general had lived his entire life in an atmosphere of hatred, a comprehensible, albeit primitive, force. Benevolence contained within it a dangerous enigma, an unpredictable threat to the very laws that governed the individual's existence. The general had never operated according to the concept of an opposition between hatred and benevolence. The execution of a deserter by firing squad was not an act of hatred but a manifestation of that justice. If someone pitied the deserter and dared to free him from his punishment on a benevolent impulse, Mohammad Bek would calmly, in the name of justice, murder them as an apostate.

The general leafed through the pages of the Tamerlane plan. Mohammad Bek thought the letter T, as the sign of the Deathchristians, most fitted this operation. As he read, he believed with satisfaction that he had triumphed utterly over his main opponent, Lieutenant General Haiduk. While the latter was cooling his heels for some years in America, the Horde's intelligence network had successfully penetrated critically vulnerable sections of the Ukrainian State. They had used bribery and blackmail to form a powerful body of traitors, delicately named agents of influence. They had planted moles in intelligence and counter-intelligence. Above all they had extirpated any will to resist in the community, instilling Ukrainian citizens with the ideal of Eurasian unity. Haiduk was utterly neutralised, even taking into account his escape from prison. However, as a worthy enemy, Haiduk deserved not pity but justice; his death.

The sole copy of Tamerlane had been produced in Arabic by the liberating army's best calligrapher. The finely wrought text aroused the general as he sat in his headquarters that he had relocated to Millerovo. He felt like a tiger concealing itself in preparation for a strike on a vulnerable target, and anticipated tearing its throat. He believed the operation contained neither hatred nor benevolence, it was a manifestation of justice itself.

85

Klynkevych's statement that the friendly forces of the Horde had been invited onto Ukrainian territory sowed an unwarranted terror in the population. Fear spread through the country with the swiftness of a wildfire, from the high officials, who had fled the Kosmichny Hall without waiting for the interval, to the most wretched of their dependants and serfs.

All Ukrainian society resonated with a foreboding of some incomprehensible and more terrifying threat approaching from the east, north and south; a July storm cloud crackling with high voltage, approaching immutably. The mass-media on Horde territory maintained absolute silence on the subject of Ukraine. They even ceased their daily assaults on what they termed 'a failed state'. They focused instead on events in India, particularly the persecution of Muslims in Mumbai.

The member states of the OGS answered Klynkevych's statement by holding a council of foreign affairs ministers in Washington. The council repeated ritualistic declarations about

386

the unacceptability of invading sovereign countries. However, it adopted no concrete resolutions and limited itself to observing the situation. An array of OGS members, above all France, called for Ukraine to be the sacrificial ram on the altar of European security. They anticipated that the Horde would push no further west than the line of the Carpathian Mountains.

Poland, recollecting the experience of Czechoslovakia in 1938 and its own fate in 1939, insisted that preventative military measures should be deployed. However, no one wanted to be the first state to engage in open warfare. The Confederation of States of North America, in spite of Shirley MacDowell's fiery speech at the Athens summit, did not deploy any concrete measures against the Horde's aggression.

The president was well aware that public opinion in her country was strongly opposed to war in Europe; 85% of those surveyed did not want American and Canadian troops dispatched to die in this little-known country, a black hole of corruption and dictatorship, when Mexican insurrectionists had seized a portion of the southern states.

Ukraine's refusal to participate in a joint operation with the OGS against the Horde aroused the wrath of congress and was viewed by the community as straightforward treachery. Furthermore, only at the end of August 2077 would installation and configuration work be completed on the Ronald Reagan Military Space Station. The vessel's field of surveillance covered Central and East Europe, opening great strategic possibilities for America's space forces command. In order not to provoke the Horde, the Confederation did not break off diplomatic relations with Kara-Khan's regime as their Kyiv based ambassador, John O'Sullivan, had anticipated. The state department only gave him vague instructions to 'prepare for an emergency situation'.

In the three days remaining until Sunday 1 August, when the Horde's forces would enter the country, the situation in Ukraine fundamentally changed. The mass looting of warehouses and stores with provisions erupted, and breweries and distilleries were torched. Long queues formed for sugar, flour, cereals and oil. People stocked up on candles, matches and gas, electronic lights and batteries for radio receivers, laptops and other gadgets. Denim, old shoes and coats, polythene and vast stocks of tortilla chips and China-Cola were swept from the shelves of those stores that still existed.

Violence did not restrict itself to plundering stores and warehouses. Local aides to the government and business men were also attacked. The three-storey individual houses of low-level state managers and functionaries were burned to the ground. Lynch courts were inflicted on the rich and police officials, hated alike by the populace. The victims hung like black bags, swollen with the heat, on trees and pillars across Ukraine.

No one could put an end to the violence because the State Guard had been liquidated. Its leadership, headed by Yulii Merezhko, had fled to an unknown location; in other words they were concealed in safe apartments prepared in advance. The armed forces, decapitated after the death of Pryadko, stood aside on the verge of collapse and spontaneous revolts, following the dishonour inflicted on them.

The television stations broadcast the images of other traitors, along with Haiduk, who had refused to swear an oath of loyalty to Vitold Klynkevych. They included Friedman, referred to as a Jewish-mason, a cosmopolitan, a traitor to Ukraine, a member of the World Government of Judeo-Liberals and one of the globe's greatest criminals. The reward for his head, two million globos, was greater than that for Haiduk's. Those making the announcement knew that Friedman, even before Klynkevych had dismissed him from the Aeropagus, had fled Ukraine after the death of the hetman. The haulier had flown to Locarno in his gold Rolls Royce terrapin. However, the people must be provided with the illusion of justice triumphant. In second place in the list of traitors, and ahead of Haiduk, was Indira Holembiyevska. She was depicted as a swindler, prostitute and maverick who, thanks to her intimate relationship with the former hetman, had risen to the summit of political life on the territory of Ukraine. She had organised the mass credit union movement known as Samodopomoha, self-help, solely to steal ten billion globos of the people's money. A one million globos reward was offered for her head. In last place among the trinity of traitors was cautious, quiet Yulii Yulianovych Merezhko, apparently a long-standing agent of Romanian intelligence. He was accused of ruining the work of the State Guard and trying to use the police and gendarmerie to further his own ambitions. A reward of half a million globos was promised for his head.

The population did not react to the exposure of new traitors accurately and regarded those currently in power as guilty of treason. They flocked to the train, bus and stagecoach stations, tried to hire trucks or horse-drawn wagons and rickshaws. Some attempted to evacuate their children, who were on their summer break, as quickly as possible; others tried to return to their homes from where they were taking their vacation, others tried to flee the districts marked for occupation. The whole state was transformed into a communal evacuation point where people, gripped by panic, stormed ticket offices in railway stations and airports. They rode on the roofs of wagons and offered extravagant sums to taxi drivers and truckers. Anything not to remain in the same place; to do something, although most did not know what they needed to do in this situation.

The hackers of the Ukrainian Liberation Front interrupted the broadcasts of the official channels a few times with their declarations and calls to action. This further strengthened the disorder gripping the state, evoking anxiety in the supreme commander of the liberation army of the Horde, General Mohammad Bek, on the eve of the invasion.

86

The young, currently naked and handsome leader of the nation, Vitold Klynkevych, triumphantly swayed over the bare derriere of Motrya, the hetman's former stewardess. He undertook his labours with thoughtfulness, absorbed in reflections befitting a statesman. The number one secure phone line rang; it was the most important state communication channel. He picked it up while he continued with Motrya.

'Who's that?' he asked brusquely, while gently caressing Motrya's silken back with his other hand.

'Your Majesty, it's General Mohammad Bek on the line.'

'I'm listening,' Klynkevych uttered somewhat more gently.

He heard the general's guttural voice saying, 'Our command is very perturbed by the situation that has arisen on the territory of the Kyiv-Dnipro District. Our representative describes it as catastrophic and uncontrolled, to the extent that it may impede the schedule for the advance of the liberating army …'

Klynkevych thought patriotically, if coarsely, Fuck you, you rancid little upstart. He was still exalted with the global renown acquired after his performance of the convicts' song during the inauguration concert. Since then he had rarely emerged from Motrya's body, having been dementedly besotted with her during Makhun's reign. This sport was also to her liking. Moaning with rapture, she tore the leader of the nation from affairs of state, receptions, telephone calls and other nonsense … her body ached for his touch. Even diamonds did not delight her as much as this love.

'Your concern is groundless, General,' said Klynkevych, considering whether he should lay on his back and plant Motrya above him. Or would it be better to swiftly conclude the call and not interrupt their pleasure. 'I completely control the situation in the state. I will deal with it and call you back later,' Klynkevych discarded the receiver.

He felt his enraptured body indifferent to where or when this moment was, in which country or in the past or future. When he returned from that other world, Klynkevych decided to deal with mundane matters.

They were at the Rohulka State dacha where the unfortunate events with Makhun had occurred. This unpleasant fact did not impede him in his pleasures. Moreover, he could easily visit the neighbouring building secreted behind a high, stone wall. This architecturally unimposing structure of dark, almost black, thick brick walls had narrow, barred windows. The building was in fact a transplanted fragment of the Kharkiv transit prison, now named the Friendship of the Peoples. The edifice was originally constructed in the eighteenth century and designed by the well-known German architect, Zimmerman. It was here that the first criminal authority was born and raised.

Semen Mohylevsky was the godfather of South Russia. His round, staring eyes were perpetually open, even in his sleep. This architectural monument had been used as the residence of the Grey Prince from that time onwards. Klynkevych passed through the secret wooden door in the wall and entered the neglected grounds, which were densely covered with trees and shrubbery. He trod an old path through the weeds. Two guards stood near the door of the building; they were wearing NKVD uniforms, blue military caps, with crimson bands, and long cavalry-style greatcoats, and were holding bayoneted rifles. They glared at Klynkevych.

Another guard point was situated immediately by the doors. Some *Chekist*s were sitting there in black leather overcoats with Mausers laying across their laps. They rose, as if on command, and with some clattering opened the heavy, metal doors from which three huge locks hung. The interior of the premises was in stark contrast to the penitentiary character of the outside. A brief walk from the harsh prison atmosphere of the nineteenth century into some rooms styled with the asceticism of the nineteen-thirties. Then an area with the enticing glamour of the twenty-twenties ... A swimming pool, with water as blue and balmy as that of the Caribbean, barred massage chambers, adorned with gold, and a banqueting hall of pink marble; beyond that a reception room with a secretary and guards. These were generals from the former State Guard and GPU, who wore black and dark blue uniforms. Klynkevych knew the faces of many of them. The Grey Prince's apparatchiks, however, acted as if they did not know Klynkevych. They opened the sturdy, oak doors before him and then peered at the heavy, tank-green, metal doors behind them; finally, they turned a huge key in the lock, with much creaking, and opened the entrance to the sanctuary of the Grey Prince.

Klynkevych had not previously visited this room. It was furnished like a single cell, with bunks, stools and a gold toilet basin in the corner. The Grey Prince sat sombrely on the bunks, wearing black satin pants and black socks on his otherwise bare legs. He drank tea from a saucer, slurping loudly. His body was inscribed with violet and black tattoos as dense as the graffiti on the Berlin Wall. He raised his head with its glisteningly pomaded, dense dark hair. His face was broad and quite pleasant, frank even, but with the deceitful dangerous smile of a Chicago gangster.

'What do you want, you ponce?' he asked.

'Your Greyness, allow me to inform you that ... Mohammad Bek ...'

'I know,' said the prince, grooming the hirsute growth on his chest. 'Don't listen to those black-assed guys. Your state is not needed by anyone and order can never be instilled there. Give the people freedom. Let the fire, axe and knife have their glorious way, for today is a holiday for my people. Free them from prison and labour camps. Apart from the politicals - kill them.'

He spoke quietly, in short sentences, without looking at Klynkevych. A portrait of Stalin hung over the bed. The dictator was screwing up his eyes as if aiming a rifle. The Grey Prince screwed up his eyes in the same fashion as he looked at Klynkevych.

'Was it you who played the *Murka?*'

'It was I.'

'Can you play the concertina?'

'I can play the accordion.'

'Learn to play the concertina. People don't love symphonies. They want something simpler, straight from the soul. I wanted to play the concertina but have you seen what they did to me?' He showed Klynkevych his hands. He had no fingers because they had fused into a solid blade, like a shark's fins. A happy smile flickered over his face, which made Klynkevych very uneasy. 'And what are you up to now?'

'Me? Your greyness, I …'

'I know,' smiled the prince benevolently, 'entertaining yourself with a babe … nice work. I always amuse myself like that after a walk in the zone … enjoy it because they'll slit her soft throat soon … and grab those diamonds. They don't belong to her.'

'Your Greyness, I ask you … that's not necessary …'

'Go now, you ponce, and don't even think about it. The shorter your life, the fewer sins you will commit. Have you ever drunk tea from a saucer?'

'Never,' murmured Klynkevych.

'A cup is like a well. Its water is dark and deep, but a saucer is like a lake, brimming with light. When you drink from one your thoughts are as broad and brilliant as its waters. Get lost now and don't be afraid of anything. A time of freedom such as rarely happens is coming.'

Klynkevych knelt down and kissed the fingerless hand of the prince. It felt cold and had a rank smell of urine.

'Go,' said the Grey Prince, shoving him away. 'And don't ruin my people's holiday. Let this land and this nation be punished for their very substantial sins, it's what they need, and don't hamper our justice.'

Klynkevych barely noticed his return to the state dacha through the shrubbery. Unconsciously he began to pray, the words finding themselves on his lips, 'Lord Jesus, Almighty God, save her from death, for all things are within your power … I will be faithful to you, only don't let her die … I love her, I pray to you, our advocate in heaven.' He looked cautiously in every direction and then crossed himself.

87

Bozhena was able to deliver the, now invaluable, American communication gadget Martha Jefferson had given to Haiduk, via Martin Husak. She also sent two fobs with the access codes to the data-base of UMI spy satellite, Sich-77. The satellite, bereft of these codes and control, was a useless piece of junk floating in space. Nevinchanyi had arrived at Irpin with these gifts on the morning of Saturday 31 July, along with the information that the evacuation of the Confederation Embassy would begin on 3 August.

Haiduk was dementedly pleased with the gadget. Its protected channels would allow him to communicate unimpeded with Bozhena. Nevinchanyi was watching the one remaining television news programme on Kreyda's Bad News Channel, swearing profusely and swigging mead; occasionally he nibbled on some tasty white, home-made cheese. Friedman's station had been closed down.

Haiduk, not wishing to impede his colleague's absorption in the news, went into the yard and lay near the fence. He could see the river and the forest on the other side. He was gripped by an even greater sense of his insignificance than immediately after his release. He could no longer smell the decaying sweetness of the wind-fallen pears. Anxiously he dialled the number of Bozhena's gadget and heard her voice.

'I missed you, honey … I dreamed …' she said in English. Then swapping to Ukrainian, 'Darling, how glad I am to hear you. How are you over there?'

'I'm OK, my dear Martian,' he said in English, before whispering in Ukrainian, 'I love you.' He was embarrassed by his feelings and did not want anyone to hear his words, even though the yard yawned emptily around him. 'I want to steal you away. Let's work something out …'

'I hope, we'll discuss this issue after tomorrow,' he heard her reply in English. He realised that either someone had entered the room or she was afraid someone was listening into the call and did not want to discuss the details of her escape plan.

'Are you unable to speak?' he said anxiously.

'I'm sorry … I cannot do it.' The call ended with those words uttered in English and at that moment Haiduk saw them. Five men, dressed in rags, ascended the slope of the track that Palii's coach had traversed. Judging by the chaotic nature of their movements, which ignored any notion of safety, this was not a special forces unit. Haiduk saw that one held a hunting rifle, while the others were armed with axes and knives. He bent low and scurried to the building.

'Bloody hell, they won't let me eat in peace,' said Nevinchanyi, wiping his mouth with his hand. He handed Haiduk a heavy IZh-107 automatic, thrusting his favourite Micro-TAR-22 into the back of his shorts. They drew a table into the corner of the room, in the dead zone for anyone firing at them, and covered it with some grenades and Kruk pistols in case they were needed.

'Don't you go out Ihor Petrovych, I will talk to them while you cover me from behind.'

Nevinchanyi opened the doors and stepped onto the verandah. He was wearing a blue t-shirt, inscribed with the words 'I Believe in UMI', and long shorts with huge outer pockets where he had stuffed his magazines of ammunition. Haiduk positioned himself so he could see Nevinchanyi through the open door, while also keeping a check on the window.

The strangers opened the gate and stepped into garden, halting before the verandah.

'Your good health gentle folk,' Nevinchanyi greeted the guests light heartedly. 'How may I help you?'

The one holding the rifle, who was certainly the leader, said, 'We have a message you are hoarding a stock of pilfered weapons and products here.'

'And who are you exactly?' enquired Nevinchanyi curiously.

'We are a military unit of the Ukrainian Liberation Front.'

'And do you have certification?' asked Hryhoriy mockingly.

'What certification?'

'A certificate with a seal; a nice round one.'

Haiduk saw the leader cast his rifle from his left to his right hand and his fighters stepped dangerously close to Nevinchanyi.

'Stop pulling the wool over our eyes,' said the rifle bearer menacingly. 'Show me what you have here. Otherwise …'

Nevinchanyi swung his hand behind his back and seized the butt of his pistol. Haiduk decided instantaneously to throw a neuro-paralysing grenade at the legs of the attackers, quickly pulled Nevinchaniy back into the building and closed the door. A small explosion sounded and a flare, like sheet lightning, flashed in the room. Leaving Hryhoriy by the doors, Haiduk leaped out of the side window into the yard. Peering around the corner he saw the five, supposed ULF, fighters lain unconscious, but gripped by convulsions. Nevinchanyi ran out onto the verandah with a role of duct tape and began to tie up and gag these assailants. Haiduk used his special forces dagger to cut off the surplus pieces of tape, and together they searched their attackers. They found Kruk pistols on two of them, and one wore the dog-tag of a State Guard agent. Two bore certificates testifying to their amnesty from crimes. They threw the axes and knives into the barn and stashed the rifle and pistols in the boot of the Ford Scorpion. The five outlaws would regain consciousness in thirty minutes. They were clearly gangsters because under the leader's dirty shirt they found a bag stuffed with pilfered gold and precious stones.

The cover of the safe house at Irpin was now blown. There was no sense in killing the attackers, it was possible they had accomplices who knew their whereabouts, instead Haiduk injected them with single dose ampules of sedative. They dragged the men into the garage and used a heavy padlock to secure the door. While carefully gathering together the things they needed, Haiduk donned the mask of Vasyl Semenovych Petrenko, which he had worn earlier. He checked the documents, which testified he was a secret agent of the newly created Minister of State Security and Internal Affairs, once more. UMI's hackers had produced the documents after obtaining a sample from Kreyda's closed servers. The document gave him permission to bear and use arms. Nevinchanyi stuck a rainbow-coloured microchip, issued by the ministry, to the windscreen and swiftly called Colonel Palii as he took the wheel.

'Shame,' he said as the car pulled away, 'it was a nice house. I didn't have time enough to recharge my batteries.'

Just before they entered Kyiv they encountered a mass of refugees who were heading for the Warsaw highway. Some travelled on rickshaws laden with a few modest possessions, others pushed wagons bearing little children, or dragged cabin cases. Old cars that ran on alcohol chugged along, emitting clouds of fetid blue fumes. Horses, who in teams of four, pulled heavy stagecoaches as they snorted and tried to head away from the gas clouds into the culvert by the roadside. Old men and women, gasping from the heat and stench, bent beneath heavy rucksacks as they moved slowly and meekly along the road. Haiduk was struck by the number of older people who had decided to abandon their homes and embark on a dangerous path into the unknown. It occurred to him that soon the mingled bodies of horses and people would be heaped by the roadside. Overturned wagons would stay alongside them, along with bags, uselessly empty, discarded by looters. His heart ached to think that his mother might well have become one of this mass and shame gripped him before these unknown Kyivans, shame for the privilege he had exploited when he dispatched her to Poland.

Occasionally they encountered expensive cars with water or electric powered engines, which would have cost between one hundred to three hundred thousand globos. Their drivers tried not to look at the refugees, the passengers were invisible behind the darkened windows. They saw an expensive burned-out Lexus with corpses strewn around it just before the Kyiv checkpoint. It was clearly lynch law.

The refugees trudged silently, paying the electronic Ford Scorpion no heed. The traffic police officer at the Kyiv checkpoint scanned the signal from the chip on the windscreen with a reader hung around his neck. As the barrier rose, letting them into the 'Mother of Russian Cities', someone from the crowd, not wanting to move off the road ahead of them, hurled a stone and yelled, 'Traitors! You sold out Ukraine! God will punish you.' The stone left a scratch on the windscreen.

The signal on Haiduk's American gadget rang as they drove along Peremohy Avenue and headed for a new safe apartment in the grounds of the polytechnic. It was located in an old, two-storey building, not far from the monument to Korolov, a prominent rocket constructor.

It was Martha Jefferson calling, 'Mr Haiduk, can you talk now?'

'Yes.' He switched on the video feed and saw Martha's anxious face on the screen.

'Who is that?' she asked agitatedly in English, switching off her camera, 'can you hear me? Where are you?'

'It's me,' he said, 'don't you think I truly look a lot more intelligent now? Do you want me to scratch my nose or stick out my tongue?' He touched the large polypate nose of the mask with his finger.

'Okay,' she laughed, 'listen to me, conspirator. We have become aware that at 02:00, that is …' she looked at her watch while he also worked out how many hours would pass until then, 'in thirteen hours, our friend will attack Boryspil Airport and try to land large military transport aircraft with armoured vehicles. Perhaps …'

'I'm not in charge of air defence forces in this country and I have no surface to air missiles,' Haiduk interrupted her brusquely. It was okay for them to sit in Washington and offer advice to a man with a one million globos reward on his head. Someone could buy three armoured Lexus vehicles for that price. But why did they offer so little for me? he thought

'Are you a military general or a fucking flake? Someone will contact you on your gadget in one hour. You can trust them completely. Work out something together. Wasn't it Taras Shevchenko who said, "Battle on and overcome?" Finally, it's your land, it's you they are occupying. Do you get it?'

The Ford Scorpion entered the quiet, empty grounds of the university. There were no students or applicants to study wandering around; only red squirrels were running along the paths between the trees.

Pulling up by the entrance to the building, Nevinchanyi began to carry their luggage to the second floor. Haiduk had not managed to ask Martha why his contact with Bozhena's communication gadget had been broken off. The old woman seemed to him like the benevolent, sharp-nosed fairy of Queen Orchids, blinking her cunning eyes and dissolving on the screen, leaving a brief glow of rose light.

Fuck you, thought Haiduk, although any notion of intimacy with Martha was far removed from his plans.

88

Boryspil Airport had long been renamed the Leonid Kravchuk airport, in honour of Ukraine's first president. Operations there were usually suspended briefly from 01:00 until 05:00. The deputy manager of the Aviation Security Service night shift, Herman Fatkhulin, adored these hours of tranquillity. All the scheduled flights had arrived and departed, transit passengers and those who had not made their flight were in hotels or on the two globos a night couchettes in the dormitory hall. Brigades of migrant workers bustled around the huge, empty halls as they cleaned the place. It was a blessed period of nocturnal calm when no air disasters or terrorist acts were anticipated.

The yellow cleaning machines trundled quietly, leaving shining paths of moisture in their wake. The cleaners sprayed aromatic disinfectants on all the plastic, metal and glass surfaces touched by the hands of thousands of passengers. Squads of joiners and installers dealt with the little mishaps; the managers of bars and cafes filled their glass cases and refrigerated cabinets with fresh food and cold drinks. Fatkhulin paid particular attention to the cleaning and disinfection of the toilets, though this was not his area it still had some bearing on passenger safety. His parents had emigrated to Ukraine from Bokhara, fleeing Kara-Khan's regime, when Fatkhulin was eleven. They had told their son about the outbreak of cholera in Uzbekistan and its causes.

Over the last few days, the airport had resembled a hive of maddened bees. Thousands of people who wanted to leave jostled by the counters for tickets on any flight to the West, stormed airline offices and slept overnight with their children in the departure lounge. They offered the airport staff huge bribes for the privilege.

Every so often fights broke out between the enraged passengers at the terminals, ending, on one occasion, with shots being fired. The security staff working the day shift were exhausted and there were not enough staff to cover the night shift. Herman Fatkhulin, who loved order and cleanliness, and highly valued his work place, was really confused by this. So, before he started on the night shift, he held a management meeting with the supervisors of the units below him. He warned them that the night would be troubled even though the last flight, which was destined for Varna, had departed at 23:00. The arrivals too had ended. Over the last few days the volume of flights from the West had declined sharply.

When he had finished the meeting he hurried towards Terminal G, whose upper storey contained the security surveillance point. Fatkhulin, an athletic, rangy man, who had graduated from the General Marchenko Intelligence Academy, watched his colleagues as they scrutinised numerous monitors. Footage from hundreds of cameras, located in every terminal, technical and office building, flickered over the screens. He wore, as always, the security service uniform, which really suited him; a short-sleeved, light blue shirt, black epaulettes, white pants and a white military cap with a blue band around it.

Fatkhulin, tanned, with black eyebrows that joined over his nose, dark-eyed and with a winning smile, enjoyed a measure of popularity among the female staff, but he was not caught out engaging in any of the usual masculine transgressions such a situation might have involved. He loved his wife, Nina, who had borne two of his children. It also helped that she worked on the counter of Kashtan, the duty-free shop in the departure terminal. He was also only too aware of the scope of the surveillance cameras at the airport. If he were not careful he might end up as an object of contempt before his colleagues, or be blackmailed. There was one other thing, however, it involved a rather sweet, blonde lady, the wife of a high-ranking Spanish diplomat. Herman had made her acquaintance in the VIP lounge when her baggage had been stolen.

After a few meetings with the voracious blond, who was half-Arab-half-Kyivan, he was almost narcotically addicted to her. He implemented her wishes without hesitation when she wanted an unusual favour from him. Two men, whom she said were fleeing the oppressive Kyiv regime, were allowed to board an Iberia flight without passing through passport control or security. However, two days ago, his beloved Isabella Nouri had asked him to allow ten Mujahideen to pass unchecked into air traffic control. They were soldiers in the Horde's guard and she had urged him to help in the name of the ultimate triumph of the Black Star of the Earth, Chief Kara-Khan. Herman felt a sharp pain seep from under his ribs to his spine as she spoke. He knew now that he had fallen into a honey trap. Although he did not love the Kyiv government, a bunch of self-satisfied cretins who had ruined a wonderful country, he hated Kara-Khan's regime even more. Promising Isabella Nouri that he would fulfil her wishes, he had quickly arranged to see his friend from the academy of military intelligence, Captain Ihor Palii. Ihor's father was a big fish in counter-intelligence.

When he returned to his office after visiting the checkpoint, two people were waiting for him; his friend Ihor and a stranger, a solid looking fifty year old with greying hair, who had the appearance of an engineer or computer technician. The pronounced nose and bright eyes that scanned Fatkhulin attentively would remain in his memory. The stranger showed Herman his credentials, indicating that he was a secret agent in the Ministry of State Security and Internal Affairs; none other than Vasyl Semenovych Petrenko.

They discussed the details of the operation in Fatkhulin's office. Luckily, he did not ask Haiduk or Palii to show him authorisation because they had none. However, Fatkhulin had decided for himself what needed doing. He telephoned a security officer in the Special Transport Service and ordered the preparation of all refuelling units and fuel tank trailers to be stationed on runway number two at 01:00. Under the pretence of orders from above, he issued instructions to the manager of the night shift's lighting and flight safety service. The manager had to be ready, on receipt of a signal, to switch off the lighting on the airfield and, if necessary, in the airport terminal buildings.

The tense atmosphere increased as midnight approached. Haiduk had managed to muster only two groups, each with ten special forces soldiers. The UMI group was commanded by Hryhoriy Nevinchanyi. Colonel Palii was in charge of the counter-intelligence troops. Haiduk, who was in continuous contact with both units, was increasingly anxious. He did not know how many troops Mohammad Bek might have located at the airport and this complicated the operation to neutralise them effectively. He knew the most significant action would develop around the air-traffic control and the airport's electricity supply stations. Haiduk stationed some of the people who had accompanied him at these sites. Herman Fatkhulin loaded all the footage from the monitors onto a single large screen. Haiduk watched the people accumulating in the airport attentively. He, along with Fatkhulin and Palii, searched among them for suspicious individuals.

Just before midnight Fatkhulin guided Haiduk into the airport air-traffic management area, which was situated on the upper storey of the ninety metre high control tower. The structure was recognised as one of the wonders of European architecture; from a distance the grace and elegance of its design resembled an ear of wheat uniting the earth and the sky. Fatkhulin introduced Haiduk to the manager of the night shift as Kreyda's personal representative. He and Ihor Palii went to the entrance of the transport zone to welcome Isabella Nouri's people.

At 23:55 a large wagon bearing the inscription 'Kyiv Catering' drew up to the gates of the cargo section. The wagon passed slowly through a special scanner used by the customs service to detect contraband. The people in the vehicle did not know that radiation was passing invisibly through the wagon, as it might through a patient passing through the cylinder of a magnetic resonance imager. The UMI special troops looked at a screen on which the skeletons of the fighters hidden in the vehicle glowed. There were twenty-two of them with three high-calibre machine guns, twenty IZh-107 automatic rifles, five portable rocket launchers, and pistols, grenades, assault knives and a radio.

Fatkhulin and Palii looked them over with alarm and reported the situation to Haiduk. However, a surprise had been prepared for these concealed soldiers. When they passed through to the airport control tower without undergoing any of the customary checks, a special aerosol sprayed them in the darkness of one of the passages. They were utterly unaware that now they were coated with a fine, special paint, the so-called 'sniper marker'.

Fatkhulin was at their head, guiding the fighters on their way. Isabella walked with him and gently held his hand. She was dressed like the rest of the soldiers, in a black jump suit with a black bandana on her head. Her beautiful, wide eyes glittered in the half light.

'Thank you beloved,' she said, pressing against him when they arrived at the empty customs room where they would stay until the operation commenced.

He smiled in reply and left quickly because he had many other affairs to attend to.

Ten metres separated this zone from the entrance to the air-traffic control area and the rapid elevators of the control tower. Fatkhulin joined Haiduk, who was listening attentively to the manager of the night shift explaining the workings of his system. The hall, although it was on the thirtieth storey, reminded Haiduk of the command chamber in a nuclear submarine; there was the same secretive atmosphere of flickering indicators and screens gleaming in the half darkness. The manager was clarifying the information received to the air-defence forces flight control information centre and their sensitive Mantia radar system. The system had detected the movement of aircraft in the Stalingrad-Kharkiv sector and a second group in the Crimea-Odesa sector. The 'Approach' system on the tower only detected aircraft at a distance of between one hundred and twenty and one hundred and fifty kilometres from the airport. At a distance of fifty kilometres it transferred the monitoring to the 'Ring' system. The 'Ring' in its turn passed surveillance of the aircraft to the take off and landing system as the vehicles were preparing to set down at the airport. Only the manager of air-traffic control could grant aircraft permission to take off and land.

Haiduk decided to lay his cards on the table. 'I represent the military wing of the Ukrainian Liberation Front, which is supported by the armed forces. In fifteen minutes the control tower will be stormed by a Horde unit. They will kill the controllers and set up their own automated guidance equipment to allow their military transport airplanes to land. Help us to stop that.'

The manager, an older, fat man, suddenly felt as if the room were stuffy. He unfastened two buttons on the collar of his blue uniform shirt. However, he did not protest, get hysterical, demand to see Haiduk's credentials or threaten to phone someone to check out the truth of this stranger's words. He believed Haiduk. He said that, above everything else, he regarded the attempt by the Horde to land a military assault force at a civilian airport without agreement as unacceptable. Under the rules of the International Civil Aviation Organisation it qualified as an act of aggression.

Haiduk asked Fatkhulin to load the images from the surveillance cameras in the customs room onto the laptop. The tension among the would-be attackers was visibly increasing. They had drawn out their weapons and lined up ready to storm the tower.

'Fire!' Haiduk ordered, speaking into the gadget.

The lights in the customs room were extinguished. The lasers from the UMI snipers in the upper gallery, which ringed the room, made the shapes of the Horde soldiers glitter. Fatkhulin tried futilely to work out where Isabella Nouri was among the images.

The lethal fire of American semi-automatic, Browning-USMC 45 rifles hailed from the speakers of the laptop. The screen was turned into a glittering melange of dancing lights. The shots from below were inaudible in the control room, but everyone watching the horrific images on the laptop was numbed by what they saw. When some of the UMI snipers descended onto the lower section of the room and switched on the lights to finish off the wounded, Haiduk turned off the laptop.

The controller of the 'Approach' system informed the manager that the first five, heavy military transport Airbus 390-XX1000s had requested permission to land. Each of these aircraft could hold up to eight hundred paratroopers and several armoured vehicles. The manager opened the audio-communication channel in hands-free mode and the voice of the commander of the landing operation was heard in the control tower; in broken English he demanded permission to land.

'What is the purpose of your flight to the airport?' asked the manager.

'We are charter flight 0895 from Delhi and are bringing humanitarian aid to the children of Ukraine,' answered the aircraft.

'Did you issue a preliminary enquiry about the flight?' asked Boryspil.

'We issued one three days ago in the name of Mr … Klyn … kevych,' said the commander of the operation, uncertainly.

'We have a problem with runway number one,' replied the manager. 'Repair work is underway there and it can't be used for landing.'

'We will touch down on runway number two,' said the voice from the sky, confidently.

'I'll hand you over to the landing control. Your course is north-west 999, with a turn in sector 017.'

'Thanks Chief. See you soon on solid ground. Get ready to receive some gifts from the south.'

The manager and Haiduk exchanged glances. Fatkhulin was not present, but when he switched on the transmission from the customs room Haiduk saw him on the screen. Fatkhulin wandered among the corpses searching for someone.

War has commenced, thought Haiduk, looking at his watch. It was 01:50. The first part of Haiduk's plan, it was now clear, had failed. The Ukrainian surface-to-air missiles, which defended the approach to the airport, had not fired a single missile at the enemy planes. They had let them pass freely into the heart of the country. Their commanders had defected to the side of the traitors.

When three minutes remained until the landing of the first aircraft, the manager of the shift ordered the lights on the summer runway and buildings to be turned off. He simultaneously severed radio communication and the operation of the automatic navigation system for landing the aircraft. Everyone in the control tower heard the harsh cries of the pilots yelling to each other and the anxious cry of the commander, 'Control tower what's happening? Are you receiving me?'

From the upper storey of the control tower they could see how, in the darkness where runway number two should have been, there were sudden blooms of fire. These transformed into burning lines, extending at three hundred kilometres an hour. A massive explosion shook the building as if it really were an ear of grain swaying before a fire. The glass facade of its upper storey flared golden, then fiery crimson, as if the sun were rising over Boryspil. Then everything turned dark; an impenetrable dark. A second explosion sounded over the nearby road and the monorail that linked the airport to Kyiv. Those in the capital who heard the blasts thought a large bomb had been detonated over Boryspil.

89

Both the first and second parts of Haiduk's plan had failed. In spite of the loss of two military transport aircraft, Operation Tamerlane was progressing successfully. The grounds of the airport were littered with mangled, dark grey fragments of fuselage, wings with their Black Star decals, detached engines, the burned corpses of paratroopers and stocks of ammunition.

Lieutenant General Yermolay Kasemi perished in the first aircraft. Mohammad Bek had appointed him commander of the first phase landings and commander in chief of Kyiv. But his death had almost no impact on the pace of the operation. A few days later Hetman Makhun Street was renamed Kasemi Street. The Ukrainian Liberation Front issued regular calls to serving personnel in Ukraine's armed forces to revolt. These were broadcast on the official state channel with the help of the front's hackers. However, with some exceptions, the Horde's forces did not encounter any serious resistance.

Three hundred students at the Ivan Bohun military college, members of LUK and URA, abandoned their military camp near Nosivka without the permission of their commanders. They headed north and occupied a suitable position in the forests alongside the E-101 road. The group attacked the M. Muravyov motorised brigade that was heading in a column along the road to Kyiv. The students used XM-507 training mortars to fire 25 mm grenades with a cumulative armour-piercing and incendiary effect. They cremated some vehicles at the front and rear of the column. The attack sowed great panic among the Russian mercenaries, who had been promised an easy tour around *Khokhol* land by the Horde's commissars. The commissars had said they would be able to take as much looted 'Little Russian' treasure as they could carry back home on their wagons and tanks.

In spite of this initial success, the imbalance between the forces was too great. The students were using old firearms, only intended for training purposes, which dated from the Ukrainian-Romanian war. They had limited stocks of ammunition and, because they were only sixteen years old, none had any experience of genuine warfare. But they would not retreat. Now they had managed to halt an armoured column they threw themselves into a protracted battle with boyish enthusiasm. The Russians, recovering from the initial shock, summoned assistance. Kazan-57 strike helicopters swooped in and dropped containers of napalm and powdered aluminium, and Kyiv's young defenders were incinerated.

Olya Hudyma's lover, URA Sergeant Maksym Borovyk, died in this battle. Haiduk only heard about this unequal conflict long after the events. The students failed to stop the advance of the enemy by the walls of Kyiv.

Haiduk, Palii and Nevinchanyi organised the cleansing of the airport building from any enemy troops who might remain. They ruined the airport's navigation systems and helped Fatkhulin, the controllers and other volunteers to flee. However, unknown to them, a group of nine Horde terrapins used the chaos to organise a landing in Kyiv. Two landed on Mount Batyieva, two at Pechersk-Lavra and three on the Dynamo Kyiv football pitch. These forces rapidly seized all government buildings. One terrapin landed on Mykhailivska Square near the GPU building, the Black Zeppelin. The last terrapin landed on Peremohy Avenue and thus sealed off movement towards the west of the city and prepared for an attack on the Confederation's embassy complex.

By 05:00 on 1 August Haiduk and his troops had just managed to cross the southern tower three-level bridge and emerge on the right bank of the Dnipro, over which a morose, late summer sun was rising. By that time the white, black-starred flags of the Horde and the red flags with a crescent moon and black-stars of the liberating military of the Eurasian Steppe hung above government buildings. Haiduk's and Nevinchanyi's blue electric car swiftly traversed the empty streets through Podil and headed for Kurenivka.

90

1 August 2077

To the people of the Kyiv-Dnipro territory

A joint address from the Head of the High Directorate, V. Klynkevych, and the Supreme Commander of the United Liberating Forces of the Horde, General Mohammad Bek

Dear Fellow Citizens, Brothers and Sisters

The previous leaders led the territory and the people thereon to

410

absolute ruination. They embarked on the criminal destruction of the fundamentals of economic and political life. They supported self-destructive processes, directed at inciting enmity between ethnic groups and nationalities.

At this tragic time your brothers, who come from the boundless Eurasian Steppe, have stretched out their hands to assist you. They come beneath the banners of freedom, the equality of all people and the flowering of the economy. The United Liberation Forces of the Horde bear order and stability, tranquility and peace, and personal prosperity to the people of the territory. They bring the principle of collective responsibility for committing illegal acts. The warriors of the Horde, along with the law enforcement agencies of the Kyiv-Dnipro territory, are developing the eternal tradition of friendship between our people. A tradition strengthened by mutual bloodshed and rich with the determination to transform a part of Eurasia into a security zone. The Christians of all hues, the Judeo-Liberal, Judeo-Christian and Zionist aggressors in the West must be warned against violating the neutrality principle of the former political creation named Ukraine.

Henceforth, all people of this non-existent creation unite in the fraternal family of the Horde.

Brothers and Sisters, give your assistance to the glorious warriors of the United Liberating Forces as they bring order and discipline to your land. Struggle against saboteurs and subversives, provocateurs from among the numbers of those vile sell-outs, Ukrainian-American nationalists. Renew industrial operations and the manufacture of agricultural resources. Do not allow the pillaging of your natural resources, strengthen law and order, and be more efficient in your labours. Now it is necessary to put an end to all manifestations of anarchy and egotism. To understand that the highest freedom is collective subordination under the omnipotent vertical power structure that stretches from Chyngiz-Saray to Kyiv. We are certain that this new Eurasian order will be supported by all the healthy elements of the population. With the aim of realising our programme we announce the organisation of the following humanitarian measures:

1. A curfew will be introduced at 20:00, according to Chyngiz-Saray Central European Time, throughout the territory of the Kyiv-Dnipro District. (See attached map for the precise boundaries thereof.)
2. Any gatherings, demonstrations, meetings or pickets, which could violate the citizen's right to tranquility and quiet are prohibited.
3. Specially Ordained Demographic Evaluation Points (SODEPs) will be opened in local police stations from 3 to 15 August for the registration of the entire population aged from ten to eighty. When registering you must bring documents that evidence your nationality, religious faith, sexual orientation, party allegiance, education, and the nationality of your parents and grandparents.
4. With the aim of improving the overall health of the population, the sale of alcohol, including beer, is prohibited, along with the sale of salo with a high-cholesterol content.
5. Women are prohibited from emerging onto their balconies when wearing only their underwear, or in the nude.
6. The male population of the district, aged between fifteen and eighty years, are permitted to have four wives each, aged between thirteen and sixty-five.
7. We will draft a limited quantity (as per our plan) of the male population of the district, aged from sixteen to forty, into the United Liberating Forces of the Horde. The draft will be undertaken in line with their military qualifications.

The failure to execute any point of the humanitarian measures is punishable by death. Responsibility for realising the above measures is placed upon the Marshall of Jurisprudence, I. O. Kreyda, and the commander of the punishment unit of Janissaries, Lieutenant General Ali Akbar Pereverzev.

The Head of the High Directorate V. Klynkevych
General Mohammad Bek

91

Thanks to the codes Bozhena had preserved, Haiduk succeeded in renewing the operation of the information on UMI satellite Sich-77. The system's essence was that every UMI officer could access an electronic intelligence network using the number of their e-post and transfer information to any other user. The net was completely secure for both the sender and receiver of e-messages. Their locations were concealed and would remain untraceable for those who strove to take control of the internet.

A number of reports and calls to action were issued to thousands of intelligence and counter espionage officers via the system. Haiduk tried to establish how many of them were prepared to participate in the struggle against the occupiers. These missives might, of course, be sent inadvertently to traitors, Kreyda's people, or other potential agents of the Horde. However, those who replied that they were willing to join the military wing of the Ukrainian Liberation Front did not know the concrete location of where their replies were sent. They did not know the location of ULF headquarters or who headed the organisation. Above all, they did not know that every reply, whether sincere or dishonest, would be analysed. Their responses were collated with their personal data and sent to one of the horizontal networks of agents, each of which was headed by already proven officers. They would determine whether an individual was fit to participate in the struggle.

Two headquarters were created. One was located

outside the occupation zone, in Chabany, on the grounds of a former horticultural institute; the second was located on Cherepanova Hill, in the middle of Kyiv, below the stands of the B. Bannikov Stadium. One of the first officers to join the ULF was the director of the UMI Lastivka and Yastrub class intelligence drone units. The summer base of these units was located at Novo-Bilychi, outside the zone of occupation.

Haiduk was suffering from lack of sleep after the nocturnal battle at Boryspil. He sat, unshaven and irritable, in the concrete chamber of the stadium on Laboratorny Lane, which remained cold even on a searingly hot day such as this. The room was the former protection centre of the grounds. Its value lay in the well-organised surveillance camera system covering the stadium. A subterranean tunnel led to the parking area where the Ford Scorpion was standing idly. Haiduk became even more irritated when he saw young men in dark red tracksuits, training on the pitch, appear on the screen. They boisterously hoofed a ball around as it glittered phosphorescently in the sunlight. Everything happening on the pitch seemed futile to Haiduk. In the depths of his soul he felt envious of these well-trained idiots. They did not comprehend what this day meant for them or for the world.

Nevinchanyi sat with two of UMI's hackers before a large computer, downloading information from the Sich-77 site. 'Bloody hell! Have you heard about this, Ihor Petrovych?'

'What's happened?' Haiduk raised his head testily.

'The Horde has prohibited *horilka* and salo,' Nevinchanyi reported excitedly. 'Now you just have to wait for a popular uprising.' After a second he added, 'The revolution might be deferred though, at least as far as men are concerned; you are now permitted to have up to four wives. Can you imagine? Well, you don't know even how to deal with just one …'

'I have fulfilled the norm of the Horde,' Haiduk replied swiftly, if inaccurately. At that moment his American gadget

414

rang, it was Martha Jefferson. It would be 05:00 in Washington. What had happened?

Martha's voice sounded agitated. 'I am in Texas and I can't speak for long. I beg you to get Bozhena out of the embassy before 01:00. Save her Ihor, like you did once before. You are my last hope.'

'What's going on with Bozhena? Why can't I reach her? You must know,' he yelled into the gadget with impotent anger, although its screen showed that the connection with Texas had ended.

After his conversation with Bozhena on 31 July he had been unable to contact her. Haiduk dialled her number with an ardent fastidiousness, but immediately received the response - No connection.

Martin Husak was also stuck in the blockaded embassy and did not communicate, which increased Haiduk's anxiety still further. Martha Jefferson's call was the harbinger of some catastrophe. Haiduk was utterly certain that the Confederation would be able to guard the embassy and evacuate the staff. They had enjoyed a window of opportunity in the three days of panic and chaos that gripped Kyiv. Some of the Confederation's military terrapins could have travelled from Poland and pierced the ring around the embassy. Perhaps, but this had not happened. Instead the situation had developed in a way Haiduk could not understand.

Immediately after Martha Jefferson's call he summoned together a crisis group of the officers who worked with him. The military attachés of the OGS countries, who were on friendly terms with some of the UMI officers, reported that there were almost five hundred and seventy people gathered in the embassy. These included embassy staff and their families, members of the OGS diplomatic corps, including the military attachés, and the personnel of international representative bodies in Kyiv. They were all convinced that the Confederation would defend them effectively and send additional units. The fifty marines who currently protected the site were obviously inadequate for the size of the area, and there was an absence of any system of special defensive fortification capable of sustaining a prolonged comprehensive defensive action.

Haiduk only had twenty troops at his disposal and participating in the defence of the building in the event of it being stormed would be suicidal. But would it be stormed? Was Martha mistaken?

The crisis group decided to strengthen surveillance of the embassy and activity within its vicinity. At 14:00 Palii arrived at the headquarters and reported that his people had captured a potential 'wagging tongue'. This was a private in the liberating army of the Horde, Akhmet Ivanov, who hailed from Bryansk Ulus, as the Horde called the former Bryansk Province. He had been bustling around a bazaar that had sprung up in the ruins of the burned out circus building on Peremohy Square.

The soldier had gone AWOL from one of the landing terrapins, intending to purchase *horilka* and salo after the Islamic commissars had banned such luxuries. He encountered two counter-intelligence officers, who were in the guise of vagrants, aimlessly wandering around the vicinity of the circus while studying the defence systems of the terrapins. They dragged Akhmet into the ruins of the circus stables, which were still redolent of manure. By pressing a knife to the throat of their terrified captive they learned there were one hundred soldiers on board landing-terrapin 052-4043. These troops were armed with mortars, close-combat rockets, laser flamethrowers, two concrete-penetrating Howitzers, IZh-107 automatics and a dozen high-calibre machine guns. The terrapin was commanded by an Iranian, Colonel Kazem Dzhalili. However, this was not the most significant aspect of Akhmet's revelations. He informed them that at 02:00 on 2 August, the embassy of the Confederation of States of North America would be stormed.

The troops from terrapin 052-4043 were required to be in position at the exits of the clinic next to the embassy by 01:00. The second terrapin would fly from the grounds of Pechersk-Lavra, along Hohol Street, at 01:00, to be ready to assist the assault.

The counter-intelligence officers did not believe Akhmet, who was trembling with fear and capable of saying anything. However, he swore he had heard this from a Russian officer who had sent him to fetch some home-brewed vodka. The Russian intended to steady his nerves before the attack; he said it would be difficult to take out the bloody Americans. The officer had told Akhmet that millions of ameros were concealed in the cellars of the embassy. The newly printed notes, with their crisp insignia, had been brought from America to hire *Khokhols* for the struggle against their fraternal Eurasian liberators. The commander of the terrapin had promised to let the officers loot the embassy's treasure.

Akhmet's testimony was confirmed by some of Haiduk's intelligence operatives who were working at Pechersk-Lavra. They reported that at 16:00, the preparation of terrapin number 052-4040 for a military operation commenced at the monastery. It was the very same vehicle that had transported the Horde's delegation to see Makhun. The soldiers from the terrapin had been led onto the square before the Cathedral of the Assumption of the Blessed Mother of God. They were broken into separate groups and officers instructed them and showed them a map or plan of somewhere. They were loading the terrapins with ammunition, ferried to the site by transport helicopters, and some unknown equipment brought from the Kovnirivsky building and concealed under a tarpaulin.

The final confirmation arrived at 19:00. An hour earlier two representatives of the high command of the liberating forces of the Horde had come to the embassy. They had presented Ambassador O'Sullivan with an ultimatum. All people within the embassy were required to leave the complex by the main exit by midnight. They would be required to undergo identification procedures and take their places on the buses transporting the agents of the American Satan and their stooges to Boryspil Airport. The Horde envisaged that an exchange of prisoners might take place. Some of the embassy staff could be traded for freedom fighters, agents of the Horde, imprisoned at the Mansfield Airbase and the Utah State penitentiary. The emissaries forgot to add that Boryspil Airport had been rendered inoperable for a long period and prisoner exchanges were forbidden by the Horde's laws.

The main demand of the occupation commanders was that nothing within the embassy should be destroyed. No papers were to be burned, no microchips with data memories were to be cremated in the furnace, nor encryption apparatus and special telecoms equipment. In the event of a refusal to comply, the embassy would be stormed and the death of the agents of Judeo-Liberal imperial Christianity would follow. According to the informer, the manager of the Ukrainian division of non-military guards at the embassy, O'Sullivan, refused to comply with the demands of the ultimatum.

Long afterwards, a senate commission would research the events connected to the storming of the embassy. It would become known that O'Sullivan had, after the receipt of the ultimatum, futilely bombarded the State Department and the office of the Adviser to the President on National Security Issues with alarmed dispatches. The missives had been sent uncoded as the day ended, but no one with any authority worked in Washington on a Sunday. The staff member on duty at the State Department urged him not to panic. They reminded O'Sullivan of the decision to evacuate the embassy on 3 August. Finally, they urged him to drag out the negotiations with the Horde for as long as possible until the president of the Confederation adopted another decision. Unfortunately Shirley MacDowell was in Texas with Martha Jefferson. They were meeting officers and soldiers of the American Legion to celebrate their triumph over Mexican narco-revolutionaries. The legion had successfully returned Houston to American control. There was no possibility of contacting her. Only a year later, in 2078, did the senate commission publish the relevant documents; with some exceptions. These included the final letter from Ambassador O'Sullivan, which was sent to Washington on 1 August at 22:30. It had gone unanswered …

On that day, at 20:00, the officers of the UMI crisis group had reached a final decision and approved the only possible plan. Hryhoriy Nevinchanyi played the main role in drafting what was known as Operation Seraphim.

At 22:00 two intelligence drones took off from Novo-Bilychi and flew towards the embassy. These were Lastivka class drones, the design of which had been passed to the Artemida factory by Haiduk's bureau three years ago. After half an hour they arrived at Yurii Kotsiubynskyi Street and approached the five-storey S-Building at the embassy.

One hovered above the flat roof of the building where, luckily, no marines were stationed. S-Building stood in the centre of the embassy grounds, not far from the ambassador's residence, which was designed in the style of the buildings in eighteenth century Virginia. The drone established accurately that the marines had selected positions along the wall surrounding the embassy. They had set up machine gun nests in the windows of buildings that faced outwards towards the most likely direction of an attack from the Horde.

The second drone was deployed to investigate what was going on inside S-Building by using its infra-red surveillance equipment. It was established that S-Building housed the embassy's secrets and was largely empty. However, on the fifth floor, in room 512, the drone observed the images of two individuals; one was sitting motionless in a chair to the left of the door, the other was pacing agitatedly, occasionally approaching the window.

Haiduk felt his heart flutter, his pulse slow, and a searing emptiness in his chest as he looked at the screen displaying the images transmitted by the drone. He really did not need to drink so much coffee. Or to be besotted with the girl from Mars. He was tortured by the question whether he had the right to risk the lives of UMI officers to free the girl he was in love with. However, a second thought emerged; no, not a thought but a cold, incredibly significant reality that was not open to doubt. Bozhena was the sole person on the earth who knew a fact that could determine the fate of humanity. What would happen if she fell into the hands of the Horde? But Haiduk could not explain this to his officers. He said only that she was a person close to the President of the Confederation and the adviser on national security, both of whom had strongly requested she be saved.

At 23:00 the final phase commenced. An ambulance headed to the Institute of Urology and Kidney Transplantation next to the embassy. It carried the somewhat ill Vasyl Semenovych Petrenko, a technologist from the Bilshovyk factory. He had been afflicted by an acute attack of pain because his bladder was blocked by a large gall stone and he required surgery immediately. He was taken to the sixth floor of the surgical block, accompanied by two stout paramedics. The operating theatres and intensive care wards there were empty because most of the patients had left in recent days. At 23:30 Haiduk and two UMI special forces lieutenants, dressed in radiation reflecting capes produced with stealth technology, which would prevent them from being detected by the embassy's radar, flew off the roof of the sixth floor. Using the flying apparatus Nevinchanyi had brought back from Israel, they ascended to an altitude of ten metres above the clinic's sixth floor, heading slowly for the embassy.

They glided quietly, like huge nocturnal owls, over the branches of Kyiv's chestnut trees, which were already shedding their desiccated leaves. The external lighting of the embassy glittered ahead of them. Haiduk gave a hand signal and they rose ten metres higher. The Israeli personal flying device PFD-X 15 appeared extremely reliable, although Haiduk recollected Nevinchanyi's heavy landing in his office. Nevinchanyi had taught Haiduk to fly using the area above the Rohulka State dacha, while UMI officers were also training in the use of the apparatus at the nearby camp. Although Hryhoriy Ivanovych had conceived of the aerial element of operation Seraphim, he would not risk flying now. He was too heavy for an angel.

The three UMI officers, in their grey stealth cloaks, hovered above the roof of S-Building. Reconnaissance drone number one had transmitted the reassuring absence of any troops there. Lowering himself onto the roof, Haiduk, Seraphim-1, left one officer, Seraphim-3, there. He and the second special services lieutenant from the Hrim Brigade, Seraphim-2, descended cautiously from the roof to the fifth floor. UMI's hackers had obtained detailed plans of the building, including the lay out of service entry points on the roof, from the files of the State Guard, which kept the embassy under close surveillance.

The corridor, sparsely illuminated by the nocturnal lighting, was empty and there was no guard at the entrance to room 512. The guard would be behind the door. Haiduk pointed to the left side of the door, indicating to the lieutenant that Bozhena would be there, on the other side of the wall. The lieutenant charged the door and plunged into the room. A shot rang out. When Haiduk burst into the room behind him, the lieutenant was laying on the floor, awash in blood. Lieutenant William Crawford stood in the left corner of the room, pressing a gun against Bozhena's head. The ruddy-haired Butcher Bill did not recognise Haiduk.

'Come in, come in,' he murmured. Bozhena was tied to

a stool and had not comprehended who had entered the room.

'I am from Rohulka,' said Haiduk, and she recognised his voice.

'Kill this slime-ball! Don't worry about me,' cried Bozhena.

'Shut up. Put the gun down,' Crawford ordered him, 'or I'll kill her.'

Haiduk realised he had fallen into a trap and the operation had collapsed. Slowly, without taking his eyes off Crawford, he lowered himself onto one knee and bowed as he began to lay his Beretta on the floor; then he grabbed it swiftly with his left hand and fired at Crawford. Haiduk saw a dazzling light, like the flare of an electrical discharge, briefly grip the face of Butcher Bill Crawford as he covered his face with both hands, but they ignited too, leaving briefly glowing bones, like an X-ray image. The bones disintegrated in the temperature of over one thousand degrees. Major Crawford's head, which had fallen on the floor, burned too under the impact of a close combat military laser. The room filled with the stench of cremated bones and hair.

The soldier Haiduk had left on the roof, Seraphim-3, was standing in the doorway. On hearing the shot he had run to room 512 and found the doors open. He had immediately assessed the situation, darted into the room, spun around and, from a distance of one metre, discharged the powerful laser beam into Crawford's face. Haiduk threw himself towards the other lieutenant, a young man he had first seen during the operation at the airport. He checked for a pulse, but the officer was dead. All three of them had agreed not to wear a bullet-proof vest so they would not to be burdened with unnecessary weight. Crawford's bullet had hit the young officer in the chest.

Seraphim-3 untied Bozhena as Haiduk noted a surveillance camera above the window and fired towards it. The bullet shattered the expensive lens, but unfortunately they had left a trace of their presence. The embassy division's security staff had the horrific recording of Central Security Service Major William Crawford being murdered. As Merezhko had once said, any operation that left some documentation behind should be regarded as a failure.

'We've got to get out,' yelled Seraphim-3. He searched the dead major, grabbing everything he found in his jacket pockets. 'You take this,' he said, not knowing what to call Bozhena, just as he did not know why she was being abducted from the embassy. 'I will take Liosha,' he added, referring to his dead colleague, 'he was the best-man at my wedding.'

Haiduk grabbed Bozhena by the arm and guided her onto the roof. The alarm would go off in just a moment. The officer laid Liosha on his shoulder and followed onto the roof; he was bowed with the weight of the body. When they reached the roof Haiduk attached one of the PFD-X15 flying devices to Bozhena and fastened one of the light grey stealth cloaks around her neck. Haiduk, without taking his hand off the apparatus on Bozhena's belt, pressed the lever to activate their ascent. They rose slowly into the air as Bozhena pressed herself to him. Seraphim-3 began to ascend in their wake, holding the slain Liosha by the belt and controlling the flying apparatus attached to the corpse. When they had flown one hundred metres from the lighted area of the embassy, sirens and shots were heard. But they were concealed in a zone of the sky gripped by the night. They soared over a huge, unlit park, away from the Institute of Urology and towards the fissures in the slopes of Hlybochytsya.

It occurred to Haiduk that even Hohol could not have dreamed up such a scene as this. Two lovers, a corpse and the killer of the corpse's killer floating in the August sky of Kyiv in the fourth world war. They fell to earth like fallen angels before being immersed in the darkness of a garage in Hlybochits, which had been looted and left in ruins. Nevinchanyi was waiting for them in the Ford Scorpion. They carefully laid Liosha's corpse in the boot before heading for Haiduk's alma mater, the polytechnic.

92

Even after Haiduk had discarded the mask of the intellectual technician, V. S. Petrenko, Bozhena remained silent, depressed and estranged. Haiduk had returned her communication gadget to her. Seraphim-3 had extracted it from the pocket of Major Crawford's corpse. Haiduk retained the other documents and computer fobs stripped from the body.

They were staying in the second floor of the safe building at the polytechnic. It retained the aroma of the technical office that had existed there since the nineteen-twenties. A leather sofa with a high back, crowned with a mirror which hailed from that period, dominated the room. It occurred to Haiduk that the old professor who had sold them the Zundapp motorcycle at Kalynivka would have sat on the same sofa where Bozhena was now sitting. Suddenly she laughed, 'Batman. A real batman,' and guffawed uncontrollably until her wild laughter turned suddenly to weeping. Haiduk sat alongside her and began to kiss her, nuzzling the tears away from her damp face and tasting their salt on his lips. Her face suddenly lost its beauty, as if she had quickly aged and returned to the state she was in when he first saw her in the limousine by the White House. Then he knelt before her and laid his head on her stomach. Everything suddenly seemed as warm and tranquil as in early childhood, and he slept.

He awoke on the floor and found he was carefully covered with a blanket and had a pillow under his head. Bozhena was sitting on the sofa and resting her elbows on her knees, gripping her head with her arms and staring at him. He leaped up because it seemed as if a drone was in the room, but it was just a small night light standing under the table. The outlines of the room and Bozhena were blurred by the half-light in the room.

'Sorry,' he said, sitting on the pillow and adding, 'kiss me.'

'Not now, it's not the right time,' she replied morosely, adding, 'I have to go now.'

'Where?'

'I spoke with Auntie Martha while you were asleep. She is really, really grateful to you. There are some Confederation people waiting for me in Bila Tserkva. All the charges against me have been dropped and I have been promoted to captain …'

Haiduk interrupted briefly saying, 'My congratulations.'

'… and appointed to the Ronald Reagan Military Space Station.'

'My congratulations,' Haiduk repeated again. During the pause he added, 'So, they are taking you away, Captain O'Connell. I'm not Batman, I am a Seraphim. My handle is Seraphim-1. But, to tell the truth, I am more Icarus than angel … and you know how the story of Icarus ended!'

And now Bozhena succumbed utterly to raw, true grief. She wept as she lay alongside him on the floor and began to tear off his and her own clothes. 'I don't want to, I don't want to, I don't want to leave you,' she pleaded with him, as if he were the one driving her away, and pushed her face close to him. It was a face that now seemed alien to Haiduk. Her body, with its concealed oases, was much more familiar. He felt the pain of a happiness lost forever and a moment of transcendence beyond his own existence. When he recovered, Haiduk saw Bozhena lying next to him, her head against his legs. Her body, which had brought him such pained happiness, did not have the lustre he had once seen.

They dressed swiftly, as if a battle had suddenly been announced. Bozhena discarded the clothes she had worn during her semi-arrest at the embassy. Haiduk had given her a new,

UMI officer's camouflage uniform. She pressed against him saying, 'Don't be mad at me sweetheart. I can't do anything else … Will you come with me to Australia?'

'No,' Haiduk said firmly, 'I am the last Ukrainian left in this bloody country. I have nowhere else to go. There is no choice.'

'And I can't live here,' said Bozhena, 'I imagined Ukraine not as it is but as the country I dreamed of. Forgive me.'

'You're not guilty of anything,' he said, 'it is time that is guilty. This bloody time of the Deathchristians. God bless you.' He made the sign of the cross on her then grazed her cheeks with his lips. Her face was dry.

'What is a Seraphim?' she asked.

'It's a bug with a head and six wings; it covers its face with two of them, its legs with another two and uses two to fly. It's an angel built with stealth technology. It is undetectable by radar.'

'When we flew you glowed in your cape like …'

'Batman.'

'No, you all, and that dead boy … looked like angels.'

Liosha has already been taken to his parents at Borshchahivka, thought Haiduk, saying aloud, 'If we were angels then we were angels of the abyss.' He kissed her lips, but felt no response from her. It was the first time they had made love since the occasion when they had lain on the floor of his apartment at Institutska. He felt his heart stutter and the darkness in his spirit grew as their love ended. Could it end so swiftly?

Nevinchanyi knocked delicately on the door. He would be taking Bozhena to Bila Tserkva.

The second night of occupation in Kyiv was ending. Haiduk still did not know everything that had happened at the Confederation Embassy during the night. The bells of Kyiv's

Pechersk-Lavra rang delightedly to welcome the day. There was some activity not far from the Gate Church of the Trinity, near the great Lavra bell tower. The construction of a mausoleum had begun there on Sansyzbayev's orders. It would house the remains of the Nazarene Rabbi who had gone to his eternal rest at thirty-three, Jesus Christ, referred to by the Hebrew word Messiah and as the Saviour in other tongues.

93

2 August 2077
18:00, Washington DC
Address of the President of the Confederation of North American States, Shirley MacDowell, to the people and the Congress of North America

My dear fellow citizens

Just yesterday we celebrated the brilliant victory of the American Legion over the narco-insurrectionaries and the gangs of Sapaterro. This triumph showed our ability to unite for the liberation of our sacred American soil from invaders.

Today we have received tragic news. During the night of 2 August 2077 a terrible crime was committed in Kyiv, the capital of a sovereign Ukrainian state now occupied by the forces of the Horde. The soldiers of a punitive unit launched a criminal and unprovoked attack on the Embassy of the Confederation of States of North America. Ambassador John O'Sullivan and eighty of the embassy staff, along with some of their family members, including children, were killed during the assault. The marines guarding the facility also perished in the attack. They had heroically defended not only citizens of the Confederation but also of OGS member states, who had sought protection in the grounds of the embassy. The loss of a hero of the Martian expeditions and a loyal son of America, William Crawford, is particularly painful.

Several of the embassy staff who survived the attack have been groundlessly arrested and transported from the premises. Their current whereabouts is unknown. The embassy is destroyed, the Confederation property at the site has been stolen, and the buildings have been burned.

This appalling crime is reminiscent of the most terrible times in human history and constitutes a gross violation of international law regarding diplomatic personnel. The American people are profoundly affected by the loss of their best sons and daughters, who served their homeland honourably and courageously. We grieve for the innocent victims of Horde aggression and express our deepest sympathy to the members of their families and all those who were close to them and who knew them.

Evil must be punished. My fellow Americans, the unprecedented criminal attack by the Horde on our embassy reminds us of another sad page in our history; the Japanese attack on Pearl Harbour in 1941, which became the cause of the USA's entry into World War Two.

I, by the power vested in me by the Constitution of the Confederation, declare that, as of 3 August 2077, the Confederation is at war with the Union of States of the Horde. I have the full support of Congress, both the Senate and the House of Representatives. I have ordered the armed forces of the Confederation to deliver a series of strikes against the military facilities of the enemy, their command points and information centres, and to deploy the newest, most advanced kinds of weaponry for this purpose. I have also ordered that the installation work on the geo-stationary orbiting Ronald Reagan Military Space Station be completed as swiftly as possible. With the assistance of that facility we will coordinate and deliver strategic blows against the Horde.

I do not promise you an easy time, my dear fellow citizens. The struggle will be complex and prolonged, and require the mobilisation of the forces of each one of us. But let us remember the immortal words of John F. Kennedy, we do these things "Not because they are easy, but because they are hard."

I want to touch on one other aspect of the tragic events in Kyiv. We have observed the events in Ukraine for a prolonged period with great concern; a once democratic, independent country, to which we are bound by our strategic partnership. Unfortunately, Ukraine became the first European country where criminal elements triumphed. Where a feudal dictatorial regime was established. Where the liberty, honour and dignity of the citizen were trampled upon by a group of oligarchs. We tried to convince our Ukrainian partners of the dangers of such a development. However, as we now know, they were engaged in secret negotiations with the Horde. They entered into voluntary slavery, acting in opposition to the national interests of their country, to this savage feudal power. They surrendered half their country to the rule of the Horde. The authorities in Kyiv have probably forgotten the lessons of 1240. Then the Uspensky Cathedral in Pechersk-Lavra, sacred to Eastern Christianity, was plundered by the army of Batu Khan.

We accuse the current leadership of Ukraine, its ruling High Directorate, of a criminal failure to execute its duties and provide reliable protection to diplomatic representatives. The blood of the Horde's innocent victims is on the conscience of Kyiv's rulers.

We are breaking off diplomatic and other relations with the Kyiv regime and have ordered our law enforcement agencies to investigate this matter. In the event of their guilt being established, the henchmen of the Horde will be arrested, along with those who sustain the narcotics trade to North America and support Sapaterro's insurrectionaries. We do not support the division of Ukraine into zones of influence, we stand for the territorial integrity of this country and its independence.

We call upon all the healthy forces in Ukrainian society to stand against the dictatorial regime in Kyiv and establish a democratic government in Ukraine. We will support a new democratic government of Ukraine. We are convinced that with the united forces of freedom-loving democratic nations we will succeed in defeating those enemies who want to subjugate humanity. They yearn to turn back history to those grim times of slavery, lawlessness and spiritual darkness. They long for the destruction of the very tenets of Christianity.

Our struggle will triumph not so much by the power of our arms as by the strength of the American ideal of freedom, and our faith in God, in his divine providence. God protect each and every one of you, my dear Americans. God Bless America.'

94

3 August 2077
To: IHDK@ GLOB.com
Secret: To be personally delivered to the Coordinator of the Ukrainian Liberation Front, Lieutenant General I. P. Haiduk.

Dear Ihor Petrovych
During this tragic time for your country, I want to address you as one of the leaders of the National Liberation Front of Ukraine with warm words of support for your work. You are battling against a double yoke, the first arm of which is the criminal regime of Klynkevych, Kreyda, Basmanov and Foshchenko. These individuals are the murderers of the lawfully elected hetman, Makhun, and have led our country to ruin. The second part of the yoke is the occupational regime of the Horde, who are terrible enemies of both Christianity and the Ukrainian people.

430

As you know, I always stood for the defence of Ukraine's national interest. Working in difficult conditions, I strove to ensure the State Guard worked for the defence of territorial integrity, law and order, and the personal freedoms of citizens. Not all this was successful of course, taking into account the vitriolic opposition of those who monopolised power and were contemptuous of Ukrainian law. They liquidated the independent judiciary and established, within the body of the state, an illegitimate punitive organ, the GPU. You, as a professional, are well aware of this. I am grateful to you for the understanding and support that you always extended to the State Guard and to me personally during the course of our, unfortunately, brief cooperation. The successful joint operations by the State Guard and UMI confirm the fruitfulness of the course of our security work.

The criminal clique of Klynkevych embarked on the liquidation of the State Guard and UMI, of their mutually linked structures and working methods, which were tried and tested, and the ruination of experienced bodies of staff. The regime chose instead to bank openly on criminal structures and gangs. This resulted in the loss to the state of both the intelligence and counter-intelligence services as vital supports of national security. Your groundless arrest and my illegal dismissal from my post are links in a single chain. The forces of the directorate are deployed for the removal of honourable professional patriots and servants of the state.

In my last letter to Hetman Makhun I warned him about the danger the Deathchristians presented to the state and proposed a number of concrete measures to work against them. In connection with this, Dear Ihor Petrovych, I remember your prophetic warning about the danger they posed during our first meeting. I would like the principles of the interests of the state, which I am sure you and I alike share, to take precedence over the trivial misunderstandings that divided us in this difficult time. I dream that the spirit of mutual respect, which united us during the war with Romania, will return to our relationship in the face of the harsh ordeals that Ukraine is destined to endure at present.

I fully support the aims and principles of the Ukrainian Liberation Front and note that several honourable State Guard and UMI officers are participating in its operations. I propose an alliance with you against the common enemy, an alliance of the State Guard and UMI, of Yu. Merezhko and I. Haiduk.

In the event of your agreement, I am ready to subordinate myself to you and allocate those resources of the State Guard that are at my disposal to the service of ULF. If we meet personally we could discuss a concrete plan of joint operations within the framework of popular resistance to the occupation of Ukraine. We certainly share the same goal of seeing our beloved Ukraine become a free, democratic country and not a vassal territory of the Horde.

I await your prompt and most active reply to my address - YYMR@GLOB.com. Our people may immediately make personal contact and arrange for us to meet within the next three to five days.

With sincere respect, Yu. Merezhko

The discussion of this letter in Haiduk's headquarters was interesting. Colonel Palii was convinced Merezhko was luring Haiduk into a trap and wanted to hand him over to General Mohammad Bek. He proposed they agree to a meeting in a location where UMI's snipers would be able to liquidate the former director of the State Guard. Two special forces' snipers supported the idea and expressed their wish to conduct this operation. However, Haiduk hesitated, having known Merezhko for many years he believed in the sincerity of this proposal from the old professional police officer. Merezhko had been humiliated by Klynkevych and, Haiduk was convinced, wished to return to power, albeit within the structures of the ULF. His knowledge of the agent network and the authority he enjoyed among State Guard officers was not irrelevant now. The support of what had been one of the most powerful structures in the state was vital. However, the ever wise Hryhoriy Nevinchanyi brought an end to their disputes.

'Ihor Petrovych, what's up with you, have you been blinded? Working with this slime-ball is the same as if, after the fall of Germany in 1945, you had arranged to meet with Himmler. Do you really not understand that Merezhko has a pathological hatred of you and detests you in the same degree as a certain Ukrainian president, whose name I forget, once loathed his prime minister? And do you know when this started? Don't you remember? When you and I captured a Romanian general and did not hand him over to this asshole Merezhko. He wanted to hog all the glory for himself. Some men from his entourage told me that he wanted to destroy you. He forgives nothing and no one. Therefore, I propose you organise a meeting and capture him. He knows a very large number of secrets. Hand him over to the courts later. If you believe him, you are the biggest idiot in the world and he will destroy you. That's all there is to this bollocks.'

They based their plans on Nevinchanyi's analysis of the situation.

95

General Mohammad Bek sat sombrely before the large screen of the computer at his headquarters. He ran through the secret reports from the command of the Horde and its agent network, the International Intelligence Directorate. The general had rejected Vizier Vadym Khlyshchenko-Khlyshchov's proposal to situate the command base above the Dnipro, in the premises of the Sejm. He held the former convict in contempt. Mohammad Bek had ordered that the red and black flag of the liberating army should instead be raised over Batii-Hrad, above the golden palace that dominated the western area of Kyiv. The headquarters of the army, the intelligence network and support structures were based in the buildings on Batyieva Hill, where the government of the territory was preparing to hold the historic summit of the USH.

The general liked his new, spacious office situated on the upper storey of Khan Batu Tower, beneath a golden dome. Three months remained until the summit. The general had decided the best gift for its participants would comprise, in part, the replacement of crosses on Kyiv's churches with crescent moons and minarets, fashioned in the style of ballistic missiles that would be erected around Uspenski Cathedral at Pechersk-Lavra and the golden domes of Mykhailivska and Sophia cathedrals. He had already set up arrangements for the army's engineering support services to develop these projects. However, the seizure of the American Embassy and the subsequent international reaction had compelled him to defer his architectural plans for a certain period.

Operation Tamerlane was not developing by any means as successfully as had been envisaged. On 3 August the weather in the Kyiv-Dnipro district had changed drastically. The African-type heat, which the general and a large part of his army were accustomed to, dissipated and the temperature plunged and the rains commenced. It would have been possible to call them tropical were it not that the walls of water sweeping over the land were mingled with snow. The movement of the liberating army slowed as tanks and wagons became mired in the black earth. The roads of this abysmal country that called itself European were in ruins because its leaders travelled in airborne terrapins. These were luxury vehicles, Mercedes Benz and BMW, armed with machine guns and missiles. Their

434

interiors consisted of salons inlaid with ivory and redwood, and their passengers would know nothing of the cratered tarmac motorways below. Only the East-West Highway was in a tolerable state because its maintenance had been supported by Friedman. His freight vehicle trains had once glided along it, earning the haulier-baron a hefty profit. However, after he had fled Kyiv, acts of sabotage were committed on the road. Explosions damaged its surface and ruined bridges, slowing up supplies of fuel and munitions. The fuel for terrapins was the source of substantial problems after a major explosion occurred at the Stalingrad chemical plant.

The deluge of rain, which lasted for over a week, generated numerous floods and engulfed poor towns and villages on the left bank. The schedule for transporting food products out of the territory, particularly the grain on which the authorities in Chyngiz-Saray insisted, was disrupted. The ceremonial meetings planned between the liberating soldiers with the local population in Donetsk, Odesa, Chernihiv and Mykolayiv did not occur. No one wanted to stand in the sleet, wearing summer clothes and gripping artificial flowers and Horde flags while depressed masses of the unemployed and factory workers besieged off-licences, demanding that sales of *horilka* be renewed. The Iranian and Pakistani police units had fired upon a number of such hostile manifestations. This had transformed the crowds into lynch mobs, who retaliated by hurling Molotov cocktails and home-made explosive devices. They had been compelled to punish the local authorities in those regions where the ceremonial welcome of the military had been disrupted. A few dozen corrupt local functionaries were hung out in the central squares of these towns.

The Horde's occupying army was only greeted appropriately in Poltava, where the military commander of the town and the city guard unit were ceremonially received in the Museum of the Battle of Poltava.

A Guiness record breaking, five ton halushka had been wheeled out on a bespoke electric vehicle to welcome the fraternal occupants. However, all those who sampled it were struck by diarrhoea a few hours later. But that minor detail did not trouble the military propaganda division who realeased news footage globally showing the gleeful welcome afforded to the liberators in this city of Russian glory.

But it was not the news, whether it was good or bad, that generated Mohammad Bek's depression. Half an hour ago he had endured an extremely unpleasant conversation with his holiness, the Black Star of the Earth and the Sun of the East, the Immortal Chief of the Horde, Kara-Khan. He had heard the wavering voice of the terminally ill Kara-Khan utter, 'What are you doing, you piece of shit?' down the line. 'Are you my deputy or a piece of camel crap drying up in the desert? Are you a human being or an ignorant ram with a small brain and big bollocks?'

'Your Sacredness,' said Mohammad Bek, inwardly cursing the old dictator who refused to die. 'I am prepared to take responsibility for my actions.'

'And you will bear responsibility for them,' snorted Kara-Khan. 'What did you do at the embassy of the American servants of Satan? I have just found out that they have declared war on us.'

He has clearly been in a hyperbaric chamber for a few days and has just caught up with things, thought Mohammad Bek, he doesn't have long now.

'Your Sacredness, there was an agent in the embassy who knew the secrets of Martian super-weaponry. I was compelled to issue an order to attack.'

'Well, so what? Did you capture her, you dirtbag?'

'Not yet, Your Sacredness, but …'

'I am striking you from the list of my potential successors,' Kara-Khan said, as his stertorous breathing echoed

436

down the line.

'Your will is the will of Allah,' said the general meekly; he understood the consequences of his fall far better than the Sun of the East.

The entire global press had screamed about the crime in Kyiv. The fourth world war had been declared, but no large-scale military activity was yet discernible. Mohammad Bek understood that Shirley MacDowell was waiting for the propaganda campaign she had launched against the Horde to have a serious impact. The percentage of Americans who supported a war against the Horde in Europe had already risen to 53% and was increasing continuously. All the Confederation's internet sites and television channels swirled unceasingly with sentimental stories of the diplomats and their families slain in Kyiv. The tale of Martian hero, William Crawford, was particularly prominent, along with a vivid portrayal of his family's suffering. Only the name of Bozhena O'Connell did not figure in the coverage.

The general had only learned about the existence of this wretched Martian and her secret on 1 August, during the day of the advance on Ukraine. His attention had been focused exclusively on implementing the operation according to its planned schedule. The director of the International Intelligence Directorate had reported to him that an American informant, code-named 'Red Pig', was based at the Confederation embassy. This asset had informed them of the presence at the embassy of a soldier in the Mars Space Legion, Bozhena O'Connell. She was Lieutenant General Haiduk's lover. Haiduk again, may he who possessed the secrets of Martian super weaponry be punished, thought Mohammed Bek.

Her knowledge could determine the outcome of the war. 'Red Pig' had proposed handing her over to the International Intelligence Directorate during the siege of the embassy in exchange for a reward of fifty-million globos. Mohammad Bek had issued an order to seize the embassy without consulting with Chyngiz-Saray. He knew that the dictator was not in a condition to make a decision then, and justifiably regarded himself as the first representative of the Black Star of the Earth. The facility had to be seized before Confederation forces began the evacuation of diplomatic personnel. It was another matter entirely that the commander of the punitive corps of Janissaries, Ali Akbar Pereverzev, had so carelessly prepared for Operation Paradisiacal Garden. He had permitted his cut-throats to perpetrate a massacre, during which 'Red Pig' and Bozhena O'Connell both might have perished. General Pereverzev was punished with fifty lashes for the failure of the operation, demoted to private and allocated to a punishment battalion in Kandahar. After these musings Mohammad Bek raised his communication gadget to his lips and said, 'Come into my office.'

The attractive Mongolian interpreter, Altantsetsen, entered, dispelling the darkness in the general's spirit a little with the glow of memories of his first love. She sat alongside him and he laid a hand on her shoulder.

'Listen carefully and interpret this.'

The International Intelligence Directorate had just sent him some material found at the Confederation Embassy that might shed light on the story of this lamentable Martian woman. He switched on a recording, obtained from the Confederation Embassy's security division, of events in room 512 on 2 August 2077 at 00:15. A woman sat, tied to a chair in a corner of the room. A muscular man in camouflage fatigues was looking around anxiously and standing alongside her, holding a Taurus army pistol. The doors opened and a figure in a strange cape darted into the room and was felled immediately with a bullet in his chest. A second figure jumped through the door and said something in Ukrainian, incomprehensible to the general, 'I am from Rohulka.' 'Kill this slime-ball! Don't worry about me,' the

438

girl in the chair shrieked back in the same language.

'Interpret,' said Mohammad Bek impatiently, thrusting his hand into a gap in her blouse where he could touch her small breasts.

'General,' she said, jerking her shoulder irritably, 'are we fucking or interpreting?'

He removed his hand.

They pondered the phrase, I am from Rohulka. What did it mean? Was it a password? The name of some locality? It was clear Bozhena and this unidentified stranger knew each other because she addressed him in familiar terms, and that she hated 'Red Pig'; there was no doubt it was he. She was ready to die herself if he died.

The general and Altantsetsen froze as they watched the third figure enter and save his colleague by turning the head and arms of 'Red Pig' to ash. Mohammad Bek scrutinised, with particularly intensity, the face of the second man that had been clearly captured by the camera; the luxuriant hair, prominent nose and narrow slits of his eyes. He had ordered the head of the intelligence directorate to conduct a digital analysis of the man's voice and search the files of the State Guard. Perhaps this man had caught the attention of Klynkevych's people.

'Go now child,' he said to her as she looked expectantly at him. 'That's all for today, we will deal with the other matter tomorrow.'

He patted her behind as she left, but found himself calling her back again soon afterwards. One of the reports on his computer particularly engaged his attention. Yesterday Klynkevych's security service and the military police had conducted a nocturnal operation in the Feofania-Pyrohovo colony. Twelve Ukrainian national terrorists were caught as a result. This represented a complete partisan unit, which had undertaken a small number of attacks on occupying units of the liberation army's forces. They had blown up a bridge on the ring road while wagons with munitions were crossing. Weapons and propaganda materials, which had been produced by the Ukrainian Liberation Front, were seized from the terrorists. Every third terrorist had been executed on the spot as was routine procedure. The others would be dispatched to special filtration sections of the Punitive Corps of Janissaries. During the process some crazy priest, when it was the turn of the person next to him to be shot in the back of the head, had requested that the police sergeant shoot him instead. He had argued this was better because the other man had two children and a third was expected. The police, struck by this episode, had allowed both terrorists to live, temporarily of course, and informed their superiors of this episode.

Mohammad Bek had ordered the mad man, who was ready to lay down his life for another, to be brought to him and summoned Altantsetsen to interpret. It struck the general that the staff uniform really suited her. It comprised a white military blouse with red epaulettes and a braided military cord, and a white aviation-style cap, with two black stars, which sat jauntily on her closely cropped hair. A silver dagger, a gift from Mohammad Bek for personal services, hung from the waistband of her black trousers.

The captive was led into the room. He was a skinny, short man with long, dirty, light brown hair, matted with rain, and a short beard, gummy with blood. Bruises lowered under his eyes and he could barely stand. The terrorist was dressed in a torn, black cassock and he held a small crucifix, which dangled around his neck, with his blood-encrusted right hand.

'Who are you, infidel?' asked the general.

'I am Father Ivan, the priest of the Feofania-Pyrohovo Church,' the priest replied.

'How did you become a terrorist? Does this not contradict the teachings of Jesus Christ?'

'Christ said, do not think I have come to bring peace on

earth. I come not to bring peace but a sword,' Father Ivan lisped as he replied because his front teeth had been smashed out.

This absurd priest had earned his death for these few words brimming with enmity towards the liberating mission of the Horde. However, there was something about the very insignificance of his person and his kind smile that compelled Mohammad Bek to continue the interrogation.

'Which church do you belong to?' he asked.

'To the Christian Church,' the priest replied simply.

'Sansyzbayev also belongs to the Christian Church,' Mohammad Bek observed.

'Sansyzbayev belongs to the Church of the Antichrist. He is a Deathchristian.'

'And do you really believe in the resurrection of Christ?'

'He rose from the dead and he is with us,' the priest said with conviction.

'And do you believe in the second coming of Christ?'

'It is very close now.'

'And how do you know this?'

'Because God is giving us signs that one would have to be blind not to see. He said that nation would rise against nation, and kingdom against kingdom. There would be famine, plague, earthquakes, brother would slay brother, and the father his child. And for the name of Christ, they would hate all of us who believe in him. And false Christs would be born …'

The general was impressed by the faith with which the captive uttered this terrible prophecy, but the calm, rational certainties of a military professional worked within him. However many wars had occurred and however often the end of the world was anticipated, the world always survived and revived. The world itself rose from the dead as the infidels insisted Prophet Isa had once risen. It was clear to Mohammad Bek that a religious fanatic stood before him; just like the Saudi, Iranian or Caucasian Wahhabi fanatics. However, the general, conquering his reluctance to cross a prohibited boundary, dared to enquire about that which he did not understand.

'Why did you want to give your life for the other terrorist?'

Father Ivan shrugged, 'I pitied him and his children. Let him live. I have no children.'

'Do you not have pity for yourself?'

'I regret my own fate, but Christ will not forsake me. His grace is sowed upon the hills of Kyiv.' Father Ivan stretched his hand towards the window where a grey wall of sleet obscured the lineaments of Kyiv's hillsides. 'His grace will stay here for eternity.'

'We will stay here for eternity,' said Mohammad Bek harshly, irritated by this crazed pontiff. He had brought the most terrible weapon to the general of the liberating army's office. That which was unnecessary for everyone and forgotten by all ... dangerous because it was motivated by nothing and no rational interests were involved - Benevolence.

'You will not stay here, foreigner,' said Father Ivan with sympathy. 'You drifted here from the Steppe like tumbleweed and you will float away on the wind. Everything that seems permanent to you will turn to ash. Remember the fate of the Golden Horde ... what trace of it remains in Kyiv? Only the name of a hill.'

'Well, okay,' Mohammad Bek said, striving forcefully to extinguish the flame of wrath that had ignited in him. He comprehended, with a feeling deeply concealed inside himself, that Ivan spoke the truth. 'And what if I had been standing alongside you? General Mohammad Bek, the owner of twenty wives and the father of thirty-seven children, and it was me they were going to shoot? Would you offer your own life in exchange for mine?'

'I pity you,' replied Father Ivan, 'for Christ teaches us to love our enemies, to bless those who curse us, do good to those

442

who hate us, and pray for those who persecute us. I have prayed and will pray for you, foreigner. And if you want to test me, stand alongside me in that line where every third person is to be shot in the head. And then you will see …'

'So you see,' Mohammad Bek gave a twisted smile, 'your goodness is selective. It's one way for the Christian, another for the Muslim.'

'You are mistaken, foreigner,' disagreed Father Ivan, 'for it is said that for Christ there is neither Greek nor Roman nor Jew. As there is no mother, no brother, no sister … there is only Him, His will, His light. I very much pity you, for I see the darkness in your spirit.'

This conversation had wearied Mohammad Bek and he suddenly felt indifferent to everything that had seemed so important to him … The army's operational reports, dispatches from the International Intelligence Directorate … even the conversation with Kara-Khan, which had denuded the general of any ambitious hope that he might sit on the throne in Chyngiz-Saray. Everything had lost all meaning and seemed very remote, a mirage in the desert. There was a bitter taste in his mouth. He barely twitched his hand to signal to the colonel who came with Father Ivan as he said, 'Take him away.'

'What shall we do with him?' asked the young officer. It seemed strange to him that the supreme commander of the Eastern European front wasted his time on this filthy dervish. This now powerless enemy could not halt the triumphal progress of the Horde.

'Hand him to Sansyzbayev to dispose of as he pleases,' ordered the general.

The captive was led out of the office. Mohammad Bek would remember the look the priest gave him as they parted … full of sympathy for the dark-bearded, swarthy, proud Arab with the soul burned utterly to ash. It was as if the general were being led to his death rather than Father Ivan.

Mohammad Bek entered the rest room next door, where there was a large marble sink. He washed his face in cold Myrhorod spring water, rinsed his hands and dried himself with an embroidered towel from Poltava. It was as if he wished to scrub away the vision of Father Ivan that still stood before his eyes.

He returned to his office and found Altantsetsen with her face pressed against the cold window, looking out on the hostile, unwelcoming city that lay before her. The interpreter turned her face towards Mohammad Bek and there were tears in her eyes. She sobbed, 'Don't kill him. Please.'

'You are free to go now,' the general replied emotionlessly. 'I am very busy. Go.'

96

Haiduk had a strange and terrible dream, like all the dreams he had been having recently. It seemed that Bozhena ran to him, roused him, grabbed his hand, and he, half dressed, ran out with her into the street. An old intercontinental-missile crawled with terrible slowness at a height of eight to ten metres above Peremohy Avenue and towards Bessarabka. The people who ran along the avenue, gripping their heads, looked up at the missile, at its central propulsion jet, its dark grey body and black warhead. Haiduk tried to identify where this solid-fuel, three-stage marine based ICBM had been manufactured. Was it American, Chinese, Russian, Ukrainian, or produced by the Horde? He could not determine its source. Could it even be one of our SS-32s with three megaton warheads? he thought with fear in his dream. Is it fitted with the Khars navigation system? He felt a cold that radiated from the propulsion outlet at the back of the missile. Impotent suffering gripped him at the impossibility of preventing this monster in its slow crawl towards the centre of the city. There were no symbols or distinguishing marks on the body of the missile. He saw his father standing nearby. The old man was wearing a white suit and was gripping a light-coloured hat made of rice straw. He was on the pavement, morose and pensive, without noticing his son or looking at the missile. Haiduk tried to pull towards his father, whom he had not seen in a long time, but Bozhena would not release her grip and cried, 'Don't go.' He turned his head towards her, but she had disappeared. It was the investigator, Belyayev, gripping his wrist and handcuffing him. The officer said, as if delivering a lesson, 'It is a mortal sin to forget your parents.' Hetman Makhun materialised, half of his head was missing, and he chorused, 'And you forgot me son. I so loved you … and you have never once visited my grave.'

Haiduk's arm, fettered by the handcuffs, grew cold and lost sensation as if it had died. He woke to find his right arm numb and he was cold because the room was cold. Mist and snow ruled the world outside the window. The rumble of metro trains, like an earthquake, shuddered around him every hour. Haiduk recollected that today was Professor Weber's birthday. The chief psychoanalytic consultant to UMI would be eighty-two years old.

Alfred Isaakovych Weber lived on Mykilsko-Botanichna Street in a dark grey, six storey building on a corner that resembled a Ukrainian letter 'Г'. The structure was known in Kyiv as 'Hrushevskyi's Building'. In reality, this creation of Stalinist classicism was built on the ruins of a private apartment building that had belonged to the head of the central parliament, M. Hrushevskyi, between 1908 and 1918. The building had once been occupied mainly by academics, but the old intelligentsia had departed. Property speculators had invested in the apartments, selling them to the nouveau-riche and diplomats. The luxuriously renovated dwellings had jacuzzis in their bedrooms, huge kitchens with bars and dining areas, billiard rooms, terrariums for crocodiles, walk-in wardrobes ... along with other alluring features from the postmodern epoch of glamour.

Miraculously, Professor Weber's seven room apartment had been preserved here. He had no wish to sell and no one troubled him because he had cured Hetman Makhun and almost all the Ukrainian elite from depression.

Haiduk and Nevinchanyi, brushing the snow off themselves and breathing heavily, carried the cardboard box with Weber's gifts to the fifth floor. The general lift, once used by the plebs, did not work; each flat owned by these new feudal suzerains had a personal lift.

The owner of the flat opened the door. He was a tiny, thin old man, always with a smile for everyone, and interested in everything around him. The bald skull of this godly old man was adorned at the back and sides with a wave of snow-white hair. His small, green eyes were hidden under bushy, grey brows. Occasionally Alfred Isaakovych would pick up a small pair of scissors and trim them. The brows would soon grow back, but as they sprang from under the scissors his eyes resembled two clear lakes ringed with bulrushes.

Haiduk removed the polypate mask of the technical intellectual, V. S. Petrenko, on the landing of the fifth floor, before they went to Weber's flat. The mask had been necessary because their documents had been inspected at the entrance to the passage into the building.

'Come in, come in,' said Weber, delighted to receive his visitors. 'I welcome you to my abode on the occasion of my birthday. You are my first and probably my last guests, but dear to me and very welcome. And what's in the box? I hope it is not a bomb?'

'It contains the things you like,' Nevinchanyi said soothingly. 'Fish, lemons and chocolate - And Virginia tobacco.'

Alfred Isaakovych had almost never ventured out of his

flat since his wife, his beloved Lusia, Liudmyla Solomonivna, had passed away. Almost no one visited him. His son, Doctor Yochanan Weber, worked at Stanford University on the West Coast of America and did not visit his father. Alfred's nephew, Hena, helped him keep up with the house. He was an old bachelor, who, on seeing the guests, immediately made himself scarce. The old, neglected flat, with its century-old furniture, was crammed with books and was reminiscent of a library compiled without any system. Only Alfred Isaakovych knew where to find a unique publication of Rilke's poetry or the newest textbook titled *Computer Psychoses and the Methods for their Treatment.*

Professor Weber was wearing a dark burgundy dressing gown with a finely patterned black and white *keffiyeh* around his neck. His own self-stated vocation was to embody Ukrainian nationalism with a human face. He was extremely proud of the fact he inhabited a building sanctified with the name of the Ukrainian historian, Hrushevskyi, whom he regarded as one of the greatest academics in world history.

The old fellow bustled around, trying to slice sausage and also lemon, which he was planning to add to the cognac he offered them. Haiduk, seeing how the professor's hands trembled, took on the responsibilities of a host. With Hryhoriy's assistance they made the dining table, which was crammed with a heap of books and a photograph of his wife, appear presentable.

'Dear Alfred Isaakovych,' said Haiduk, raising a glass, 'you are our great teacher. You always instructed us that, even in the most difficult circumstances, we must remain human. You are the bearer of the best humanitarian traditions of European science …'

'You are overdoing it Ihor. A touch too much pathos,' the professor interjected, although it was apparent the toast was to his liking. 'Let's just have a drink, and thank you for not forgetting.'

'To you,' said Haiduk and Nevinchanyi, clinking glasses with the professor.

Nevinchanyi went to the next room, where he had a good view of the street and the entrance. Prior to the occupation, guards from the diplomatic protection corps had watched over the building, in a small structure ten metres away from the entrance. Two of Haiduk's UMI special forces troops were now positioned in this abandoned guard point to control the adjacent approaches to the building. The Ford Scorpion was parked around the corner of Pankivska Street.

Haiduk and Weber remained alone. Alfred Isaakovych picked up his favourite pipe, a Dunhill Briar, which had been finished in hot oil with a stem of red wood. Haiduk had presented the pipe to Weber for his seventieth birthday. At that time Alfred Isaakovych was working near to Washington, in a laboratory of experimental psychology in electronic systems. The professor unhurriedly extracted a pinch of Golden Virginia from a smooth metal tobacco tin. He stuffed it into his pipe bowl with his thumb and lit the pipe, as he inhaled the smoke his eyes glowed bright with the sweetness of tobacco.

'So, tell me, what's going on,' he said.

'You know, Alfred Isaakovych, how far removed I am from politics. Or I was.'

'But was politics distant from you?' Weber laughed.

'Politics erupted into my life like a hurricane. And not only politics, but religion. The Deathchristians, the Risenchristians, Islam … I have been compelled to act several degrees above my level of competency. I am clearly a technician and a spy rather than a politician, and I was confused. In addition, there is the national question. As a cosmopolitan technocrat I was indifferent to all that as recently as six months ago. But now I can no longer stand aside.'

On a number of occasions over the last twenty years of

448

their acquaintance, Haiduk had gone to Weber as to a confessor. He could not confess to a priest because he did not trust any of them. However, the conversations with Weber eased his conscience. Alfred Isaakovych had a marvellous gift for reaching a precise conclusion. He would reel it in like a fish from the chaos of conflicting facts, assumptions and tangled hypotheses, as clear sighted as an experienced angler. He was by no means a prophet. However, it was only recently that Haiduk had understood Weber's advantage over the majority of experts. His wisdom grew from his vast love of humanity and the powerful religious ideal of responsibility before God. He was, of course, not a pure psychologist, psychoanalyst or psychiatrist. He was an integrator, who joined his knowledge of medical biology with political science, and historiography with philosophy and information technology. His first book was published in 2023 when Weber, a graduate of, and lecturer at, Kyiv-Mohyla Academy, was twenty-eight. He had written a number of books, but it was his third work, *The Paranoia of Political Correctness and the Loss of Europe,* published in 2030, that led to Weber being elected a member of the Royal Society in London. He was also awarded a professorship at Harvard, and moved to Boston. Isaakovych's five years at Harvard concluded with his work, *New World Demons, the Psychopathy of Globalisation* (2036). In this work he demonstrated that globalisation ruined the psychological equilibrium of traditional societies and would be the principle of geo-political catastrophe in the future. The research he undertook for *A Dangerous Psychological illness; the Criminalisation of Societies and States* (2058) became the theme of a number of special debates at the UN.

The UN subsequently drafted a list of criminal states, which included Ukraine and Russia. This aroused the ire of both the upper echelons of government and national radicals alike. The governing elite compelled Alfred to emigrate to Switzerland for a number of years. No one took note of the fact that Friedman, one of the 'heroes' of the book, had become an arch-enemy of Weber after its publication.

Weber replied to Haiduk's remarks after a few moments. 'When, Ihor, you referred to me with absolutely sincerity I believe, as the bearer of the best humanitarian traditions of European science, you cannot have imagined how my heart ached.' The pleasant aroma of tobacco filled the room. 'This so-called humane European science bears a heavy weight of guilt before humanity. I feel this very acutely now, as we all feel it, you included.'

'Are you disillusioned with science?' Haiduk asked.

'Science murdered God. This is its greatest crime before humanity. Technology has given humanity the sense that all is permissible, that they are omnipotent. It is only now that a group of scientists, I among them, have begun to renew God. Without the concept of a creator or a general constructor, God in other words, it is impossible to comprehend the world. We find traces of God everywhere in the creation of the Universe, through the Big Bang and the behaviour of elemental particles, in the nature of archetypes, and in the genetic code. However, how can we now demonstrate to the pagans who rule this world that God really exists? But, forgive me, instead of listening to you I have confessed all my own sins ...' The old professor poured out a little more cognac and the bottle chimed against the crystal glasses. 'Let's toast Lusia ... I wait to meet her again from day to day ... I expect she is in paradise and has chosen a good spot for us. Only I don't know if there is a library there? Or a computer?'

They drank for a moment in silence.

'I have read your *Psychology of Hatred* a few times,' Haiduk said, 'but even you cannot imagine the depth and extent of this phenomenon now. I feel how hatred utterly subsumes me, hatred for the Horde, for the regime of traitors, for the investigators, politicians, for the American major who raped

450

my girlfriend, for the Ukrainian turncoats who have gone to work in the police assistance units of the Horde, for the Poltava dumpling himself, for Kreyda, and for the Egyptian who sits on Batyieva Hill and governs Ukraine. I would announce the slogan of 'sacred hatred' for the occupiers and their collaborators. But hatred is not sacred, it is primitive and dark, it burns all that is decent in me and murders my soul. Do you know the greatest pleasure I have enjoyed recently? When I saw how the face of that American major darkened and burned in an assault laser; how it turned to ash.'

'You are obviously not a Christian,' Weber laughed, 'but neither are you the antichrist. Why are you surprised? Hatred was inherited by us as far back in the evolutionary chain as the dinosaurs. Hatred, terror, revenge, anger, fear they will take your food, your spouse, your children, your life ... Hatred inhabits millions of people. This is a very intense and, in some ways, positive feeling. Hatred and the desire for vengeance engender profound discoveries and great works of art. But only when hatred is built on great love. We inherited love from the dinosaurs also. Love and hatred are twins. God, the great dialectician, instilled our spirits with both angels and demons and now observes us to see who will be overcome.'

'So the human soul is like a dormitory inhabited by squabbling angels and devils.' Haiduk laughed; his spirit felt at ease now, having unburdened itself to Weber. Perhaps the secret power of the confession just lay in someone listening to you.

Weber, drawing on his pipe with relish, went to the shelf and extracted a leather-bound folder, which he handed to Haiduk.

'What's that?'

'It's the Nobel Committee report on my joint nomination with Professor Armstrong for this year's Nobel Prize,' Weber explained with great satisfaction. 'You are the first person I have told about it. Do you remember Armstrong? You played golf with him when you came to our laboratory. The core of our research,' he said, beginning to whisper, as if afraid someone might be listening in, 'lay in our discovery of the televisual virus. The virus strikes the human brain, generating a psychotic illness and a syndrome that incorporates debilitation, dulled emotion, and a state of aggressive hatred. The most difficult aspect was the discovery and research of the mechanism by which the virus is transmitted from the televisual screen to the human brain in a form of digital code. However, we proved this experimentally and isolated the virus in its pure form. We have named it TDV - Television Debility Virus.'

'This is a terrible discovery,' said Haiduk, conceiving of the menace it presented to humanity.

Weber gathered the folder from him and groomed his bushy, grey brows with his fingers. 'This is not a discovery but a tardy explanation of the sad fact of humanity's progressive degradation. It is unclear how it can be prevented. So, my dear Ihor, when you are the leader of the Ukrainian State, you must consider what to do with television.'

'I'm not planning to lead anything, Alfred Isaakovych,' said Ihor sombrely.

'Oh, you will, you will,' echoed Weber cheerfully. 'You cannot get away from it because it is your destiny, you are a natural leader. If we may be serious for a moment, it is a challenge, but you must not run away from it. Listen to some advice from an old man. Ukraine must be renewed. The country could be renamed Ukraine-Rus. All the rights stripped from the Ukrainian people must be returned to them: language, national pride, history, liberty, national wealth, without these this place will remain a wilderness. I urge you to become a Ukrainian nationalist and to salvage this country.'

'I have practically become one already,' Haiduk acknowledged dejectedly.

'No, not yet. You don't really know this earth, its songs,

or why people die for it. Only do not think that nationalism is hatred for others. It is love for yourself and for your people and others. Do not listen to those who weep continuously over Ukraine's unhappy fate, who cry and whine and wipe the tears away. This state of chronic national depression will only kill off Ukraine. Rise above history and above the mundane. I heard that some movement had emerged called "I am the last Ukrainian". It is a mistake and contains the seeds of defeat. Imagine instead, that you are the first and that everything is ahead of you. Begin to write the history of Ukraine on the new leaf you turn over. What do you lack for this task? You have an honourable name and an unblemished biography. People trust you. They know you in the West, and you and your people have not only the future but also a glorious past in Kyiv-Rus, a great state that existed one thousand years ago, and Christianity. The Steppe has come here, but will depart as soon as the grass perishes and winter begins.' Weber looked out of the window where snow fell and mingled with pouring rain. 'The Steppe horses will lack hay ...'

The old guy is confused about which century he's in, thought Haiduk. He is losing his mind. Now it is not the horses of Batu Khan, but terrapins and tanks from the Nizhny Tagil factory.

'Forgive me for being blunt, Ihor,' Weber continued, 'but why the hell are you sitting here in Kyiv playing at conspiracy games and creating a partisan unit like that of Sydir Kovpak, Bandera and Che Guevara? This is ineffective. You need to be occupied instead with saving Ukraine. You must immediately go outside the zone of occupation and announce to the entire world that you are creating and leading the government of a renascent Ukraine. You must immediately organise a meeting of all opposition forces from the left and right banks of Ukraine. The best place to hold this is Vinnytsia, the capital of Podilia. Only I beg you,' Weber said, coming from the table and leaning over, 'not to fall into the childish disease of so-called democracy. It matters not whether they are rich or poor; the rule of quarter, of half intellectual types, of the mass. That stage in the development of humanity is behind us.'

Alfred Isaakovych began to stroll around the room as if he were lecturing his students. They had nick-named him marathon runner because during the course of a lecture he would cover a great distance. 'I will reveal to you one more secret. There may be no true democracy, for people are not in any respect equal; this has been proven by genetics.'

'And what about the French Revolution? Liberty, Equality, Fraternity?' responded Haiduk.

'The equality of victims and executioners? The fraternity of the beggar and the millionaire? The liberty to slay enemies of the people?' Weber paused for a moment, looking in surprise at Haiduk, as if he did not know the basics of the psychology of history. 'People are not equal, eighty percent of them are grey, average, contaminated with TDV. So electoral democracy is the democracy of the grey mass. Of course, as human beings, as God's creations, they have the right to a secure life, good governance, social justice and education for their children. However, power must belong to the professionals. Therefore, there must be no parties, no elections, no majority rule. Elections must be held only at the basic municipal level. The country must not be ruled by bureaucrats but by managers employed for that purpose.'

'And who will control them?' Haiduk asked.

'A united civic society. There will be no presidents or hetmans in the state. The country must be governed by professional minds, a council consisting of economic, financial, social educational, ecological and security managers. Right now, Ihor, this possibility is unbelievable. You think it is a utopian fantasy of an aged professor, but remember that a new period in human history is beginning. The old projects for developing civilisation are exhausted, above all the so-called democratic project, the rule of the majority over the minority. As a rule it is exceptional bastards and arrogant paranoiacs who become chiefs, hetmans and presidents. And quite apart from that one person, even the greatest genius cannot realise the will and the wishes of millions of people. A pitiable epithelial cell cannot control the human organism. The mind must rule the body. New ways for the construction of society must be sought. The thoughts of God are certainly not akin to our thoughts and God's logic is incomprehensible to us, but Christ understands and pities us. Do you know who He loved the most?'

'Who?' Haiduk managed to squeeze in a word.

'Sinners, those who repent. For in repentance there is movement, there is life, from the transgression to the absolution. Those who are pristine and just lack that movement, that life, Christ always suspected them of Phariseeism. God directs the large-scale processes, punishing entire people. These were harsh, large scale punishments, perhaps unjust. And Christ supports the individual offering hope of justice.'

Nevinchanyi entered the room. 'We have to go now, two armoured vehicles from the Janissary corps are coming this way from the university, and a platoon of Ukrainian police. They've been held up at the junction of Tolstoy and Pankivska streets, but won't be for long,' he said.

Haiduk approached Weber, who smiled dreamily as he recollected the spring. 'Alfred Isaakovych, come with us. We will take you to a safe place, and, if you want, we will go together to Vinnytsia. I beg you. Gather up your important papers, get your coat and ...'

Weber laughed and it was unclear if this was the merry, carefree laugh of the Epicurean or the bitter laugh of an infinitely old man ready for death.

'The sole safe place for me is alongside Lusia ... Who will bother me anyway? Someone my age isn't interesting. No, Ihor, thank you, I am going nowhere away from here. This is my home … You go now, go, and God bless you.'

Haiduk embraced the meagre body of the professor and kissed his bald pate. The thought that he would never see Alfred Isaakovych again was unbearable. Haiduk would learn a little later that he had caused Weber's death. When the guards stationed by the entrance had seen the mask of the technical intellectual, V. S. Petrenko, on Haiduk's face, they realised this was the prison bird for whom a hefty reward was promised. Their computer showed that this was a dangerous traitor. However, they delayed phoning the confidential informers' line only because they had a long argument about how to split the money three ways. They finally settled the matter and when the two fugitives exited the building one of the guards tried to detain them, intending to acquire the lion's share of the reward. He and his colleagues were shot in the face, but that didn't save Alfred Isaakovych.

97

10 August 2077
Kyiv
For distribution on internet and television channels
Report

The member of the Higher Directorate and Marshall of Jurisprudence, General Prosecutor of Ukraine, I. O. Kreyda, has recently had his attention drawn to footage broadcast on the state television channel. The footage apparently shows the murder of former Hetman K. D. Makhun being undertaken by his legitimate successor and current head of the state V. Ya. Klynkevych. Citizens have addressed the GPU with numerous requests for an explanation. Is this a further falsification from the so-called Ukrainian Liberation Front or is it factual? Our starting point is the presumption of the innocence of any citizen until their guilt is proven in court. The GPU aims to support the rule of law and justice and has assumed control over the case of the possible murder of General K. D. Makhun. We therefore announce:

1. The conduct of a comprehensive analysis of the recording and the scene of the murder to establish the identities of those involved and/or if the recording is false.
2. The summoning of Lieutenant General V. Ya. Klynkevych to the GPU for questioning as a witness, and asking him to sign an agreement that he will not leave the country, with the agreement of the command of the Horde liberating army.
3. The exhumation of the body of K. D. Makhun so a repeat post-mortem examination can be carried out, and a ballistics investigation.

The GPU will regularly update the public regarding the results of the investigation.

I. O. Kreyda

98

The Grand Master of the Church of Christ's Death, Father Kalerii, aka Sansyzbayev, and a dozen of the warriors of light, the sacred priests/guardians, were freezing in the sleet. They were waiting for the authorities to hand them Father Ivan, as promised. Before them reared the nine-storey building of the former ecology ministry, painted in garish greens and yellows. The military command of the Batyiska special division was based in this building, which was situated not far from the Victims of the Cheka Square. Father Ivan had been brought here after his interrogation by Mohammad Bek. Their wolf skins and the bottles of home-brewed vodka they passed around did not prevent the guardians from suffering in the cold and rain. Only Sansyzbayev haughtily refused to gulp down any of the Buriakivka home-brew because he was afraid someone might notice him breaking Sharia law.

The Deathchristians quarrelled loudly about the best location for killing Father Ivan. Some suggested Lysa Hill, but it was dangerous there in the ruins of the academic nuclear reactor. Others wished to take the priest to Pechersk-Lavra. However, the military commandant there, a major in the Horde police, forbade the conduct of any large demonstrations on the territory of the military unit. Eventually they agreed to crucify him on Batyieva Hill, above the gully in whose depths the River Lybid coursed. The whole city would be able to see. The more they drank, the more they became convinced that Father Ivan would depart this earth as the last advocate of the Risenchristians. Kyiv and the entire territory of the district would be under the control of the Deathchristians.

Eventually, two guards pushed Father Ivan through the doors of the building. The Deathchristians had prepared a standard T-shaped cross for the crucifixion of Father Ivan in advance. It was moulded from plastic because nearly all the trees in the city had been felled by citizens preparing for winter.

They surrounded Father Ivan, cackling and swearing as they fastened the crucifix to his back. They harried him through the Solomianske Cemetery. The priest felt neither pain nor cold. His ancestors had been buried here once, but in the third decade of the twenty-first century a home for elderly State Guard officers had been erected on their bones.

Will my forebears, priests from generation to generation, be unable to welcome the second coming because their bones have already perished? Father Ivan wondered. He dragged the plastic T-shaped cross fettered to him. Although it was not as heavy as wood, it was cold and slippery and slid from his back. Sansyzbayev's Deathchristians would then reward him with a lash of their whips.

The guards, in their warm raincoats and wellingtons, did not embroil themselves in the acts of savagery. They respected local traditions and simply trudged indifferently at the side of this weary procession. There was almost no one on the streets and the chance passers by who saw the Guardians fled into the subways. One of them made an audio-visual recording of the procession. The streaming rain washed away the blood from Father Ivan's brow. His eyes gleamed with suffering and a superhuman stubborn insistence on dragging his cross to the end. Some impoverished women, wearing headscarves, joined the procession in spite of the threats of the Guardians.

Sansyzbayev, in his red, waterproof mantle, walked a little apart from his wolf pack. He cursed Mohammad Bek inwardly. The general had ostentatiously ignored him. He had not appointed Sansyzbayev as head of the civilian occupation administration established by the Horde. He had not provided the excavators and bulldozers required for the erection of Christ's mausoleum. He is not who he appears to be, this Mohammad Bek, thought Sansyzbayev.

They passed the golden palace of Batii-Hrad on the left, passing through the camouflaged battery of Grad rockets targeted at the city. Eventually they merged into a small clearing over the gully from where, on clement days, the vast panorama of Kyiv-West was revealed; but the town was now covered in grey mist. The warriors of light slithered on the wet clay soil, swearing profusely, and dug a hole wherein to plant the crucifix. They were weary of this drawn-out affair. The women approached Father Ivan and, kissing his hands, pleaded for him to bless them. The guards did not try to prevent this strange benediction.

Sansyzbayev, however, approached the priest and snarled at the women, so that they fled into the shrubbery. 'You chose death for yourself,' said the grandmaster, as if justifying his actions.

'It is not I but Christ who chose this destiny for me,' Father Ivan responded.

'But you are not afraid of death, for you will rise from the dead,' continued Sansyzbayev, mockingly.

The rain streamed down Father Ivan's face, or maybe those were tears. 'Christ is Risen,' he said, crossing himself. 'Leave me now Antichrist and let me pray.'

'Your Christ died and you will die like a dog. Then there will be nothing, only darkness,' bellowed Sansyzbayev, as he left Father Ivan. But it was the Deathchristian who felt powerless, hopelessly sick and of no use to anyone. 'Finish this,' he ordered his guards, who were delighted that soon it would all be over.

They threw themselves upon Father Ivan, tearing away his outer garments and laying him with his back on the cold crucifix. The warriors of light tried to nail the arms and legs of their victim to the crucifix, but the plastic did not give. They only succeeded in driving holes through his wrists. Then they twisted barbed wire around his arms and legs to bind him to the cross. Father Ivan cried out, losing consciousness for a moment, but recovered quickly.

They began to raise the crucifix over the gully, turning Father Ivan's face towards Kyiv so he might better see the world he was losing. However, he no longer perceived that external world or what happened around him.

All around Father Ivan was immersed in darkness. He managed to think about whether the Saviour had really forsaken him before he died. In this hour, the dark energy held sway over Kyiv. Rain, snow and climactic changes worked together to immerse the city in the depths of a freak weather event. Night fell early, as if it were midwinter.

Father Ivan died from wounds, the effects of being beaten and hypothermia on Friday 13 August 2077.

99

To all citizens of Ukraine
13 August 2077
Distributed by ULF hackers via the internet and state television channels
REPORT OF THE UKRAINIAN LIBERATION FRONT

Citizens of Ukraine
As a result of the successful operation conducted by Ukrainian Military Intelligence in one of the European countries, incontrovertible evidence of treason has been revealed. The evidence shows the betrayal was planned by Ukraine's ruling elite over a number of years, when they were involved in a criminal conspiracy with the leadership of the Horde.

Today, the ULF has launched two websites, which are accessible to both the Ukrainian and global communities, http://www.zrada.ua and http://www.corrup.ua. Anyone who wishes may find lists of agents of the Horde on these domains, detailed facts, names of individuals and companies utilised, and the payments made. The site also details the involvement of highly positioned individuals in Ukraine, members of the Aeropagus, national and local government, and officials from law enforcement and military bodies. These individuals systematically plundered the Ukrainian people and the country's national wealth. They transferred astronomical profits outside the country without paying taxes. Simultaneously, they became the Horde's agents, fulfilling the instructions of the so-called Ukrainian research centre established by Kornilov-Kyseliov. This was created by the military and political leadership of the Horde as it prepared to undertake military aggression against our native land.

The general prosecutor, I. O. Kreyda, played, and continues to play, the most heinous role in the process of

Ukraine's subjugation. He is one of the most dangerous drug barons and organised crime bosses. Kreyda formed an alliance with the Mexican drug baron, Sapaterro, and supplied him with arms. He also has a joint narcotics business with the family of the former Vice-President of the Confederation of States of North America, Sara Lou Lane. Kreyda secures the link between Ukraine's governing elite and the so-called 'Grey Prince'. He is a criminal-in-law and the leader of the criminal underground to which V. Klynkevych also belongs.

Both sites provide striking evidence of Ukraine's transformation into a criminal state through the subjugation of the law enforcement bodies to the Grey Brigades. These criminal groups were, in reality, governing the state, plundering its treasures and the national wealth, which belonged to the entire people. Recordings are provided of the negotiations between the conspirators and their foreign-based bosses regarding the so-called 'Magic Nine'.

What does this phrase mean? It is a selection of the nine strategic types of raw material, without which a modern radio, electronic and defence sector would not exist. These include such substances as vanadium, cobalt, germanium, niobium, lanthanum, zirconium and others. Many deposits of these and other extremely important metals are to be found in the eastern, central and western areas of Ukraine. The locations of these fields and the estimated volumes of their deposits are a state secret of the highest category. The materials obtained during the course of the intelligence operation unambiguously illustrate that these high-level traitors handed these secrets to the enemy. They acted thus for their own personal advantage and out of a hatred of independent Ukraine. This resulted in irreparable financial losses to the country and transformed Ukraine into a raw materials colony of neighbouring states.

A series of events occurred in connection with another strategic resource of our native land - grain; during a period when one of the major threats to humanity is the insufficient production of grain and the consequent famine this will cause. Those individuals who transformed the people into serfs, who usurped the people's right to control their own resources, simply handed the fertile earth of Ukraine to the agents of foreign states. It is clear from the materials made public that almost 40% of Ukraine's most productive land was sold to foreign owners. This represents treason and requires due legal punishment.

The materials presented on these sites illustrate the profound moral decline of the so-called Ukrainian elite and the degeneration of a caste of those above the law. Their degradation stretched from utter hypocrisy to absolute shamelessness, to the cynical public flaunting of treasures plundered from the people. The Ukrainian Liberation Front has initiated the creation of a Kyiv tribunal, the aim of which is to try the leading perpetrators of treason as traitors to Ukraine. The preparation is also being undertaken of an international trial for the functionaries of the armed forces and punitive organs of the Horde. This will encompass the collaborators from the local population who have also committed crimes against Ukrainian citizens. Independent lawyers, human rights activists, international experts and representatives of civic organisations are invited to participate in the Kyiv tribunal. Their participation will guarantee the impartiality of the proceedings, and the examination of the cases and the objectiveness of the verdicts.

The Ukrainian Liberation Front hopes the secret files that have been made public will hasten the destruction of this debased regime of Deathchristians and Horde agents, and secure Ukraine's liberation from foreign occupation and the renewal of statehood.

100

Major Boiko of the medical service telephoned Haiduk from

the Kyiv military hospital. He picked up the call in the Ford Scorpion as he travelled to Vinnytsia with Nevinchanyi and Palii senior. It was difficult to catch the voice on the other end of the line, perhaps because of the rain and snow that gripped Ukraine in a prolonged siege. It was also probable that the intelligence and defence services of the Horde had begun to control more, and monitor stringently, conversations transmitted via the UMI satellite.

'Ihor Petrovych?' Haiduk heard Boiko's voice through a screen of crackling and buzzing. 'Do you recollect the patient who is occupying a bed in our haematology department?'

Haiduk recollected the meagre face of the Russian, Rear Admiral Feoktysov, who he had transported from the Island of Evia and placed in the hospital. They had located a distant relative of his in Kyiv, who had agreed to care for the patient and often went to the unit to give him fruit and vegetables. Feoktysov's condition had greatly improved.

'What's going on with him?' Haiduk asked.

Nevinchanyi, swerving around the mud-filled potholes on the road, even refrained from swearing so as not to hamper Haiduk's conversation. Boiko's voice penetrated the white noise, 'Things are very bad, Ihor Petrovych. This morning some of the Janissary regime collaborative unit came to us, wanting to take away the admiral. We only just managed to stop them by insisting that he was going to die imminently ... but they will come again in the evening and if he has not died ...'

'Are you capable of doing anything at all?' Haiduk replied, beginning to seethe, 'Are you Grandma Dunia or an officer?' he added, think that the major was like some ineffective old woman.

'Which Grandma Dunia?' asked the major, not understanding Haiduk's metaphor.

'Fuck you,' Haiduk cursed quietly. Then said in a louder voice, 'Tell me precisely what is happening.'

'Half an hour ago Feoktysov gave the order to launch.'

Now it was Haiduk's turn not to understand, 'What launch?'

'Are you a general or Grandma Dunia in epaulettes?' said the major irritably. 'The word launch, in accord with military statute, means an operation directed towards the discharge of missiles.'

'And how do you know this?' Haiduk asked.

'I heard him give the order myself. At first I did not understand, I just heard him speaking what sounded like some kind of codes, probably coordinates, distances, the devil knows what, and then he said I am issuing the order to launch. I understood then. I tried to take his gadget from him, but he turned blue, I felt sorry for him … but what if he has targeted the missiles at the hospital? That is at Kyiv? Can you hear me?'

'Stop!' Haiduk ordered Nevinchanyi.

Hryhoriy and Palii exchanged glances, while the former steered carefully to the right, so as not to flip over in the culvert, and headed for the edge of the forest. Haiduk exited the vehicle into the cold rain, shook off the water and snow, and ran to the short pine trees nearby. For some reason he remembered how he and Bozhena had driven to an area covered with wet aspens near Kyiv, not far from the ring road. It seemed to have happened one hundred years ago.

Nevinchanyi and Palii exited the electronic vehicle reluctantly because it was wet and cold, and they had no idea what had happened to Haiduk.

'Switch off the engine and batteries and block everything electric. Wrap all the gadgets in the stealth cloaks and bury them. Do it!' Haiduk ordered so harshly he disturbed his subordinates.

'It's so cold Ihor Petrovych, and the soil is wet,' Nevinchanyi said, trying to persuade Haiduk to amend his order.

'It's getting warmer now,' Haiduk replied.

The rain ceased suddenly and the sky turned its immortal August shade of pale blue. The trio of intelligence agents looked upwards, as if seeing its secret depths for the first time. They noticed some strange, level, white lines that plaited the heavens from west to east. The sun over Vinnytsia had already sunk low into the west when a second sun was born on the eastern horizon. A younger, more energetic sun, which bathed Eurasia in light, as if the day had been reborn before it had perished. Then the light died, leaving a green lustre that filled the sky and all around, evoking a fluorescent effect. The UMI officers, the Ford Scorpion, the short pines at the edge of the forest, the pitted road and the telegraph poles with their wires, all glowed silver. Then they were extinguished, as if the landscape had been covered with a stealth cloak.

101

One hundred years after the events described, historians gathered at a global congress dedicated to the causes of the Fourth World War. There was no one to interview about what had really happened in August 2077. Only a very few documents had been preserved from that period. After the thermo-nuclear explosions in the atmosphere and space, most satellites storing significant information were seared by the heat. Earth based computers were either destroyed or damaged by electromagnetic radiation. Many of those who might have remembered these events had perished. There were almost no paper documents providing testimony to the events of this period.

The congress was held in Kyiv, on Ivanova Hill, in the Palace of Nations, which was built after the war because the local branch of the UN was situated in Kyiv. The delegates of the gathering, particularly those who had never seen the capital, delighted in the city's parks and the fountains and quiet pavilions, which rendered the August heat imperceptible. The highest point of the hill loomed above a gully, offering a view of the pure abundant waters of the River Lybid and the western part of Kyiv.

A huge, T-shaped crucifix, fashioned from black Zhytomyr granite, was erected there, bearing a forty-two metre crucified Christ, cast in dazzlingly bright composite metal. They said that the sculptor had used an antique video recording to create this work. The footage showed the crucifixion long ago of an unknown priest on this hill. It was said that the corpse had disappeared on the second day after his execution, never to be found …

At the congress, as would be expected, sharp disputes occurred between representatives of various schools of science and historians. A group of historians from Great Britain argued, citing the materials of a senate research commission, for the hypothesis that the President of the Confederation, Shirley MacDowell, knew of the timing and goals of the attack on the embassy. They asserted she had consciously concealed this intelligence from the American public. In their view she believed that only a sacrifice, the deaths of diplomats, would convince the citizens of the Confederation of the necessity to launch a war against the Horde on the territory of Eurasia. The researchers referred to the deployment of a similar trick by President F. D. Roosevelt. He had been aware of the planned Japanese attack on Pearl Harbour in 1941, but did nothing to prevent the threat to the USA's Pacific port. However, the treacherous Japanese attack and the casualties incurred by the fleet roused the American people from the lethargy of isolation.

A second group of historians from George Washington University contradicted this absurd hypothesis. They argued, on the basis of the available documents, that the Ambassador of the Confederation in Kyiv, John O'Sullivan, bore the entirety of the guilt. He had supposedly allayed the concerns of the State

Department and not insisted on an immediate evacuation of embassy personnel.

A special sitting of the Congress was dedicated to the military aspects of the Fourth World War. Implacable disputes between various groups of historians also broke out. It was regarded as an indisputable fact that on 15 August 2077 a series of nuclear missile strikes had been delivered to the capital of the Horde, Chyngiz-Saray. The centre of the Horde's military-attack coordination complex, the city of Nizhny Tagil, had also been struck. Missiles had targeted facilities in Turkey, Pakistan and Iran, resulting in the destruction of the Horde military's command structures. Their technological potential and the locations where their forces were concentrated were also destroyed. In total, approximately ten million military personnel and civilians perished.

The most terrible blow to the earth's population was the five thermo-nuclear explosions in space, at an altitude of two hundred to four hundred kilometres. These detonations, with a combined force of eighteen mega-tonnes, created the doomsday effect. Several western historians, for whom, even now, the defunct Russian empire presented the greatest threat, affirmed that these nuclear explosions were caused by an attack of cruise missiles and ICBMs launched from Russia's strategic nuclear submarines, based in the Eastern Atlantic. Several missiles did not follow the stipulated course and exploded not far from their launch point. Some were destroyed by the Horde's missile protection system. Two missiles strayed sideways and fell onto the northern part of the Sahara Desert. Others reached their intended targets.

This version was sharply criticised by experts from the Prussian Higher Academy of Geo-politics, who ascribed it to the ranks of standard Russo-phobic phantasms. The Prussians argued convincingly that the ageing missiles borne by the Russian submarines would, at the time of the launch, have been degraded to the point of being scrap metal. The global navigation system utilised by Russian missiles was destroyed after the fall of the Empire of the Double-Headed Eagle. A significant quantity of the explosions and their power did not accord with the quantity and categories of nuclear device onboard the Russian submarines. The Prussians expressed the view that, under the cover of the Russian launches, another entity had launched a major nuclear assault against an enemy that threatened western civilisation. This entity may have been the Confederation of States of North America, acting independently or in co-ordination with the military command of the OGS. The research undertaken by military experts at the site of the ground-level military explosions showed the strong probability that a number of American missiles had been utilised. These may have been the ground based LGM-318 W Revenger-XI or the space based SGM.

The Prussian geo-politicians insisted on dropping the charges of committing a crime against humanity and initiating global nuclear apocalypse against Rear Admiral Feoktysov. No trace of any remnants of the submarine based MBR SS-60 ICBMs or Harpoon-2 cruise missiles was revealed at the sites.

The most paradoxical view was offered by researchers from the Shanghai Institute of Artificial Intelligence. In their view no Fourth World War had occurred. The Chinese historians insisted that a chance occurrence of circumstances was involved, which in total gave the effect of a war. The researchers connected the collapse of the Horde, not with the nuclear strikes but with the death of the Kara-Khan and an acute internal conflict, which caused the collapse of yet another empire. The Chinese scientists affirmed that there were in fact no nuclear explosions. In August 2077 the earth had collided with an enormous asteroid, causing the effect of a huge flash followed by a great darkness.

The paper by the renowned theoretician, Doctor

Moshe Weber (Israel), grandson of the famous historical psychoanalyst, Alfred Weber, was of particular interest. It concerned the sense of a Second Coming, which seized a substantial portion of humanity after the nuclear catastrophe of 15 August 2077. Doctor Moshe Weber analysed, in detail, the feeling of apocalypse that emerged in people's consciousness and its physical and psychological causes. As a consequence of the explosions in space and the subsequent pulsation of electro-magnetic impulses, the entirety of the global mass-media were in chaos. Radio systems were inoperative, telephone, television and internet connections were destroyed. Large-scale electronic mass information was lost permanently. An Information Night gripped humanity for many years. Continents were immersed in darkness, both metaphorically and literally, with the aviation links between them broken. Humanity lost over two billion of its population during this period. Large states collapsed, to be replaced by small-scale local communities, similar to those in the middle ages, gripped by the fear of doomsday.

M. Weber's discovery of an article by the unknown researcher R. H. Friedman, titled *On the Eve of the Great Darkness* (2070) was of particular interest. The author, utilising the theory of magical mathematical cycles in history, via the method of associative-numerical prediction, provided an accurate prognosis of the events of 2077. Weber convincingly argued that after the Great Conflagration, a caste of seers had appeared. They wandered from village to village and town to town bearing the tidings of Christ with the words, 'I am the first and the last. I am he that liveth and was dead; and, behold, I am alive for evermore, and have the keys of hell and of death, Amen.' Not everyone believed in these seers and some of them were murdered. However, the majority of the population, striving above all to save their children, listened to the seers and believed in the imminence of the Second Coming of Christ.

Doctor Weber analysed the text of the Book of

Revelation and collated it with the testimonies and documents that remained after the period of Humanity's Informational Darkness (HID). He found striking similarities in the modes of thought, legends and phobias of the different communities, located significant distances apart, during the HID. Moshe Weber showed how, during the conditions of the Information Night, the absence of information and the fear of death in the consciousness of modern people provoked ancient, genetically conditioned feelings.

Weber's brilliant, generously illustrated paper evoked a stormy discussion among the participants of the congress. Many spoke against the conception of fear and restrictions on behaviours as having engendered Christianity en-route to the renaissance of faith. The majority of the researchers supported the ideal of educated hedonism as the engine of progress. The congress affirmed that the period of darkness and fear in newer human history had fortunately concluded. The recent past had seen the rebirth of scientific-technological and industrial potential, global trade and the functioning of the state. The revival of large-scale armed forces and the geo-political struggle for the resources of the mechanisms of dominance and influence had returned global human life to its pluralistic form. There were renewed attempts by some to cast God from his throne and occupy his place.

The excursion to Sophiiska Square in Kyiv was particularly instructive for participants of the congress. They heard a lecture about how, on the second day after the destruction of the Horde, a penetrating explosion occurred at the site of the Black Zeppelin. The GPU was transformed into an abyss from which crawled tens of thousands of black, dark blue and grey rats. The animals ran, screeching along the metro tunnels, to the banks of the Dnipro and disappeared, leaving a repellent aroma behind them. This chasm gaped for years in the centre of the city. Those Kyivans who survived during the darkness were afraid to venture near it. Eventually the chasm was filled with soil and disappeared, to be replaced by Cathedral Square, which united the mesmerising gold of Sophiiska and Mykhailivska churches in a single area above the Dnipro. The cathedral of Christ's Resurrection was built at the former site of the ministry of foreign affairs.

102

27 September 2077
Secret
For the personal attention of the Son of God, Jesus Christ of Nazareth

Given that the earth's system of telecommunication satellites has been destroyed, I do not know if my epistle will reach you. I am typing this letter on my communication gadget, which by some miracle has survived, in the hope that in some way you will hear my voice. I want to talk to you for the first time in my life without any intermediaries. That is why this letter is designated 'secret'. I have a sufficiency of time and am in no rush to go anywhere, for all the world is immersed in a green twilight in which all shadows have disappeared. Time has stopped and has become a smooth, featureless space, two dimensional, like a figure in a medieval geometry textbook.

After the Great Conflagration I spent almost a month returning to Kyiv on foot. I said goodbye to my subordinates, for each of us had to choose his own path. I walked without encountering any people, cars or other vehicles on the road. It was as if life had stopped and become transfixed. I was not afraid of radiation because the explosions had occurred a great distance from Kyiv and the monitor on my gadget indicated an absence of heightened levels of radiation. I was afraid of my own solitude, of the savagery of people turned wild again, of outbreaks of motiveless hatred and violence. Though I was well armed and could respond to any attack on me, it was hard to convince myself as to whether the prophecies were being fulfilled. Had brother risen against brother, son against father, people against people?

However, I personally encountered no conflict of this kind. Heading towards Kyiv on rural roads, I visited serfs' houses, where people shared bread and milk with me, and allowed me to stay the night.

In one of the villages a young woman, whose husband had gone to work abroad in Portugal and had disappeared, asked me to stay with her and wept profusely when I refused. In another the mother of a soldier, who had been taken captive by the Horde, gave me a pair of sturdy boots when she saw my worn shoes with gaping holes. I walked to Kyiv in those boots.

People were afraid to go out onto the streets, they were oppressed by fear and did not comprehend what was happening. The radio, internet, television and mobile connections had all ceased functioning. Nevertheless, people remained hospitable. Icons hung in every house everywhere, and I saw none of the symbols of the Deathchristians. On the contrary, when they talked about the Great Conflagration, people were convinced that You were giving a sign of Your coming. Many of them waited for doomsday and the resurrection of the dead.

In the border areas of occupied Kyiv, that is the ring road, I saw no Horde patrols nor MSSIA checkpoints. The road was clear. The streets of Kyiv remained empty. Only here and there did I see human figures with buckets of water or sacks of provisions. No one knew where the military forces of the Horde had disappeared to or what had happened to the regime of the High Directorate. Chaos reigned in the city.

The elevator in my apartment building on Institutska, as in other buildings, did not work. I barely managed to ascend to the twenty-ninth floor. My apartment, where I had not been since the events of 7 July, had been looted. The doors were broken down, the furniture was smashed, and rags were strewn around the floor. The wall safe, where I had stashed money and weapons, had been seared open with a blow torch. There was no water or electricity, and the drainage did not work. Amazingly my coffee making machine was preserved, an anachronistic exhibit from another era. There was no coffee, water or sugar.

I went out onto the balcony, which was covered with ash, like after a volcanic eruption, and looked at Kyiv. In the dark green twilight, denuded of the lights and bustle of a city, the landscape seemed dead, but this was an illusion. Here and there the feeble light of lanterns flickered and I sensed the warmth of life. And then, Jesus, for the first time in my life I composed a brief prayer and whispered it to you. Bless and protect us all powerful and compassionate Jesus Christ, the only one in whom I believe and in whom I will believe. Son of God, I am sorry for the suffering You endured in the name of each one of us and I believe in Your resurrection. Have mercy on our home, our Kyiv, on Ukraine and all other countries, have compassion for our people and other people; pity those who dwell in towns and villages. And have compassion on me, sinful as I am, and on those I love, respect and know, those whom I am close to and those from whom I am distant. And punish me for this, that I came to see you clearly so late, that I bowed to false prophets, that I believed in a mirage, that I lived with the laws of the wolf pack, that I followed values of little worth, that I served the forces of hatred and not of true virtue.

If I may speak the full, pitiless truth, I am a Deathchristian. So, I betrayed myself and for all my life I served them, those who destroyed God in themselves and in other people. I betrayed the people dearest to me. My father, whose funeral I did not attend because the circumstances of my work prevented me; some routine, idiotic instance of espionage with a sample of some new British weaponry that we stole from New

474

Zealand; because of that I did not hear my father's last words. He loved me so and believed in me, and I inherited my technical gifts from him. As he was dying my father called me, expecting to see me up until his last moment of life.

I betrayed my mother by not listening to her prayers and not believing in prayer. I dispatched my mother to Poland, having no way of contacting her or meeting her. I do not know what has become of her. Is she alive? I betrayed my sister, Kateryna, because, having quarrelled with her husband, I broke off all contact. Now I do not know her fate and it is unlikely I will find out what happened to her. I betrayed Shirley MacDowell, whom I loved truly, dementedly, so I was ready to die for her, loved her as I never loved anyone else. I betrayed her, abandoned her for my career when she was pregnant. I was carrying out the orders of Merezhko and Makhun, who threatened to cease payment of my government stipend and throw me out of the intelligence service. My heart turned to stone after this and I lost the gift of love forever. But perhaps I was never able to love in reality. I betrayed my own wife, Lara, whom I never truly loved, though she loved me. I married her, a relative of Natalia Havrilivna Makhun, because I tried to forget Shirley. But I could not forget her. Lara was a ballerina from the Kyiv Theatre of Opera and Ballet, and what did a ballerina and a military intelligence agent have in common? If it were not for her pregnancy, and for Krystyna, I would have abandoned Lara soon after our marriage, for she did not give me the same pleasure as other women. But now I realise I was brutal and unjust to her, quarrelling at every step she made, every word of hers irritated me. Even when she was pregnant and not looking her best and she wept, I had no sympathy for her. I lost Lara and with her Krystyna. I betrayed my daughter, taking little interest in her, trying to forget her and strike her out of my memory. However, I thought about her all the time and suffered because I had lost her. I betrayed Ukraine, which my father had taught me to love. If I know a little of its history it is from my father. I served not Ukraine but her enemies and her masters. Although I did not always understand that, it does not excuse me.

The criminal ruling regime, whatever slogans it covered itself with, violated and destroyed the people. It drove them into poverty and servitude, denuding them of nationhood and criminalising them. I placated myself with the thought that I served Ukraine, seeking out new categories of weapons, organising technological exchanges, seeking out new and still newer secrets. Why and for whom did I do this?

When I realised that I was being transformed into the last Ukrainian on earth it was too late. I am guilty of the death of Viktor Bezpalii, for I knew his arrogance and his weakness for women and money, but I did not send him home. On the contrary, I told him about the secret files and was thus instrumental in bringing about his death. Similarly, I am guilty of the deaths of Linda Kenworthy, Zaur Khamzyn, special forces soldier Liosha, and other of my UMI colleagues. At the risk of my own life and those of my subordinates, I compiled files on the traitors of Ukraine, on criminals within the state, who presented the greatest threat to national security. I was proud of this because I believed it was necessary for Ukraine. However, when these files were made public on the eve of the Great Conflagration it became clear they were of no use to anyone, except perhaps historians. The people hated and were contemptuous of their rulers irrespective of my archives.

The fact that I knew of many state secrets gratified my egotism and flattered my pride, which constitutes a great sin. And Professor Weber? My criminal negligence, when I failed to change the mask I was using for a fresh one, led to Alfred Isaakovych's death. Is it possible to forgive this? I am guilty before Bozhena, who made me happy here, in this flat where her voice and the light of her body remain. I am guilty in that I did not leave immediately for Australia with her that night when her

476

body glowed. That I did not cast aside this goddam state work, this vampires' ball which adorns itself with contrived honours, purchased titles and undeserved ranks. I lost Bozhena forever; though her body and spirit were maimed, perhaps she was my last hope of true love and there is no way I can be forgiven for this. I do not know if she stayed in Washington or if she was burned in orbit along with the Ronald Reagan Military Space Station.

I am guilty before Nataliia Havrilivna Makhun, whom everyone turned away from after the assassination of the hetman. She only did good to me and I had no word of thanks for her. Perhaps it was necessary to help her get to Poland, to my mother. It would have been easier for them to survive the Great Darkness together.

But my greatest fault is that I participated directly in the preparation of the Great Conflagration. I did not protect Ukraine before the aggression of the Horde, or raise up a revolt against the traitors who controlled Ukraine. I just watched impotently as it was transformed into Europe's wild field. There is no forgiveness for all the mistakes and crimes I committed after returning to Ukraine. I did not track down the Grey Prince, though he was somewhere nearby. He needed to be located and destroyed, but instead I collated pointless files on his servants. And now a myth about me as a future leader of Ukraine is circulating. I am, it is said, an honourable person on whom my poor people may rely. Is this not a terrible blasphemy, a betrayal of those ideals in which those unfortunate people believe, who want to see me as head of state? Is this not a crime for which there may be no amnesty? My pride and self-confidence mixed in with my weakness, my indecision and my fear of taking, albeit some desperate, steps in time is my unforgivable sin. Perhaps only Jesus may take these sins away from me.

I slept for one last night in my apartment, sleeping on some rags on the same floor where I had made love with

Bozhena, before leaving in the morning. I walked to Ivana Mazepy Street, past the empty, burned Sejm building, dragging with me a cabin case on wheels, which I had found on Sadova Street. I had put my coffee maker in there for some reason, without understanding why.

I entered a small church, which was still open, near Askold's grave A number of candles were burning and women crossed themselves to the sad declamation of the priest. I lit a candle for the peace of the soul of Askold, Bozhena's brother, and for the health of my mother and all those close to me. Then I descended the hill towards the Dnipro waterfront and the capital highway.

I turned right and came to the empty ring road. I decided to find out what had become of the inhabitants of the village where Askold and his family had dwelled, along with Father Ivan. I learned of the priest's death as a martyr when I was on the road to Vinnytsia. When I reached the access road from the highway I saw there was still a rusted sign for the Feofania-Pyrohovo zone. I reached the entrance to ZEK-116. There were no guards there and the iron gates painted with roosters had been torn off their hinges, as if a tank had battered them down. I reached the top of the hill where I had stood with Nevinchanyi not so long ago in June. Superficially it looked as if nothing had changed, but the green twilight and fluorescent aura around things would not allow me to assess the view of the settlement which lay before me. I descended the hill and approached the church. Both it and the village had been burned, but through the open doors I saw flickering candle flames and the gold lustre of an icon. People, mainly old men and women, had gathered around the church. One of the old men explained to me that it was the Festival of the Exaltation of the Holy Cross. To my shame I did not know what that signified.

Seeing none of the O'Connells near the church, I was gripped with a terrible foreboding and went to their house. It

478

was burned, but in the yard I saw some people near the shed that had survived. Drawing closer, I saw Askold sitting at a table with a baby in his arms. Lykera was pouring out some kind of food from a pot into bowls for the children, Yarema and Mykhailina. They joined hands and prayed and then I understood, Son of God, that only Your will and Your mercy had protected the family of Askold O'Connell. I hid behind the trunk of an old pear tree and looked at this blessed image. Yarema and Mykhailina, who were quiet in a way that was not childlike, the tearful but happy Lykera, and Askold, haggard and grey haired; his face was blissful as he held his three month old boy against his chest. The baby, his back warm against his father, looked into the distance and in that non-childlike gaze, a calm thoughtfulness glittered. I can find no other words, although I am writing about a baby, it seemed that the quiet child saw something that none of us has the gift to see.

In the name of the Father, Son and Holy Ghost, Amen.

Former Lieutenant General in Ukrainian Military Intelligence and now the servant of God, Ihor Haiduk

To be continued ...

18/07/2010 - 19/02/2011

Also available from Kalyna Language Press

Episodic Memory by Liubov Holota

Winner of the 2008 Shevchenko Prize

Episodic Memory, published in Ukraine in 2007, is the story of a young girl, Sofia, growing up in a Ukrainian village, and her return, as an adult, to be at her dying mother's bedside. While staying in her parent's house after the funeral, she is haunted by memories of a vanished world where Gypsies sang their way over the Steppe and the post man, a KGB informer, hurled the mail at their gatepost as his wagon hurtled past.

Raven's Way by Vasyl Shkliar

Winner of the 2011 Shevchenko Prize

In 1921, after four years of war, the Bolsheviks conquer Ukraine, but Raven and Veremii hide in the forest with other Cossacks and continue their struggle. When Veremii dies in battle, the communists secretly follow the burial party, but when they dig up the coffin they find a cryptic note instead of a corpse.

The novel brings to light the desperate resistance of a guerrilla army that fought until 1926, conducting daring attacks on Soviet forces and concealing themselves in underground lairs that could hold hundreds of Cossacks.

Kaharlyk by Oleh Shynkarenko

The novel began on Facebook as a series of bulletins from an alternative reality, and is written entirely in blocks of 100 words. It is set in Ukraine after a war with Russia. A man has lost his memory because the Russian army have used his brain to control military satellites. He regains consciousness in a mysterious hospital-like building and begins a pilgrimage to find his past. He journeys to Kaharlyk, a town where time has stood still following the testing of an experimental weapon.

The book is an Odyssey as magical as Alice's tumble through the looking glass or Gulliver's first footprints on the sands of Lilliput.

www.kalynalanguagepress.com/shop